Harem Hex Healer

Harem Hex Healer

A Reverse Harem Monster Romance

Imogen Knowed

ISBN-13: 979-8-9874825-0-6

Dedication

I dedicate this to all the readers out there who aren't satisfied with a single love interest in a book and wish they would all *just bone already.*

Content Warnings

This book has explicit descriptions of sexual acts. While all sex is consensual, some may be considered coerced. There is mention of sexual assault, but no detailed descriptions of it.

There is some mention of miscarriage, but no active detailing. Additionally, a character is pregnant throughout the book.

There is some violence, domestic violence, and gore.

Body shaming and some ableist language are also present.

1

What the fuck is going on? It's too bright. My head hurts. There are so many trees, but their leaves provide enough space for light to pierce through them. The beams are like knives cutting directly into my skull. My migraine is still kicking. The meds I took are not working. Why am I in a forest? Or is it woods? What is the difference? Does it even matter? I am fucking stuck in them!

I stand, lifting myself from the ground, and brush the debris from my butt. I'm not even going to bother trying to brush off my back. I pull some sticks and leaves from my hair.

Keep it together, Astrid. I hug myself and rub my arms attempting to warm up a bit. It's cold. I'm happy I have my hoodie. I want to lie down and hide my face in my hood, but I need to figure out where I am. I need to figure out how I got here.

Did I fall asleep? Am I dreaming? Migraine medication tends to give me vivid dreams. This doesn't feel like a dream. They were new meds. Maybe they affect me differently than my usual pills. Perhaps I shouldn't have taken migraine meds I bought from a literal drug dealer. The stupid pharmacy wouldn't give me any more of my prescription, though. They said I could only have ten pills a month. I have migraines that last a week and need at least three per day. How the fuck is ten supposed to last?

I can't see anything other than trees and these sharp light beams. Ugh, the light. I'm sure I'd think it was pretty if it wasn't so damn painful to look at.

What should I do? Where should I go? I suppose left is as good a direction as any. Whenever I play video games and come to a fork, I always go left. Not for any particular reason other than being left-handed and a bit arrogant about it. Alright. Left it is.

This can't be real.

Am I the star of some goofy isekai anime? I audibly giggle. Maybe I'll collect a harem of hotties and fuck my way to becoming the most powerful being in all the lands. I giggle again and stand in a superhero pose at this thought. What is wrong with me? I'm about to die in the woods. Why am I giggling about boning hot anime dudes? I groan in annoyance so loudly I startle myself. I stop moving and look around frantically to ensure no creepy forest creatures heard me — the dirty perv stuck in the woods … or forest.

The brush is thick. I wish I had a machete. Funny. I was joking that weeding through the code I was trying to debug this morning was like fighting my way through a forest with a butter knife.

I'd kill for a butter knife right now.

I'm not wearing any shoes; just socks. If I'm dreaming, thinking about shoes hard enough will give me some shoes. Shoes. Shoes. SHOES. FUCKING SHOES. Okay, I guess I am shoeless in a forest. Or maybe it's woods. I just have to watch where I walk.

If I walk in one direction long enough, I'm sure I'll find something that can tell me where to go. I just need to keep my eyes on the ground. I need to watch where I step and stop the light from entering my eyes. I pull my hoodie up to cover my forehead and hang it above my eyes. That feels a bit better. I'm slightly warmer. The light isn't as bad now.

The trees form a semi-decent canopy. I can't really see the sky through it. That's good. At least the trees make me feel like I'm indoors. My therapist would be so proud of me. I'm outside! I start to panic, thinking about the sky and how expansive it is. I know if I look at it, I'll feel like I'm falling upward through it—hurling through the atmosphere to an expanse of nothingness. Snap out of it, Astrid. There are trees above you. You'll be okay. Just don't look up.

"Forward. Just move forward one step at a time. Eventually, you'll get somewhere," I whisper to myself. Or I'll die of starvation. Or thirst. Or hypothermia. Or some weird worm will wiggle its way through my socks and into my bloodstream. Bury itself in my heart. Make lots of little baby worms and take over my body. Then I'll be the worm puppet walking through the woods … or forest. That probably won't happen. It's not muddy here. There are no wiggly, sock-penetrating worms, Astrid. I'll keep an eye out for puddles, though, just in case.

This is my worst nightmare. I'd be the first to die in a zombie apocalypse and the first to die in the woods. I have no survival skills. My skills are NOT transferable. Sure, I'm smart, but being good at writing code isn't going to save me. It turns out, being able to write a sorting algorithm is completely useless information. Not only did I never use that info while making video games; it's knowledge that I won't use anywhere—especially the fucking woods. FUCK. Or is it a forest? GAAAH. Stop fixating on that! It does not matter if you are in a forest or woods or a jungle or a grove. Oh, God. Am I in a grove? What even is a grove? You're going to die, and it will not matter either way. You'll die not knowing the difference between woods or forests or groves. At least I know it's not a fucking jungle.

Ok. Suck it up, buttercup. Walk. Of all the times to be a lazy, crazy, fat ass, this is not one of them. My therapist says I need to stop using negative self-talk and labeling to motivate myself. Well, she hasn't taught me how to do that yet. Negative self-talk has gotten me through the last thirty years. It got me through school. It got me a six-figure job in a field run by douche-bros. It'll get me through these stupid fucking woods. Forest? Grove? God damn it. Stop it, Astrid!

Is wandering around really the right thing to do? Google would be super helpful right now. I'd search, "What to do when you suddenly find yourself in the woods." Actually, I bet I'd just find a bunch of unhelpful ads for products I can't buy right now. So, probably not that helpful.

I feel like I've been walking forever. Maybe I should stop moving, stay here, and wait for help. Who the fuck is going to help you in the middle of the damn woods, Astrid? You know who? Fucking wolves, you stupid fucking cunt. Just fucking keep walking. Just fucking do it, you scaredy cat piece of shit.

I don't have my watch or phone. I do have my bracelet that spells "Fucking do it" in Morse code. That is going to be super helpful. I roll my eyes at myself. I bought it hoping it would motivate me to work out and do other things I don't want to do. It doesn't usually work, but it's cute. Maybe it will work now. I run my fingers over the beads. Okay, Astrid. Just fucking do it. Just walk. You'll be okay.

I have no idea what time it is. If I could see the sun, maybe I could figure it out — do that thing where you stab a stick in the ground and see how far the shadow has moved. But I guess that wouldn't work since I'm walking. Also, besides those beams of mind-splitting light, the light isn't casting many shadows. Maybe I could use those beams of light to determine my direction and estimate the time of day.

But, what the fuck good will that do me? I don't know where I am. How would knowing time and direction even help? I guess I'm going north. Maybe I should go south to get warmer. I laugh a bit because I realize how stupid that is. Not only am I stuck in the woods, but I'm also the crazy lady who keeps laughing to herself in the middle of the fucking woods. Or forest. Maybe it's morning and I'm going south already. God, what the fuck is the difference?

I step into a sort of clearing. There are no trees or tall bushes—just dead leaves on the ground. It seems like there should be a road here, but there isn't. Oh, hey, my migraine is gone.

A weird fog rolls in. It's an extremely thick fog with well-defined edges. I've never seen anything like it. It looks like perfect whitish-grey, smoke streams rolling off a cigarette. It's almost like a layer of touchable cloud. It seems cozy. I kind of want to curl up in it and fall asleep. I reach out to touch it. Before my fingers can graze the smoky tendrils, they pull back out of the clearing — almost as if someone sucked them back to wherever they came from.

There's a crunching sound behind me. Was that a twig snapping? What was that? Oh my God. Did I jinx myself when I thought about wolves earlier? How cliché of me. The headline would read: Dumb girl gets stuck in an undefined collection of trees, hears a twig snap, then immediately gets torn apart by wolves.

It's fine. Just look behind you. You won't see any wolves, Astrid. It'll be a cute fluffy fucking bunny or something. I turn to face my fears.

I squint to peer through the surrounding vegetation, and my heart stops. Fuck. That's not a bunny. A group of large, dark figures is hiding behind the row of trees at the inner edge of the clearing. They're not doing a great job at concealing themselves, though. A shock wave starts in my chest and washes all over my body, as I process what I am seeing. I can't tell what these giant figures are, but they are terrifying. I can see the glow of some of their eyes, reflecting the little light that reaches them and piercing through the shadowy darkness with a purpose. The purpose looks like desire.

They're too large to be men. Are they bears? What is it that you do when you see a bear? Act big and wave your hands around? Scream at it? Play dead?

I'm frozen in fear. I suppose I'm not surprised I'm reacting this way. I'm scared of everything. I can't even leave my house. How am I supposed to stare down a group of scary bears in the woods? Woods or a forest? Why are you focusing on that right now?!

One. Two. Three. Four. Five. Six. Seven. Lucky me. Seven bears here to maul me. Goldilocks and the seven fucking bears. Or Goldy-Brownish-Locks and the seven fucking bears.

They aren't approaching me. They're just hiding behind the trees—watching me. It's almost like they're curious about me. Maybe they're not going to kill me. Perhaps they're more scared of me than I am of them. Maybe I should make myself big and intimidating. How would I do that? Okay, spread your hands out and scream in the deepest, burliest voice you can muster—no sudden movements.

I can't even move my hands or make a peep. I just stand here—staring back at them. I'm like a dumb prey animal who freezes and waits for the predator to pounce. Like a deer. Or a bunny. Or a possum. Should I play dead?

I can't make out their shapes. I only see dark shadowy outlines of most of them. One appears to be ethereal, its shape ever-changing. I am unable to get a full read on it. Another has large antlers like a deer. The rest appear as simple black masses peeking from behind the trees … almost human-shaped. Oh, God. They're going to eat me.

One to my left stirs. I focus my gaze on it only for a moment, terrified that turning my head, and taking my eyes off the rest, will cause them to attack. It sidesteps from behind the tree. I can see its full features now. It's even more terrifying than I thought.

It looks like a man in a bird costume. He has a long beak. Is he wearing one of those plague doctor noses? No. His arms are fully covered in long black feathers, with hands that spread wide to form wings. The rest of him is a fully nude man. A completely naked and highly aroused man.

He approaches me slowly. Tiptoeing. Turning his head side to side in a bird-like fashion as if he is trying to figure me out. I can hear him inhaling loudly and passionately. After each inhale, he moans with pleasure—like he smells the most delicious cake. As he gets closer, I turn to face him, trying not to position my back toward the others. I am unsuccessful in this attempt and my back faces the smoky, ethereal one.

I try not to look directly at the birdman, as he approaches. I'm afraid direct eye contact will provoke him. His body is lean but muscular. Except for his arms and head, he looks just like a man—a man almost entirely covered in feathers. He shudders, inhales loudly, and lets out a sound of pure ecstasy. This time, I can see as he inhales, that his penis jumps, almost as if it is enjoying whatever it is he is smelling. I've only seen a few penises in my life, and despite this one still being a few feet away, I can see it more clearly than if it was right in front of my face. I can see now that his entire body is covered in short downy black feathers. Well, not his entire body. His dick seems to be featherless.

He tilts his head down as if to see where I keep glancing and realizes I am looking at his erection. He tilts his head up and makes a cawing noise. Is he pleased with himself? One of his feathery hands shoots down to his member. Oh my God, is he masturbating? He makes a soft, seductive moan. What the hell?

Oh, fuck. Is he going to rape me? Does looking at his penis constitute consent, in his mind? Does he even understand the concept of consent? Does he even care?

I shake uncontrollably. I hadn't shaken like this since I once stood outside in a Minnesota winter with nothing but a thin wool peacoat. A single tear rolls down my cheek. I croak out very slowly and barely audibly, "Please, don't."

He stops. Did he understand me? He takes a single step back as if my words wounded him. He places the hand not holding his dick to his chest and says, "M'Lady, I would not." He can understand me? He can speak!?

I take a step back. This time it is me who is struck back with words. My foot catches on something. A log? I don't know. But I know that it scrapes at my heel and hurts. I fall backward. If a chubby girl falls in the woods, does she make a noise?

Before I hit the ground, a soft pillow engulfs me from behind. Did I fall onto a fluffy cloud? That doesn't make any sense. White, cloud-like, masculine hands reach around me, gripping me under my breasts. I feel the unmistakable pressure of a very large and very erect penis pressed against my back. A face, or the approximation of a face, appears against my left cheek and coos softly in my ear, "Watch your step, darlin'." The white tendrils of clouds I saw earlier emanate from him and swirl around me. It's that cloud thing. It can speak, too?

He puts his nose in my neck and does what I assume is an inhale. It's hard to tell what he's doing. He made a noise similar to an inhale with what looked kind of like a nose, but it lost its shape against my neck. His body seems to ripple as the air enters his body. His cock gets even harder, and since he had to bend down to sniff my neck, it is now wedged perfectly between my ass cheeks.

Once again, I am frozen in place. My body trembles in fear and, embarrassingly, arousal. I can feel a tingling between my thighs I have not felt in a long time in the presence of another. My nipples tighten and perk up. They're now distinctly visible through my hoodie. I entertain the idea of turning around and taking this stiff, cloud dick inside me. Maybe giving the bird a go, too, but I am too scared to do anything. My arousal causes me to instinctively push my backside against him, but only slightly. I catch myself and stand straight. Don't fuck the cloud, Astrid.

Almost as if they can sense my arousal, the other five emerge from the forest. I can see them clearly now. All of them are naked. All of them are obviously aroused—their dicks are in full view. Well, except for one. And all of them are, for lack of a better term, monsters.

The one closest to my right looks like he walked out of the ocean. He's like a squid trying to impersonate a man. An incredibly well-built, handsome man. His arms are about as big around as my waist. And I'm a big girl! He is holding his penis in his hand, rolling his thumb over the head. I can see tiny beads of semen pool on the tip. He licks his lips and inhales in that same lustful way the birdman had. As he does so, more pre-cum oozes out.

Next to him looks like a tree with deer antlers. No, just branches in the shape of deer antlers sprouting from its head. It appears to be growing and changing shape as it moves. Almost like it must grow its legs to where it wants to step. It creaks as it moves—that same sound a large tree makes when it bends in the wind. It doesn't have an erection. I don't see a penis anywhere on it. I do, however, see two perfectly round tree knots that look remarkably like voluptuous breasts. Is it a tree woman?

The one to the right of the birdman slinks out from the shadows. Is that a werewolf? He puts his hands out and motions to the others to calm down, "Now come on, boys, you're scaring the poor lass." This one seems to have a bit of modesty about him because, while his dick was in full view when he tried to calm his compatriots, he's at least trying to cover it now.

"She's not scared. She's dripping wet. Can't you smell it on her?" the squid guy says.

"Come on, Osric, don't be crass." The next creature walks out in a strut, swaying side to side while his striped tail sways back and forth. He licks the back of one hand and rubs it over his ear. Now there's a cat?

"You would say that, you fucking pussy," says the one I am guessing is named Osric—the squid man.

"Original," the cat man says and waves his hand as if he doesn't care about the squid man's opinion.

The last monster enters the clearing. His body is covered in scales. He looks a bit like a mini-Godzilla. His long tongue slithers out while he eye fucks me. He has … OH … MY … GOD, two dicks!? He is built like a linebacker and stands at least a head above the cat.

They're all less than five feet from me. I'm standing on my own, but the cloud man is still holding on to me, smelling me.

The rest are slowly strolling toward me, smelling the air loudly. What the fuck are they smelling? Oh my god, it is me! They're going to rape me, then eat me!

I pull myself away from the cloud man's grip and stumble. I turn my body to face them all.

I put my hands out and scream as loud as possible. If a dumb girl screams in the woods, can anyone hear her? What about if she screams in a forest?

They all stop. All seven of them stand before me, eagerly awaiting my next move.

I turn and run. This new angle reveals a bit of the sky above the treeline. Oh, shit. There are no trees above my head. I accidentally look up. Fuck, not now. I envision myself falling upward into the clouds, engulfed in their fluffy nothingness. My heart was already pounding, but now it's racing so fast I can barely distinguish its beats. As I'm blacking out, I feel the clouds embrace me and whisper, "Damn, darlin', you sure are somethin'."

- - - -`♥´- - - -

I awake and my vision is blurry. I appear to be moving quickly down a dirt road. Wait? I'm on a horse? I'm sitting sidesaddle and feel like I might slip off. There are two masculine arms on either side of me—holding the reins and keeping me in place. My head is pressed against a strong silk-covered chest. Oh, no. One of the monsters is whisking me away to their lair to eat me later. I jolt up and look at my abductor.

What looks back at me is the face of the most attractive man I have ever seen in my entire life. He looks like he'd be the favorite in a boy band. Hair dark and shining. Skin flawless. No stubble, but a strong chiseled jaw. On top of his head sits a crown with dazzling jewels. He looks down at me and smiles, revealing even more dazzling teeth before saying, "It's okay, babe! I got you. You'll be alright. I'm taking you home with me."

What is going on? I woke in the middle of the woods surrounded by monsters and now a gorgeous man with a crown is taking me home with him. Oh, my God, I am in an isekai anime!

2

"What happened? Where are the monsters? Did you kill them?" I ask weakly. I'm almost more afraid of this man than the monsters; he's so handsome. My social anxiety screams at me to get away from him as quickly as possible before he tells me how ugly I am. I look at him, trying to memorize his face without obviously staring. Does this guy even have pores?

"Oh, beautiful, don't worry. I've got you," he says. Beautiful? Who the fuck is he talking about? It can't be me. I'm too afraid to ask.

"I heard your scream as I was riding through the woods," he continues. Ah, so it is the woods and not a forest. Maybe now I can stop obsessing over those damn trees. That's not the thing to focus on here, Astrid! Get your head in the game!

"I found you on the ground with those naked barbarians surrounding you. They were getting ready to take advantage of you and spoil that gorgeous body of yours." Okay, there it was again. A compliment. He is talking about me.

He continues, "I rode them through and snatched you up. Sadly, I couldn't take the time to kill those brutes. I couldn't risk one of them defiling you while I murdered the others. I grabbed you as fast as possible and rode out of there. Don't worry. Fancy here is the fastest horse in the country. She'll get us home in no time. Then you can lay that pretty little head on silk pillows and forget all about those heathens."

Just knowing the sky is open above me is making me dizzy. I tempt fate, turn, bury my face in his chest, and nestle into the crook of his arm. His smile is so reassuring. His voice is so comforting. His smell is so soothing. My fear is melting. Just don't look up, you fat hog. I hope he doesn't push me off him in disgust.

He places his hand on my head and pets my hair, "Now, now gorgeous. I got you. You can rest now." I think I hear him smell my hair, but I am uncertain. I am, however, certain of the erection that presses against my side. What!? Am I seriously arousing this gorgeous man? How can that possibly be? I look up at him, and he gives me a half grin and a wink. No way!

Ok, Astrid, you got this. Say something to him. Ask him his name. I pick my head off his chest to speak, but I am too scared to look at him. Too frightened to speak.

"What is your name, gorgeous?" he asks.

"I'm Astrid."

"Divinely beautiful. Aptly named." How does he know the definition of my name? Why is he hitting on me? Is he blind?

I laugh nervously, "Yeah, my mom had a crush on a girl named Astrid in high school and decided to name me after her." Why did I tell him that? He doesn't need to know that.

"I'm Thadius. It means 'gift from God.'" He lets out an assured single chuckle. Aptly named. This dude is a gift I'd love to unwrap.

Unthinkingly, I rest my head back on his chest, close my eyes, and nuzzle against him. I am sure he smells me this time, and I feel his penis hop, popping me against my side. Fuck, this guy is hot.

I let out a slight "ope" in surprise. My Minnesota vernacular peeking out its horny head.

"Sorry about that, angel. You're just so delectable." Oh, no. Is this handsome man going to eat me? Why do I instantly think everyone is going to eat me? I've seen too many cannibal horror films. "I'm ashamed of my body's reaction to you. As the king, I should have more self-control. But it is taking all of my willpower not to stop this horse and make love to you in every bed of flowers we pass." The king? Beds of flowers? I like that idea. Let's do that.

"Delectable?" I ask.

"Yes, angel. That smell of yours …" he inhales, "is like nothing I've ever smelled before. It is ravishing. It's making me a bit delirious with lust if I'm honest. You're not from around here, are you?"

Should I tell him the truth? I think I'm from another world in some weird anime with hot dudes and monsters. Honestly, I don't know what the truth is. I don't know how I ended up in those woods. The last thing I remember was climbing into bed with a migraine and taking one of those suspicious pills, praying to no God in particular that it wouldn't kill me. Did it kill me? Is this heaven? Do I get to have sex with hot kings who find me irresistible in my afterlife? It can't be. I wasn't religious. And… there's the rapey monsters, so it can't be heaven.

I need to try to figure out where I am before I go jumping to conclusions and sound like a crazy person. "Where exactly is … here?" I pry.

"Well, currently, we are in Prailyra Woods—the woods right outside of the city of Prailyra. That's where my castle resides," he smirks.

I have never heard of this place before. I'm pretty sure I am in a whole other world, but I need to make sure. I don't know the name of every city in the world, after all. "And your kingdom. What is it called?" I ask.

"The kingdom is called Laerean. My family has ruled it for many centuries." Okay, I have definitely never heard of that before. I'm decent at geography. I got a one-hundred percent on every one of my tenth-grade geography tests, which had me write out the names of as many countries as possible on a map. But I didn't write every single one.

"Okay, and, um … the world. What is it called?" I ask, unsure how to ask the questions I need to ask.

"The world? It's called Earth." Fuck. Am I really just in some weird tiny kingdom in the middle of Europe or something that I've never heard of before? What is going on? Ask better questions, Astrid.

"What year is it?" God, he's going to think I'm such an idiot.

He chuckles and declares, "It's 1700 AX. How do you not know where you are and what year is it? Did those monsters hit you on the head or something?" What does AX mean? Maybe I should just go with the amnesia excuse. Instead of trying to explain that I think I died and, like, I don't know, rematerialized in a different world, a different dimension? That sounds crazy. Why would I rematerialize with all my clothes but no shoes or watch?

"I honestly am not sure where I am or how I got here. The last thing I remember is having a bad headache, taking questionable medicine, dozing off in bed, and then I woke up in the woods." Suddenly, I realized I am wearing exactly what I was wearing when I fell asleep. I usually don't sleep with my socks on, but I'm happy I did because my feet would be freezing without socks right now—even though I have a hole at the bottom. Oh, no. Did a worm get in? I notice a pain emanating from approximately the same place the hole is. No, idiot. This is where you tripped earlier. You must have ripped your sock when you fell.

I suddenly realize I am without a bra, and my boobs are painfully bouncing due to the horse. Big boobs can be such a hassle. I'm also freezing. The front of the saddle is digging into my side; my hips are too wide to sit like this. I've been so preoccupied with figuring out what is going on that I haven't noticed any of the signals my body is sending me. Astrid, you need to be more self-aware.

I lean back and swing my leg to the horse's other side. This new position hurts a bit. It pulls my legs a bit wider than I prefer, but it's more comfortable than sitting sideways. Now I can't bury my face in Thadius' chest anymore. Fuck, maybe I should have stayed the way I was—dealt with the painful welt building up.

I hug myself across my ribs to get warm and stop my breasts from bouncing. "So, maybe you are an angel? You fell from the clouds to grace us with your voluptuous body." He notices me hugging myself. "Oh, you poor thing, are you cold?" He wraps his left arm across mine to keep me warm. The tips of my breasts are resting on his arms. His palm stops just under my right breast and almost cups it. Is he trying to feel me up? Slyly? Kingly? My breath quickens. This is terrifying and exciting. Heat rises to my chest from where he touches me and spreads across my body.

After a while of riding, I can feel his thumb caress my nipple through my hoodie. I try not to, but the swell between my legs causes me to grind against the saddle slightly, pushing my backside into Thadius' cock. It takes all my willpower not to moan, grab his hand, jam it down my pants, and use the horse's movement to pound against his fingers. Maybe I should. Maybe I should just fuck this dude on this horse. No. He doesn't want me. He's a king, and I'm a … nothing.

He breathes heavily. He moves his head down toward my neck and inhales. I can feel his cock pulsate with excitement against my back. He shifts his weight as if he's uncomfortable. I can tell the horse's movement is about to get him off, too. "Perhaps, we should, um, stop and take a break," he says breathlessly.

"No, don't stop!" I involuntarily shout. I'm seriously about to cum. I grab his arm and pull it tight against my chest. I squeeze my legs together and grind my hips down toward the saddle. I thrust my butt backward to get a better angle and more friction against my clit. I know he knows what I'm doing. He knows I know what he's doing. But we're still trying to pretend we're just respectably riding this horse rather than dry-humping each other to completion.

A wet burst of sparkles lights up between my legs and explodes its way across my body like a wave. There is a deep pressure in my uterus as it releases itself from contraction. I sling my head back against Thadius, unable to maintain the facade much longer, and moan as the pleasure washes over me. My feet thrust out, and my toes curl. I bite and lick my lips in satisfaction. At that moment, Thadius presses his face into my neck, inhales deeply, and pulls me tighter toward him. He presses his dick so hard against my back that I swear I'm going to get a bruise. I can feel it jerk with pleasure as he cums. Wetness rests on my back, soaking his clothes and mine.

For a few moments, we both sit, panting and recovering from our post-orgasm exhaustion. The horse continues to move forward and doesn't seem to mind that we just got off while riding her. I feel a bit guilty using her in such a way. At least I came on the saddle and not the horse. I don't need that level of guilt in my life right now.

He coughs, clearing his throat. "Do you mind if we stop now?" I'm sure he wants to go clean himself off. We stop, and he dismounts. He disappears into the woods with something rolled up in his hands. I lean forward on the horse so I am languidly lying on her while I wait for him to return. I stroke her hair and whisper, "Do you think he likes me, girl?"

I'm about to fall asleep when Thadius returns wearing a new set of clothes. These clothes are also made of silk but seem a bit more casual. The shirt is open deep across his chest, revealing a deep crevice between his pecs. His chest is hairless and smooth. I want to rub my hands over it. How am I aroused again? As he strolls back, he runs his hands through his hair. I wish I could do the same. It looks so soft.

He clears his throat and smiles knowingly at me. "Sorry for the delay, my dear. Let's get you to my castle." After he saddles up behind me, I notice his erection, which has been raging against my back for our entire ride, is gone. Geeze, it must hurt to have one that long. Don't think that, Astrid. The concept of blue balls is a misogynist talking point.

3

We've been riding in silence for quite a while. I nod off until he jolts me from my sleep by solemnly speaking. "Those monsters who attacked you in the woods—I know of them. They have lived on the outskirts of my kingdom for years—dragging the beautiful women of my country into the woods, only for them never to be seen again." Oh my God, am I in a place with rapey, woman-stealing monsters?

"You're a king. Don't you have an army or something? Can't you, like, go get them?" I ask. He seems to bristle a bit at my question. Should I not have asked that? That seems like a sore spot. Did I make him mad at me?

"I have tried. We cannot defeat them," his tone changes to one even more solemn, "I have lost more soldiers trying to fight them than I have lost women to their abductions. As a king, I had to make the hard decision to learn to live with them. They have slowed their abductions in recent months." He pauses, presumably for dramatic effect. "I'm worried that encountering you has relit their loins, though."

Earlier, he said he didn't kill them because he needed to save me. Is it actually that they are too strong for him to kill? If his army can't take them out, how could he? Maybe he was trying to make me feel safe and convince me they weren't as scary as they actually are. Now that the threat has passed, he can tell me the truth. Something about the story doesn't sit right with me, but I'm not sure what it is. I want to ask more about what happens to the women the monsters abduct, but I'm scared to hear his answer.

He stops speaking for a minute. He looks off into the distance like he fondly remembers something. His lip quivers. "Five years ago. They … they took my wife."

I cover my mouth gently. This poor man. He's been through so much. "I'm so sorry. That must have been very hard." I want to wrap my arms around him and comfort him, but I'd have to fully turn on this horse and face him. Where'd I put my legs? Around him? Perhaps I can unbuckle his pants and … stop, Astrid. Wrangle in the dirty perv and show some compassion. He just told you about his wife being murdered.

He looks as if he is about to cry but doesn't. "It was difficult." The guilt I feel for just picturing myself riding his dick is enough to cool me down.

We're out of the woods in an open field now. I'm starting to get dizzy by the vast expanse of sky. It's overcast, and, for some reason, that makes me a little more comfortable—like the sky has a floor and I can't fall through it.

I force myself to glance upward hoping to give myself a bit of exposure therapy—something my therapist constantly tried to convince me to do. Maybe being cradled by the king will give me some strength. I suddenly hear a loud, cawing noise from behind us, and my curiosity outweighs my fear. I whip my head around to look and see a dark figure following us. Thadius turns, too, and grimaces. What is that? It's the birdman from the woods. He's flying toward us.

"Fuck. It's Alistair," Thadius says. The birdman has a name? I guess the squid one had a name. But wait. How does the king know his name? Maybe they chatted during their fights? That's weird. I guess I know the squid's name, so it's not so odd for him to know the bird's name.

"The birdman is named Alistair?" I ask. He does not answer my question but instead stops the horse and turns to face the oncoming threat.

"Sit up straight. Hold on. I don't want you falling off now." He snaps the reins, and the horse runs faster toward the dark mass. I sit up straight. My head taps against Thadius' chin while the horse bounces up and down. I hope he doesn't bite his tongue. I congratulate myself for not going down a sexy spiral at the thought of his tongue.

We're close enough now that I can see the birdman has a spear of some sort. Thadius must notice when I do because he unsheathes his sword. I did not notice the sword on his hip before, but now, with it held out in front of me, it glistens with some sort of iridescence. The iridescence isn't a reflection of light. It's overcast. It's a greenish, moving iridescence. Does this world have magic? Maybe I'll ask Thadius about it if we make it out alive.

"Thadius, let her go! Give her back. You cannot have this one, too!" the birdman screams. What does he mean by "have this one, too?"

"Shut your dirty mouth, you filthy bird!" Thadius shouts. His tone is mean, angry, and intimidating. I struggle with men yelling. It causes a deep panic in me, even if they're yelling to protect me and not yelling at me. I shiver, and he nuzzles the side of my head as if to assure me. His hands are full of reins and swords. "It'll be okay," he whispers. It's him I'm afraid of at this moment, so this action does not reassure me. It sends a jolt of fear through my body.

We rush toward the monster. I can now see that the spear is in the birdman's beak. His arms are steady, allowing him to glide.

We are within striking distance when Alistair dives downward toward us. He takes the spear from his beak and grabs it with two hands. He falls like a sinking stone—spear pointed down, directly at us. I lift my hands to cover my face as I imagine it slicing through me.

Thadius releases the reins and hugs me tightly against himself, protecting me. Alistair balks and puts the spear back in his mouth. He spreads his wings to slow his descent. It causes a wave of wind to engulf us and whips my hair into my face. Why did he stop?

Alistair is now a much bigger target. Thadius takes this opportunity to stab at him. He shoves his sword in the direction of Alistair's chest, but Alistair twists at just the right moment. He is stabbed between the wing and breast instead. He howls in pain as a shimmering green wave overcomes him.

The birdman crashes to the ground, slipping off the blade and landing hard on his back. A cloud of dirt puffs up around him as he lands with a thud. I hear his head whack against the ground. Blood splatters behind his head.

Blood is glistening off the sword. Thadius turns the sword from side to side, admiring the blood, and smirks. He notices me watching him and immediately wipes the side of the blade on the horse to remove the blood.

Why would he do that? That's strange. "I am sorry you had to see all that blood, beautiful." His erection is raging against my back again. I can feel him grind slightly against me. I am torn between feeling slightly aroused by this and a feeling of uncertainty I cannot shake. Did he just use me as a human shield? Is that why the birdman didn't attack?

I place my hands on the saddle in front of me between my legs. I press myself against my arm hard in an attempt to relieve the pressure building up at my crotch. I hope Thadius doesn't notice. I look up at him. He is smirking. Maybe he does see what I'm doing. Or maybe he's pleased with his kill.

I look at Alistair's body writhing in pain on the ground. Blood is pooling under his arm and head. I feel nauseated. My arousal has dissipated.

Thadius turns the horse as if to leave. "You're not going to just leave him like that, are you?" I plead.

He must assume I am afraid of the threat this birdman may still cause, "Don't worry, babe. He'll die soon enough and won't be able to come after you again." I'm not worried about that. Well, I guess I am, but now I mostly feel extreme sympathy for this creature. His wails of agony sound like that of a real man. It doesn't seem right to leave him like this. I don't press the subject—afraid to show empathy to the creature that killed Thadius' wife.

We ride away, and Thadius seems to sit with a bit more confidence. It's almost like he's jauntily walking away from his conquest. The sound of Alistair's head hitting the ground rings in my ears. I picture myself falling from this horse, with the same fate—head smacking against the ground and my brains splattering across the dirt. I tap my finger to the beat of the horse's hooves as we trot and count the steps to calm myself. If I keep counting, I won't fall. Three hundred, three hundred one, three hundred two.

4

Thadius gently jostles me awake, "Astrid! Wake up. You'll be able to see the castle against the sunrise and it is so beautiful."

"Thad, I'm sorry I keep falling asleep and leaving you alone. I normally have a really hard time sleeping. I must be exhausted from the stress."

"Thad?" he chuckles and looks at me with a questioning look.

"Oh, I'm sorry, can I call you Thad?"

"Yeah, I like the sound of that on your voice."

We reach the cusp of a hill and I can see the castle and surrounding town in the distance. It looks like something out of a fairy tale.

"There's the City of Prailyra and at its heart, you can see my castle," he states.

"It's beautiful!" I exclaim.

He chuckles. "Thanks."

Based on everyone's clothing, I feel like I woke up at a Renaissance fair. Now that I think about it, Thadius is dressed like he works at a Medieval Times restaurant. My brightly colored hoodie with a rainbow unicorn and pajama pants with kitten faces all over them look ridiculous in comparison. They always look ridiculous since I'm a thirty-year-old woman wearing clothes that look like they belong to a child, but I am suddenly embarrassed by them for the first time.

We ride through the town, and I am surprised by a palpable sadness hanging in the air. Missing women posters are posted on nearly every surface.

The missing women posters look like photographs. There are no cars—just horses. There is absolutely no technology. It looks like the 1400s. Or earlier? Honestly, I suck at history and have no idea when the Middle Ages were. Or was it the dark ages? No, Astrid, don't start obsessing over this now. How are there photographs? How does that work? That's a bit anachronistic. I look around and don't see any other signs of technology. Where and when the fuck am I?

Dogs are barking in the distance. I hear weeping. A deep agonizing wailing rings out beside us. It is excruciating to hear—it drenches me with so much empathy that it feels like a cold bucket was dumped over my head.

A woman approaches the horse while waving a missing woman poster. "My king, please, save my daughter! The monsters must have abducted her." The poster contains a color photograph of a gorgeous woman with big round green eyes and bright red hair. Her lips are the same red, adding a beautiful symmetry to the image.

"I assure you, madam, I will do everything in my power to find your daughter. Now step aside," Thadius says with a wave of a hand. That was a bit cold of him. I'm sure this is all very stressful for him. To be king of a kingdom that has such a hardship must be very difficult. My eyes well up in tears for the woman. I watch her as we trot past her. She looks me in the eyes, and I give her a sad smile. She melts into despair, arms drooping down, face to the ground, and slowly folds like a discarded pile of clothes. Fuck, was smiling the wrong thing to do? Two young men calling "Mama!" run up to her and lift her. They carry her as she drags her feet, her face pointed to the sky and wailing. She looks like a toddler throwing a temper tantrum in a store.

Tears burst from my eyes, and I bury my face in my hands. Thadius brushes my hair behind my ear with his left hand and says, "You sweet thing. I'm sorry that you had to see that."

We continue through the village, and the crowds of people part for the king. "My liege," they sigh as we pass. I can hear the occasional, "Who is she? She is gorgeous!" I feel like they can't be talking about me until I hear someone say, "Oh, my god, can you smell her? I have never smelt something so amazing in my life. His Majesty is truly a lucky man."

What is with these people? I am below average to average at best. I'm overweight. I don't see any overweight people here. Maybe they think plumpness is hot? I'm nothing compared to the woman on that poster.

As I scan my surroundings to see the hotness level of the people here, I notice there are no women of reproductive age. What is that about? Maybe this is just the "dude and old lady district." That's stupid. Surely, I'd have seen some younger women by now. Perhaps they're all hiding, afraid of being abducted by monsters.

"Is there an inn or something I will stay in?" I ask.

"Don't be absurd. You're staying with me in my castle," he states.

The whole time we've been together, Thadius has said I was coming home with him. I just thought he meant coming home to his town, not his actual castle.

"Oh, I don't want to impose!"

"Nonsense. It is no imposition. Besides, do you have money for an inn?"

"Oh, I guess I don't."

"See! It's settled. You'll stay with me. I have more than enough room. It is an expansive castle, after all." He winks at me and grins his big, brilliant smile.

I realize it is no longer overcast, but I do not feel like the sky will swallow me. On this horse, between Thadius' arms, feels safe. Like a little room that is all mine. The thought of getting off and walking around is terrifying. I still don't tempt fate and try to look at the sky or the top of the castle when we get to the gates. I wish I could look to the top of the castle and really get a good view of its architecture, but I know glancing up will only make me feel like I'm falling down.

At the gates, a man shouts from a lookout tower, "Your Majesty! Your guards have been running around searching for you all day! Where have you been?"

"You do not presume to question me, do you?" Thadius barks at the man.

The man stumbles back and seems shocked to be yelled at, "Of course not, Your Majesty. I will send out birds to signal your arrival. Everyone will be most glad you are safe."

"Why would I not be safe?! I am the king!" Thadius' jaw clenches and I can almost feel the anger emanate from him. It makes me extremely uncomfortable and I pull away from him slightly.

The guard realizes he cannot win and opens the gate without further word. My gaze is transfixed on Thadius' face. He is scowling and the muscles in his jaw are throbbing as he grinds his teeth. When he notices my looking at him, he instantly smiles back at me and says, "Sorry, I'm just so tired."

Yes, I suppose he must be. I have been dozing off this whole time, and he has been riding without rest. "Oh, I completely understand." I accept this as an excuse for his cruelty, but I am still a bit weary of him. Men, particularly angry men, are terrifying and I'm worried he will get mad again. He rubs his jaw, perhaps to loosen the muscles that have tightened.

We enter through the gate and turn to the left, where the stables are. I wish I could stay on this horse forever.

We dismount Fancy and leave her with a young boy who does not speak to us, only bows. I thank the young boy. Thadius laughs at me as if I am being silly. I give the horse a good nuzzle and pat its nose. I've never been around a horse before, but I assume she will like this. She seems to and leans into my touch. I tell her, "Thank you for rescuing me." I want to say, "and for the best orgasm I've had in a decade," but don't.

As we exit the stable, I am overwhelmed by the vastness of this wide-open space and recoil a bit. Thadius asks me if I am okay. I tell him truthfully, "Just a bit overwhelmed. I have problems with open spaces—with being outside."

"Oh, you sweet thing," he says while he grabs my hand. "Does this help?" My heart races, and now I'm panicking for a different reason. If I had my watch, it would scream at me about my elevated heart rate. I flush and look at my toes. Dang, my socks are dirty. The dirtiness of my socks almost distracts me from the dirtiness of my mind.

"Actually, yes, it does," I say with a soft smile and scoot closer to him. His presence is comforting and makes me feel grounded. I am a bit embarrassed by how pathetic I am being.

He seems genuinely pleased with my response. "Don't worry. I will protect you from everything. Just stay with me, and we'll get you inside. That should help." He was right; it would. He pulls on my hand, and I walk demurely behind him. I'm too scared to look up but too curious not to and steal glances at my surroundings. When I can't stand looking around, I look at his perfect, perfect ass. My fear subsides as I watch the muscles in his backside flex and tighten with each step. I wonder what it looks like under those pants. Gosh, I wish those pants were tighter.

He drags me through the outer court. Various men appear to be training with swords. As we pass, they all lift their faces to the air—stopped dead in their tracks. One is knocked off his feet with a bloody nose from the fumble. They all turn to us and stare. No, they aren't staring at us; they are staring at me. I can see them all grab at their pants, adjusting. Holy shit, are they all getting aroused because of me!? One whispers a bit too loudly to his companion, "Look at those breasts!" I blush with embarrassment. I look at my toes while I hide behind Thadius. Please, Thadius, get me out of here.

Thadius hears him and shouts, "Get back to work, you louts!" I jump at the sound of his voice and recoil. I really don't like it when he yells.

"Oh, my sweetling. I did not realize how frail you are. I won't raise my voice again. Jacobson! You have caused me to upset my frail companion. Apologize to me and her at once!" he says sternly, but not as loudly. He has softened his voice for my comfort, but you can still hear the anger in it.

The man known as Jacobson, the one who commented on my breasts, says, "My deepest apologies, Your Majesty. My sincerest apologies, My Lady." He tugs at his tunic, attempting to hide his erection, and lifts his leg to adjust himself a bit. Thadius glowers, seemingly unhappy with Jacobson's futile attempt to hide his arousal. The sparkle in his eyes that I've admired is gone. Perhaps, he's not as nice as I thought he was. Maybe I've made a mistake coming here with him.

"Very well," he says. "Back to work." He's not yelling anymore, but there is a level of authoritativeness to his voice that still surprises me. Is this the same man who chuckled and smiled the whole way here?

The men get back to fighting each other. I think one of them throw some kind of fireball. I slow and tug at Thadius' hand. "Was that magic?" I ask.

"Of course," he laughs at me like I am the silliest thing in the world. Okay, I'm definitely in a different world. Magic? I want to ask about magic but am easily distracted by the small structure we pass that looks like a chapel. It has a symbol on the steeple I have never seen before. It's a pitchfork of some kind. A trident, maybe? I wonder what their religion is called.

We approach a second gate, and a man in full plate armor runs to the king. "Your Majesty. Welcome home. I see you had an eventful excursion," he says. I think he is looking at me, but I cannot tell due to his helmet.

"Yes," Thadius says to the guard. He then leans in toward him and whispers something I cannot hear. I think I hear "Jacobson," but I am not sure.

"Right away, sir," the guard salutes and then hurries toward the outer court.

"Jacobson isn't in trouble, is he? I really hope it's not on account of me." My heart races thinking about what will be done to the man.

"Oh, don't worry your pretty little head about it," he smiles and gently pulls me forward. I do worry my pretty little head about it. I worry my pretty little head about everything. I hate that I'm letting him lead me around like some weak little puppy. I am a fucking smart, strong woman. What is wrong with me? I know exactly what's wrong with me. It's easy to pretend I'm fearless when I don't leave my house and don't speak to people except online. I'm always a pathetic mess when I speak to people in real life. Especially since the pandemic.

COVID hit three years ago and I hadn't left the house since. My agoraphobia and social anxiety have always been a problem. But once I was permitted to never leave the house again, and finally allowed to work from home, I embraced it. Too much. All of the bravery I had learned how to fake while in an office, all of the social anxiety I was able to pretend away, had overcome me again during the pandemic. During the allowed isolation, it has all evaporated.

And here we are, outside! In a fucking world I've never been to, where people throw fireballs and I think everyone wants to rape me. Of course, I'm scared. Thadius has been kind. He saved me and he hasn't taken advantage of me. What happened on the horse, that was … that wasn't taking advantage of me in my fragile state, was it? Is there a power dynamic I am not considering? I shake my head. Stop it. Stop spiraling and overthinking. One foot in front of the other. One, two, three. I count my steps.

We approach a large open gate. Past the gate is a mote. I stop abruptly. Thadius' momentum, combined with my sudden stopping, causes him to stumble slightly. He looks back at me with gentle concern.

"I'm… I'm sorry. I am scared of water. I'm scared of bridges." On the other side of the moat, the castle doors begin to open for us. I tremble and crouch to the ground. I release his hand and hug my knees.

He smiles. I think he's trying to be reassuring, but it looks sinister. "Okay, well, if we just get over this bridge this one time, you will never have to cross it again. The water is not that deep. The bridge is not that long," he says while pointing at the door to the castle.

I look at him with a pleading look of desperation. I shake my head in protest and bury my head in my knees.

"Will it help if I carry you?" That is even scarier. What if he gets halfway across and decides to chuck me into the water? I see the castle after the moat and know that once I cross this bridge, I can be inside again. I know my legs will not move on their own. I feverishly nod my head up and down. I squeeze my eyes shut and wait for him to lift me. What if he can't pick me up? I weigh almost two hundred pounds. There's no way he'll …

Mid-thought, he lifts me, like a husband carrying their bride across a threshold—with minimal effort. He doesn't even make a noise. I open my eyes and look at him in surprise. "Don't worry, babe, I got you." God, this is so fucking hot. I wrap my arms around his neck. All the distrust I had for him seems to melt away and is replaced by a warm and fuzzy feeling. Am I in love with this guy already? My body has stopped trembling in fear and now trembles in desire. I want to stay like this forever.

I cannot enjoy this tingling happiness for long because he's already walking toward the moat. I freak out and bury my face in the crook of his neck. With my face here, I can smell his armpits. They smell, but in a good way. It's that sour, musty smell of a men's basketball game. How I can be both terrified and horny at the same time is a character trait I will never understand. My nose and lips are pressed against his neck. I want to suck—hard. I want to bite his neck, gain vampiric powers, and drain his blood—fill myself with him. I squeeze my legs together to feel something between them.

Before I know it, he gently places my feet down on the solid ground.

"It's all over. We're here," he says. I open my eyes.

We are in a large courtyard with stunning shrubbery and plants. "Wow," I gasp. I am blown away by the beauty.

"This was my mother's garden when she was alive. It was her pride and joy. I make sure to keep it beautiful in her honor."

"Oh, I'm sorry for your loss," I say quietly. I never know what to say in situations like this, but "sorry for your loss" always seems to be a good catch-all.

"It's okay. It was a while ago. But thank you." He smiles at me and places his hand on my shoulder. I blush like a virgin who has never been touched. I've definitely been touched before, but definitely not by someone this hot.

To my left is a small area of apple trees. It makes me wonder if we are in a climate that snows. It was the dead of winter when I fell asleep back home, but this seems almost like the fall season. "Does it snow here?"

"Yes, it does. I have fire mages here around the clock in the winter defrosting the roses." Mages. Wow. I cannot believe this is happening. I need to find out how magic works here. Maybe my high intelligence would make me an excellent mage if it's like a video game. I giggle to myself because that is a pretty stupid idea, and I've been acting like a moron since I arrived here, so maybe I'm not as smart as I thought I was.

He drags me through the garden, and we finally approach the enormous castle doors. A slew of men and women are standing outside the entrance waiting for us. They all bow and immediately follow behind us as we pass them.

I breathe an immense sigh of relief as I finally get to be indoors again.

We enter the castle and the foyer is gigantic. The people who greet us at the door all wait patiently for the king to give them orders. He looks toward one of the women dressed as a maid. "Has the Rose Tower been cleaned recently? Is it able to accommodate our guest?"

"Yes, Your Majesty. We tended to it just this morning," she replies.

"Perfect," he says, then barks orders as he leads me toward a hallway at the end of the room. "Have the kitchen prepare the lady a meal. She has not eaten in a while and is also quite thirsty. Bring her a change of clothes and send someone to bathe and change her." He's leading me forward with such precision and force that I barely have time to look around.

"Yes, Your Majesty," they say, bowing and scurrying off.

"This is my home." He says motioning around with his arm. "I'll give you a tour later, but for now, let's get you fed and cleaned. I'm sure you are quite exhausted and don't feel like trekking around this huge castle." He was half-right. I did not feel like trekking around it, but I am deeply curious to see it. However, my fear of new places beats out my curiosity.

"Yes, that would be lovely. Thank you," I say.

As we enter the hall, he places his arms around my shoulders and leads me down the hall. He points to the various pictures on the walls telling me who each person is—all previous kings and queens. My shoulders burn with the warmth of his touch and the desire within me is raging. I am so focused on his touch; I can't concentrate on his words. I'm in a daze. This is all happening so quickly. We reach the end of the stairs and are confronted with a steep, narrow spiral staircase. No, not stairs. I work out sometimes but not enough to be able to go up a flight of stairs without embarrassing myself.

Thadius gestures to the stairwell and says, "Your room is up this way." He walks in front of me, because there is not enough room for us to walk side-by-side, and his ass is right in my face. I want to reach out and bite it. It is so perfectly taught and bubbly. He grabs my hand and pulls me up the stairs.

Are we going up a tower? Am I seriously going to get a room at the top of a tower in a fucking castle?! I suddenly remember I'm afraid of heights and regardless of how romantic it sounds to sleep on a pile of pillows at the top of a tower while, perhaps, Thadius kisses my entire body, I'm going to be scared. Just stay away from windows, Astrid.

I am out of breath by the time we reach the top. I am desperately trying to not let Thadius see me heaving. Breathing long drawn out, pained breaths through my nose. Him seeing me pant after sex—acceptable. After doing other physical activity—unacceptable. As expected, the stairs end at a door. This is the top of the tower! A stitch builds up in my side and I pretend it away. I can't show him how pathetic I am.

The door is white with carved ornate roses on it. I wonder if this was Thad's mother's room. I'm not brave enough to ask. Plus, I can't fucking breathe. Talking would give me away.

As Thad opens the door with a key, he grins at me and states, "I recall you telling me you have trouble sleeping. I thought this room would be good for you. It is the quietest room in the house and happens to have the softest bed." Did he remember that? I only said it in passing.

"This can be your room. Consider it and everything inside it yours from this point on."

He opens the door to an extremely large, round, opulent room with a spiral staircase in the middle that leads to a second level. One side of the room is hidden behind folding screens. I assume it is the changing and bathing area. The other side contains a huge canopy bed. In the middle, near the stairs, is a seating area with a small dining table, couches, and chairs.

I gasp in wonder—and exhaustion. I clap my hands together and look at him like he just offered me the greatest gift in the world.

"Really!? I can stay here?" I squeak out breathlessly. It is so beautiful. I would have paid tons of money to get a hotel room like this back home.

"You like it?" He does that adorable half-smile and almost blushes at me.

"Oh, my God. I love it. This is so sweet of you, Thad." I scurry around the room looking at everything. When I reach the window, I forget my promise to myself and gaze out at the gorgeous view.

"I can see the whole kingdom from here!" I exhale—still breathless.

"Well, not all of it. Laerean is the biggest kingdom in the world after all," he chuckles.

I lose myself in the excitement and look down. The world spins around me. We are so high up. Directly below me is the moat. Shit. Astrid, you weren't supposed to go to the window.

I pull myself back in quickly before I get sick. I can't pass out. I can't get sick. I can't freak out. Not now. Not when I get to be in this beautiful room.

I move to the other side of the room. There's a chamber pot and a huge clawfoot tub. There is also a dressing table with many bottles of lotions and potions. A woman did live here. As if it wasn't already obvious with all the pink.

"May I go up the stairs?" I ask and point to the spiral staircase in the room.

"Of course!" he waves his hands in a way that emphasizes I should go.

Wait. Maybe I shouldn't. I've only just got my breath back. Take the stairs slowly, Astrid.

Up the stairs, I find a lavish sitting area. There is another window with a telescope pointing toward the sky. Okay, so they have cameras and telescopes. There are also easels, paints, yarn, threads, and fabrics. A foot pedal sewing machine (tech item number three), a loom, and a yarn-spinning wheel sit on one side of the room.

"These were my mother's personal chambers. She was an artist." He looks a bit sad when he says this.

"Oh, Thad, you really don't have to let me stay in here. I don't want to disrespect your mother's memory," I say.

He looks at me with a sad smile, but it brightens as he says, "I appreciate your concern, but, no, it's okay. It has been a very long time since a woman enjoyed this room. I think it would honor her for you to use it."

"Oh, thank you!" I say. I run to him and wrap my arms around his neck to give him a big hug.

"Erm," he says, holding his hands behind my back as if he wants to hug me back, but is unsure if he can. He gets an instant erection that presses against the top of my pelvis.

"Oh, I'm sorry," I say as I back away. "You are a king. I shouldn't be so familiar. We don't have royalty where I'm from so I don't know how to act."

"Well, I suppose I can teach you." He says bashfully, with his hands folded in front of his crotch covering his erection. This man is so smooth. If I hadn't just felt it raging against me, I'd never know he was rock hard right now.

He clears his throat and walks down the stairs. I follow him.

In the main room again, he turns to me and says, "Well, I suppose I should leave you to rest. I will send someone up later to feed you and bathe you." Bathe me? "I would love to have breakfast with you tomorrow. Would it be okay if I come tomorrow at daybreak?"

"Daybreak? That's a bit early, isn't it?"

He chuckles. "You are so amusing, Astrid. How about you send for me when you wake?"

"That would be amazing, Thad."

"Great," he says. We look at each other, unsure of what to say or do. Should we kiss goodbye? Should we hug? Do I bow? What does one do when one wants to say goodbye to a king?

He clears his throat and spins on his heels while saying, "Well, until tomorrow!" and lets himself out.

I spin around and take in my surroundings. I giggle, jump, and clap like a little girl. I can't believe this is happening.

5

I walk over to the basin in the bathing area and splash some water on my face. I find what I think is soap, rub it on my hands, and wash up to my elbows. I feel pretty gross after the day I've had and am happy I can clean up before eating. I wonder what kind of food they'll bring. I hope there's cake! I hope it's edible. What if they have weird food indigestible by my foreign body?

As I'm scrubbing, there is a knock on the door. Three men enter the room holding trays of food. They are all obviously overcome by me and almost drop their trays. They compose themselves because, after all, they are professionals. Men getting erections at the sight of me is a bit annoying, but … if I'm being honest with myself, it's also awesome. I wouldn't consider myself particularly attractive, so provoking this response is a whole new experience. I've got great tits and a symmetric face, but my hair is always in a messy bun and my ass is always in some form of sweatpants. I went through a slutty hot girl phase in college, landing on a different dick almost every night, but that was nearly a decade and fifty pounds ago.

All the food is covered with cute silver covers. The men place the trays on the large table in the middle of the room and position things around the table. They remove the covers and wait for me to inspect the food. There are meats, vegetables, fruits, different types of bread, and, as I had hoped, cakes. It looks like my own personal thanksgiving feast.

"Is this all for me?" I start drooling, but I need to uphold some facade of being a proper woman. I wipe my mouth to hide the unseemly response.

"Yes, M'Lady," one of the servers says as he pours me a glass of water. Another pours me a glass of wine. They set the wine in a bowl of ice and the water pitcher on the table. They bow a little lower than normal, presumably to hide their erections, and stay hunched as they hurry out of the room, anxious to escape me. As the door shuts, it sounds like it locks. Did I just get locked in? No, that can't be. I consider getting up to check the door, but I am much more concerned with eating at the moment.

I survey the table of food and grab at the closest thing. I am alone, so it's okay that I eat like a ravenous beast, stuffing various items in my mouth. I am determined to try each thing.

I eat until I feel like I might burst, but I haven't tried the cakes. I overdid it and may throw up. I lay on the bed, spread out, with a hand on my stomach, trying to digest my food. In my other hand, I have a cupcake of sorts, waiting for the right moment to shove it in my mouth. Right now, the thought of anything passing my tongue makes me want to puke, but I know from experience this feeling will pass shortly, and I can get right back at it.

"M'Lady, may I enter?" I hear a rap at the door and a soft feminine voice. Oh, yeah, I'm supposed to take a bath. I shove half the cupcake in my mouth, afraid whoever it is will see the fatty cuddling the cupcake in bed.

"Yes, you may," I sing, before engulfing the other half of the cupcake.

A gorgeous brunette woman walks in with what appears to be clothes draped over her arm. She glances at me when I am mid-face-stuff, and I am sure I look like a damn squirrel stuffing her face with cupcakes for the winter.

"Good evening, M'Lady," she says with a giggle. I am taken aback by her beauty. Her hair is voluminous, wavy, and long. Her eyes are big and brown. Her cheeks are a perfect shade of pink. She looks like a porcelain doll—a porcelain sex doll—dressed in what my weeb-self would describe as a Lolita maid attire—and an even stronger weeb would probably correct me on. She's wearing a corset over the dress, and her breasts are pushed to their maximum height. Her top dips so low that I am surprised her nipples are not showing. The top is a little too tight, so the fatty part of her breast is bulging out a bit. It's so fucking hot. My body heats with lust and embarrassment—a feeling I am incredibly familiar with. I wish I could see her form underneath the many layers of skirts. I gulp down the cupcake still nestled in my cheek comically loud.

"Hi," I say pathetically. I am utterly stunned by her beauty.

She doesn't allow me much time to gawk. She hurries in and pulls the various items of clothing off of her arm and laying them around the room. She speaks hurriedly, a woman with shit to do. "I have for you a gown for your breakfast tomorrow. Don't worry. I will assist you with putting it on in the morning. I just wanted to check and see if it would fit and if it was to your liking. Oh, I heard you were quite voluptuous and guessed at the size. It looks like I was right." She eyes me in a way that I am unsure if she is complimenting me or hitting on me. She continues running around the room as she places various fabrics in their specific places. She continues to chatter quickly, "I also have something for you to wear tonight while you sleep. And here is a robe for you to wear as I bathe you. I also have these undergarments for you. Here's an extra blanket in case you are cold."

As she is fluttering around the room, young boys begin carrying heavy buckets of steaming water and pouring them into the tub. They struggle to lift the buckets over the edge and look like they may break in half. I feel bad for them doing this for me. Especially considering they had to lug the buckets up the stairs. Who is going to drain the tub? I wonder where they bring the water from. Maybe there's a pulley system we can get together to bring water up from the base of the tower—save these poor boys' backs.

She pulls out a bottle of small pills. Okay, they have pills here. "His Majesty told me that I am to do whatever it takes to help you sleep tonight, so I brought you some of these dried cherry seeds with a hint of sleeping magic cast on them."

I take the bottle. "Oh, thank you. Should I go ahead and take one now?"

"Yes, these take a while to take effect. Combined with a warm bath, it should help to make you drowsy. If the bath and the cherry seeds don't work, there are other things I can do to help you sleep." She half-smiles at me and batts her eyes.

Wait, what? She looks me up and down. Okay, is she hitting on me? Is she offering me sex? A small firework goes off in my pants. No, that can't be what she means, but just in case it is, I say, "Oh, um, that won't be necessary. Thank you." I picture her head buried between my legs and running my hands through her hair.

"Well, just let me know." She brushes off my protest, like the school lunch lady who knows you want two slices of pizza but won't push when you say you want one. She knows she'll see you later.

As the last boy leaves, he takes the dirty dishes and the rest of my cupcakes with him. No, I was going to eat more of those. She moves to the door and quickly closes it. I watch her move back to the bath. Her hips move with a gentle sway, and her breasts bounce ever so slightly. I'm still ogling her breasts when she begins to pour various concoctions into the bath, making it bubble and foam. I am excited to get in there. I feel filthy, and it looks so relaxing.

"Okay, let's get you out of these dirty … Oh, my. What are you wearing?" She is just now noticing how ridiculous I look against this medieval backdrop.

"I, um…" I am so embarrassed. I look like an idiot.

She doesn't wait for my reply and leans in to look closely at the zipper of my hoodie, trying to figure out what it does. I pull it down, and she gasps in excitement, "Amazing!" I guess they don't have zippers here.

She doesn't let herself be amazed for long because she almost instantly pulls at the hoodie's sides and drops it to the floor. My t-shirt is even more ridiculous looking to her than my unicorn hoodie. It contains the entire cast of Sailor Moon on a tie-dye background. She giggles and says, "I love this!" as if it isn't weird. She grabs the bottom seam and yanks it upward. I hesitate for a minute when it gets to the bottom of my breasts, then breathe and lift my hands over my head. I squeeze my eyes shut in embarrassment when the shirt gets hooked on the bottom of my boobs, making them pop out the bottom and bounce their way into position like a set of anime tits.

I quickly cover my breasts with my arms. She wryly smiles at me. "It's okay. Your body is beautiful!" I pretend not to hear her. I'm too embarrassed. I am usually pretty proud of my breasts, but the thought of this gorgeous woman seeing me naked and comparing herself to me makes me want to crawl into a hole and die. I imagine her insulting me, screaming at me that I'm repulsive. Then in the next breath, telling me I'm a dirty girl who needs to be taught a lesson. Men yelling at me scares the shit out of me. But women yelling at me, degrading me … gets me a little hot. It makes me want to prove to them that I deserve their love. My therapist and I were starting to unpack these parts of my psyche. Oh, well, I guess I'll never figure it out now.

She doesn't leave me much time to feel the shame because she instantly hooks her thumbs into my pajama pants and underwear and tugs them down with a quick jolt. I'm left standing there, naked, except for my socks. I remove one hand from my breasts and cover my pubic region.

"Okay, now, this way." She says and leads me to step out of my pile of clothes. She places her hand on the small of my back, gently nudging me toward the bath. A cold sweat breaks out all over my body. The smell of her, combined with the fragrance from the bath and her hand touching me, makes me a bit delirious.

My socks are still on. She notices as I step out of the pile of clothes. "Oops, we forgot something," she says and bends over in front of me, reaching for my socks. Her face is mere inches from my crotch. Oh, God. I look down at her. I'm sure my whole body is beet red with embarrassment and excitement. She looks up at me while I lift my legs to allow her to remove my socks, and all I can think about is her mouth on my clit. How beautiful she'd look, those big doe eyes staring at me while I grind away on her face. My bush engulfing her cute little nose. Stop it, you dirty perv, before you leak all over the place.

I hurry to the bath, hoping for some way to hide my body.

She holds my hand as I gingerly place my toe into the bath water. Jeeze, that is hot. I pull my toe back.

"Too hot?" she asks.

"Just a little? But I'll get used to it." I'm sorry! Please don't be mad at me. I can take it. I can take the heat for you.

"No, no. I will fix it." She blows gently, waving her head over the water. Tiny snowflakes pour from her mouth, instantly melting in the water.

I look at her in amazement. She notices me gawking and says, "My magic's not good for much else," and laughs embarrassed at herself.

"No, that's amazing! I bet you could do all sorts of amazing things with your mouth." I quickly turn away immediately regretting my word choice. She giggles and seems to blush before motioning for me to try getting in the bath again.

I dip my toe in, and it is perfect! Hot, but not too hot. I send my whole leg into the depths and grin stupidly in awe at her, saying, "Wow, it's perfect! You are amazing!" This time she definitely blushes. Use a word other than "amazing," Astrid. You know other words! She's going to think you're an idiot.

I grip the tub's sides and slowly lower myself into the warm liquid. I feel all my worries leave my body instantly.

"I put some calming potions in there. It should make you feel nice and relaxed." It does.

"I'm Astrid. What's your name?" Dang, I am feeling chill. I can't believe I'm talking first.

She seems genuinely surprised I asked. "My name? Oh, it's Genevieve."

"That is a beautiful name, Genevieve. It suits you," I say lazily as I sink further into the liquid, letting the bubbles reach my chin. At least you didn't say "amazing," Astrid.

She blushes again and stutters out a, "Thank you."

She composes herself quickly. "I am going to wash your hair and body. Normally I would do more, but I am sure you'd rather take that time to sleep, so let's just do the essentials. Sit back, relax, and let me know if you need anything." I sink so the bubbles are covering my mouth. I close my eyes and nod my head sleepily.

She washes my hair. As she lathers my hair, she slowly massages my head and rubs her thumbs in a circular motion on my temples. "Where were you the last time I had a migraine?" I sleepily breathe out.

She giggles and pours water over my head multiple times to thoroughly remove the suds. I am trying hard to stay awake, but it is so relaxing I can't. I doze off as she washes my face.

I awaken when she starts scrubbing my feet. I giggle and squirm. She laughs at me and brings the sponge up my thigh. Hey now. Where are you going with that sponge?

One of her breasts dips into the bath as she reaches in, her arm fully submerged, and the bottom of her sleeve is drenched. As she lifts, I can see her nipple through her top—my own personal wet t-shirt contest with one contestant—the winner. I shift uncomfortably, trying to ignore the building pressure between my legs. I can't stop staring at her breasts—at her beauty. She notices me staring, pushes her hair behind her ear, and gives me a half smile. I look away quickly and blush.

"Remember, I am here for whatever you need, M'Lady. Anything, anything, at all." She grins at me. Does she know what I am thinking? I'm pretty sure she is offering to please me, but I cannot ask her to do that for me. Maybe I should tell her she might be more comfortable if she takes off her shirt. No, stop being a dirty perv. You could never. The power dynamic would make you a predator. Even if she is offering, you would hate yourself in the morning.

I inhale, and the flowery scents of the bath seep into my body. Everything gets hazy, and I feel instantly calmed. "Um, what is in this water? It feels like it is going to my head."

"Well, I did brew quite a few inhibition reducers for you. His majesty told me you were a very stressed woman." That was sweet of him. I am a stressed woman. But right now, I'm a super horny chill woman. The sound of Thad's name triggers images of him on top of me, pumping into me as I bite at his shoulder. I shake my head, trying hard to be in the moment and sober up a bit.

"So, you can do magic other than the cold thing?" I ask.

Once again, she seems genuinely surprised I am asking about her. "Oh. Well, yes. I can do the 'cold thing,' as you called it. But I am also quite adept and brewing different baths for different moods. Whatever kind of bath your heart desires, I can concoct it. Um… not to brag." She definitely wants to brag.

"You can brag! You're quite amazing," I said. There you go with that word again, Astrid … amazing. This time she stops scrubbing for a minute and bites her lip in a half-smile. I swear the tub's water height went up an inch after a rush of lusty liquid expelled itself from my body. She's so cute.

"We should probably get you in bed," she says.

I agree. I'm tired, and I need her to leave so I can rub one out.

She grabs a large towel and holds it out, beckoning me to stand. I grab the sides of the tub and slowly stand, the effects of the tub wear off a little, and my anxiety returns. I picture myself slipping and breaking my head open on the side of this beautiful tub and watch it fill with blood. Genevieve is screaming—her tits bouncing right out of her top—her nipples stiff with fear. Do nipples get hard with fear?

She wraps the towel around me, arms and all, almost hugging me in the process. I feel so comforted by it I let out a little satisfied moan. I pull the towel to my face and nuzzle against it before I remove my arms from under it and tuck it on the side—stopping it from falling when I remove my hands. She offers me her hand, and I step out, dripping all over the floor.

"Oh, no! I'm going to ruin the floor!"

"It's okay," she states, "the floor has built-in drainage." She leans over and unplugs the tub's stopper. I bend over to look at the floor and notice I am standing on a grate with tiny holes. There is a tube exiting the bottom of the tub.

"Ooh, neat!" I'm happy those poor boys don't have to come back to remove the water.

She grabs the towel off my body and drops it to the ground. Before I have a chance to be embarrassed, she's holding a robe for me to step into.

"Okay, sit at the mirror, and I will be right there." She hurriedly tidies up, wiping down the tub and a bit of water on the floor that missed the grate.

I lustfully watch her bend over. I can almost make out the shape of her ass in this position, and it really does look like her breasts may pop out any minute. Now that I know precisely where her nipple is, I see that wish isn't thoroughly impossible. Her breasts jiggle back and forth as she wipes. I am not proud that I quickly grind against my wrist as I pretend to adjust the chair. I consider reaching into my robe quickly, but she's already at my side, picking up a comb.

She moves the comb through my hair, which quickly and easily passes through my locks. I am shocked as my thin hair tangles so easily. I have to apply a deep conditioner to stop it from creating a bird's nest after every shower.

She grabs a bottle of some liquid and shakes it into her hand. Oh, it's body oil. Please don't rub that on me. I cannot take it.

She rubs her hands together, spreads the oil in her hands then grabs my feet. She massages the oil firmly and gently into my skin. She starts up my legs. Oh, God. I can't.

Lucky for me, she doesn't linger on my inner thighs. If she did, she'd find her hands wet with something other than oil. She pours more into her hands and smooths it into my hands and arms. Please don't reach into my robe, please don't reach into my robe. I can't handle her touching my breasts and torso right now. I also don't want her to see the way my stomach looks when I'm sitting. She reaches for the opening of my robe, and I grab her hands to stop her. "No, that's okay, I'm good," I say, flushed. "I think I'd like to go to sleep now."

"Okay, let's get you into your night dressings," she says as she stands.

She ushers me to another section of the room—a small sitting area next to a standing closet. She grabs the undergarments and sleeping clothes she placed on the chair for me earlier.

The undergarments are just a thin dress. I've never not worn panties before, but when in Rome. I pull the robe off and let it drop to the ground. No sense in being modest now. She slips the undergarment over my head, and I can see my pubic hair and large nipples through the thin fabric.

She places the nightgown over my head, and I slip my arms through its long sleeves. I expected the fabric to be scratchy, but the undergarment is some kind of silk, and the night dress is the softest cotton I've ever felt. I hug the material to my body and say, "Thank you."

"You are most welcome," she curtseys.

She hurriedly picks up all the towels and robes we left in our path, along with my clothes. "I will have these clothes washed and returned to you."

She stands in the doorway, holding my dirty clothes. "Is there anything else, M'Lady?" I stand in silence, considering. The water is still draining slowly from the tub, and the sound is all we can hear.

I shake my head quickly after a moment. "No, thank you. Good night."

"Okay, well, you see this string. It rings a summoning bell. Ring it whenever you need me. His Majesty directed me not to wake you for breakfast and wait for you to call. Ring this bell in the morning, and I will be up to dress you for your visit with His Majesty. Oh!" she says, remembering something. "I didn't show you the dress I picked for you!" She hurries to the dressing area and grabs the dress she hung there. She presents it to me, holding the top with one hand and lifts the skirt with the other. "What do you think? I think it will be beautiful with those gray eyes of yours." The fabric is a light blue; it reminds me of a video game ice level.

"I love it!" I exclaim.

"Oh, great! I'm so excited to be able to dress a lady again!" Again? Who else has she dressed? She returns it to its perch and hurries back to the door. She bows slightly to me, "Goodnight, my lady." And lets herself out. I think I hear it lock behind her. But why would it lock from the outside? I don't bother to check. I've got more important things to do.

The sleeping cherry seeds Genevieve gave me are taking over, and I need to do something before they knock me out. I'm finally alone! Time to do what I've wanted to do all day.

I quickly run to the bed and leap into the pillows. I flip over and spread out. I have a little energy burst, unable to contain my excitement. I kick my feet and bounce on the bed. Enough of that; down to business. Dirty business, I giggle to myself.

I grab the extra blanket she gave me because I know I will get cold in the middle of the night. Also, I know I need it for what is coming next. I scramble to tear the blankets down and wiggle my way under them. I roll the extra blanket into a long body-pillow shape and lay down on it on my tummy. I lift my dresses to my chin and jam my left hand down between my legs. My right-hand pinches my nipple.

My fingers slip inside me for just a moment. Holy shit, I am wet. I am going to ruin this blanket. But I can't care about that right now. I pull them upward, flatten my three fingers against my clit, and press hard. I grind against my hand and the blanket, biting at the blanket in pleasure.

As I masturbate furiously, images of Thadius entering me flash in my head. Then visions of Genevieve's face at my crotch, looking up at me. Then images of Thadius thrusting at me from behind, playing with my breasts, while Genoveva eats me from the front. I get a giggle thinking about how this might not be physically possible, and his ballsack may smack her chin away, but whatever, it's a masturbation fantasy. I can think about whatever I want.

Wow, that only took about fifteen seconds. As I climax, I moan loudly, and pictures of the seven monsters flash through my head. I come even harder and instantly fall asleep in this position.

6

I wake up in the same position I fell asleep—straddling the blankets with my hands at my crotch and breast. I'm drooling all over the blanket and have a terrible taste in my mouth. Ugh, I guess my mouth was wide open all night. I try to remember my dreams but am unable. Dang, I knocked myself out cold last night.

I sleepily shuffle to the bathing area and wash my hands in the basin. I look around for a toothbrush and see a bunch of small brushes, but I am not sure which will work. I'll ask Genevieve when I see her.

I ring the bell to summon Genevieve and she walks in a few minutes later. I feel guilty thinking she's been sitting around waiting for me.

She helps me get dressed. The dress contains a corset she has to tug hard at, and I feel like I may pass out. It's low cut, and makes my tits look huge. If dudes were creaming their pants when I wore a hoodie, wait until they see me now.

I notice Genevieve is getting flustered at the sight of my body. I wonder how my "make people horny by being smelly power" works. Does it affect anyone attracted to women? Does it only affect those who would have been attracted to me to begin with? Does it affect everyone? I may have to perform some experiments to find out. Maybe I should ask her how she feels. For science, of course—not because I keep staring at her tits whenever she bends over. Why does everything she does have to make them look like they're about to jiggle their way out of her dress?

She gives me a cloth to rub on my teeth and something to swish in my mouth and spit with. Thank God, I was so worried about breathing my rancid morning breath in her face. Good thing I didn't try brushing my teeth with any of those little brushes. I wonder what they're for.

She brushes my hair and braids a small crown around my head, letting the rest of my long wavy hair fall to my shoulders and kiss my breasts. She also puts a tiny bit of makeup on me. I look kind of cute. She's really good at this.

As she leaves the room, she turns to me, her whole face red, to say, "I will tell His Majesty you are ready to see him now." Is she flushing because she's aroused, or is she flushing because squeezing me into this thing was hard work?

I wait, standing nervously, fidgeting, and unsure of what to do. Should I sit? Should I stay standing? Should I lay on the bed in a way that makes my hips pop out and squeeze my breasts together? That's probably not what I should do, but I wish I could. I imagine Thad's hands running over my body, ripping my clothes, popping my breasts from their sheath, and taking them in his mouth.

I'm standing there, rubbing myself over my skirts, unable to handle the pressure I've built up in my body, when he opens the door. "Sorry, it took me so long, babe. I had some papers to sign," he says as he saunters in without knocking. Shit. Did he see me touching myself? I hope he didn't. Well, maybe I hope he did. Perhaps he'll take it as a cue that we can skip this whole breakfast date and jump right to fucking. Well … I am hungry, though. How am I hungry after gorging myself last night? Being horny 24/7 must burn a lot of calories. Okay, we can get to the fucking right after the eating.

He stops in his tracks when he sees me and gawks. I give him a bashful smile, doing my best impression of a pure, innocent princess rather than the raunchy, defiled programmer I actually am. He gains his composure and slyly shifts his erection, so I won't see it raging in his pants. He clears his throat and says, "You … you look stunning."

"Thanks. You do, too," I blush and look toward the ground. He is the most handsome man I have ever seen. He's dressed much more nicely than when we met, but I struggle to look at and admire him. Having social anxiety while being a complete and total horndog has proven difficult in life; today is a prime example of how. I want to push him to the ground and grind so hard on his dick that he cums before he can even whip it out, but I can barely look at him without my heart racing and imagining all the terrible things he must think of me.

He chuckles, "Well, I'm all dressed up for a meeting with the king of a neighboring country later today. I need to make a good first impression. I was worried you would sleep so late I'd miss my meeting with them." Would he have breakfast with me over meeting with the other king? That's sweet.

There is a knock on the door. "Come in," Thad says brusquely.

The three men who brought me food last night scurry in and set the food up around the table. We walk over and take our seats. "It all looks so yummy," I exclaim.

Two of the men leave, but one stands at Thad's side, holding a pitcher, waiting to refill our drinks. Thad says, "Leave us. Leave the pitcher," and points at an open spot on the table. He bows and leaves. I noticed the men all seemed to look incredibly uncomfortable, and I am happy they won't be standing around while we eat. I'm also hoping he asked them to leave so he can fuck my brains out while feeding me toast. Maybe I can slather butter on his dick and spread it on my toast. Why am I getting so hot for toast?

We nibble on the various delicacies in front of us. I look down at my plate the whole time, but sneak glances at Thad. When I see him staring at me and smiling, our eyes meet. I get flustered and look back down quickly. He chuckles a little each time. Just look at him, you dumb cow. Talk to him!

"How did you sleep?" Thad asks.

"Quite well, thank you," I say shyly. I want to scream, "Fuck me, Thad!" My imagination is running wild. My fear is overwhelming. I am sweating and I can feel my hair stick to my face. I imagine the makeup Genevieve put on me running down my face and dripping on my breasts. I pat my face dry with a napkin and place it on my lap. Oh, yeah. I have tits. I press my elbows in so that my breasts lift and squeeze together. I lean forward to give him a good look. I don't look at him, but he clears his throat the moment I do this, so I know he sees. Oh, Thad, is innocent 'ole me arousing you with her huge supple breasts? I can show you other things if you'd like.

We don't know what to say to each other. I'm trying to think of topics, but I don't know anything about this world, and all I want to do is drag his beautiful ass to the bed and sit on his face. I fantasize about doing just that when he asks if I need anything brought to my room to make it more comfortable.

"Oh, no! Everything is wonderful. I will let you know, though."

After we finish eating, he stands and says, "I'm sorry, babe, but I have to go meet with the King of Laila. Politics." I think for a minute about the fact that another king came all the way here to speak with him.

"Wow, the King came to see you himself? He didn't send someone in his stead? You must be really important." I say, my mind racing considering all the reasons they may be meeting.

"I am. He is here to convince me not to take his kingdom from him. I suppose he thinks if he does it in person, he has a better chance of convincing me." He smiles, almost wickedly, and stands to leave. Take his kingdom from him?

I stand, too, and follow him slowly like a sad dog who's about to be left home alone all day when her owner is at work. I don't want him to go. I want him to stay and chat with me. Stay and fuck me. Stay and cuddle me. I should have talked more. I should have been charming. I know how to do it. I just need a bit of practice. My heart races as I look at him, my eyes welling up with tears. He gives me a pitying smile, and I look back down at the ground. "When … when can I see you again?" I muster.

He lifts my chin with his fingers so I can look him in the eyes. "As soon as possible." And kisses me gently on the lips. The kiss feels like a fire that spreads through my body. He pulls back, and I'm trembling, making fists in the fabrics of my skirts.

"Hopefully, that's very soon," I say meekly. He smiles and looks back as he shuts the door behind him. The feeling of his lips on mine is still etched in my skin. I place my hands to my lips to try to hold the feeling even longer. Well, now I have to masturbate again.

- - - -`♥´- - - -

The king visits me often. He always brings small gifts, like books of poetry or candies. I get braver around him. I start to believe he isn't just being nice to me; he actually likes me. He isn't faking a smile at me while thinking about what a fat ugly, stupid slut I am. His smiles are genuine.

He consumes my mind. Time flies by in a daze. I'm dizzy with lust. I sleep all the time. When he is not here, I am either masturbating, sleeping, or bathing. I'm in a perpetual state of sleepy, happy high due to Genevieve's pills and the intoxicating baths she brews me. I live only for the moments Thad visits.

We steal small kisses at each visit, pulling ourselves away from each other, not daring to let ourselves go any further. The kisses are quick, gentle, and sweet. I rush to my bed and masturbate after every visit, with the taste of the kiss lingering on my lips.

As the days progress, the gifts get more extravagant, the kisses more passionate. The orgasms I have the moment he leaves get more intense. When we kiss, his hands move their way to my ass and across my breasts, but he always pushes me away before anything further happens. He leaves me there, panting, begging him to stay "just a few more moments." I like to think that he, too, is running off to furiously rub one out while thinking of me, unable to stand it much longer.

He brings me more gifts. More candies. More jewelry—big gorgeous necklaces that look like they belong in the museum of a heist movie. I cannot believe necklaces like these exist, and they are all mine! One night I lay them all across my naked body and touch myself with them, bathing in them—like a desperately horny Scrooge McDuck.

The best gift he brings is a golden cage with two love birds. The cage is so large the butlers who carry it up struggle to get it in the room. Thad is annoyed that the big reveal of it to me is "ruined" by two butlers fumbling with physics and geometry when he tries to rush them in. I go to him and place my hand on his elbow to calm him. I put my head on his shoulder, the first time I've done this since we were on the horse, and say, "thank you, My King."

"They sing beautifully. I thought they would be good company," he replies after calming down.

Genevieve, or Gen as I call her now, bathes me nearly every night. I have grown used to Gen bathing me, and the baths no longer turn me on as they first did. They are, however, some of the most cherished moments of my day. It gets lonely in the tower all alone, with nothing but my birds and yarn to keep me company. I find myself lying around waiting for her or Thad to visit most days—if I'm even awake.

A few nights ago, I asked Gen why she locks the door behind her every time she leaves. She says it is to protect me from the people who find me irresistible and cannot control themselves. I suppose that makes sense. I ask why I don't have a key, and she does not have a good answer for me. She says perhaps the king will give me one. When I ask him, he says he will have one made, "But aren't you afraid to leave, my flower? I would hate for you to pass out and fall down the stairs. Perhaps you should wait for me, and I will take you outside." He's right, I am afraid. When he said that, I picture myself tumbling down the stairs, limbs twisting and convulsing—an unrecognizable blob of goo and limbs by the time I hit the ground floor.

I've considered asking Thad to take me somewhere. Maybe the garden. Anywhere to leave my tower, but the thought of the world outside this room sends me into a panic. "One day. But not today," I say to myself every single time the thought arises.

Tonight, I am wearing the most recent necklace Thad has given me—the biggest one yet, while Gen bathes me. It catches the light and reflects around the room, making little rainbow circles appear wherever I face. I am playing a little game with myself where I make the light circles point at various items in the room.

I stroke lovingly at the large necklace on my chest as Gen washes my legs. We chat about random things. She and Thad now know I am not from this world and she enjoys teaching me about its history, geography, religion, and magic. She cannot fathom how the people of my world lived without magic. I try to explain to her we have electricity, but she doesn't quite understand it. How does one define a video game and the internet to someone who has never seen a lightbulb or a telephone? She says, "Sounds like magic to me," so frequently it's become a little inside joke with us. I try to explain things as fantastically as possible to get her to say it.

She notices me petting my necklace and says, "The king must really like you. His perfect little pet." What does she mean by "pet"? "I supposed he'll be proposing soon," she continues.

I sit up quickly, my breasts bouncing, floating at the water's edge, my nipples peeking out from behind the bubbles. Water spills to the ground. "Propose?!" I ask in almost a shout.

"Of course," she giggles. "Did you think he wanted to just remain friends?" using air quotes around the world friends. When she does the air quotes, my mind wanders, thinking about how similar and different our two worlds are. I shake my head in an attempt to clear my thoughts and focus. These bubbles tend to make me more spacey than I usually am.

I lean back and grin with delight. I giggle and squeal like a schoolgirl and kick my feet excitedly, splashing the water up. Holy shit! He's going to propose to me. I'm going to be queen. I'm going to be married to Thad. I'm going to be able to kiss and hug and hump and fuck him as often as I want! He's going to be all mine.

"Watch it!" Gen chuckles as the water splashes her face. She reaches into the bath, scoops a handful of water, and throws it at me, snapping me out of my little episode. I do the same, thoroughly drenching her neck and chest. Her nipples are visible through her now soaking-wet top. She looks down at her nipples and sighs. "Look what you did!"

"Sorry," I say as I sink, so the bubbles cover my mouth. I have been so consumed with my lust for Thad that I've forgotten how sexy Gen is. I sneakily touch myself under the bubbles, sure she cannot see.

That night I come harder than I think I ever have. I imagine a crown bouncing on my head. My having to hold it to keep it on while I bite at Gen's perfect little nipples and get pounded from behind by the king—my king.

7

It's morning, and Gen comes to my room, particularly flustered. She usually flutters around my room like a busy little hummingbird, but today she is buzzing about to an extreme level. Gen brings me a dress and insists on doing my hair up. "What's wrong with the dress you brought me last night?" I ask.

"Oh, nothing, it's just a little plain. I thought this would be better for today," she says with a sly, knowing grin. She raises her eyebrows at me as if trying to hint at something. The dress she presents to me is dazzling. It is a deep red with jewels sewn around the trims.

"Wait, what's going on? Is something happening today?" I squint at her with a confused expression.

She leans in and whispers to me, who she thinks will hear I do not know, "The head waiter overheard the king talking to his advisor about you. I'm sorry to ruin the surprise, but he is proposing to you this afternoon! He'll be here shortly!"

Oh my God! Oh my God! Oh my fucking God!

"They'll want to preserve the moment in a picture, and I'll be damned if you don't look like a ravishing goddess during that moment," she says while tugging at me.

"My picture?"

She remembers I know nothing of magic. "Yes, the king has a royal memory mage. He can preserve images in his mind's eye and transfer them with paint to canvas with a flick of his hand. He is so talented. His pictures look so realistic. You can't even tell they are painted! They look like real people standing there. And they're life-sized."

"Oh, that must be how the missing woman posters were made. We have something like that in my world; they're called photographs. They work by

…" I begin to ramble but stop when I see she is frowning. Tears pool in her eyes. She stops pulling at the various ribbons and fabrics on my dress.

"Are you okay?" I say and place a hand on her shoulder.

She covers my hand with hers. "Sorry, I … I just miss a friend … well, a lover. She went missing right before you arrived."

She is into girls! That is not the thing to focus on, Astrid. You're an awful person. This is sad, and you're about to marry the king, so stop thinking about how you can fuck your best friend.

"Oh, my God. I am so sorry. I did not know," I say, trying to focus and express empathy like a normal person.

"Of course not. I didn't tell you," she says sadly and starts dressing me again.

I grab her hands, stopping her from lacing up my bodice. I look her deep in the eyes. "You can tell me things. You are my best friend. You're my only friend other than Thad. I care about you. I am here for you. Do you want to talk about her?"

She sniffles back a tear. "Thanks, but …," she sucks air into her lungs through her teeth sharply, "we have a proposal to prepare for." She fusses away at me again with a big forced smile. I can tell she's putting on a show for me and I feel bad suddenly realizing how one-sided our relationship has been. She doesn't want to talk about it right now, so I will not push it.

"When you're ready to talk, I'm ready to listen." She doesn't respond. She keeps adjusting my fabrics and hair. There is a method to her madness, but I'm not sure exactly what it is.

When she is done, I stand in front of the mirror and am in shock. I am beautiful. She has made me look attractive before. She always does. She's a genius with makeup and fabrics. I never knew how to apply makeup or wear clothes that fit my body type. I didn't even know how to do my hair. I always looked like a frumpy potato with tits, but she knows how to play up my features and can transform me into something attractive. If she lived in my world, she'd probably be an internet beauty guru or something, making tutorial videos on how to cover double chins through contouring. I'd follow her.

Today, however, she has outdone herself. "You, you are a miracle worker," I say as I turn to admire myself from all angles, gently touching my hair, face, and body in disbelief.

"Hush, I just work with your natural beauty," she says, while she places a hair on my head back in place that I accidentally dislodged while touching myself. "Hands off the hair! At least until after the proposal."

"Okay," I blush. She adds powders to my chest to cover the redness arising from embarrassment for being such a loser. Why can't I let myself look nice for even a minute without messing myself up somehow?

How do proposals work here? Does he get down on one knee? Will there be a ring? Do we consummate after the proposal? God, I hope so.

There is a knock on my door, and Gen hurries to open it. Thadius is standing there, taking up the whole doorway, and bows to her. She bows back and slinks out of the room as he enters. As he's closing the door behind her, I notice other people in the stairwell with Gen. Who are they?

"Go…good morning" He doesn't usually stutter. He's always so confident. He must be nervous. Oh, my God, he is going to propose!

Thad walks toward me, places his hands on my elbows, and says, "Astrid, I am so happy I found you that day in the woods. Since you have come here, I wake up each morning and think of nothing but you. I cannot concentrate on my work. You consume my thoughts." He pulls a small box out of his pocket and gets down on one knee. They propose with rings here! "I must make you mine, Astrid. I must have you. Marry me!" He says as he opens the box. I notice he doesn't ask me to marry him; he tells me to. I love that. I gasp and cover my face in surprise. I begin to cry. I remove my hands promptly, knowing Gen would be so upset if she knew I was touching my face.

"Of course!" I say through tears. He places the ring on my finger, pulls me toward him, and kisses me with such passion I almost fall back. His cock digs into my hip, and I swoon. I bet we look like that classic sailor and nurse photo. I place my hand on his face and feel the tension in his jaw relax.

He breaks out of the embrace. "Perfect," he says, clapping his hands together. "We will marry tomorrow. I have already made all the arrangements."

"Tomorrow?" I say with a surprised croak. He already made the arrangements? What if I had said no? Who am I kidding? I'm so pathetically obvious in my lust for him. There was no way I would have said no.

"Of course! I can't wait one moment longer to have you," he says with a smirk. Does he mean fuck me? Because honestly, I can't wait for one moment longer for him to fuck me, either. I picture sitting on his face while he lays back, spread eagle on my bed, dick pointing to the sky, jacking himself off, and cumming on my back.

He grabs my hand and turns me to face the door. "Come in now." He bellows, and people flood into the room, congratulating us. Gen is there giggling happily and crying, waving. She runs over to me and rubs a cloth under my eyes, cleaning up whatever mess I've made with my makeup with tears. She congratulates me and tells me how lucky I am.

When Gen finishes fussing at my face, Thad says, "Smile." At that moment, a mage at the front of the crowd mutters an incantation. Sparkles emanate from us, follow where the mage points, and land on a canvas one of my butlers is holding. Our image materializes on the canvas as paint swirls and pools into place. The picture is gorgeous. Gen did such a good job; I am sure she is pleased. For once, I think I actually look like someone a king would want to marry.

"I did leave one task for you and your lady to do," Thadius states.

"What's that?" I ask.

"Your dress. Your lady has such a good eye for you; I didn't dare pick it myself. Plus, I hear women enjoy that part of wedding planning. Dozens of dressmakers have come. They are waiting in the stairwell right now with all their best work for you to pick from. If there is not one you like, they are instructed to make one to your specifications. They will spend all night working if necessary."

I look at him and cannot believe my luck. I tear up. He wipes the tear from my cheek with his thumb. I smile and push my cheek into his hand, holding it to my face. I'm sure Gen doesn't care so much about my makeup now that the picture is over. He says, "From now on, you get only the best."

"It's bad luck to see the bride in her wedding dress before the wedding. So, I will leave you ladies to it." He and the others that entered pile out of the room, taking the picture with them. I was hoping to get a better look at it, but I'm sure I'll have time eventually. Gen leaps next to me and grabs my hand. We both squeal in excitement.

I'm sad Thad didn't kiss me goodbye, but I suppose we have a lot to do and dry humping in front of all these people is probably not the most royal way to behave.

He enters the stairwell, and I hear him harshly say, "You first." A dressmaker scurries in at the command.

Gen and I fawn over all the beautiful dresses, gleefully running our fingers through the fabrics and twirling around as we hold them to our chests. As she holds one against her body, showing me the material, I can't help but think how beautiful of a bride she would make. "That one would be gorgeous on you!" I say.

She lets out a single "Ha," and says, "well, unfortunately for me, I'm not getting married tomorrow."

I muster up bravery and say to the dressmaker, "Leave this one with us. It will be a gift for my friend."

She looks at me in disbelief. "Astrid! You can't."

"I can do what I want. I'm going to be queen." I say confidently, unsure if I actually can do what I want.

Her eyes widen in excitement, and she looks at the dressmaker. He nods and says, "The king told us to give her whatever she wants." She jumps excitedly, still pressing the dress to her body, and runs to hug me. She carefully puts it down on a chair. She looks at it with such love and admiration you'd think she was laying a baby to rest. Her eyes sparkle with tears of happiness.

I notice the dressmakers look very nervous when we say we're not interested in specific dresses. I bet this would make a massive commission for them—selling a wedding dress to the future queen, so I can see how it may be nerve-wracking. Plus, the idea of having to stay up all night sewing me a dress if I don't like one is probably not precisely exciting for them. And then, there's the erection thing. Poor guys. Their hearts are probably about to explode with anxiety.

I picture myself going full-on bridezilla. Yelling at each dressmaker that their creations are terrible and not befitting their new queen. Making them stay up all night, sewing me dresses based on vague and terrible directions. Their fingers bleeding. Barking orders at them and degrading them until sunrise and I find one I am only slightly satisfied with. Screaming, "Well, I guess this hideous dress will have to do," as they silently weep. I will not do that to them, but I suppose they expect I will. After the first three dressmakers leave, I am worried we will not find something we like.

When the fourth dressmaker walks through the room presenting a dress, his procession of employees following, Gen gasps and points. "That one. That is the one!" she exclaims.

She's right. It is the one. It is perfect. Its bodice is fully encrusted in diamonds. It is sleeveless. It is so puffy on the bottom and reminds me of a dress one of my old Barbies had. We approach the dress, and the dressmaker unrolls it, revealing a train. We gush and giggle. I escape behind the dressing wall with Gen. She helps me put it on. "Oh, my God! And your eyes will sparkle with the Aquamarine necklace his majesty gave you last week!"

"I look like a princess," I whisper to her.

"Incorrect. You look like a queen. No, a goddess!"

I whisper, "Queen," to myself in the mirror. She places her head on my bare shoulder as we sigh in unison at my reflection in the mirror. We giggle and return to the main area of my room. The dressmaker stops with a start. He is utterly stunned by his work, and I don't blame him. We tell him this is the one; we will take it. We call him a genius. He takes a moment to process the news and to slyly adjust his erection. God, I wish I didn't have that effect on everyone. It is getting super old. His face lights up, and he claps his hands together. Tears of pride and relief well in his eyes. "Oh, thank you, Your Majesty, thank you!" he bows profusely. Your Majesty? I can get used to that.

He hurries out of the room, twittering away to his companions in delight. Gen pokes her head out of the room and tells the others waiting in the stairwell, "We found the one; the rest of you may leave." I hear grumbling and sobbing and many footsteps descending the stairs. How many people are still out there?

"Okay, well, let's take this thing off so I don't mess it up." We take the dress off and place it carefully on a hanger in my dressing area.

It is approaching evening, and I cannot believe how much time has passed already. We spent all day looking at dresses.

I sit on my bed, "I cannot believe I'm getting married tomorrow," I say.

"Don't get too cozy!" Gen says, "We still have to get you ready for tomorrow."

"What else is there to do?"

"You need to bathe and get your hair wrapped into curls. I'm picturing that long hair of yours curling under a crown!" she pauses, thinking, "And we need to shave you."

"Shave me? My hair is so blond and thin I never shave my legs."

"No, we need to shave," she stops talking and points her finger at my crotch.

"Oh, I guess we can do that."

"It is a tradition in this country to shape it into a heart for the wedding night. It's a joke. During the ceremony, the priest will say something about the king piercing your heart, and everyone will giggle."

I picture Thadius between my legs, spreading my lips with his fingers so he can pierce my heart and get wet.

We realize neither of us has eaten all day. I ring the bell three times to signal, "bring dinner."

Gen and I have never eaten together before; she usually arrives after I have already eaten. She hesitates when I tell her to share the food with me. I remind her that she hasn't eaten, either. Her face lights up in pure glee as she places the various delicacies in her mouth. I imagine I looked the same way on my first night here. I am disappointed in myself. There is always way more food for me to eat and so many leftovers when she arrives each night. I should have offered her some before. I make a promise to myself to have her eat with me again.

She smiles, satisfied, hand on her belly, as we finish the last bites we can muster. I bet this is the look she makes after she comes. "This has been such an amazing day, Astrid. Thank you for the dress and the food. I probably shouldn't say this, but … you've made me feel like a princess." I get a bit sad. I've had the power to do this for her all along, but I've been so focused on myself. I will make up for it.

After we have digested our food a bit, she bathes me. I daydream about being a queen, fucking Thad, sitting on a throne—my belly swollen with the future prince or princess. My daydream is interrupted when she casually brushes against my labia while washing my legs. This is par for the course with her now, and I am used to it, but I still enjoy it immensely. I'm sure she knows what she's doing to me, but we don't discuss it, and I don't act on it. It's our unspoken secret. Now I picture her sitting on the throne next to me, beaming at me as we rule together.

After my bath, she wraps my hair around some cloth. "This fabric is very absorbent. It should be dry by morning. Your hair will be so beautiful in curls," she states in that breathless way she does when complimenting me.

After the curls are set, she jumps up and exclaims, "Okay, time to shave you!" Is she excited to do this? She walks to the dressing table and returns with a straight razor and some creams.

"You're going to shave me with that?" I point at the straight razor, terrified.

"What else will I shave you with?" She seems genuinely confused by my surprise. I shouldn't be. She shaves under my arms with it most nights, but the thought of it against my crotch, slicing through the large veins in my groin, is terrifying.

"Come on now; you need your beauty rest. Let's not dilly-dally. Go, lay on the bed." She's recovered from the daze stuffing her face had given her and is back at her usual hyper speed.

I lay on the bed, and she lifts my sleeping gown to my breasts. I close my eyes, too scared and honestly too aroused to do anything other than lay there paralyzed in fear. I'm afraid she will cut me if I move, and she hasn't even started yet. I picture her hand slipping and cutting my vulva clean off—her running out of the room screaming in horror. Thadius rushing in, screaming "I can't marry her now! Throw her in the streets and bring me someone with a pristine pussy—one I can wrap my lips around." Okay, that won't happen, but I lay completely still, just in case.

She spreads my legs open and lathers creams on me, rubbing around my vulva, inner thighs, and lips. She runs her finger through my ass crack. Oh, God, I hope she doesn't shave my ass crack, too. Her fingers flick at my clit, and the look on her face makes it seem like she knows what she's doing—it is no tangential accident. Please don't make me buck upward, not now. I know a deep pool of juices must be accumulating at my vaginal opening. I hope she either doesn't see it or confuses it with the creams she rubbed on me.

She flicks the razor open and says, "Okay, do not move." She looks like a greaser in an old gang movie, ready to slice me open for kissing her girl.

She places one hand firmly on the top of my thigh, holding it down. She drags the blade across my labia with her other hand. The cold steel sends sparks down my leg. I pant in fear and pleasure. My clitoris is throbbing. I want to hump at her fingers as they graze against it, but I dare not. I'm sure it's three sizes too big right now. Just poking its little head out between my lips. It's yelling at her, "please kiss me, you gorgeous fucking woman!"

After she completes one side, she moves her body next to mine and positions herself so that her face is inches away from my crotch. Her hips are inches away from my face. She pulls my leg open further, and I hope against hope she will place her mouth on me. Instead, she reaches down and begins to shave. FUUUCK, I need this woman.

I wish her fingers would slip into me, just for a second. Accidentally, of course. I look over at her hips, her skirts hanging down to the bed, and picture myself grabbing her ass. I could easily slip my hand up that skirt and bury my fingers deep inside her. My hand lifts for a second, and I catch myself. I cannot surprise her and make her cut me. I cannot cross that invisible line in our friendship.

Please, please, please accidentally enter me, Gen. I moan quietly. I'm fucking getting married tomorrow. I should not be imagining sixty-nining my best friend right now. "Don't worry; I'm almost done." Did she hear me moan?

She finishes her work, pops off the bed, and jumps to the foot to admire her work. I am spread eagle, full view. "A perfect little heart," she says. She is panting. She is sweating. She wants me, too; I can feel it. I can see it in her eyes. I look down between my legs and see the cute little heart-shaped pubic mound. I'm still covered in creams, though.

She walks toward me, a cloth in her hand, and places it on my pubic hair. She then pushes downward with it. My body was so anxiously awaiting her touch that I start to come as she wipes me clean. She tries to pull her hand away from me, but I grab her wrist and press her hand down hard against myself so that I can finish my orgasm.

I moan in pure delight, and she looks at me, surprised. As I am coming on the cloth, she gently pokes the tip of a finger inside me. Did she do that on purpose, or did I force it in there when I grabbed her hand? I finish and realize what I have done. I can't believe that simple touch sent me over the edge. I can't believe I just forced my best friend on me.

"Oh, my God! I am so sorry! I can't believe I just did that. Please forgive me, Gen." Fuck, I'm a dirty perv, best friend rapist. I deserve to die.

She giggles. "You do not need to apologize. I've been waiting for you to do that since we met. I can't believe it took you this long. I've been teasing you for weeks." She steps away and grabs a few things. She gets her dress and hugs it to her chest while smiling at me. "Thanks, Astrid!" I sit up, still fully naked, still spread eagle. No, thank you, Gen.

"Good night, my queen." She says as she shuts the door behind her, dress in hand, and locks the door.

8

Gen arrives in the morning with many other women to prepare me for the wedding. By the time they are done, I have on more lotions and makeup than usual. The white powder they place all over my body makes me look like a porcelain doll—a porcelain doll with a huge rack. My skin feels like silk.

Gen and I don't speak of last night, and, other than the stolen knowing glances, we don't act differently than usual.

The whole morning is a blur; before I know it, they are rushing me down the stairs. I realize this is the first time I have left my room since I arrived. As we descend the stairs, I get dizzy with anxiety. I begin to faint, and someone catches me from behind before I fall. "Is she okay?" Someone asks frantically.

"It's a big day; she's just nervous," another says.

"Did we remember to give her something to eat and drink?" says a third.

"She's scared of leaving her room," Gen speaks up. I am sitting on the stairs, face in my hands. Blackness begins to engulf me—sweat pools on my chest. A hum builds in my ears. Gen squats, so she is face-to-face with me. "Now, now, you're going to smudge your makeup," she says as she removes my hands from my face. She inspects me and sees I have not done much damage. She licks her thumb, rubs it under my eye, and says, "powder." Power appears in a hand as if from nowhere and is placed into hers. She pats it on my face, where she just rubbed. "There, perfect," she smiles.

I realize the church is on the other side of the moat and begin to hyperventilate while rocking back and forth. "I can't do this. I can't go outside. The church is too far away. Please take me back to my room," I say.

"Don't worry. His Majesty knows you are afraid to go outside. He has arranged for the wedding to be in the ballroom. The priest has come to you.

All you have to do is go down these stairs and to the hall. The ballroom is just on the opposite side of the castle. You can do this. You are brave. You will get your happily ever after," she says. "But, just in case, I have a little magic to help you." She pulls out a bottle of pills and slips one in my mouth. "Swallow." I swallow, not even asking what it is. "This will help. These are magic calming capsules. They shouldn't take too long to kick in. Let's wait here for a bit while they work their magic."

She reaches up my skirt, and I think she is about to finger me right here on the stairs, surrounded by all these people, when I realize she has slipped the pill bottle inside the belt wrapped around my leg. "Just in case you need them tonight." She winks. She sits beside me and rubs my back in a circular motion, humming quietly to me while I rock.

They take effect quickly. I feel drunk, happy, and warm and fuzzy all over. When my breathing calms, she smiles at me reassuringly. She grabs my arm and walks me slowly down the stairs. I stumble. If it weren't for Gen and the others, I would not be able to walk. I think she gave me too much. The din in my head doesn't disappear; it just changes tone. It is no longer terrifying but instead comforting—engulfing and soothing.

The rest of the trip to the ballroom is hazy. I recognize the pictures of ex-kings and queens from my previous walk down this hall with Thad, but cannot remember who any of them are. The look at me judgingly. I imagine them crawling out of the paintings and yelling that a fat, ugly slut like me is not good enough for their Thad. That I will taint their bloodline with my filth. I say, "I am actually pretty clean," out loud while pointing at the nearest painting taunting me.

Gen laughs and says, "yes, you are."

I am rushed around so quickly, and I am so fucking high I hardly know what's happening. Two large doors open, and loud music begins playing. Fuck, is this my wedding? Everyone stands. Gen gives me a little nudge and stays at the door. I walk down the aisle formed between chairs. Women cry—likely sad they won't be able to marry Thad now. Ha! He's mine, bitches! Men grab at their crotches. I giggle to myself. "The queen that everyone wants to fuck," I whisper into my bouquet as I march. When did these flowers get in my hands?

I look down the aisle and see Thadius standing by a priest. The priest looks like a Roman Catholic priest with one of those tall hats. I feel like I remember some dick joke about a bishop's hat. Something about chess pieces? I can't remember it. Rather than a cross, the symbol on the front of the hat is a trident—like the one I saw outside of the church on my first day here. Gen told me a bit about this religion, but I can't remember anything about it or even its name at the moment.

Thadius is dressed in puffy purple velvets and has his largest crown on. He looks so stunning. I stop in my tracks for a second to admire him, and everyone gasps. Walk, Astrid. Don't worry, everyone. I'm not going to turn and run. I'm just high and horny for your dazzling king.

There is a crown on a cushioned stool in front of where I should stand. Oooh, that's mine! I guess weddings here are pretty much the same as in my world.

I get to where I assume I am supposed to stand, and everyone sits. I realize there was no rehearsal, and I have never seen a wedding in this world. I'll act like I'm in one in my world and hope I don't make everyone think their new queen is a royal fool.

The priest speaks in some language I've never heard. It sounds a little like Latin and is a speck more guttural. After a few moments, everyone giggles. That must be the heart-stabbing part Gen told me about. Thadius raises his eyebrows at me and smirks. The whole room is thinking about Thadius slipping his dick into me, and I wish I could go ahead and let them see what it looks like. I wish I knew what the priest was saying. This is like signing a contract without reading it.

Suddenly, someone behind me puts a crown on my head. Everyone stands and claps. Thadius pulls me close and kisses me. Was that it? Am I married now? I can't believe I was so high I barely knew what was happening.

Everyone is clapping, sobbing, and smiling as we walk down the aisle holding hands. I force myself to smile and walk. I try waving, but the motion is too complicated for me. I am walking on rails and have to remind myself to do simple things like smile, walk, and breathe. Gen is peeking around the doorway and wiping tears from her face. I want to scream, "you'll smudge your makeup," to her like she did to me, but I think better of it. I lock eyes with her the rest of the way down the aisle—anxious to be with my friend.

We enter the hall, and Gen says, "You did great!" She gives me a thumbs up as we walk past her. No, I don't want to walk past her. I want to walk with her. I want to reach for her, but Thadius moves me forward too quickly.

Everyone follows us, and we enter another room: a banquet hall. How the fuck big is this place? There is a table at least twenty feet long with many other round tables.

We sit, and we eat. Thadius sits beside me, caressing my thigh through my dress the whole time and using his other hand to eat and drink. I finally start to sober up just as Thadius grabs my hand and says, "I cannot take it any longer. I must have you. Now." Guards usher people away from us, blocking them as they try to approach while we jog through the banquet hall.

We rush down the hall and up some stairs, running and giggling, as I trip. We're not going back to my room. Where are we going?

A butler opens two heavy wooden doors to reveal a vast room. It's so big; it's bigger than my house from my past life. In the center is a bed big enough to fit a football team, with dark wood banisters and dark red velvet drapes. There is a large fireplace with a fire roaring. I can feel the heat on me all the way over here, a good twenty feet away. There is a bear skin rug. Gross. Is that real? There's also a large desk to the left. Does he work in this room, too? I picture a football team having an orgy on that big bed, helmets still on, dicks glistening in the firelight, while the bear watches and Thadius signs some papers.

He picks me up and carries me across the doorway—a groom carrying his bride over the threshold. He walks very quickly to the bed and places me on it. The large doors make a loud, startling, ominous bang as they shut behind us.

There is so much tulle and fabric on my dress. I press it down to see Thad standing over me at the foot of the bed. I giggle and lay down, still drowsy from the magic pill Gen gave me. He pulls at the skirts, trying to get to me, only to be blocked by a continuous stream of fabric. He lets out a slight yell and rips the fabric into pieces. "Thadius, don't. It's beautiful," I say, but he does not respond; he just rips more.

He's scaring me a little. It looks as if his eyes are glowing yellow. It can't be. It must be the reflection of the fire. He's chiseled away at the skirt, and I now lay there, with my lower half exposed, nothing put a bodice on—my heart-shaped public hair begging him to pierce me.

He looks ravenous as he lunges his face down between my legs. He licks my slit from top to bottom, and I shudder. He lets out a wail that sounds almost animalistic. I must still be high. I'm imagining things. He slips his fingers inside me and presses his lips hard against my clit, flicking his tongue over it. His tongue is so wet. I am so wet. The moisture is building, and I am losing myself in pleasure.

His crown bounces off his head as I fuck his face harder and harder. He stands, fingers still inside me, and grabs the crown from his head. He throws it to the side of the room, letting out a loud, hungry growl. It lands with a crash. Something shatters. I look in its direction but can't see what happened.

He removes his fingers with a wet pop and reaches to my diamond-covered bodice. My mind plays tricks on me as his nails appear to get longer. He sinks his fingers into the corset and rips down the center in one sweeping motion of his arms. Diamonds fly off in every direction. No! It was so pretty. I picture the dressmaker at the foot of the bed, holding the corpse of my wedding dress weeping, as Thadius and I fuck. The two of us looking down at the dressmaker with royal disgust.

He grabs his clothing and rips them off, leaving it in a shredded pile at the foot of the bed along with mine. So much beautiful fabric ruined. I sit up on my elbows and admire his body. My eyes widen when I see him, and

I audibly gasp. He is gorgeous and engorged. The firelight casts a shadow on every single ab. I cannot believe how ripped he is. He stands there and lets me admire him, getting off on my gaze. His dick is way bigger than I expected. I thought I had a good idea of its size as much as it has been pressed against me, but I was wrong. He holds it in his hand, rubbing his finger over the tip, licking his lips at me. "Wow," I say.

Almost in one single movement, he grabs my feet, pulls me closer to the edge of the bed, and enters me. I let out a wail of both pleasure and pain as he enters. It's been so long since I've had anything bigger than a few fingers inside me. He lifts one of my legs to his chest and kisses at my calf as he pumps hard and fast. Holy fuck. This is too much, I place my hand on his hips to slow him down, but he does not. He grabs my hand and pushes it over my head, pinning me down. My leg bends forward, knee on my breast, as he does. He's going so deep now. With each thrust, I let out a breath of air, and I picture his dick hitting my diaphragm, even though I know it's impossible. He grunts, snorts, and breathes hard on my neck—releasing one exhale with each pump. We are both breathing in unison with his thrusts. I can smell the sweet wine from the wedding feast on his breath.

He lifts himself to look me in the eye, smiles and lets out a moan that resembles a low growl. His body seems to vibrate with the noise. He leans his head down and sucks hard on my nipple. He is pumping so hard and fast that I yelp with every push. It doesn't help that my leg pushes the air out of me. He thrusts deep and hard one final time and almost howls as he twitches and releases his cum into me. He stares me in the eyes and licks his lips. I think his tongue looks slit, and his eyes look yellow, but I am sure my eyes are just playing tricks on me in the light. I am still so high. I wish I could have been sober for this—maybe I could have come.

He collapses beside me and snores loudly. I did not come, but I'm so happy he did. I'm so happy I pleased him. I look at his beautiful face, and I cannot believe how lucky I am. I cannot believe this gorgeous man could find any sort of pleasure inside my repulsive body. I can't believe I am queen! I sneak under the covers and silently pleasure myself as he sleeps—staring at his gorgeous face and brushing my breasts against his powerful arm. The sensation of his skin against my nipples is enough to help me finish.

After I finish, the largeness of the room begins to envelop me. The belt around my leg survived the ravishing I just experienced and I reach into it to find the bottle of pills Gen snuck me. I take two. When the magic fully sets in, I cuddle against Thadius and fall asleep.

9

Thadius wakes me with a thrust. He is inside me and licking at my nipples. I grab his ass with a smack and pull him deeper into me. He looks at me with a startled look on his face. Is he surprised I'm awake? Surprised I smacked his ass? Surprised I want it deeper? I lift my legs higher and arc my back so his face is buried in my breast, and his cock is buried deep into my core. He chuckles and pumps faster and faster. I ooh and ah and lick my lips. I'm honestly not enjoying this that much. I prefer more clitoral stimulation, but I want him to feel good about himself. With every noise I make, he gets closer to completion. Finally, he unloads himself into me when I say, "You're … so … big!" in his ear and bite at it. I wail with him, pretending I'm coming at the same time.

I'm anxious to return to my room. Thad orders breakfast and tells me we'll go back as soon as we've finished eating. During breakfast, I cut one of Gen's pills in half. I take it with some wine. His room is gorgeous, but it's so big and unfamiliar I struggle to relax. Being here makes me nervous, but I don't want to get as fucked up as last night. I hope half a pill can get me through the walk back to my room.

It begins to wear off when we finish breakfast, so I take the other half of the pill for the walk to my room. We walk hand in hand slowly while leaning on each other. Occasionally, he strokes at my nipple, and I pinch his butt or trace his abs through his shirt. As we cross the path of various workers, they stop, say, "Your Majesties," and walk the other way. We don't care if they see us groping each other.

"Your Majesty. I like the sound of that," I say.

"How do you feel about 'My Queen'?" he says in a silky voice.

"I love it. My King." I realize I have not told Thadius I loved him. "I love you, My King." He does not respond, only smiles.

When we get to my room, I am quite dizzy with love and magic. My inhibitions are gone when I take a running leap to the bed. I get on all fours, turn to face Thadius, point my ass at him, and say, "Take me, My King."

He's already walking toward me, removing his clothes. He lifts my skirt and buries himself deep inside my sopping-wet vagina. He's rolling his hips, hitting all my edges. He holds my hips and pumps me up and down on his cock.

This time is gentler, but it's still rough. I let out a wail with every thrust because it hits this spot that is so sensitive. I have to bite down on the blankets to keep from screaming so loud the guards rush in, thinking their new queen is being murdered.

I pump myself back and forth on his cock, faster than he's pushing me back and forth. I reach back and press my fingers hard on my clit, forcefully rubbing them in a circular motion. I always think I could be an excellent DJ when I do this. DJ Queen Pussy would be my name. DJ stands for "disc jockey." Maybe it would be CJ Queen Pussy—C for clit. God, I'm cheesy. I bite and claw at the blankets. I wail out in pleasure as I actually come.

Thadius laughs haughtily, loudly, and proudly. He pumps me even harder against him. I can feel his cock pulse and jump within me as he fills me with his royal seed. He smacks my ass, and I say, "Thank you, My King."

"If we keep this up, I should have an heir in no time," he says as we crawl into the bed under the covers. I cuddle against him and place my head on his shoulder as we fall asleep.

We spend the next week fucking, sleeping, and eating. I have not seen Gen all week, as all my bathing is done with Thadius, and, let's be honest, I don't need anyone to dress me—I have been naked this whole time.

We do take breaks occasionally. He tells me how his mother was an artist and that he inherited some of her skills. He asks me to lay naked while he paints me. It is pretty good and does capture my essence; however, he throws it into the fire and says he "cannot risk anyone else seeing it." He then carries me to the bed for us to fuck once again.

Things are perfect, and I am so smitten, so sexually satisfied. I am giddy. My life is one endless stream of pleasure. Fucking. Eating. Sleeping. Magic drugs.

One night after a rather raucous love-making session, I lay next to him, stroking his chest and say, "I wish we could stay like this forever."

"Me, too, my pet," he says and kisses me on the forehead. "But, tomorrow, I will have to get back to work. Political negotiations with Laila have not been going well. The king and queen came to the wedding, and I need to meet with them before they leave."

"Oh, I'm sorry. Is there anything I can do to help?" I ask.

He laughs as if my helping is the most ridiculous thing he's ever heard, "You can give me a son."

"What if I gave you a daughter?"

"I'd prefer a son." He says a bit coldly, rubbing my shoulder and pulling me close so he can kiss me on the forehead.

Since I've been here, I haven't been doing a great job of tracking my menstrual cycle. In fact, I haven't been tracking the days at all. The time with Thadius has been one big blur. I think it's been at least three months since I've been here and I have only had one period—about two weeks before the wedding. I should have gotten another by now.

My breasts hurt. I haven't had any nausea, but I think I might be pregnant.

We're sitting at the table, eating breakfast, naked, when I ask, "What day is it?" with a confused look on my face. He tells me the day, and it means nothing to me. I have no idea what day I got here, what day my last period was, or even how their calendar system works. What the fuck does "the fifth day of Sommulan" even mean?

"Thad, I think I need to visit the doctor."

"Why, what's wrong? Are you sick?" He leans forward, worried.

"Umm, I think I might be pregnant."

"WHAT! Really?" he says, rushing to my side, kneeling beside me, and placing his hand on my belly. He looks at me with a stupid grin, and I have to kiss him.

"In my world, we have these sticks you can pee on, and they tell you if you are pregnant or not."

He wrinkles his nose and lets out a little laugh as if I had said the most absurd thing, "I thought you didn't have magic in your world."

"It's not magic. It's science. They put these chemicals on these absorbent sticks that react to the hormone in your pee that only occurs when you are pregnant. It changes color if you're pregnant."

The look on his face is utterly bewildered.

"We don't have any science pee sticks, but we do have magic. And mages can tell if you are pregnant or not with a potion."

"The potion won't hurt the baby if I drink it?"

He looks touched, happy to hear I am concerned for the wellbeing of our future child, and laughs at my naivety, "You don't drink it. I do!"

"What!?" That makes no fucking sense. I look at him like he's the dumb one now.

"I drink it, and then I, um, will be able to tell with my penis if you are pregnant."

"Are you messing with me? Are you just trying to get laid?"

"A little. It will work with my fingers, too." He giggles and looks at me with that sly smile of his. He jolts up in realization. "OH! It works kind of like your science pee stick. My dick will change colors if you are pregnant!"

I give him a skeptical look.

"Oooor my finger … if that's what you really want," he says, rubbing his hand on the inside of my thigh and pouting out his lip exaggeratedly. It isn't what I want. He knows it. I try to shove his cock in me every chance I get, and I don't need an excuse like this to stick it in there.

I can't believe it. I can't believe I got a happily ever after.

10

I may have been an anti-social hermit in my normal life, but I stayed busy. Idle time makes me anxious, and I tend to work when I get anxious. I would work 16-hour days. I worked until I passed out from exhaustion, which sometimes wasn't until 48 hours of being awake.

My free time was scheduled to ensure I had self-care time and "relaxing time." If I didn't put it on my calendar, I would forget to do it. I am terrible at reading my body and sensing impending burnout. I would schedule thirty minutes a day to exercise. I'm finding it hard to exercise in this room and am getting fatter than I already was—it's not just from the baby, but from all the binge eating and lying around. When I took time off from work, I would have multi-day gaming sessions, forgetting to eat or sleep if I didn't schedule it. Every moment of my day was planned, and every moment was fully utilized. Having an empty slot on my schedule would cause me extreme anxiety.

Now that I am here, in my room, alone again, I find my anxiety skyrocketing—unsure of how to spend my time. Luckily, I had some skills in crocheting and cross-stitching before I came here, so I try to crochet things. To paint. To cross stitch, but it's been months, and I am bored out of my mind.

I can't sleep—which makes the boredom even worse. Nothing like lying awake at night with nothing to fucking do but flick at your own clit while your husband lies dead asleep next to you. I can't get up and do anything because it will wake him. He got pretty mad at me when I accidentally knocked something over when I tried sneaking up to my art room in the middle of the night.

I am depressed. The only thing that breaks my depression is visits from Thad and Gen. Once we found out I was pregnant, I had to stop taking

Gen's magic pills. She says it probably won't hurt the baby, but Thad doesn't think it's worth it and won't let her bring me any more.

I'm struggling to adjust to this unplugged, sober lifestyle. I miss my calendar. I miss my video games. I miss social media. I can't believe I miss social media and all the stresses that came with it.

I miss my thyroid meds, anti-anxiety meds, and sleeping pills! I miss Gen's pills! She reduces the magic she puts in my bath water and makes me take cold baths now, saying hot baths and magic can cause miscarriages. We fight about it one night. I tell her if she's my friend, she will do these things to help me, but she says the king would kill her if she obliged. I tell her she's exaggerating, and she looks at me like I'm missing something. I don't say a word to her the rest of the night as I sob—exhausted, lonely, and sad. She tries to rub my back to calm me down, as she did when I freaked out on the stairs, but I push her away.

At first, my time here was a vacation, but now, it feels like a prison. I never thought I'd want to go outside, but I am so fucking bored I'm considering it.

I'm starting to understand the isolation people felt at the beginning of the pandemic. As an introvert with social anxiety and agoraphobia, I relished in it. Now, I get it.

Thaddeus brings me books occasionally. I read them so quickly that I'm done before he even returns. I don't even care what they're about. I consume them and beg him for more when he arrives. He makes a joke, "I remembered when you begged for my cock when I arrived, not just dusty old books." He seems genuinely annoyed.

He can get quite cold with me when I'm not fawning all over him. I've learned that complimenting him, begging him to fuck me, and calling him "My well-endowed king" tends to turn the tides in my favor.

I spend every day crocheting nothing in particular and talking to my birds. I spend every night chatting with Gen and getting fucked by the king. This is not the woman I am. I used to have drive. I used to have passion. I was self-sufficient. Sure, I was a scaredy cat who couldn't leave the house, but I was accomplished and powerful (from behind my keyboard, anyway). I cannot spend much more time like this. I feel like I'm rotting away, just waiting to die.

The only time I left my room was my wedding day. I think it's time to try to leave. To branch out. To be brave.

A butler sees me reaching the end of my book one evening and mentions I may enjoy visiting the library in the castle's south wing. I bet I could do that! I bet I could leave … if only I had my pills. Oh, how amazing it would be to see a library. To pick my book!

I ask Thad about it the next day, and he says the butler was mistaken—we do not have a library on the castle grounds. I want to ask the butler to clarify the following evening, but I he doesn't return. The books Thad brings me are okay, I guess. But I want to learn about magic! I want to learn about this world. I want to read romance novels! I don't want to just read whatever Thad finds interesting—which tends to be books about war and his family's power. I need to get out of this room!

I mention to Thad I'd like to see his mother's roses; maybe we can walk in the garden. "The fresh air may be good for the baby," I say, trying to appeal to his fatherly instinct.

He shuts me down immediately, "Now, you know you can't leave this room. The sky is so expansive outside. You'll pass out. That can't be good for the baby. Plus, there's the moat." I think I could do it if he holds me tight, the same way he got me through my first day here, but he changes the subject to the baby before I can protest.

I wonder why everyone locks my door when they leave. Initially, I thought it was to make me feel safe—to keep me safe from rapists aroused by my scent. But now I think it's to keep me prisoner. Whenever I ask Thad about my key, he says he'll have it made and reminds me I am afraid to leave. I think Thad doesn't want me to leave. He wants me here whenever he is craving a fuck. His smile is a bit less dazzling to me now.

Tonight, I am restless. I need to get out of here. I am considering different ways in which I can ask Thad to leave. I need to say something that makes it his idea. I need to stroke his ego when I ask. Perhaps I can make up some story about dreaming of fucking him on the horse, finishing what we started the day we met.

Wait a minute. I didn't hear the door lock as the men who brought my dinner left. Did they forget to lock the door? I tiptoe my way to my door and give it a gentle tug. It cracks open. I peek my head out the door and don't see anyone. I returned to my dressing area and put on a coat and some shoes. I had one pill left. I have been hiding it from Thad and Gen for a special occasion. I bite it in half and then in half again. I need bravery. I don't need stupidity.

I creep out of the room, shutting the door slowly behind me. I glide down the stairs. I have no idea where I'm going, but I need to see what this castle looks like. I'm the queen, for fuck's sake. I should know what it looks like. Thadius has never explicitly told me I can't leave, but I very much feel I should not be. I am terrified I will be found.

At the base of my stairs is a hallway. I know this leads to the castle's front door, the ballroom, and the rest of the castle. There is a door at the base of the stairs. I hadn't noticed the three times I've passed this way previously. Let's start with this door. I know I'll be found if I go down the hall, but who knows what's down here.

It's another spiral staircase. That's weird. Why would stairs go down? There are torches on the walls, but the curve of the stairs makes it very dark wherever there is no torch. This is scary. How far down does this go? Maybe I should turn back.

Right as I begin to turn back up the stairs, I think I hear crying. Is that a woman crying? I descend deeper—my curiosity (and the quarter of a magic pill) overcoming my fear. The torches are fewer and further between, and it feels like I'm descending into complete darkness.

I finally reach the base of the stairs. It is lit well enough to see a hallway ahead and a hallway to my right, but I can't see much else.

The crying has gotten louder. It is not just one woman crying. It is multiple women crying. It's down the hallway in front of me. It's dark. I can faintly make out the shape of the hall. Are those bars? Are these cells? Is this a dungeon?

I peek into the first cell to see where the loudest source of wails is coming from. There is a naked woman curled on the floor. She has deep red lashes on her back. Like she's been whipped. Her hair is red and curly. So red it glows in the torchlight, even under a thick layer of dirt.

I don't know how to process what I am seeing. What did this woman do to be imprisoned here? I glance down the hallway as more cries ring out. How … how many people are down here? Are they all women? All the cries sound like women. I try to count the cells but cannot; it's too dark. There are at least ten cells on one side alone, but I know there must be more.

The door at the top of the stairs opens and closes with a loud creak and thud. Fuck. I should not be here. I run down the hallway to my right only to be confronted with … no. This can't be real.

My brain cannot process what I am seeing. The mutilated corpses of men and women lay in a pile to my left. Various torture devices, blades, and tables are to my right.

Chained to the wall by the neck, naked, skin partially flayed, is Jacobson. The man who commented on my tits when I first arrived. He is too delirious to notice my arrival. But he is alive. Has … has he been here since that first day? It's been months! No. This … this can't be.

The footsteps are louder behind me. Someone is coming this way. Should I hide? Where?

I go deeper into the room only to find one of the men who used to bring me food. He is lying on a table, his intestines pulled out and laid on the table. He omits a terrible stench and heat. Two nights ago, his erection accidentally brushed against my wrist when Thadius was dining with me. Thadius said the man had been reassigned at the man's request. He was too embarrassed to be seen by me after. Why would Thadius lie to me?

I retch in my hand and fall to my knees. Heaving. The smell is too strong. The sight is too much. I am on the ground vomiting when I hear a loud booming voice behind me, "How did you get in here?" Thadius is standing above me, his eyes on fire. I've seen this look. It is not the reflection of the firelight. This is his eyes. His eyes are golden and enraged.

He grabs my wrist hard and yanks me from the ground. I feel like my arm is being pulled out of its socket. Jacobson's eyes open, and he moans. Thadius pulls hard and drags me so fast that I struggle to keep my feet under me. I'm still retching—vomit trickling down my chin.

We pass the hallway with cells. An arm from the cell closest to the entrance grabs my leg. Thadius and the arm are pulling me in opposite directions. I feel like I'll be torn in half. I look toward my foot in terror. It is the redhead. Holy shit. It is the missing woman from the poster the old lady showed me on my way to the castle.

She is bruised. She is dirty. Her face is swollen and nearly unrecognizable, but I'd never forget that hair. I'd never forget those eyes. "Let me out!!!" she screams. Her eyes burn into me, and I feel her profound despair.

Thadius drops my wrist, and I fall to the ground. Before she can do anything, he kicks hard at her hand around my leg. The kick lands on her hand, but also my leg. She lets go. I feel a sharp spark of pain zap through my body. The redhead and I wail out in unison. "Look what you made me do, you stupid, fucking cunt!" he screams at her as he kicks at the cell bars. I sob and grab at my leg.

"Now, now, pet, it doesn't hurt that badly," he says and scoops me up, carrying me as he did when he brought me here. As he did on our wedding night.

He carries me up the dungeon stairs and to my room. "How did you get out? You should not be leaving your room. I will have Gen come to clean you up. You look like a total mess," he says calmly. As if what happened had not just happened. As if what had just happened was all my fault. I suppose it was.

He places me gently on my bed and says, "Okay, now get some rest. Gen will be up shortly." He kisses me on the forehead, and I look at him in horror.

"DON'T YOU FUCKING LOOK AT ME LIKE THAT," he screams. I cower and turn away from him.

"LOOK AT ME!" he yells. I turn back, afraid of what he will do.

"I'm not a bad guy. See," he says, pointing at his dashing smile.

He places his hand on my leg and scowls when I flinch at his touch. "Now, this, this is something WE ARE NOT going to do." I cry quietly as I look at him in fear.

"STOP CRYING!" he screams. I snort and sniff the tears up. I know this drill. I must not cry. I must not show fear. I force a smile. "There's my pet. You don't want me to give you something to cry about, do you?" he says with a smile so sweet you'd think he just told me he loved me. My dad used to say that to me when I'd cry. Said he'd give me something to cry about. My therapist says it's why I have such a hard time describing my emotions to her because I have spent so long trying to repress them. I didn't need her to tell me it's also why men raising their voices frighten me so much.

"You've had a big night, huh? Look at you, leaving your room. I'm proud of you." He smirks. "I'm sure you need your rest. How about you clean yourself up and go to bed? You can see Gen tomorrow. I'll be by for breakfast, and we can discuss this. How does that sound?"

He gently pats my leg exactly where he kicked me. Pain rushes up my leg. At first, I think it is a coincidence. He just happened to touch where he kicked me. Until he squeezes my leg, making me writhe in pain, "HOW DOES THAT SOUND?" he commands.

"Goood. Goooood. Yes." I wail out. I half expect him to say "Yes, what?" the way my father would whenever I would say "yes" instead of "Yes, sir." So, I correct myself before he has the chance, "Yes, My King!"

"Good. I will see you tomorrow," he says as he kisses me on the cheek. He wipes my face and then grabs my breast and gives it a jiggle. He chuckles and leaves. The door definitely locks behind him.

I lie awake all-night crying. I see flashes of the dead bodies that are piled up directly below me. My overactive, brutal imagination doesn't need to imagine anything tonight.

I cannot believe I was duped by a bright smile and a big cock. I should have known better. I used to read stories of women who fell for toxic men, and I would wonder how they could be so stupid—confident it would never happen to me. But here I am, the dumpy girl with a crown who's so easily smitten by a simple smile.

The following day I am still in bed when the king enters my room, not bothering to knock. He comes in all smiles and kisses and sits next to me on the bed.

"So, last night, you weren't supposed to see that. Why did you leave your room?" he coos sweetly.

"I … I was bored." He bristles at my response. I should have said it was because I missed him. Fuck. He stands and faces me, making himself big.

"Haven't I given you a nice place to stay? I give you everything you need. I eat your pussy when I visit. I even gave you the hottest lady-in-waiting to fuck when I'm not around. See, I'm not a jealous man. I am not an evil man."

I stand, determined to fight back. He steps back, surprised I am standing up to him—literally.

"You've given me a nice cage!" I yell. "I want to leave when it is my choice!" I push him back, and he stumbles. Knocking the back of his leg against the chair he sits in when we dine together. He turns, grabs the chair, and smashes it hard against the table—breaking both the chair and table into pieces.

He turns to me, and his eyes are golden flames. He hisses and growls and begins to morph. His lower body extends to reveal a long tail with a poisonous tip. He has four legs. His arms transform into large pincers. He is a half-man, half-scorpion. A scorpion-centaur? That's not a thing. His eyes are golden fire, and he lunges at me. He grabs my wrist with a pincer and says, "YOU ARE MY QUEEN. YOU ARE MY PET. YOU STAY WHERE I PUT YOU. YOU FUCK WHEN I FUCK YOU. YOU ARE MINE. YOU ARE NOT YOUR OWN." He screams in my face. I recoil and cower. I instinctively place my free hand on my belly.

He pauses as though electricity traveled through his body and drops my wrist. I fall to the ground and look at him in horror. His tone changes to something much calmer when he says, "You're lucky you're carrying my child. Otherwise, I'd rip you in two and throw you in that room with those men who thought of fucking you." I thought you weren't jealous, psycho.

"This is your fault. You made me into this. I was cursed many years ago, and I can control the curse by having that room downstairs. That room downstairs lets me be your handsome king. But you HAD to FUCKING go downstairs, you selfish bitch."

He sighs. "I didn't want you to see this part of me." He motions toward his body with his claws. "I am ashamed of this part. You just had to leave your room, didn't you?" he scowls.

I decide in that instant that I must not cower. I must play along. I will tell him what he wants to hear and get what I want. I will bide my time. Play the role of the perfect wife—the perfect queen. I will escape when the time is right.

A numbness washes over me as I disassociate from myself. I put on the mask of a submissive sexy queen who is not scared of her king—a queen who worships her king unconditionally. My face instantly softens to demonstrate love, but not pity. He'd hate that. "Oh, darling. I am sorry you have been carrying this burden. This explains why you have been so protective of me. I'm sorry you felt you had to hide this from me. Come here, my love." I reach out my arms, beckoning him for a hug.

He looks like he might cry. He slowly returns to his human form and grabs me in a big hug. He is stark naked, the transformation having ripped his clothes to pieces, except for a few shreds that hang tattered on his body. He sobs in my breasts. I let him kiss me passionately on the mouth, and I kiss back.

I slip my tongue into his mouth and gently turn him, so his back faces my bed. I push him back until his knees hit the edges, and he is forced to sit on the bed's edge. He usually likes me to be submissive, but I need to be aggressive to prove to him that I love him. If I'm too submissive, he'll think I'm scared. I need him to think I accept all of him or I know he will make the rest of my life miserable—or take it from me entirely.

I maintain eye contact with him while I unbuckle his pants hurriedly. I kiss him hard on the mouth, neck, and chest and work my way down until I am on my knees, eye level with his cock.

Fuck, am I really going to do this? Yes, I must. This will seal it in his mind that I am complacent and he has nothing to worry about. I kiss the tip gently, and it jumps a bit, popping me in the nose. I giggle. I want to vomit. I hate him with every fiber of my being.

I look up innocently at him, my eyes wide. I move my shoulders inward to make my breasts pop and say, "Do you think it will fit in my mouth?" and make an innocent pout. It is bigger than usual. Transforming must change its size or something. His body was significantly bigger when he looked like a half-scorpion. It must take a while for the effect to disappear entirely.

He says, "Well, there's only one way to find out," and laughs.

I wrap my left hand around the base and place my palm on his abdomen, jamming my thumb behind his balls to reach his taint and press firmly. I lick and tease. I run my lips up the side getting it wet. I rub my hand up and down the shaft, spreading my saliva. I place my lips on the tip and press his dick into my mouth, wrapping my lips around my teeth as I do so. I do this for quite some time, moving my hand and mouth in unison, hoping he doesn't grab my head and push himself in deeper.

When he starts to twitch and moan, I keep my hand on him and lean him back onto the bed. He jumps a little so that he is fully sitting on it. In one movement, I climb on him and insert him into me. I'm surprised I'm so wet. I'm disappointed I'm so wet. I guess even a monster can't stop the dirty perv in me from creaming her pants at the sight of a huge cock. I hate myself. I hate that I'm able to play this part so easily that I almost convince myself I want this.

I press my breasts into his face and bounce my ass up and down as fast as I can. I am getting minimal pleasure from this; I'm just doing what I know will get him off the fastest, but I let out a shriek every time he reaches his deepest point to make him think I am. I put on the show I know he loves, biting my lip, wailing, saying, "fuck me harder," the whole nine yards. I make sure my ass and tits jiggle as much as possible as I push him deeper into my loins. I can tell I will have a bruise on my mound from pumping so hard. He grabs my ass hard and squeezes me toward him so he can be as deep as possible when he cums inside me. As he does so, I thrust my tongue into his mouth and flick it around.

"That's my big strong king. Don't worry, baby; I understand now. We'll work this out. I'm sorry I made you show me that side of you. But I feel so much closer to you now." I say with my head against his chest. His heart is pounding. His breath is heavy. Maybe I can kill him; he's so vulnerable right now. Stab him right in the heart. I don't have anything to stab him with. Maybe I'll sneak a knife under my pillow after my next meal.

It's been about ten years since I used my body as a weapon against a man, but riding a dick is like riding a bike—you never forget how to do it.

11

I spend the next few weeks trying to determine an escape plan. My belly grows as I scheme. I hate this child inside me. I hate that I am carrying around a piece of him. I lie awake at night and wish for a miscarriage. I envision giving birth. Thousands of tiny scorpions pour out of my body as I scream in pain and horror or a baby-hand-sized claw piercing its way through my abdomen.

I need to fake my death; otherwise, he will continue to look for me after I escape. He will lock me up if he finds me. I'm sure anything I decide to do will not be particularly convincing for a very long time. So, I need to buy myself some time to get as much distance between me and this castle as possible.

Maybe I can fake suicide—make it look like I jumped into the moat and drowned. I can jump into the moat and then swim away. Since the moat drains into the river, my body could theoretically get washed away after jumping in. Thadius incorrectly assumes that my fear of water means I can't swim. He doesn't know my fear of water actually stems from my father teaching me to swim by throwing me into the deep end of a pool. I can swim; I just prefer not to do it. Jumping out into the moat and swimming away might work. But I'd have to make them think I jumped when they weren't looking. I can't have them see me swimming away. Maybe I could leave a torn piece of fabric from my dress on the windowsill to make it look like I had jumped.

I don't know. I don't think I can risk that. What if I jump and I break my legs hitting the bottom, or I actually do drown? I have no idea how deep that moat is. No idea how far I will sink from this height.

I suppose I could start a fire in my room. That would definitely be a way to fake my death, but unless everything is completely incinerated, they will wonder why they don't find a body. It would buy me some time to escape, though. They'll be so busy trying to save me I can use that time to run as far away as possible. I can be halfway to the next kingdom when they realize there's no charred body.

Perhaps I can combine these two ideas. I can set fire to my room—knock a small candle onto my bedding. I don't know how good their fire forensics are here. I can jump into the water to save myself from the fire. They'll think I drowned trying to escape the fire.

Wait, I can't jump in the water. I might die trying that. How do I make it look like I jumped into the water? Anything I could leave behind to make it look like I jumped into the water would probably burn. Maybe I don't need to leave anything. Maybe they'll assume I jumped.

What if I waited until the moat was iced over and threw something into the moat to leave a human size hole? That could work.

But how do I get out of the tower if I can't jump into the moat? Maybe I can shimmy down with rope—tie my bedsheets together like a cheesy prison movie escapee. But how would I get the rope down, so they won't know I obviously climbed my way down the tower? They need to think I jumped. They need to believe my body is missing. Well, actually, the fire could burn the rope after I am done with it—removing any evidence of it.

I think that could work. It's a harebrained idea, but I don't have a better one. I will set the fire on the other side of the room so that it will take a while to get to my rope. I will throw something heavy into the ice to make it look like I jumped. Then I will shimmy down and hope the fire consumes the evidence.

I'll wait until the end of winter right before spring when the ice is not so thick. I will do it then. That should give me more than enough time to prepare. I will watch for the first sign of birds singing and flowers blooming. That way, the ice will be thin enough to break easily.

How pregnant will I be by then? Fuck, I'll be very pregnant. What if I go into labor while trying to escape? Maybe I should wait until after the baby is born. Traveling with a baby will be difficult, though. Perhaps I can leave the baby with him. I can't do that. I don't love this baby, but I can't leave it with a monster. Plus, who's to say he won't murder me the moment this thing pops out of me? Fuck. I guess I'm going to have to do this pregnant.

I must be brave. I must prepare. I'll start by looking at that fucking sky from my window. I can't pass out the moment I get outside. I have to force myself to get used to it.

- - - -`♥´- - - -

Thad and I lay in bed together after having sex. He'll leave soon, but for now, he's just hanging around, waiting to catch his breath. I faked an orgasm tonight to help hurry things along. While I lay here and wait for him to leave, I contemplate my escape plan.

What do I do once I get out of the tower? I don't know where I am. I don't know where to go. I know Thadius told me there was another city about three days ride from here. I can go there. Fuck, I don't have any other ideas. But how will I find my way there? I have no fucking clue where I am or where the city is compared to here. I need a map.

How can I get a map? I supposed I could ask Gen to get me one, but I don't want her involved in my escape plan. I can't let her get hurt because of me. I know she cares, but I also know she won't do anything without Thad's permission.

Fuck, maybe I can just ask Thad for one. What excuse can I give him that will stroke his ego enough, so he doesn't ask me too many questions about my intentions?

"Darling? Can I have a map of the kingdom and surrounding kingdoms?" I ask, gently stroking his chest with my fingertips.

"What? Why would you need one of those?"

"I want to know the kingdom my son will one day rule over. I want to describe it to him when I sing to my belly at night." Thad loves that. He loves to hear me calling our child a son and a ruler.

The next night he returns, ready to fuck, like always, but he has a map this time. I ham up my excitement. I kiss him profusely. I waddle my way to the bed and unroll the map. I study it. He's looking annoyed that I am not fawning over him.

"Wow! I didn't realize how large the Laerean Kingdom is! You rule all of this?" He beams. I get up and walk to him. I feign admiration and stroke his arm. "Your kingdom is the biggest I've ever seen. It's bigger than all the others. It's so big it reminds me of your huge, fat cock." He's convinced. He's hard as a rock. God, he's stupid when he's hard. He scoops me up and throws me to the bed. The map falls to my side. As much as I hate him, I do still enjoy fucking him sometimes. Being pregnant makes me so horny—and I thought I was horny before.

He rips my dress off my body, tearing it to pieces. I giggle. I loved that dress. Fucking asshole. "Fuck me, my king!" I say breathlessly. He doesn't bother taking off all his clothes or foreplay. He drops his pants to the ground, stands next to the bed, pulls my legs toward him, and enters me with a deep, painful thrust.

He's a bit too rough with me, and it hurts, but I know if I tell him it hurts, he will pump harder. "Oh, that feels so good. You're so deep. I love it when you fuck me with that huge cock." I moan, lick my lips, pinch my nipples, and act like I'm enjoying myself. "But, maybe, you should pull back a bit. I'm scared you'll hurt our baby." Turn on the doe eyes, Astrid. Make the tits bounce. He looks at me with actual concern.

"Of course, babe." He tones it down a bit, and I actually start to enjoy myself, but of course, he cums, pulls out, and doesn't bother to finish me. Not that I expected to come. I'll finish later. He has gotten more selfish since I found out his secret. He doesn't go down on me anymore and always skips foreplay.

He pulls up his pants and lays beside me on the bed. I stay there naked, semen running down my leg, but I grab the map and look at it again. He seems annoyed that I am looking at it and not him. He prefers me to stare at his cock while I masturbate after sex. He huffs a bit.

Fine, you fucking narcissist. I stroke my belly and talk to it, "One day, my little prince, you will rule over the entire Laerean Kingdom." He visibly calms. He is so easy. I have him thoroughly convinced that I care for him and his demon spawn. He places his head on my shoulder and strokes my blooming belly, as well.

I need to memorize this layout just in case he takes the map with him. "To the east, over the sea, there is the country of Laila. To the west is Tranzen. They are smaller than Laerean. One day you will rule those kingdoms, too, because, just like your father, you will be brave, strong, and powerful. You will subjugate the people and absorb their countries into ours." I look down at Thad and give him a wry smile, "That is if your big, strong father has not done so by then." How does he not see this for the big crock of shit it is?

"That's right. I'll do it first," he says, his hand slipping from my belly to between my legs, stopping to twirl my pubic hair. He slips his fingers right down the track and buries them deep into me. Now that I've stroked his ego, he wants to get me off.

As much as I hate this asshole, I still yearn for his touch. I hate this so much about myself. As I grind on his fingers, I curse myself. I come quickly. He pulls his fingers back in surprise. "That was quick." He licks his fingers and then wipes them on my bedding.

"Learning how big your kingdom is got me all hot and bothered. Just looking at that map makes my pussy hot and wet." I generally dislike the word pussy, but he loves it when I talk like this.

He kisses me hard on the lips. "Then I'll leave it here with you."

Map acquired.

I set my plan into motion. I spent the next few weeks collecting any food I can find that seem non-perishable. I request jam; say it's a craving. I empty jars and bottles to store water in. I hide everything under my crocheting chair. Thad never comes to my art room anymore, so I don't think he'll find my stash. I crochet a bag to carry it all.

I found a piece of the broken chair under my bed. The maids did not collect it when they cleaned up the fragments of the furniture Thadius broke the night he transformed. He told them we broke the table fucking. They blushed and giggled, surprised he would speak to them like that. How does no one know what a monster he is? Why do they think he is charming? I scowl at them and call them dumb hogs under my breath. I check myself and remember I, too, was a dumb hog fooled by his smile and nice clothes. My rage is misplaced in their direction. I whisper sorry—not that they heard me the first time.

They count my silverware when they collect my food, so I can't take a knife with me. I bet Thadius told them to do that. He probably expects I'll slit his throat in his sleep. He's not wrong.

While I eat, I slowly whittle the chair leg into a shiv. It takes me a few days, but I don't have shit else to do. Having a goal keeps me sane. If my escape plan fails, maybe I'll learn to whittle properly.

I stuff blankets and other warm items in the sack with the food and shiv.

The last part of the plan is the rope I will need to escape. I spend the next few weeks carefully fashioning a rope with any material I can gather that won't cause suspicion.

I keep pretending my sewing needles break and bend them to hooks. I can fashion a fishing pole with branches and some thread when I am in the woods.

I will need money when I make it to the city. I can't exactly ask Thad for money, but I guess I don't need to. I stuff a few of my more elaborate necklaces into the sack. As I load one in, I stop and look at it. Tears well in my eyes when I remember I had planned to give it to Gen. Our relationship has changed since I saw that room. I barely speak when she visits. I think she thinks I'm mad at her. I kind of am. I worry she knew what a monster he was. She had hinted at him having a temper, like when she stopped giving me warm baths and said he would kill her. I suspect she knows he has a dark side. I doubt she knows how deeply dark it is, though. I suspect she was all part of the plot to placate and trap me—maybe unwittingly—maybe not. I wish things could go back to how they were before I got pregnant. While staring at this necklace, I mourn the loss of our friendship. I mourn the loss of a husband I adored.

I weep all the time. Gen asks me what's wrong. Why do I seem so sad? I cry every night while she bathes me before the king visits. I tell her it is hormones. "Being pregnant makes women crazy," I say. I desperately want to tell her my plan. Have her run away with me. But I can't put her life in danger. I hope she is sad, but not too sad when I'm gone. I hope that she didn't trap me because it was just part of her job. I hope she did actually care about me.

I do push-ups in the mornings before breakfast. I lift my furniture when my belly gets too big to do push-ups. I know I will need to be strong to shimmy down that wall.

I still have three-fourths of a singular magic calming pill. I took only a fourth of it the night I found Thad's secret dungeon. I have considered taking them when Thad visits—he can sometimes be so rough with me. Some nights I am so angry and scared of him that I struggle to fake my love. I know I will need them to deal with my time outside. I cannot let the sky engulf me; I need all the bravery I can muster to get out of this fucking tower.

When the rope is done, the last piece of my plan is complete. I look outside, and the ice appears to be melting enough to possibly leap through. Tonight is the night. Thad will not be visiting because he is on one of his night hunts. God, I don't want to know what that means. I used to think it was deer—which was upsetting. Now I doubt it and wish it was just deer.

I place my hands on the golden cage of my love birds. They are my only friends. They are the only thing I will miss about this place. I guess I'll miss Gen, too. I still love her even though I don't trust her. I release my birds and tell them I love them. I worry they won't make it on their own. I worry I won't. But I can't sacrifice them to the fire I'm about to start. I may be fucking a monster. I may be carrying the spawn of a monster in my belly. But I am not a fucking monster.

- - - -`♥´- - - -

It's around midnight, and time to put my plan into action. I grab my bag from under my chair and take inventory. Everything seems to be in place. I put gloves on to save my hands from the cold and the rope. I loop around my room and ensure there is nothing else I need. What if I run into Thad in the woods? He can smell me a mile away. No … I can't stop now. I have to go. If I don't go now, I will never go.

I tie my rope to my bed. This bed is huge and should have no problem holding me. I hope the rope also has no problems. I drop the rope at the foot of my window. It makes a loud, hollow, thump noise when it hits the floor—almost startling me. I hope no one thinks I fell and comes running in to check on me.

I grab the sack I've filled with various small, heavy objects. I peer out the window and down at the water. Please be heavy enough. This thing has to weigh at least twenty pounds. The acceleration from this height should make it hit the ice hard. Please, please, please break the ice. I place it at the base of the window with my rope.

I go to my table and break off one of its legs. I then jam it under the crack of the door. I don't really think this will do much to stop anyone from coming in, but I hope that will slow them just a bit. Even a moment will be helpful. Hopefully, I'll be halfway down the wall before they notice the fire.

Ok, everything is in place. I just need to start the fire. I bundle bedding and other flammable items into a pile in my bathing area—the area furthest from my bed. This is an obvious arson scene and I truly hope most of the evidence is gone before anyone can get in here.

"Moment of truth," I whisper to myself. I light the candle in my hand and drop it on the pile. I watch it burn for a second and turn on my heels, bag strapped to my back. I look at the matches in my hand and realize I fucking forgot to pack matches. I stuff them quickly in my bag.

I grab the rope in one hand. I hold the heavy sack in the other and scoot up to the window ledge. Fuck. Can I do this? The fire starts to rage behind me, heating my cheeks when I turn to look at it. No choice. The smoke is burning my nose and eyes already. This fire won't be a secret much longer.

I drop the heavy sack out the window. Please break. Please break. It hurls toward the frozen moat and pierces through the ice leaving a perfect, human-sized hole. Yes! Part 1—done.

Ok, now to descend. The fire is raging faster than expected. Fuck, I need to go. I start to repel down and lose my footing almost immediately. I fall and dangle. My belly slams against the wall. Sorry, baby. I hope your head didn't just get smashed in. I can't worry about that right now. Luckily, I wrapped the rope around my hand, and the bed is heavy, so I don't plummet to my death. Not yet, anyway.

I'm nearing the bottom when I notice the flames are at the window. Fuck. I descend faster. I'm about ten feet off the ground when my rope snaps, hurling me down to the ground. I turn to land on my hands and brace my fall. Bad idea. My right wrist breaks on impact—sending an electric shock up to my elbow and into my teeth. The pain pops into my ears. I'm no doctor, but an intact wrist doesn't turn in that direction. FUCK. The pain took a second to kick in, but as I get up, it rages at me. Throbbing. Maybe I should put some ice on it. I look at the moat and don't see myself being about to dislodge any. No time. I must go. Suck it up, Astrid. You have to run. Just be happy you're left-handed.

The rope is still wrapped around me. I can't leave it here. I quickly coil it up and put it in my bag. I hoped the fire would hide the rope for me, but I guess this is better. The rope felt like the worst part of my plan. Picturing it left dangling or piled at the tower base kept me up at night. I'm sure a rope will come in handy. I don't know how, but I can't see how it can make things worse.

I put a mask on, struggling to do so with my wrist barking at me. I stifle the wails of pain as best I can. I pull my hood up. I hope all the extra clothing will be enough to mask my scent while also hiding my face.

I realize I probably should have screamed to make it so people suspect I jumped. It's too late now.

I run along the side of the castle. A loud bell chimes incessantly. Fire alarm? I hide in a bush when guards running past me. I hear them say "fire" and "Queen." I look back, and, fuck, my whole tower is in flames. I hope it doesn't spread to the dungeon—trapping all those women. Fuck, I didn't think this through enough.

I'm out, though. I sneak my way out of the castle grounds effortlessly. Everyone is too busy rushing toward the fire to look at me. I didn't expect it would be a distraction in this part of my escape. I have to get as far away from this castle and as far away from people as possible.

Oh, thank God. There are no guards at the gates. They're all trying to put out the fire. I honestly didn't have a plan for what I'd do if they found me. Seduction? Murder? I'm happy I don't have to do that. I didn't have an excellent plan for getting through the castle's outer walls and to the woods; I just knew I needed to do it. So, this is going better than it probably should.

I am out of the castle wall and in the town. I hurry through the streets, dipping through various alleys and staying out of sight. Everyone is concerned with the tower fire, even the townspeople, so no one notices me sneaking around. They don't seem to smell me! The extra clothes and padding on my neck, pits, and crotch must be working. I don't know where the scent comes from, but I figured it was one of those places.

I reach the outskirts of town and can see the woods. I run as fast as I can—which feels painfully slow. I slip behind the trees. When I am deep enough that I feel hidden, I stop and turn to look back. I can see the sky raging orange through the trees where the fire burns. I still can hear people yelling. Still hear the bell chiming. I bet Thad can hear it and see it from wherever he is, too. I've got to get out of here.

I turn back to face the woods and run deep into them. I made it! I fucking made it. I run until I can't run anymore.

12

I'm back in the fucking woods. Great. I've been walking for five days. My wrist is killing me and I've used some of my rope to tie it to my chest in a sling so I stop reaching for stuff with my hand. I never realized how much I used my right hand before.

My map shows roads and streams. There is a road that leads directly from Prailyra to Sailoria, but I have to avoid the paths. I can't risk being found. I've just been walking in the overgrown woods this whole time and it is making it difficult to determine where I am.

The map I have doesn't have a legend or scale indicated on it. I attempted to make my own based on tidbits of information I garnered from conversations with Thad. He told me Sailoria was about three days ride from the Prailyra. I divided the distance between the two cities by three and I'm using "a horse day" as my primary unit of measure. It's about as long as the distance from my thumb tip to its first knuckle, so I'm using my thumb to help me estimate time. I don't know how true it is, but I feel like I heard once that the inch was based on the length of some king's thumb from my world. I find it funny that I am now using a queen's thumb.

I know when a horse walks it actually doesn't walk much faster than a human, but they trot and run significantly faster. I've blindly estimated that a horse on a path travels five times faster than a pregnant queen stomping through the woods who needs lots of breaks. So, I assume each thumb length is about five days of me traveling.

I try to determine where I was on the map when the monsters found me. The map doesn't indicate any clearings, but I was only on the horse with Thad for about half a day or so. I worry I'm near where they found me. I hope they don't find me again. The last thing I need right now is to be raped by a bunch of monsters.

It's so cold. The first few nights, I was too scared to light a fire. I worried it would make me spottable by any knights or kings searching the woods for me. Tonight is so cold I have no choice, but to make a fire. I use the matches I brought and realize I only have a few. This will not get me through this trip. Fuck. It's much colder than I expected.

I am so thirsty. I ran out of water yesterday. I don't know why I thought the two jars of water I brought would be enough to last. Dehydrating and freezing can't be good for the baby. As much as I hate Thad and this child, I don't particularly want to miscarry. I especially don't want to miscarry in the middle of the fucking woods. God, maybe I didn't think this through. I look at my belly and place my hand on it. I feel a little kick like a bubble popping against me. Oh no … will it puncture through me with hideous claws? It kicks again—that kind of tickles. I giggle and smile at my belly, calmed by the feeling. I don't want to care for this thing, but I am already caring a little anyway.

I study my map by the firelight. Supposedly there is a stream is directly south of the castle. It runs perpendicular to my route, so I shouldn't miss it. I thought I would have found it by now. I let out a growl of frustration and slam the map to the ground. What good is a map without units of measure? I have no idea how far away Sailoria is. I have no idea how far away the stream is. I have no idea how fast I can walk through these woods. It's all so fucking useless. This sounds like a stupid joke. How fast does a pregnant woman walk in the woods? Not fast enough to not die of thirst.

The following day, I wake up and pack my things into my sack. I did not sleep well. Despite the fire, I was still quite cold. It is hard enough to get comfortable with a huge belly in a bed fit for a queen. How I thought my fat, insomniac ass was going to sleep on the ground of the woods is beyond me. My hand is swollen to twice its size. Dreams of monsters raping me woke me multiple times throughout the night. It has not been good sleep. I stomp at the fire's embers to disperse the ashes and cover my tracks.

It is freezing. Maybe it will snow today. I can refill my water jars with snow. But the snow would also leave tracks and get me wet with cold. Maybe

I don't want it to snow. It would be nice to have some snow to pack on my wrist, though.

I walk for a few hours and hear the sound of running water. I pick up the pace, and find the small stream. Thank GOD. I gulp down the water and refill my water jars. Visions of my dead body in the middle of the woods in a pile of my shit flash through my head as I drink. Is dysentery a thing in this world? They have horses. They have birds. Why wouldn't they also have diarrhea causing bacteria?

The map says the city of Sailoria is southwest of the castle. If I follow the stream west, I should get to the approximate location of the city. I might as well keep a water source handy and follow it for a while. My speed and distance calculations are totally fucked, so I have no idea how long I need to follow the stream. In a few days, I guess I will go south again. Fuck, I have no idea. Maybe I should give up on making it to the city. Maybe I should just try to learn how to live in the woods.

It's getting dark, and I need to set up camp. I look around for some hidden area that has enough flatness to lie down. Is that a cave? Sleeping in a cave will be much better than sleeping under the open sky. I'm handling this whole *being outside* thing better than I thought, but still not great. I took the last pieces of my magic pill to deal with the fear and the pain in my wrist my very first night, so sleeping under the sky still scares me. I hope there aren't any bears or unimaginable dangers in there.

I sneak up to the cave and peek in. It's shallow. I don't see anything here that looks like a nest or a pile of bones or anything. I guess it's safe. I wouldn't know what a bear nest looks like, anyway. Maybe shed fur all over the place? I will probably die in these woods no matter what I do, so I will take my chances to get from under this sky.

This cave is shallow, but deep enough to hide me from the elements if it were to rain or storm. It's by a water source. Maybe I should just stay here. Adopt a couple of wolves as pets and raise my child with them. The idea of having to raise a child in a cave sounds horrid, but honestly, the idea of having to raise Thad's little monster scorpion child in his castle sounds horrid, too.

The temperature seems to have dropped even further. I'm happy I waited for it to warm up before leaving, but it is still so cold, and I am so fucking pregnant and pathetic. I need to start a fire. I desperately want to just lay down in this cave and fall asleep, but my coldness is taking precedence over my exhaustion. I drop my bag in the cave and wonder if it's okay to leave it there. It's not like anyone is going to steal it, Astrid. But maybe someone will find me because of it? The cave has a little alcove that can't be seen from its entrance. I hide my bag there. That's where I'll sleep tonight.

I return to the woods and gather some underbrush for kindling and some branches to burn. Maybe I can try catching a fish with the hooks and string I brought.

I return to the cave, looking over my shoulder the whole time to make sure no one sees me enter. I turn into the cave to the little nook I tucked my bag in and see a dark figure crouched down, riffling through it. It's the birdman! "Alistair," I involuntarily say aloud and drop the fire kindling I have in my hands. Fuck.

He turns quickly and stands, an unopened jar of jam in his left hand.

He looks at me and instantly becomes erect.

Fuck. Fuck. Fuck.

"Please, don't hurt me! I am with child!" I say, placing my hand on my belly. I hope this whole pregnancy thing will make him have sympathy for me. Or maybe turn him off, so he doesn't rape and murder me. Fuck. What if he eats babies, and I just made my irresistible-smelling ass an even tastier morsel?

"M'Lady, I would not." That's what he said the last time we met. He notices I am staring, horrified at his penis. He drops the jam to cover his manhood with his wings. The jam jar smashes to the ground, red goo splattering all over the cave wall and floor. "Forgive me. I cannot control it. You smell …" he stops talking and inhales lustfully.

Oh, my God. He's going to rape me. I will be raped and murdered on a puddle of jam and broken glass in this dirty cave. My blood will mix with the red jam, and people won't be able to tell the difference between my gore and the jam. He's going to cut my stomach open with a shard of that jam jar's glass and rip this baby from my guts and eat my baby while I watch! All because of this stupid fucking smell! I step back from him slowly, too scared to breathe. Please don't kill me.

He looks down at the broken jar and crouches down to grab the glass. No, he is going to cut me open! I should not have brought the fucking jam. Maybe I can find something to hit him with. I glance around, trying to find something to bludgeon with him while he's down there.

He quickly scrambles to pick up the pieces. "I am so sorry. I didn't mean to drop it." He cuts his wing on the broken glass and winces but keeps going. Is he just trying to clean it up? "Please step back, M'Lady. I don't want you to cut yourself. I am so sorry. Please forgive me. Please forgive me."

"Don't …" I say and reach toward him slightly. He's hurting himself with his clumsiness. Those feathered wings of his are not meant to pick up small pieces of glass—or do anything dexterous. "You're hurting yourself."

"Please, please forgive me, M'Lady." He looks at me helplessly, like a kicked dog still trying to please its evil master. "I didn't mean to break your jar. I saw the bag in my home and was curious about it." So much for my checking to make sure nothing lived here already.

"I should have left it alone as soon as I smelled traces of you on it. Please forgive me. I can make you more jam. There is a wild berry patch not far from here. I can get the berries right now. It will take a while since I cannot fly, but I will run there now." Tears are rolling down his face. I have never seen such a nervous man. He … reminds me of me when I first came here. My empathy drive kicks into gear, and I want to show him kindness.

He tries to run out of the cave past me. I grab his arm and say, "Don't. It's okay." Why the fuck am I touching him? What is wrong with me? Why am I grabbing at the monster? His arm is hard and muscular. The top of his arm, where I've grabbed him, is covered in soft downy feathers. The contrast of soft fluffiness and hard muscles is surprising.

He hangs his head and covers himself. I've never seen a creature look so ashamed before. His bottom beak quivers. Is this like a lip quiver? Is he going to cry? He refuses to look at me.

We stand there—him recoiling with my hand on his arm, me looking at his eyes—for what feels like forever.

Eventually, he says, "Did you call me …," he gulps. "Did you call me Alistair? How did you know my name?"

"Thadius told me."

His head snaps at the sound of the name Thadius, and he rushes to the cave's opening, holding onto the side and peeking out. "Is he here? Did he bring you here as bait to hunt me?" He makes a weird noise clicking his beak quickly. Is he afraid?

"No, I ran away from him," I say.

"You did? How on Earth did you manage to escape his prison?" He looks back at me. His head tilts to the side at an almost ninety-degree angle. I wonder if he can look behind himself like an owl.

I hug myself tight and shiver. Not in fear. I am no longer afraid, just wary, but I am cold.

"Oh, you are cold. I will start a fire," he says and cautiously slinks over to me. He grabs the bundle of wood I dropped to the ground and walks back slowly, careful not to turn his back to me. He's not making any quick movements and I'm not sure if he's scared of me or scared of scaring me. He slinks to an area in front of the cave and piles the kindling and branches. He smacks some rocks together, and it catches fire. He is much more adept at making a fire than I am, and I am grateful he's the one building it.

He stands by the fire and motions to it with his two wings for me to come closer. I walk toward the fire, slowly, cautiously, arms still folded. He says, "Wait!" and grabs some moss he didn't use for kindling. He lays it flat out on the floor. He fusses and fluffs at it a bit and motions for me to sit down on it.

I sit and look at him cautiously. I wait for him to do something. He slinks to the other side of the cave, far away, probably not getting any warmth. He squats, hugging his legs and watching me.

I decide to answer his question. The silence is killing me. "He kept me locked in a tower, but I set it on fire and climbed out the window with some rope I made. I hope he thinks I am dead, but I doubt he does." He seems reassured by the sound of my voice. He sits in what looks like a less nervous and more comfortable position, crossing his legs and placing his hands on his knees. He watches me intently while I speak. "I hurt my wrist when I jumped." I show him my wrist, and he winces. "Everyone was so preoccupied with the fire. I was able to get out of the city easily."

He does not say anything. We just look at each other in silence. After a long while, he speaks. "Um, I have some fish. They are fresh." He points at a pile of fish at the entrance. I had not noticed them until now. "Are you hungry? I can make some for you."

I nod nervously. Fuck, yes, I'm hungry. I've been rationing my food, but I've been ravenous this whole voyage.

He crab-crawls to the fish, afraid to stand and startle me. He scales the fish with a stick while I watch. I look at him, and … he's sort of hot. Maybe it's my pregnancy hormones, but my labia pulse while I watch the muscles in his arms. The motion of scaling a fish is making the firelight bounce off all his arm's curves as he flicks back and forth. Why am I finding a bird monster scaling a fish erotic? It's been a while since I've enjoyed a good deep dicking and—stop it, Astrid. Reign in the dirty perv. I gulp and try to compose myself. I look at the ground for a long moment and watch an ant scurry across the dirt, leaving a little groove in his wake.

The silence is deafening, so I speak again. I feel an intense need to tell my story to him. I haven't been able to talk to anyone about the ordeal and I just need to get it out. "He was so sweet when we first met. We got married. I was so stupid." I begin to cry.

"You were not stupid." He whispers. Alistair stops scaling the fish and jams them on the end of long sticks. He sprinkles some kind of herbs on the fish. I'm surprised by his use of herbs in a cave. It seems weird.

"Yes, I was! I was seduced by him, drugged by him, impregnated by him. How could I let him do this to me?" Why am I spilling my guts to this bird? I chuckle, thinking about how I would spill my guts to the birds in my tower. I guess I just like birds.

"No, you were not, M'Lady. His Majesty is maliciously charming. You are not the first to fall for his act. Please, do not blame yourself." At least this bird talks back. He seems to know a lot about Thadius.

"You … you know Thadius well then?" I ask.

"I know him, yes. I was a chef in his castle before he did this to me." He motions toward his body.

"Chef? What do you mean? What did he do?"

"He's the one who cursed me with this form—he's the one who made me and my friends monsters. We were human before he did this to us."

13

"Wait! He made you a monster? How did he do that? Why did he do that?" I ask, utterly confused. Alistair's kneeling in front of the fire, and his erection has not subsided. I'm worried he will burn the tip of his dick off. I stop asking my questions to stare at it, completely distracted by it. It is pitch black with the same blue sheen his feathers have. The light reflecting off of it is mesmerizing.

He opens his beak, but before he can answer my barrage of questions he notices where I am staring and awkwardly shifts to hide his erection. He begins to apologize to me, "Please forgive my state, M'Lady. I do not mean to disrespect you. Oh, I suppose I should call you Your Majesty. Forgive me." God, I am such an asshole. The man has been cursed and I care more about his cock than his predicament. I giggle. Pre-dick-ament. Ugh, I suck. Get it together, Astrid.

"It's okay. Thad explained to me the effect I have on people here. And, I think I prefer 'M'Lady'. 'Your Majesty' makes me think of him."

"Here?" he asks and raises a tuft of feathers on his forehead that resemble an eyebrow.

"I'm not from this world," I say as I wave my hands around, trying to motion to the entire planet, but probably just looking like a crazy person. I brace myself for him to ask me tons of questions now.

"Oh, just like Serena."

"Who is Serena?"

"She was His Majesty's wife. She was from another world, too." Thadius never told me her name. Why did I never think to ask? I guess Gen wasn't the only person whose life I was too preoccupied to learn about.

"Oh," I say, feeling ashamed for not knowing her name. Why hadn't he told me she was from another world, too? When I finally revealed to him my true origins, he acted surprised. He acted like he doubted me and it was impossible. I suppose it was just that—an act.

"He murdered her about a month before you arrived."

"WHAT!? He told me you and the other monsters murdered his first wife five years ago!" He seems to bristle at me calling them monsters. I probably should stop doing that.

"No! We would never hurt Serena. We were all so fond of her. We tried to stop him from killing her. He murdered her and then hexed us with the same curse that had once been cast upon him." I look at him in shock. I realize I know absolutely nothing about Thadius or this world.

"Okay, um … this is a lot to take in. Let's back up a bit." I'm not sure what to ask, I want to know everything. "Can you … can you tell me about Thadius? About Serena? Can you tell me what happened? Can you explain how you knew them? Can you tell me about your friends?" I have so many questions I can't get them all out.

"Okay, I'll try to start from the beginning," he takes a deep breath and seems like he's trying to figure out the best way to explain all of this to me. Alistair seems as eager to tell me his story as I was to tell him mine. I scoot closer to the fire both for warmth and to get closer to him. I need to learn this story. I need to learn what is really going on.

"Most of what I know about His Majesty I learned from the others—from my friends. The other … monsters," he pauses before the word "monster", obviously uncomfortable calling himself and his friends that. "Even though I had been a chef at the castle for quite a while, I didn't interact with him much before Serena arrived." I think back to him putting herbs on the fish and I guess now it makes more sense now that I know he was a chef.

He hands me a fish on a stick, and I nibble on it. It's hot, so I blow at it and wait for it to cool, but I can already tell it tastes great. He does not bite at his fish but jams the non-fish end of the stick into the ground to make it stand up. It looks like a fish being punished for misdeeds—spiked on a stick—an example to all the other naughty fish in the kingdom. I do the same while I wait for mine to cool.

He rubs one of his wings with the other, almost like he's trying to pet himself—to comfort himself. "Osric was his Majesty's best friend in childhood who later became the royal cupbearer. He said the king was a selfish child who always got his way—which is to be expected of a prince, but Thadius also had cruelty about him. Osric said that once His Majesty realized the effect he had on women, he would use his princely manners and good looks to seduce as many as he could. It was a game to him. But once he bedded them, he'd treat them cruelly and never speak to them again."

"Which one is Osric? Oh, the squid one! Right?" I ask, remembering someone saying his name in the woods.

"Yes, he is the squid one. According to Osric, his Majesty acted this way for many years until he slept with a beautiful woman who turned out to be a powerful mage. After sleeping with her, he was instantly cruel and embarrassed her somehow—I don't know the full story. She hexed him to the form of a monster, saying something about how he would remain in that form until he found someone he loved who would accept him in his monster form. I think the phrase was, 'once she accepts your body and heart into hers, you will be cured of your curse.'" Alistair shifts his weight and sits more comfortably to continue his story.

"Gideon—the cat—was the royal scholar and physician appointed to the castle. He and Thadius spent months studying, trying to break the curse. During this time, the only people permitted to see the king were Osric, Gideon, and His Majesty's royal guard, Lysander. Lysander is the lizard. Lysander sent the army out to search for the mage, but no one could find her. Gideon and His Majesty surmised that His Majesty had to sleep with a woman he loved, who loved him and accepted him in his monstrous form."

True love's first fuck? This can't be real. Is this whole long story a pickup line? Is Alistair just trying to get me to sleep with him? Is it some fucking incel pickup line? I look at him, incredulous, trying to determine if he's telling the truth, but it's hard to read emotions on a beak. His eyes look honest, though.

"Eventually, his Majesty sent Lysander to bring women to the castle to live in the Rose Tower. He would try to convince them to love him, but none would. Until that is, he found Serena. Serena was from a different world like you. She was special. She saw past the king's monstrous form, fell in love with him, and cured him of his curse. For a time, they were happy."

I tried to imagine what Serena looked like. The way Alistair says her name leads me to believe she was loved. I bet she was beautiful.

"What happened to the women who didn't cure him?" I ask.

"Lysander will not tell us what happened to them. But, when he tells the story, the way his tone changes, the shame on his face. You can tell bad things happened to them. Cordelia—the um, tree woman—acted as their lady-in-waiting. She would see the king interact with them. The women would tell her how the king was getting impatient and forceful with them. She thinks his Majesty would eventually force himself on them. When it did not work to cure him, she believes he killed them. He would tell her they went home, unable to love him when she asked after them. She tried to believe this story. But when Lysander would not answer our questions, she knew her worst fears were true."

So, Gen wasn't their lady-in-waiting. That makes me feel better. I still don't know if she knew Thadius was a monster, but if she had been theirs, I would have even less faith in her.

"He lived with Serena for a few years. But, his desire to steal women had sunk in. He continued to abduct them. When Serena found out about it, she confronted him and hit him. He entered into a rage and turned into that scorpion form. He murdered her."

"Florian—the wolf—was the queen's guard. He and Lysander fought valiantly to stop him but were unsuccessful. The rest of us just happened to be there. We tried to stop him, too, of course. We held her body and tried to save her, but it was no use. While we sat with her, crying over her, he hexed us all with the same curse that had once befallen him. He said, 'I am your king! You should love me, not that whore I found in the woods. I put my curse upon you until you understand the true meaning of love!' We were cast out of the castle and banished. We tried to stay in the city, but we terrified everyone. So, we hid in the woods."

"Wait, Thadius knew how to cast the spell, too?" I ask.

"Gideon said up until that point, Thadius had never used magic before, but must have learned how to perform the hex or curse, sorry, I don't know the difference, while studying to break his affliction."

I try to process what he has just told me. I need to ask him questions about this.

"So, wait. All the missing women? That is ALL HIM?" I already know the answer. I don't know why I'm asking.

"Yes. Some he keeps. Most he kills."

"How … how does he get away with this? How do people not know he's doing this?"

"He takes them to the woods and sets them loose. He chases them down, rapes them, and murders them. He … hunts them in his beast form. When we first were banished to the woods, we tried to save them, but he is powerful in his beast form and brings his army to protect him. He didn't kill us when we fought him. He just had us held down and made us watch him rape them and then murder them." I am sick to my stomach. So, maybe the city folk don't know what the king is up to, but his guards do. All those men that were training. They are in on it. They help him murder the women of the city.

"Why did you stick around? Why didn't you leave instead?" Maybe I shouldn't push him with so many questions. He looks like he may burst into sorrow.

"Well, after he took you, we did. Well, everyone except me, that is. After I recovered from my injuries, I returned to our cave here, and everyone was gone. We stayed so long, hoping we could save at least one. But, something about how he grabbed you, I think it was the last straw for my friends. It was the last straw for me. I stopped trying to save the women. I am a monster, inside and out."

"You did your best. That does not make you a monster." Alistair weeps silently, ashamed of himself. The silent weeps turn to uncontrollable sobs and my heart aches for him. I consider getting closer and patting his back or something, but it feels inappropriate. Instead, I pull my fish from the ground and nibble at it, to see if it is still hot. It has cooled enough to eat. It is surprisingly good for dirty stream fish with mysterious cave spices. While I chew, I steal glances at his cock. I am such a heartless asshole. I never know how to console people—or monsters.

He composes himself and says, "I'm sorry. It's just a lot."

"I'm sorry I pushed you. I should have stopped asking questions."

He sniffles and says, "No! No! I want to tell you everything, M'Lady! Please, ask me all the questions you have."

"Why can Thadius still transform into the beast after the curse was broken?"

"According to Gideon—the cat—if a cursed man can make love to a woman who truly accepts him, then he can accept the form unto himself and call on that form, in a much stronger state, whenever he needs it. He saw something in a book about using the curse's power to protect your love. Something about sharing the curse with the one who truly loves you. But he didn't protect Serena, despite her great love for him." He wipes a tear from his eye at the mention of her name.

"Who were you to Serena? You obviously cared for her."

He lights up and shifts his weight to get more comfortable. He puts one hand over his chest and says, "I was her personal chef! She taught me so many amazing recipes from her world! She was a great baker, but couldn't handle cooking meat. It grossed her out," he chuckles. "She knew what was in the dishes, though, and told me what to do. We would spend a lot of time together in the kitchen. I miss her every day."

"Did you and Serena ever …?" I make a little face and glance down at his penis. He looks seriously wounded that I would ask such a thing, and I immediately regret it. Not everyone is a dirty perv like you, Astrid. I was just hoping to hear a naughty story. And maybe hear someone do something secretly to hurt Thad.

"Of course not! She was my queen. My friend. I would never touch her. I did not think of her like that. I cared for her very deeply, though."

"But, did she have the smell? The smell from another world?"

"She had the smell, but it worked a bit differently than yours. It didn't cause arousal. I think maybe it caused deep feelings of friendship and kindness, though. You'd want to be a better person whenever you'd smell her."

I'm feeling a bit jealous of Serena right now. I would prefer people be nice to me rather than point boners at me all day. I mean, I am flattered by the boners, but I also kind of hate it.

"Can you tell me about the day you found me in the woods? What happened after I passed out?"

"We were in the woods discussing what to do. Florian first smelled something he described as 'cute' on the breeze."

"You can smell cute?" Why am I flattered? Maybe the smell isn't that bad.

"He can. He has a really good sense of smell in his cursed form—he's the wolf. It's so good he can see shapes with it. I don't fully understand it. Eventually, we all smelled it and became extremely aroused. We could not contain our curiosity and followed Florian to the smell."

He continues, "We saw you aimlessly wandering around and talking to yourself." Great, they heard me talking to myself. "We watched you for quite a while before you saw us. We didn't want to scare you."

I think back on that day and remember them all approaching me menacingly and talking about fucking me. "Why did you try to rape me!?" I can't trust this bird even if he does have a cool dick, nice eyes, and cries.

"What! We didn't! We would never!" He falls back at the accusation, like I have seriously wounded him.

"But … you all walked toward me with erections. The cloud guy grabbed me!"

"Oh, M'Lady, I think you misinterpreted the situation. We approached slowly. We stopped when you asked. Augusten, or the cloud guy you call him, didn't grab you. He caught you. You tripped and fell."

Oh, yeah, I did trip. "Why were you naked?"

"When we transformed into our monster forms, our clothes were destroyed. We were chased into the woods and couldn't return to get clothes. Clothes became a low priority for us during that time." I suppose that makes sense.

"But what about what the squid guy said? He said something about raping me. What was his name? Osric?"

"Osric is a bit crass, but he wouldn't have hurt you. He thought you were … um, in the mood and approached the situation as such. You smelled … forgive me for saying, aroused." I'm not sure if I believe this story. This sounds convenient. I was aroused, though, so maybe he's not lying. I recall the feeling of the cloud guy's dick against my back and get a bit wet. Oh, shit! Can he smell me right now getting wet?

"But even you were stroking your dick!"

A look of pure horror and shame crosses his face. His beak flies open, and he caws in surprise. "What! You thought I was touching myself? Oh, no, no, no, M'Lady. I was trying to cover it—so you wouldn't have to see it. I am so ashamed. This whole time you thought I was …" He sobs and wails.

I look at him, still unsure if I believe this story, but I am starting to. If he's acting, he's a better actor than Thadius. But, I'm afraid to trust a man again so soon.

He composes himself. "M'Lady, I am so sorry we scared you. I would do anything to go back in time and fix that. You passed out before we could speak to you."

"We watched over you for about half an hour, waiting for you to wake up. Not one of us touched you inappropriately. I swear!" I'm still unsure of this story, but the look in his eyes is so sincere. Despite the beak, his face is recognizably emotive because of those eyes.

"How did I end up with the king?"

"He … was in the area with a woman he was hunting. He saw us with you, and I guess he decided he was more interested in you than his recent prey."

"He let her go?"

"Unfortunately, no. He … he ripped her in half in front of us."

My heart sinks. How did I spend so much time with a man capable of such atrocities? Flashes of his bright, beautiful smile appear in my head. It's hard to believe this is all the same Thad, but I know it's true. I saw that room.

"He threw her corpse aside and then ran his horse toward us. We tried to protect you, but please forgive us, M'Lady. If we were stronger, we could have protected you. He overtook us and grabbed you."

"Why did he take me? Why didn't he kill me?"

"I cannot speak to his intentions, M'Lady, but perhaps you seemed collectible to him? He likes to collect rare women. Perhaps you reminded him of Serena. Perhaps he planned to kill you, but you did something to win him over. I could not tell you why he chose to keep you rather than kill you, but I am happy to see he did."

A tear runs down his cheek. "I cannot imagine the unspeakable things he did to you." He buries his face in his wings and sobs. "I am so sorry, M'Lady. I am just a chef. I am not a fighter. I tried to catch you. I tried to stop him. But when he put you in the way of my spear, I could not get close to him for fear of harming you."

I think back to when Alistair chased us. I remember thinking Thad might have used me as a human shield. It sounds like he did. I think of what he said. "You cannot have this one, too!" That is starting to make more sense now.

"How did you survive that attack?" I ask.

"I almost didn't. I lay in that same spot in the dirt for days. He had almost severed my wing. I can no longer fly. I dragged myself back to where I thought my friends would be, but they were not here."

I sit for a long moment absorbing the story. I turn it in my head to find holes. I cannot be fooled by a man again. I will trust him for now because I am tired, he knows how to make a fire, and I think he can cook. I also can't think of a way to escape. I'll get him to trust me and then run in the night.

He waits for a long moment. I think he, too, is absorbing the story he just told me because I can see multiple emotions run across his face, none of them pleasant. I am surprised how much emotion he can convey with a beak. "Even with a warrior like Lysander on our side, we could do nothing to protect you. Nothing to protect Serena. Nothing to protect those women." He puts his hands in his wings and weeps loudly. The wails echo through the cave, and I feel cold thinking about how he needs to tone it down before someone hears him.

14

We spend a few days together in the cave. Alistair does not touch me and recoils if I try to touch him. The first time he touches me is to reset my wrist. The swelling has not gone down, and it bends at a weird angle. I wail in pain as he pulls it. "I'm sorry, M'Lady. I'm sorry. If I didn't do it, it wouldn't heal correctly." He then places a salve of sorts he mushed together on my wrist. The pain doesn't completely disappear, but it reduces slightly. I doze off in a small nest of blankets and moss he has made me, delirious from the pain.

I wake up from a dream of the seven monsters tangled in an orgy with each other—me right in the center. "Al. Couldn't you have cured the curse from each other? I mean, you care about each other, right? Wouldn't, um, wouldn't that have worked."

He looks a bit bashful. "Um, some of us tried. It didn't work." I blush and desperately want to know more about this story. Who tried with who? Why didn't it work? How did they know it didn't work? I get wet thinking of all the combinations of "some of us" and swallow to moisten my dry throat.

I don't want to push him to expand, but he can tell I want to ask more. "Perhaps we did not accept each other as we were and wished each other to be who we were before the curse. Perhaps, the curse didn't appreciate us trying to find a loophole. Curses have minds of their own; since we don't know the original caster, we don't know all the rules. We only know small details Gideon had learned when he originally tried to help cure His Majesty." He doesn't say anything else, but instead turns from me and continues with what he was doing. Damn, I was hoping for some more lurid details.

I turn in my bedroll, unable to get comfortable. My belly is so huge, and I prefer sleeping and masturbating on my stomach. Being pregnant fucking sucks. I'm also always fucking horny and can't do anything about it with Alistair here all the time. I try to get him to leave so I can masturbate, but he is too protective of me, and by the time I get in a comfortable position, he is back. Well, maybe I can do something about it with him here.

Alistair is tending to the fire while I lay in bed. Every night he has kept it lit for me until I fall asleep. He says we can't leave it up overnight, or we could attract predators or die from the smoke choking us. I think about how you're not supposed to fall asleep with your fireplace on because of carbon monoxide poisoning, and believe him.

I look at Alistair and try to picture him before he changed into a monster. He is tall and lean, but muscular. Most of his body is covered in either long black feathers or a short downy fluff. The feathers gleam blue when the light hits them just right. It is a beautiful color. Even with the feathers, I can still see the outline of muscles on his strong back. His feathers on the top of his head fall to his shoulders resembling long, thick, black hair. The kind of hair so thick it grows outward for months before gravity can even take hold of it. He looks so soft and cuddly I want to rub my nipples against his chest.

Other than the beak, he is handsome. Over these last few days, I have often found myself staring at him and getting aroused thinking about him. I get aroused now. He's not looking at me, so I lay on my side and stare at him while I slip my hands inside my bedroll and gently press my clit over my clothes.

The sexual tension between us has been palpable. I don't think he can tell I'm feeling it on my end; he's so shy. It's apparent on his, though. He is so attentive to me. He is so sweet; I find myself tingling all over whenever he does something for me. I guess my love language is acts of service because I'm falling for him faster than I fell for Thad.

He has gotten used to my presence and can now control his erection a bit, but if I accidentally brush against him, his penis jumps to attention instantly. I'm surprised he doesn't pass out with how fast the blood rushes to his dick and out of his face whenever this happens. He freezes in place and looks like a man who has never had an erection before—he's just learning how to deal with himself, hiding behind his wings.

I made him a little loincloth with some of my fabric to save him some grace, but it almost makes it worse when he gets erect as it lifts right up and flaps away at me. I try to convince him to wear some of my clothes, maybe a dress, but he refuses to "defile my clothes with his filthy feathers."

I giggle a bit, thinking about his loincloth waving at me. I slip my hands inside my skirts, no longer satisfied with the over-the-clothes action, to flick gently at my clit. It's soaking wet. I can't go full out. I can't have an orgasm here with him in the room. Or can I? I flick faster and hump against my hand in my bed. If he turns from the fire, he'll see me. He'll know what I'm doing. The thought of him seeing me masturbate while staring at that strong back of his gets me going even harder. I've always had a thing for back muscles.

We have been together for a few days, and he has been nothing but kind. He has not tried to take advantage of me, even though he definitely could have. I don't suspect an ulterior motive with him, but I haven't been the best judge of character lately. I am easily swayed by a hottie. And … he *is* hot. How the fuck do I find a bird monster hot? It's the hair. The eyes. The strong back.

I ache for him. I want him inside me—bad. If I sleep with him, I can cure this ache. I can also probably cure his curse. I want to do this for him. I want to save him from his curse. I want to fuck him so badly. I've finally admitted it to myself. Playing with myself slyly under the covers while I stare at him should be obvious enough, but it's hard to admit I want to fuck a monster's brains out.

Ok, how am I going to do this? Should I say, "Alistair, please fuck me until I see stars?" No. I don't think that will go over well with him. He's too timid. I need to seduce him. He needs to feel like he's helping me.

I remove my hand from my crotch and groan loudly, faking pain. I wasn't a theater kid, but with the acting I've been doing the last few months, you'd think I was.

Alistair perks up quickly and rushes over to me. He kneels beside my bedroll and frantically looks me up and down, his hands hovering over me, not daring to touch me. "What's wrong?! Are you okay? Is the food hurting your stomach? I was sure those herbs were not poisonous. Maybe it was the fish. Oh, M'Lady, please forgive me!"

"No, no," I say breathlessly. I wince this time. "It's my back. It hurts so much." I poke out my lip trying to sexy pout. Okay, that was a bit much. He's going to see through this. There's no way that face was believable.

"Oh, of course! You're a queen, and I have you lying on a dirt floor! How could I be so careless? I will find some more padding for you right away. Perhaps some moss. Yes, moss, that would be perfect." He talks so fast I can barely speak. I touch his arm to stop him before he gets up.

He stops in his tracks and waits patiently for my next words, too worried to recoil from my touch. "No, that's not it. It's just from being pregnant. I felt like this at the castle, too. The only thing that will help is a back rub. Can you do that for me? Please, Alistair?"

He gulps. "Yes, of course, M'Lady! But, are you sure you want me to touch you?"

"I am sure."

"My hands, they aren't the same as human hands. They …"

"It's okay, Alistair, just try your best," I grin and roll over to my side with my back facing him. It's too painful to get on my stomach. God, I wish I could get on my stomach and let him lay on top of me while he enters me from behind, and I grind against the ground. Okay, focus, Astrid. Stop daydreaming. He'll be inside you soon enough if you play your cards right.

He rubs my back with what feels kind of like palms. I moan in pleasure. It feels good but not as good as I'm making it out to feel. His feathers tickle against my chin, and I giggle a bit. He pulls his hands back "Don't stop," I tell him.

He seems startled by this reaction, but pleased that he pleases me. I'm going to have to ham it up for him a bit to get him to catch on. I moan in delight, even louder. If he could grin, I'm sure he would be. He shifts his body so that he is on his knees, kneeling next to me, kneading away at my back in the best way his biology allows. His feathers tickle my legs, and I giggle and moan. This is hard to keep up.

I know he must be hard as a rock right now. He gets hard from me just walking past him. How can I get him to do something about it? I turn slightly with a moan trying to get him to grab at my breasts when he rubs me, trying to get him to reach between my legs, but he pulls back and concentrates on my back. This dude is not going to fall for my, "Oh, no; your fingers slipped in. You should just keep going," tricks. I am throwing myself at him, and he is not catching the hint. Or he is choosing to ignore it out of politeness.

Maybe it's just time to tell him I want him. I roll over on my back and look him in the eye. "Oh, do you want me to stop? Was it good? Did it help?"

"Yes, Al, it was good. It did help. But I do not want you to stop. I want you to do the front." He looks at me utterly bewildered and turns his head in the birdlike way he does. "I want you to do it here," I say as I open the blanket and gesture to my crotch. God, this is so desperately cheesy of me. This is not remotely smooth, but his raging erection tells me I don't need to be smooth. He'll fuck me.

"Wait, you can't mean…." He looks bewildered, his beak agape.

I turn to face him and prop myself up on my elbow. With my free hand, I place my palm flat against his beak. His beak snaps shut and he shudders. "I do mean. Please, I need you," I whisper and kiss him gently on the side of the beak.

I swear I can feel his heart stop, and he falls back a little. "Um, um, are you sure?" Kicking the dirt up as he moves away from me. Watch it dude, I don't need dirt in my eye.

"Yes, I am sure; I want this very much," I say while lying back down on my back. I lift my bed clothing over my head, revealing my fully naked body to him. My belly heaves. My pubic hair is already moist and my breasts are swollen from pregnancy and arousal. He takes it all in. His beak drops open again as he reaches out. He places his hand on my belly, and I look over at him. His loin cloth flaps at me as if waving, "Hey, lady, I'm gonna fuck you."

I grab his feathery hand and place the tips where my thighs meet. A burst of pleasure grows where his feathers graze. He snatches his hand back quickly. Did I push him too far? Was I too aggressive?

"I … I can't kiss you. My beak."

"I don't need to be kissed."

I half expect him to plunge right into me, but he doesn't do that. He waits. He admires my body. He runs the tips of his feathers around my nipples, and I grind upwards in a moan. Damn, dude, this is nice, but fuck me already.

I reach over and snatch the loincloth off him to see his dick. It points at my face and I can see that beautiful black and blue iridescence wave over it. He shuffles to the side preparing to straddle me. Here it comes, Astrid, that worked.

He takes the cue and moves his leg between my legs so I can press against it. I moan in delight as I slowly slick his leg with my juices.

He leans his head down and turns his face to the side so his beak does not stab me. He rubs the side of his face against my breasts while he strokes his penis. This time I take his cue and grab his penis in my hand. He moans so loudly, almost caws; I'm surprised he doesn't blow his load all over the side of the cave walls. Maybe it does have tiny feathers on it, because the texture is very, very soft. Not quite like skin. I can't wait to feel it on me.

I rub my thumb over the tip, and he pushes his body against mine. He slips out of my grip and grabs himself again. I'm confused. Does he not want me to touch him? He uses his knees to spread my legs out so he can get between them. He rubs his dick around my slit slowly. He moves it up and down, moistening his dick with me. He stops, pushes it hard against my clit, and rubs it in a circular motion, tracing my tip with his. Oh, shit. This feels good. I buck on him, making it slip inside slightly.

I'm about to cum when he stops. No, don't stop. I lift my upper body a bit to see what he is doing. He moves beside me and lies on his back. Wait? Is he done? What the fuck?

He puts his left arm under my neck. His feathers are so soft, like a fantastic pillow. He scoots up beside me, lifts my leg, and puts himself and his dick between me. The fleshy lips between my thighs wrap around his cock, and I am not proud of the fact that I think of a hotdog bun. Oh, this is nice, too.

I grind on his dick, getting it sloppy wet, not putting it in yet, just sliding it back and forth between my lips. As good as this feels, I can't take it anymore. I reach down and shove it so that it pops in, making a squishy noise in the process. He convulses. I squeeze my legs around his leg and move my upper body further from his to get a good angle. I hump and grind in a circular motion on his dick and leg. I like this angle a lot. I can get some excellent friction on my clit off his leg while his dick rolls around in me. Most positions have been uncomfortable with my big stomach, but this is great. Nothing is lying or pushing on my big belly and I still get to lie down.

He reaches around and pets my breasts with his feathers. He gets brave and softly nips at my right nipple. I don't stop him. I'm a little afraid his beak will bite it right off, but it doesn't. The fear adds to my pleasure. For the first time, I see his tongue as it slips out and flicks at my nipple. He nips at it again.

I moan in relief and gratification. The wet movement between my legs is about to climax when he reaches around so that both wings are engulfing me, tickling every part of my body with his feathers. There it is! I grab his leg and grind harder as I have a skyrocketing orgasm. I push myself hard onto him as I finish. I lay there resting for a moment when he whispered gently, "Did you come?"

"Oh, yeah."

He turns me slightly so he can leverage his weight, lifts my knee higher, as much as the belly will let him, and pumps into me rapidly. He reaches crevices he had not before, and I think I might come again. "Can I cum in you?" he asks. I realize he had not thrust the entire time I was getting off on him. He let me do all the work. Let me use his body for my own pleasure.

"Yes," I moan breathlessly, and for the first time in my life, I have a second orgasm. As he cums inside me, his body stiffens, and his feathers slowly recede. His beak begins to disappear. He has transformed into a man. He flops to the side and uses his human mouth to give me a slow kiss on my neck.

He stays inside of me as we both start to doze. Finally satisfied, the raging boner he has had this whole week slowly shrinks inside me. His semen starts to spill out. Fuck, we've made a mess. And we left the fire on. Oh, whatever, I don't care. As I fall asleep, I think, "How about that? He wasn't lying about the curse's cure."

15

I awake in the middle of the night and notice Al is not with me. He has extinguished the fire and put extra blankets on me. He is sitting at the edge of the cave, knees to his chest, staring at the stars. I sit up. "Al, you okay?" He's human. He somehow looks exactly the same and completely different. Where there were once long, thick black feathers are now luscious locks of black hair. His back is still the same back I was lusting over before, but now that it's not covered in downy feathers, I can see the outlines of muscles more easily. I do miss that mesmerizing black and blue sheen, though. His feathered arms have been replaced by lean muscular arms and hands with actual fingers.

He turns to look at me. He's been crying, but he smiles. "Yes, I very much am, M'Lady." Wow, I passed out before I got a good look at him. Even in this pale light, I can see he is gorgeous. He has those same big dark eyes, with long eyelashes that convey so much emotion that he was able to smile even with a beak. The lips that have replaced the beak are beautiful. I weep for the world that had lost them. I feel sorry for the fact that there was once a universe where these lips did not exist. They are full and in a permanent pout. I need to kiss those lips. Hard. Or ram them into my crotch. God, how am I horny again already?

I start to get up. "No, don't get up. I'll come to you. It's cold here." God, this guy is sweet. I shiver a bit; he is right. I pull the blankets up to my chin and get snuggly. "Do you need me to relight the fire? I can stay up with it?"

"No, no. Just come keep me warm."

"I can do that," he smiles with all his teeth.

He gets in the bedroll beside me and adjusts the blankets so they mainly cover me. His back is naked against the cold air. "Are you not cold?" I ask.

"No, I'm okay. You get warm."

I wonder if he feels the wind's chill now that his back is bare. Did the feathers help keep him warm? I look closely at him. I inspect his new face and body. I run my fingers over his chest and notice a scar on the front of his shoulder. I trace it with my fingers. This must be where Thad almost removed his arm. It's raised high and pink. I see another scar on his chest over his heart. It is white, old, jagged, and angry looking. It looks like someone stabbed him directly in the chest with a knife and pulled out his heart.

I sit up quickly. Thad had this same scar. It was the same shape, same color, and gave me the same weird empathetic tingle when I touched it. "What is this?" I demand. My heart is racing. Is this Thad in disguise? Is he using magic to trick me? I have no idea what magic is capable of in this world.

"That's the curse. It starts at the heart and grows outward. When cured, it returns to the heart but leaves a bit of itself right there. I'm still technically cursed—just less cursed, I guess. I had it before; you just couldn't see it in the feathers." I run my finger down the edges of the scar and shivers run through my body.

"Does it hurt?"

"No. It feels nice when you touch it, though. Like, I can feel your love radiating through it." He smiles warmly and closes his eyes. He looks genuinely at peace. Since he's so anxious, I suspect I won't see this look on his face often. He must be feeling the same tingle I'm feeling, but for him it is soothing—for me it is a confusing feeling I've never felt before. It causes a bit of panic in me, but I suppose the feeling could be love, as well.

"You seem a lot less anxious than usual. Are you always this chill after sex?"

"Well, if you didn't notice, my dick had been really hard for, like, a week. That can be a bit … stressful," he laughs.

I smack him softly and flop down. "You sure have gotten cocky since getting your dick wet." His nose crinkles at the crude phase, and he chuckles.

I hope you don't find vulgar talk offensive, Al, because if so, you've saddled yourself with the wrong gal.

"I'm joking. I'm just really happy. I never thought anyone would ever cure my curse. I wasn't exactly a ladies' man before it, so it felt a bit hopeless. You make me feel … safe." He pauses and looks toward the ceiling. "Plus, I'm really happy I got my 'dick wet.'" He laughs, jumps up to straddle me, and kisses my neck. Those lips. God, those lips are soft.

I grab his face between my two hands and examine him. I squish his cheeks—making his lips pucker like a fish. Dang, he's adorable.

"You are beautiful," I say—moisture building up between my legs, begging him to insert himself into me. I'm surprised he wasn't beating women away with a stick before the curse.

"So are you," he says and smiles. I swear he's lighting up the room with those teeth. I didn't think I'd see a smile more brilliant than Thad's, but this one is. I realize it is because it is sincere.

I pull his face toward mine and kiss him on the mouth. I slip my tongue in and am surprised he doesn't taste bad, given I know he hasn't brushed his teeth. I mean, he literally had a beak just a few hours ago. His dick is stiff, poking the bottom of my belly.

He pulls away and says, "I love you, M'Lady."

"I love you, too." Did I really just say that? I just met this guy. But I do. I love him. I love him more than I have ever loved anyone. What is wrong with me? Why do I keep falling head over heels for these men so quickly?

He crawls his way down my body, kissing every inch of me. He kisses a big circle around my belly and boops my nearly non-existent belly button with the tip of his nose. "I missed having lips!" he exclaims.

He keeps kissing and kissing, and I giggle and squirm until he reaches my pubic area. I freeze in anticipation. He brushes his nose against my pubic hair and breaths in. I don't know if I'll ever get used to these dudes smelling me. He gently sticks out his tongue and licks the peak where my lips meet. Very gently—teasing me.

"And I missed having fingers!" he exclaims, lifting his hand in the air and wiggling them at me. He reaches below me and traces the line formed by my slit. He raises one eyebrow at me and then dips back down to work. For a man who hasn't had a mouth for months, this dude knows what he is doing. He knows where my clit is and knows it's not all about tongue flicks but about wet, sloppy pressure and steady, methodical movement. I'm starting to doubt he wasn't a ladies' man in his past life because he definitely has practiced this.

How he knows exactly what I want when I want it is beyond me. He has at least two fingers inside of me, scratching upwards as if to beckon me forward. I grab that beautiful hair and pull it closer to me. I wish I didn't have this big belly blocking the view. I want to see him between my legs. I grind his face until I scream in pleasure. He stays there and waits for me to finish fucking his face and I gently push him away. I collapse on my side, panting.

After I have fully basked in my post orgasm glory, I reach down, grab his dick, and shove it into me. I'm not particularly in the mood to continue, but he did such a good job he deserves to get his dick wet on the fruits of his labor. He enters me with a moan of pleasure.

He sucks on my nipples, and while I know I won't cum again, I am still enjoying the ride. This time he doesn't ask before he cums in me; he just does it. It takes him less time than before to finish, and I'm glad because I am exhausted. He lifts his upper body and digs his lower body deeper into me. My uterus contracts down on the sensation. He cums for a long time. He pulls out and wraps me up like a little burrito, tucking me in. He scootches up next to me, wraps his arms around me, and pets my hair until I fall back asleep.

I awake to the smell of food sizzling and Al singing to me, "Wake up, M'Lady, you can't sleep all day. I've made you breakfast." Al seems to have cooked me a feast. What a grateful boy, I giggle to myself.

I walk toward him with the blankets bundled up over my shoulders.

"Where the hell did you get a frying pan!?"

"I can fly again!" he says.

"Wait, what?"

"Yeah, check this out." He puts down the frying pan, backs into the cave entrance, and poof, all his feathers grow back. But now, he's much bigger and looks more like an actual bird than a half-man/half-bird. His wingspan is significantly wider. I feel a bit of a tingle in my body when he does this. Is it arousal? No, it's something else.

"Gideon said he thought lifting the curse would give us the power to control our form and make our form stronger. He was right!"

He returns to his human body and walks back to the pan, flipping the eggs.

"So, what? You flew to town and got a frying pan and some eggs?"

"Yep! It was awesome! No one was scared of me! They were a bit concerned with a naked man walking around, but I stole some clothes that were out drying. Then everyone just ignored me."

"Where are your clothes now?" I ask. Not particularly annoyed that he's still naked.

"Oh, yeah, I had to take them off to transform, and I'm just kind of used to being naked. Let me go put them on. I think I look rather dashing in them."

He puts the eggs he was scrambling onto a plate and hands them to me. He rushes to the side of the cave to grab the new clothes he found and present them to me.

"Are you not going to eat?"

"No, I can't eat eggs anymore. Not after …" he lifts his hand, and it turns to feathers. Then quickly returns it to the hand of a human. "The idea makes me sick. I had some fish this morning." Can he turn just parts of his body into a bird now? That's super cool.

"That makes sense. I don't have to eat these if it makes you uncomfortable."

"No, no, you eat. You need protein, and you shouldn't be eating so much fish in your condition. It's good for the baby's brain but can be dangerous if you eat too much of it." I'm not sure how much science is behind this statement, but I don't fight it because I love some fucking eggs for breakfast. He's a chef. He probably knows what he's talking about.

"Wait, you ate this morning? What time is it?"

"It's well after noon."

WHAT? "Wow, you really fucked the insomnia out of me."

He laughs and says, "I can do it again tonight if you'd like. Or right now?"

"Oh, no. I need a little break. I'm kind of sore. Plus, I gotta eat these eggs."

"Sore!? Did I hurt you? Oh no, was I too rough?" He sits beside me, legs crossed, still naked, and inspects me. "I'm so sorry, M'Lady. I will be more gentle next time. Listen to me, presuming there will be a next time. Forgive me, My Lady. Oh, my god, did I hurt the baby?" At this point, he is standing back up, pacing—emotionally spiraling. I love this about him. It reminds me of me, except he says all his worries out loud and I internalize mine.

"Calm down, Al. I'm good. Just worn out. This is a good feeling." That sex was so gentle compared to the ramming I'm used to receiving from Thad, but I'm not going to tell Al that.

He sighs in relief. "Okay, good," and he slips his new outfit on. He's wearing a white blouse (do men wear blouses?) and tan pants. I have to admit, as awesome as he looks naked, he looks fantastic with some clothes on. He looks like he walked right off the cover of a period romance novel.

"You know, I'm happy you still have those feathers," I say.

"Oh, really? Why?"

"Well, there's the practicality of you being able to fly. That's going to be super helpful. But I liked when you teased me with them." I say, blushing at the ground.

He looks quite pleased with himself. He then gives me this look out of the corner of his eye and lifts his eyebrow—smirking. It's obvious he's asking me if I want him to please me right now.

"No, not right now," I giggle. This guy might be hornier than I am. Not that I'm complaining.

"Of course not." He says, looking slightly disappointed and shaking his head.

While eating my eggs, I sneeze, and some feathers pop out of my hand holding the fork. My hand is covered with the same downy feathers that covered Al's body, but they're not black. They're almost the same color as my golden-brown hair. When I turn my hand the gleam with golden iridescence against the light. We both look at it with amazement. What the fuck!? Since I've been pregnant, a little pee squirts out each time I sneeze. I don't know if I can handle feathers also squirting out of me.

I look at him and think I might freak out when they recede. "What just happened!?"

He grabs my hand and turns it, inspecting it. He's not a bird anymore, but his head still turns like one—just not as much.

"I think … maybe you absorbed some of my curse," he says, frowning at me contemplatively. I wish we understood the rules of this curse, but he seems cured, and that's good enough for me for now. I try to make it happen again but can't figure out how.

After a few minutes of us staring at my hand with me making faces at it and fake sneezing, Alistair speaks up, "So, I was thinking we should go find everyone else."

I stop looking at my hand. "What?"

"I think I know where Augusten is. I saw a cloud that looked like him when I flew to Sailoria to get your breakfast. We should find him. He might know where the others are." Al starts pacing again and waving his hands in excitement as he talks. "We can band together and fight the king. You're the rightful queen. You can take over."

"How long have you been awake? It seems like you have a whole plan ready."

"A while."

"You're talking about us essentially going on a quest to find your missing cursed monster friends and then overthrow a king."

"Yes."

"But, haven't you all tried to fight him before and failed? They won't be of any help."

"Well, there's another part to the plan." I look at him wearily. "You can maybe change them back? I am so much stronger now that my curse is cured. I can feel it. I bet they would be, too." he says while shrugging, wondering what I will say.

"Wait, what? That would mean I would have to …."

"Yeah."

"With all of them."

"Yep."

"And you're okay with that?"

"Definitely! I don't own you. And I love them like family."

"Even Osric?" I remember the crass tentacled monster.

"Yeah, even him." He pauses for a long moment. "I would never force you or ask you to do something you don't want to. It wouldn't work if you didn't want to, anyway. Remember, you have to want it for the curse to lift. So, how about we just find Augusten and see where things go? If you want to, you will. If not, then we'll still be stronger with one more person. If he knows where Lysander is, that could be a great help! Even in his cursed form, Lysander is powerful. Much stronger than this pathetic chef." He looks down at his feet.

I know we can't stay like this forever. We need to leave this cave. He looks like a human now, so perhaps we can go live in the town without people being afraid of us. My original plan was to go to Sailoria; we should go there together. I cannot birth this baby in this dirty ass cave. So, we should leave anyway.

"You are not pathetic. And you do look quite handsome in that outfit." I smile. "We'll look for Augusten."

He gets on his hands and knees, grabs my hands, and thanks me. "Thank you. Thank you, M'Lady!" Seeing him like this, maybe I am ready to go again. No, I need to eat. That takes precedent. Then, we'll fuck. I scarf down my eggs quickly, wondering how many more people I will be sleeping with in the coming days.

16

We leave early in the morning. I'm not great at waking early. Since I've been with Al, my insomnia has subsided; all I want to do is sleep. I'm assuming I'm emotionally and physically exhausted from the escape, being pregnant—and of course all the fucking we've done in the last few days. Despite my grogginess, I know we need as much daylight as possible, so I try to muster the motivation.

Al said he thinks he saw Augusten in a clearing near the town of Sailoria. Apparently, Augusten moves around by turning into smoke and streaming through the world. Al believes he saw something like his incorporeal form flittering through the woods in the distance, but by the time he reached the location, he could not find Augusten. He hopes, however, that if we return to where he saw the smoke, Augusten will have left some clue or, better yet, returned.

Al is pretty sure he can fly with me on his back and offers to fly me, but there's no way in hell that's happening. Just thinking about riding on his back at that height makes me panic. So, instead, we are walking. He occasionally jumps up, flies around, and gets a bearing on our surroundings. I have to stop frequently, and Al tries to carry me, but I find it uncomfortable.

I explain the concept of a travois to Al, "We need two long sticks. We'll cross them at the top to make kind of an X. The top part of the X is the handles you drag it with. We'll use the bottom part of the X to build me a bed. We need a bunch more sticks to go across the bottom of the X to make it something I can lay on. It's like a gurney you drag."

Al still doesn't get it, but I'm sure it will make more sense to him once we put it together. He gathers a bunch of large sticks to build the X-frame contraption. We cut the rope I used to escape the castle to secure the branches into position. I'm happy I have it with me. It really has come in handy. We spend a lot of time padding it with moss and some of the blankets and clothes I brought to make it more comfortable. I climb aboard, and Al drags me behind him through the woods. He is careful not to hit rocks and bumps, but it's impossible to miss them entirely. It is not incredibly comfortable, but it's better than walking!

Al said the city was about a thirty-minute flight southwest from the cave. He wasn't sure of the distance. But we have already walked for at least eight hours. The breaks I need to stretch my legs and pee have slowed us down. Al gets more anxious the longer we walk, wanting to leave and scout more frequently—especially since the sun will be setting soon. He tells me his vision is much better in his bird form, and he can see at night, but he worries he won't be able to see Augusten's smoke in the dark.

He takes off his clothes so he can transform, folds them neatly, and places them in a bag that he has draped around his neck. He puts the map in the bag, as well. I'm realizing, though, that dude has no sense of direction and cannot read a map. We all have our strengths, and this is not one of his. I ask him to guess approximately where we are based on the map before it gets dark, anyway, because I need some idea of where we are, even if it's wrong.

He jumps high into the air, and a cloud of dust billows out from where he leaps. I get a flash of the memory of the puff of dust that billowed around him when he fell to the ground, bleeding after Thad stabbed him. This image of violence rotates in my head, and I start to panic in the woods by myself. Where is he? Is he okay? What if he loses his powers mid-flight and falls to his death, his head splatting against the dirt, but this time his brains splash out?

Ok, I need something to focus on. I look through my sack for something, anything that will distract me. God, I miss my cell phone. It's been months, and I still jones for it in times like this. I count the leaves on a nearby tree and rock myself in an attempt to calm down.

He said from the cave to the city was a thirty-minute flight. It seems like he's been gone for at least an hour. I'm not sure exactly because I don't have a clock, but based on the number of leaves I've counted, it's been a while. Why has he been gone so long? We are much closer to the city now; it should be less than thirty minutes—definitely less than an hour. Maybe Al is as bad at approximating time as he is with directions. You'd think a chef, whose whole career is based on being able to time things, would be good at perceiving the passage of time.

The built-up anxiety and fear feel like a pressure about to explode through my head. I feel like my skin is too tight. Like I'm a balloon about to pop. I want to scream at the top of my lungs, but I know I can't. It's unsafe. Who knows what the fuck is in these woods ready to eat lost preggos. Maybe even Thad is around. I shudder at the thought of him finding me. "Oh, you're alive! Not for much longer, you stupid cunt!" he'd say.

The world spirals around me. I get dizzy, and my vision gets cloudy. I sit on the travois and hug my legs to my chest as best I can against my swollen belly. The baby kicks at my thighs. I calm down a bit. The baby almost has a magical ability to ground me. To comfort me when it kicks me. My therapist was always trying to teach me grounding techniques and was mostly unsuccessful. It turns out I just needed a swift kick in the uterus to bring me back to the here and now.

I realize that the cloudiness I thought was all in my head is actually not in my head at all. It IS cloudy. These are the same thick, tangible clouds I saw in the clearing when the monsters approached me on my first day in this world. It looks so soft and touchable.

I lock eyes on a stream and walk toward it. It swirls right in front of me. I am hypnotic. I reach out to touch it.

"Careful, darlin'. If you touch me like that, I might not be able to contain myself." I hear a voice whisper from the smoke. I recognize this voice. I've felt it whisper in my ear before. It's Augusten.

The smoke pulsates and rushes around me like I'm in the middle of a whirlpool. It comes in closer and closer and then stops in front of me. It culminates into the shape of a man. He looks at me, with his body waving—not taking a wholly formed shape. He has a location where eyes would be, but no eyes. Just darker smoke. He towers over me. I'm slightly below average height for a woman, and he's at least a whole head taller than me.

Most of his body is an approximation of a human, except, of course, his penis. It is a large, raging, hard boner that looks solid and corporeal. Of course. I guess if the curse took away their dicks that would be a bit unfair—they'd have no way to break the curse.

Al said Augusten would never hurt me, but when you see a naked man standing in front of you with a raging boner all alone in the woods, it's hard not to be terrified. This man is enormous and could overpower my weak pregnant body—my center of balance is not the best right now. I picture him pushing me to the ground, my head hitting the dirt.

I step back defensively, and he kneels to one knee. He puts his arm on his knee, hangs his head in a bow, and says, "Forgive me, darlin', I mean you no harm. I apologize for scaring you."

I clear my throat. "You are Augusten, correct?"

He looks up at me in a jerk. There is not much of a clear expression on his face, but the smoke where his face should be shifts and moves. I think he is surprised. "You … you know my name?" He creeps me out more than Al did in his monster form. I could see the emotion in Al's eyes. With Augusten, I can only see a movement and a slight color variation that I think is emotion.

"Yes, I have been with Alistair. We are looking for you," I say.

"Al!? Where is he?" He looks around almost frantically for his friend.

"I'm not sure. He flew away to determine our location a while ago and has not returned. He should be back by now." I start to cry. I am too scared to look at the sky to search for him. Why can't I be brave for Al? I've been in the wilderness for days, and I'm still scared of the sky. This is the ultimate exposure therapy! I should be cured by fucking now.

"I am sure he will be back soon. Let's make a fire. It's going to be very cold tonight," Augusten says.

I hiccup my tears back. "Okay," I say, sniffing in my snot and pouting like a little girl. "I'll get some firewood," I state and grab my stomach.

"No, no, no, darlin'. You will do no such thing. Sit. I will get it."

"Please don't leave me alone," I look at him with my most pathetic puppy dog eyes possible.

"No problem, darlin', there is enough right here for me to make a fire."

"Okay," I say as I slowly lower myself to the travois.

Augusten methodically gathers various things to burn. He turns things over in his hand and examines it before deciding to add them to the pile in his arm. Watching him scrutinize each piece of wood is weirdly calming.

Augusten is building a fire when Al swoops down unexpectedly. We didn't even hear him approaching; he just appears in front of us. He lands with a thud. An apple falls from the sack that he had strapped around his neck.

"Al!" Augusten and I say in unison. Mine sounds more like a statement, and Augusten's sounds more like a question. I suppose he hasn't seen Al in this new, upgraded bird form yet.

"Auggie, you're here!" Al says and approaches his friend while transforming into his human form.

Before they can continue their greeting, I say a bit too tersely, "Where the fuck have you been?! You left me all alone! I was scared you died!"

Al notices me struggling to lift myself from the travois on the ground and leans over to help me up. He lifts me so I can yell at him more—what a good guy.

"I am so sorry, M'Lady. I got anxious and began looking for Augusten, then I saw some apples and picked them for you because I remembered you said you were craving apples. Then I … I got a bit lost. Before I picked up your scent, I had to fly around a bit."

This is a perfectly reasonable explanation. But I'm still mad. Logically I've forgiven him, but emotionally, I have not.

I place my hands on my hips, look to the side and say, "Okay," in a humph.

"Please, forgive me, M'Lady," he says. His big eyes plead and sparkle in the firelight. He reaches out and grabs my hands at my waist to pull me toward him. I lose my balance slightly, but he doesn't let me fall.

"Do you forgive me?" he says as he places his forehead on mine. My belly pushes against his hip and it gives a little kick. I wonder if he can feel it.

"Yes," I croak with a pout, still not fully ready to let go of my anger.

"Thank you, M'Lady," he says and kisses me on the nose.

During this exchange, Augusten has stopped dead in his tracks, and I assume he is gawking at us (if I could see an expression on his face, I'd know for sure).

Al snaps out of the trance of our embrace and says, "Oh, apologies, Auggie! I am so pleased to see you! We have been looking for you!"

Auggie snaps out of his bewilderment and says with less sugar in his voice that he had previously, "Yes, she told me as much. Um, you're a human?"

"Yes! She lifted my curse!" Al says, pulling me close to him.

"Is … is that, your child?" Augusten asks, motioning toward my belly.

"No, it is Thadius'," I say.

The smoke that makes up Augusten's body shivers and waves and changes a darker ominous color. "WHAT?"

17

"Where did you all go?" Al asks Augusten while roasting an apple over the fire for me. I've never had a roasted apple before, and I'm salivating. I'm so focused on it that I'm struggling to pay attention to the conversation around me.

"We thought you were dead and decided we needed to give up on our quest to kill the king … to … save the women … and accept our fate. We should try to live our lives as best we can. I made myself a nice little hut by the city, just at the edge of the woods. You know me. I'm not a wilderness kind of guy. I'm a silk and chiffon kind of guy. I felt being near the city would be best for me. I could get supplies when I needed them."

"Do you know where any of the others are?" Al asks.

"Cordelia stayed with me for quite some time, but she just silently walked into the woods a few weeks ago and never came back. I worry that she took her own life. She saw a girl that reminded her of Serena in town and became deeply depressed. She got so depressed she couldn't even do her magic anymore. I look for her every day. I was looking for her when I stumbled upon y'all."

I remember Al telling me Serena was Cordelia's lady-in-waiting and best friend. I can see why this would cause her to lose her last will to fight.

"I'll be honest. When I look for her, I look for her corpse. But, how does one tell the corpse of a wood woman from a tree?" I cannot see it on his face, but I can hear the extreme sadness in his voice. I want to ask him about the others, but I know the respectful thing to do would be to ask more about Cordelia.

"Are you and Cordelia close?" I ask. I make sure to speak of her in present and not past tense.

"Yes, we are. She, Serena, and I were all very close. Cordelia would help me design dresses for Serena. We spent many, many nights staying up late, designing dresses … snacking on Al's cupcakes," He chuckles sadly. "Life was so different then."

These men have been treated so badly by Thadius. He has ruined their lives, and they have done nothing wrong.

"I'm … I'm so sorry for what Thadius did to you. I'm sorry for your loss," I say, trying not to urge the conversation forward until he is ready.

He looks at me and says, "It's okay, darlin'. You didn't do it." I always get flustered when people respond with that. I'm over here, trying to express empathy, and they turn it on me. What else am I supposed to say other than "I'm sorry that happened to you?" I hate that I respond with frustration when people say it—it's not about me, after all. But I struggle expressing emotions and finding the exact right thing to say, so when they make it seem like I said the wrong thing I worry about what I am actually supposed to say. Now I'm scared to talk.

We sit in silence for quite a while. "If I know Gideon, he's near the Library of Astica. He's drawn to books. The others I do not know. They didn't say where they were going, just that they were leaving. I'd guess Florian and Lysander are together; you know them. Osric may be with them."

I pull out my map and find the Library of Astica. It is past Sailoria to the southwest. "Okay, so let's go to Saloria and get some supplies. I'd love to stay the night in an inn. Maybe get some horses. We can then proceed to the Library of Astica." I look at Augusten for a moment and realize I should mention Cordelia. Shit, Astrid, express empathy like a normal human! "We'll look for Cordelia, as well, of course. She couldn't have gone too far, right? Maybe Al can find her with his flight and eagle eyes? Maybe she'll find me with my scent like you did. We can ask around the city if anyone spotted a walking tree."

"Okay," Augusten says. Augusten can't come to the city with us; people would definitely freak out at the sight of him, so we'll have to figure something out.

"We have no money for an inn, M'Lady," Al says.

"I do!" I exclaim, and I show him the jewelry I brought with me.

The City of Sailoria is massive! It's even bigger than the City of Prailyra, where the castle is. It is also more modern. There are more people, too, since the women aren't cowering in fear of abduction from seven rapey monsters. Or should I say, one rapey king? Thad's bright smile flashes in my mind. Stop it. Stop thinking of him. I'm ashamed I still get aroused thinking of that bright smile between my legs.

Augusten is waiting for us in his hut while we gather supplies. He marked it on our map so I can find it. I hold on to the map because I've learned it's useless in Al's hands. I feel bad for leaving Augusten alone, but he can't walk into town in his current form. After we get some supplies, we will go back for him. We cleaned up a bit before coming to the city, but the people here are dressed so beautifully. Even after cleaning, I'm still dirty, plus my pregnant ass has been tracking through the woods for days. I look like a hot mess.

As we walk through the city and see beautiful women, I fuss with my hair, trying to improve my appearance. People stop and stare at me as they did before. I'm sure my barely-bathed body smells even more potent than usual. The people here don't actively approach me, but they do gawk. I am getting self-conscious.

I tell Al that maybe my being here isn't the best idea. Perhaps I should stay with Augusten while Al shops. "If that is what you wish, let's go back." As we turn to leave, a man holds a paper and points at me while talking to a guard. The guard looks at me, makes that 'I just got a huge boner face,' which I've become accustomed to, and marches purposefully toward me.

"Did you see that? What was that paper he showed him?" I hide behind Al.

"I don't know," Al responds.

"You there! Stop!" the guard shouts, pointing at us.

"Run!" Al yells while grabbing my hand. We run down an alley. As we run, I notice wanted posters with my picture on them. It's my proposal picture! And they say, "WANTED ALIVE!" on them. Fuck, Thad knows I'm not dead, and I just showed my face in a city. He'll know I'm here soon enough. I can't run very fast and the guard is catching up to us. We reach a dead end and panic sets in as I imagine the guard dragging me off to Thad's dungeon to give birth in the pile of dead bodies.

"What are we going to do? I can't go back to that castle, Al! He'll kill me after this baby is born! I know it! Especially now that I've run away."

"I'm sorry, M'Lady, but I must do this," he says with a gentle and concerned smile.

"Huh?"

Before I can ask him what he is talking about, Al transforms into his bird form, wraps his legs around me, and bolts up into the sky.

FUUUUUUUUCK. I scream like I am going to die because, fuck, I'm going to.

Arrows whiz past us, but Al is way too fast and agile. He's too high before they can even figure out what is happening.

This is both terrifying and embarrassing. Here I am, literally pissing my pants, dangling from a bird with his legs wrapped around me. Of course, his dick is hard and jammed against my back. He's enjoying this. I guess he keeps his human dick in his bird form. Or do birds have dicks?

He looks down at me, and I scream. "Put me down!"

"We'll be there soon. I'm sorry to grab you this way. I had no choice. Next time you can ride on my back." There will be no next time!

"I grabbed one of those posters as we ran past it. You look so gorgeous in it."

"I don't care, you fucking pervert bird!"

"Sorry, just trying to distract you."

Al hovers just above the ground when Augusten's shack is in sight to allow me to place my feet flat on the floor. He gently places me down. My knees buckle, and I immediately collapse to the earth. "GET ME INSIDE!" I scream. I need a roof over my head. I need solid ground under my feet. I need a blanket wrapped around my body. I realize I'm being mean to Al; he doesn't deserve this. I'll apologize to him later, but for now, I need to get inside.

Augusten runs out, "What happened!?"

"There were wanted posters. I had to fly her out quickly," Al says as he places me on Augusten's bed and wraps me in blankets. "She's terrified of heights."

"Don't give her that pillow! Here give her this one!" Augusten frantically runs to the other side of the room and brings back a fluffy silk pillow. "This one won't scratch her face." Al takes it, lifts my head, and places it under my face. It is nice. It calms me a bit, but I am still freaked out.

They stand over me, staring at me, unsure what to do with me—both naked. Boners raging—right at eye level. I really don't feel like looking at their dicks right now. I turn my back to them and face the wall. This is nicer, anyway—a smaller space.

I peed my pants in the air, and I squirm in my discomfort.

"Al, could you get me a change of clothes, please? I have some in my sack," I say meekly.

"Oh, yes, of course," al responds.

It takes me a while to feel safe enough to leave my little blanket cocoon to change my clothes. Al helps me dress and redress while Augusten changes the bed linens I've tangentially soiled. I am so embarrassed. Augusten replaces the fabrics with much nicer ones. He does his best to avert his eyes while I change, and Al blocks the view with his body the best he can. Why's he blocking the view? I thought he wanted me to fuck his friend. Changing your mind now, are we, Al?

I quickly jump back into bed once my clothes and the bedding are changed. I pull the blankets up to my chin. Al tucks the bedding around me, making me a little burrito again. He knows I love this. I giggle when I think, "I'm a little burrito broad." I stare at the texture of the walls.

For a shack, this place is lovely! It's obviously hand-built by someone who has no idea how to build a shack, but there are wallpapers, pillows, and all sorts of soft fabrics. It's a full-on silk lounge.

I lay like this a long time before my heart rate returns to normal.

Al and Augusten sit and chat quietly in whispers: formulating plans, worrying about me, catching up, and reminiscing.

Al approaches the bed, leans down, and places his hand on my head. "M'Lady, I will go back to town and try to get some supplies on my own. Auggie has given me some new clothes, and I stand the best chance of going through town. The guard saw my face, but it was just one guard. I should be okay. I will take one of the jewels from your necklace and be back in a few hours. Is that okay with you? Will you be okay?"

I nod, still staring at the wall and refusing to turn to him.

He bends down and kisses me on the back of the head. I pull the blankets up higher over my head, burying myself completely.

"I'll be back soon, Auggie. Please take care of her. She can be a bit frail. There are some snacks for her in the bag." Frail? Am I really frail? Is that how he sees me? He's talking about me like some fucking child. God, I'm so fucking pathetic. I'm a queen. I'm going to be a mother. I was a boss bitch in my world. I am better than this. I tell myself to get out of bed. No, no I'm not better than this. I'm a sad, pathetic mess who is nothing but a burden to those around her. All this misery is my fault. If only I weren't so fucking pathetic.

Augusten leaves me there in silence for quite a while. My self-hatred spiral doesn't last long. This is such a cozy little nest of blankets, so I doze off. A loud crashing sound wakes me. I bolt upright and yelp. Augusten had fallen asleep in a chair, but I startle him awake with my fright.

It's just thunder. Rain pounds hard on the top of the shack. Al can't fly in the rain. I hope he'll be okay. I look at Augusten and he looks back at me.

"Do you need anything, darlin'?" he says.

"No, I'm okay. Thank you for watching over me. I'm sorry I'm such a burden."

"You're not a burden, darlin'. We all have our fears. We all have to take care of each other sometime." We look at each other in silence for a while.

"Where did you get all this stuff?" I ask.

"I stole it. I sneak into people's homes in the middle of the night and take all their best fabrics," he giggles. I'm surprised they haven't come hunting in the woods with pitchforks for the fabric-stealing smoke monster.

He is wearing a very sharp outfit. He must have dressed while I slept. "If you don't mind my asking … you can wear clothes?" His body seems like things should pass right through it. I'm wondering about the physics of it all.

"Of course, I can!"

"Then why were you always naked? Showing off your dick?" I giggle and raise my eyebrow accusatory.

"No! It's just once I start floating around, I lose the clothes. I was tired of them getting dirty and lost all the time. I was a dressmaker! I love clothes. I much prefer wearing clothes. Why do you think my dick is something I should show off?" Now he's the one giggling.

I ignore the question about his dick, because the answer is yes, he should be showing it off. "The clothes have nothing to do with me being around?" I ask.

"Well, yes, I do think it is more appropriate if I, umm, don't constantly affront you with my manhood. I apologize, but I just can't control it when you're around."

"It's okay; I'm used to it. Supposedly it gets a bit easier to control after a while if that makes you feel any better." He's wearing clothes for my sake. That's sweet. If only he knew what a damn dirty perv I was.

The rain slows, and Al opens the door. He startles us because we didn't hear him coming. He's so quiet I suspect he will be startling me and Augusten a lot in the near future. He is soaking wet.

"SHOES!" Augusten yells, motioning to the muddy shoes. The carpets and silks in here definitely would be ruined by them.

"And here, get out of those wet clothes! Don't drip on the silks."

I suppose muddy boots aren't a problem for Augusten, being smoke that floats around.

Al strips his clothes off, tripping over himself to remove them as quickly as possible. "I found Cordelia!" He exclaims excitedly, jumping on one foot as he pulls his boot.

Augusten stops fussing over the wet clothes and silks. "WHAT!?"

"She's near the middle of Sailoria. A big beautiful tree just sprang up there recently. The people have no idea how it got there. They are debating burning it down, thinking it may be evil because you feel a deep sadness when you approach it."

Augusten hands a towel to Al to dry his hair. At this point, he's nude except for his undergarments, and even those are wet. I can see the dark pubic hair through the material and the outline of his penis. It's not erect; he must be getting used to me finally. But, fuck, I kind of wish it was erect because he looks hot standing there dripping.

I lick my lips, knowing he can tell what I'm thinking because he suddenly becomes erect. Score.

Augusten seems unphased by this interaction; his full concern is focused on his lost friend—even though he, too, has an erection, as he has the entire time I have been here. They are facing each other, dicks pointed directly at one another. I think of that meme of Spider-Men pointing at each other, but I picture them pointing at each other with their dicks. I giggle, hoping someone out there has drawn that picture. Al looks at me quizzically, wondering why this dirty perv he's hitched himself to is giggling about during a serious moment.

"We have to go get her! Now!" Augusten says as he heads toward the door.

"Not so fast. I think she's in a vegetative state. I tried talking to her, but she didn't react."

"Are you sure it's her? Are you sure it's not just some magical tree that popped up in the middle of the city and makes people sad?" I ask.

They both look at me like I said the most ridiculous thing in the world. "I know for a fact it was her. They were her leaves. They were her flowers. It was her."

"So, how can we wake her up?" I ask.

Augusten announces, "She's done something like this before. Become an unwakeable tree. She did it right after we were all cursed. Remember, Al?" Al nods his head.

I look at him as if to say, "Well?"

"We have to play her favorite song to her," Augusten says sadly.

"Oh, okay. That sounds easy."

"It would be, except Gideon is the only one who knows how to play it."

Of course. A side quest.

18

"I have something to show you!" Al tells me excitedly.

He grabs my hand and pulls me to the door. I'm thankful the rain has stopped because I don't want to get wet.

Outside the shack stand three horses: two pulling a covered wagon and a third tied to the back. Awesome! This will be much more comfortable than the travois!

Within the wagon are tons of supplies. He got lots of rations, new clothes, blankets, and medicines.

"I thought we could use the horses. Now that we're going to the library to get Gideon, they'll be really helpful," Al says with that same big prideful grin he gives me after making me come.

"Nice work! You got all this with just one jewel from the necklace! I can't imagine what the whole thing would have bought you," I say, completely stunned. I realize I'd lose miserably at any Price Is Right game show in this world.

"Yes, the merchant was so excited to see it that he threw in some jugs of water for free."

We return to the shack's interior. We will rest and leave in the morning. "Hey, Auggie, I couldn't help myself, but I got you this feathered hat," Al said.

"Al, I love you, and I appreciate you and this thoughtful gift, but I will not be wearing that hat," Auggie says very dryly.

Al looks confused, and I fully know where this is going, but I am along for the ride. I wish I had some popcorn.

"That, sir, is the ugliest damn hat I've ever seen!" he chuckles. I wish I could tell what kind of expression he had on his face right now because I am sure it would be priceless.

Al puts it on and says, "What!? I thought it was quite dashing," while touching his chest, feigning offense. He looks to me for support.

"Sorry, but he's right. It's hideous." He laughs and puts it on top of my head, covering my eyes.

I tilt my head up and look at them from under the bridge of the hat sultrily and make a pouty, kissy expression like I'm posing for an early 2000s duck face photo. They both stop chuckling and clear their throat.

"What?" I ask. Do I really look that stupid?

"Well, it looks good on you," Augusten says. I guess they like duck face here. I'll keep that in mind.

I laugh and toss the hat to the side of the room.

We all settle into the cozy bedding Augusten has assembled for the night. Al spoons me while we sleep, and his hard dick pushes against my backside. This makes me so aroused. I press back at him, moving my butt hard on his dick, making him grind me.

I am so wet and horny, but it doesn't feel right to do it here when we're all like little sardines in this shack with Augusten.

I slip his fingers up my skirts and cum pretty quickly. I'm pretty confident I was sneaky enough about it that Augusten didn't notice. Al kisses me on the top of the head and dozes off.

I think I hear Augusten moaning softly in the background and suspect he is masturbating, but I fall asleep before I am sure. I'm probably not as sneaky as I think.

The next morning, we prepare for the journey. Al tends to the horses and double-checks the supplies. He straps the supplies down so they won't shift on our travels. Auggie brings most of the rugs, silks, and pillows from the shack and makes a luxurious sleeping area for me.

I feel helpless, useless, and super fat, just standing on the sidelines watching them prepare for the voyage.

"Thank you so much, Auggie!" I say as I look into the wagon and admire the bed he made for me. This is the first time I've called him by his nickname.

He bows and says, "Well, I know you were really looking forward to staying in the inn, and I know you are super uncomfortable, so I tried to make it as fit for a knocked-up queen as I could!" I giggle.

"Why thank you, sir." I curtsey, and he helps me climb into the back of the wagon. He's taken to wearing clothing around me now, and his fashion design skills are unmatched. I can see the shape of his body much more easily now that he's clothed. I am quite impressed. The way the fabric stretches over his broad chest catches my eye more often than not. I don't let go of Auggie's hand immediately while I lustfully stare at the shape of his body.

"Ready, everyone?" Al asks as he positions himself at the helm of the wagon.

"Yep!" Auggie says, letting go of my hand. He saddles onto the free horse, and we set out.

I lay back in my nice little bed and touch myself thinking of Auggie's chest. The rocking of the cart is particularly arousing, and it is so comfy in here. Before I can really get to it, Al yells back to me, "Would you mind being the navigator, M'Lady? As we both know, I am not good with maps." Fuck. I suppose an orgasm will have to wait. I haven't been able to have sex with Al since we met up with Auggie, and I am desperate for a deep dicking. But I guess I should help Al out.

"Sure," I say, a bit exacerbated. He doesn't hear the tone in my voice, and I'm pretty thankful for that because I'm kind of being a bitch.

I look at the map, placing my thumb on it trying to get a sense of how long things will take us. "So, if Auggie's shack is where I think it is in relation to the city, we just need to travel south for about a day's ride before we find the main road. There's no path from here to the main road, but the terrain looks pretty flat, so it shouldn't be too hard for the horses. Once we hit the main road, we will travel about two days west until we need to turn left at a fork. That road should take us all the way to the library. My map doesn't have units of measure on it and I'm not sure how far a horse can go in a day, but based on the fact that Prailyra to Sailoria is a three-day ride, I'd say it will take us about five days. I suspect we can't ride more than half a day or so without resting them, especially these two here who are having to pull my fat ass. So, we'll see how far we get today, and I'll recalculate."

"You're so smart!" Al said.

"Well, yeah, when I was in my world, I had a pretty brainy job."

"Your world?" Auggie asks, "Are you from another world like Serena?"

Oh, I guess that hadn't come up. "Yeah, I am."

"It all makes sense now." He says and chuckles. "I didn't even have raging boners like this when I was going through puberty. I knew there was something up with that smell of yours."

They both laugh. "It's awful, isn't it!?" Al says.

"Yeah," Auggie says.

"HEY! I'm right here, guys!"

"Sorry," they say in unison.

Ok, fuck these boys. I'm going to go masturbate, and they can stay up there in silence and just live with their "awful" erections. "Okay, I'm going to take a nap," I lie. "Wake me if you need more directions."

I giggle as I sink deep into the blankets Auggie has piled up for me. He really has put a lot of care into this. I try to find some that aren't silk to position myself over. I don't need to get those all wet and give myself away.

The gentle rock of the cart is honestly all I'm going to need to get this done. Ugh, being pregnant really makes this challenging. It's hard to reach down because my belly is in the way, and it makes it almost impossible to get on my tummy.

I pile the blankets up in various places to easily prop myself up and glance around. Maybe there's something I can use to help me out. Something long and hard. I don't see anything, so I bundle up the blanket to make something nice and dense to grind on.

I hump the blankets, licking them, and reaching down to myself as best I can. Despite this awkwardness, I'm still able to get off really quickly. The best part of being pregnant is the orgasms. I'm always wet, always aroused, and the way my uterus contracts when something is actually in it just makes it that much more intense. I get a little skeeved out thinking about how the baby inside me helps me get off and try to push the thought out of my head as best I can.

I giggle to myself, "Stupid boys. Who needs 'em?" Even though thoughts of them both railing me at the same time are what really sent me over the edge.

Al sleeps with me in the wagon at night. Auggie volunteered to sleep outside so that we can have some time together. I feel bad that Auggie has to sleep outside on the ground, but Al and I are busy rocking the shit out of this wagon; there's no room for Auggie in here, anyway.

After about three days of traveling, fucking, and, masturbating, I am feeling quite ripe. If I'm being honest with myself, I was probably quite ripe before I got in the wagon. We pull over to a stream to rest and clean up.

Auggie naps in the wagon while Al and I bathe in the stream. Al helps me clean myself, and I'm reminded of Gen. I hope she's okay. I hope Thadius doesn't think she helped me escape.

We're in knee-deep water as Al runs the cloth over my body, scrubbing my back. I push my ass against his crotch. And bend over. I snap my head back to look at him with a smirk. He shakes his head, and I wonder if I'm too much for him. Is he getting tired of being with the perpetually horny girl who is afraid of everything? He says nothing but slips his dick deep inside me.

My tits look great from this angle. Hanging. They're huge from pregnancy. He pumps himself inside me, one hand on my tit, one on my clit.

My free tit bounces back and forth. I notice that Auggie is peeking over the ledge of the wagon and can see us. The wagon rocks. Is he? Yep, he is definitely masturbating.

I picture Auggie's dick in his hand and get even more aroused. I grab Al's hand and suck on his fingers. Now both of my breasts bounce. I want to give Auggie a show. I stare at Auggie so he knows I see him. The wagon rocks back and forth more furiously. Al and I come, almost in unison. He knows exactly where to touch me and always waits for me to come before he does. He's the exact opposite of Thad. As Al and I are coming I notice the wagon stops rocking. It looks like we all finished at the same time.

Al and I finish cleaning up, and Auggie walks past us to the water to bathe. Hm, I guess smoke needs to wash, too? As we cross paths, he locks eyes with me, and I blush while I push my hair behind my ear, feigning innocence. His color changes slightly, and his smoke waves. I like to think he's blushing, too.

19

It's the final morning of our trip, and I am getting a bit stir-crazy. Lying in the wagon, sleeping, masturbating, waking occasionally to assure Al of the directions, and rocking the wagon with him at night is getting a bit old. Well, maybe not the wagon-rocking part.

Sometimes I lay in the wagon and think of baby names. I'll probably give the baby a name from my world. It's my baby, after all. Fuck Thad. I don't care what he thinks. But this baby is the future queen or king; maybe I should give it an approachable name. I'm starting to get a bit excited to see it. Until now, I've thought of it as a burden, some shitty thing Thad did to me. But I'm growing fond of it. God, please, don't let it look like a scorpion.

I'm lying there thinking about baby names when I think about giving birth. Oh, God. I have to squeeze this thing out of me. Okay, baby, maybe I don't like you after all. It kicks me as if to say, "Mom, I can hear your every thought. Stop being a bitch. You'll love me." Yeah, I probably will, baby. Wait, I hope the baby can't actually hear or see my thoughts. The things I think are not for the eyes of the young. Shit, some of the things I think aren't for anyone's eyes. It's all gore and genitalia up there.

I need something to distract me. I sit up and look at Auggie on his horse. I like Auggie. He's thoughtful like Al but better at directions. He's silly. I'm sure walking around with a raging boner all day while two other people fuck like rabbits and one masturbates furiously on a bed of pillows you made for her must be hard. He's been respectful and hasn't approached me to break his curse or even tried to touch me.

I kind of wish he would, though. I catch myself fantasizing about him bending me over a large log we pass by, railing deep inside me as I scream into the night. His smoke tendrils wrapped around my legs, working their way through me, reaching crevices no one else can. Fuck I'm horny. Oh, I also have to pee.

We stop on the side of the road. I go off into the woods by myself to pee. The boys wait close by protectively. "Holler if you need us," Auggie states. I dismissively wave back. I know the drill.

Al got some toilet paper when he got supplies. I whisper to the heavens, "Thank God for Al," as I wipe. Thank God they have toilet paper in this world. If they didn't, I was going to have to invent it. Toothbrushes—I will invent those as soon as I am queen again. There is a large globule of goo left on the paper. It has a hint of blood, but mostly it's a gooey whitish-yellow pile of goop. What the fuck is that? I bring the paper closer to my face to get a better look at it. I don't dare sniff it. It looks a bit like an egg yolk. It's not Al's semen, is it? I have never seen this before. Is this something to do with the pregnancy? I feel okay. I don't feel like the baby is about to leak out of me. I decide it must just be a big gob of discharge that dislodged. I've been so horny, so filled with cum, and laying down a lot. Maybe it just came loose now. I shudder thinking about how gross that is and want a bath desperately. I hope the library has a way for me to bathe in something other than river water. I miss showers.

We return to the wagon and continue on our journey. I hear Auggie call from ahead, "Oye, Astrid! I can see the library." Thank God! The library is in sight. I am so uncomfortable, and my belly keeps cramping up a bit. I can't get in a good position. Everything I do is just wrong. I shift my weight in an attempt to get more comfortable, and a small gush of water bursts between my thighs. Did I just piss myself? What the hell? I got it all over Auggie's silks. He's going to be so upset.

I get on my hands and knees and try to clean it up, but the road is bumpy, and I fall over, landing hard on my bad wrist. My wrist is definitely still broken, but the split the boys made for me keeps it from hurting too badly most of the time. The splint can't help me if I fall directly on it, though.

"OOOOW!" I roar.

Al turns around, panic in his voice. "Are you okay? What happened?"

"I fell and hurt my wrist. I'm okay." I then grab my belly and wince.

Al looks at me questioningly. "Um, you don't look okay."

"It's okay. I just can't get comfortable. Every way I sit seems to make my stomach cramp up … and I think I peed myself. Please don't tell Auggie I ruined his silks."

"Are you in labor?" he asks loudly.

"Did you say labor!?" Auggie yells.

"No, no, it's just a little cramp. OWW." Am … am I in labor? Fuck, I think I might be. Was that my water breaking?

Shit. I'm in labor. NO! A look of panic sweeps over my face as I realize I am, in fact, in labor.

"Crap. We're almost at the library. They'll be able to help." Al says.

"How the fuck are a bunch of virgin book nerds going to help me?" I scream in pain. There's no denying that this is labor now. The pain has increased exponentially. It feels like I'm being picked up by a giant and he is squeezing me as hard as he can and wondering if my head will pop off or I will poop.

We stop for a second, and they help me clean up. Auggie ties his horse to the back of the cart and takes over the reins so that Al can be with me. Al climbs in the wagon and rubs my lower back, whispering reassuring sweetnesses to me. I wish he would fuck right off and leave me alone. I don't want to be touched. But I didn't realize how badly my lower back hurt until he started rubbing it for me, so maybe he can stay. I decide not to yell, "Stop fucking touching me!" at him.

"We're pulling up now. This road is cobbled, so it will get a bit bumpy. Brace yourselves." Auggie says.

The bumps are intense and make me nauseated. Luckily, we only have to deal with it for a few minutes, and I don't have a contraction while we're on it.

The wagon comes to a stop, and Al slides out. "I'll be right back." He says and rushes to the library doors. Why did he leave? I guess Auggie can't go because he's a fucking scary smoke monster. Al is a hottie chef who can go places.

I prop myself up so I can see out the front of the wagon and get a good look at where we are. This looks like a giant Gothic church: stained glass, steeples, and gargoyles. It is quite beautiful. As I admire it, Auggie crawls into the back to sit with me. "Do you need anything, darlin'?"

"No, I'm okay," I say breathlessly as I shift my weight, trying to get comfortable. Then, I howl in pain.

"You don't sound okay, darlin'."

"I'm so scared, and this hurts really badly," I say with tears in my eyes.

He scooches up toward me and grabs my hand, "It'll be okay. The smartest and best doctors in the world are here." I squeeze his hand so hard that the smoke pours between my fingers. He makes a little noise of discomfort but doesn't protest. He then proceeds to rub my back as Al had done.

"My momma had a lot of children. I know she really liked her back being rubbed like this when it was time," he said.

"I didn't realize it was time. I thought I had a few more weeks," I say. "I'm scared something is wrong. I'm scared I'm going to die. I'm scared the baby is going to die. This is going to hurt so much!"

"You're so brave and strong. You can do this. The doctors will help you." His voice is so calm. How can he be so calm right now? I guess he's not the one about to be ripped in two at the groin by a human scorpion baby thing.

"What if … it's a monster like Thad?" I whisper to Auggie.

He doesn't haven't time to respond because, at that moment, Al comes bursting out of the library. "Look who I found!?" he yells. A cat man follows behind him, pushing a wheelchair. Is that Gideon?

"Gideon!" Auggie yells.

Auggie helps me crawl out of the wagon and picks me up effortlessly, placing my feet on the ground. I was almost two hundred pounds before I got fully knocked up. I am impressed he's able to lift me with such ease. My feet crumble because the moment I touch the ground, a contraction starts.

"AAAAAAAAAAA!" I howl as I feel like something is pulling all my muscles in opposite directions. Auggie holds me up by looping his arm under mine and looks toward the others.

"She's in active labor!" Gideon says sternly. "Get her on this chair."

Auggie picks me up. I'm reminded of when Thad picked me up to cross the moat, and thinking about him makes me freak out a bit. Auggie gently places me in the chair, and they rush me through the door. I realize I am soaked with sweat and piss. Well, I guess it's amniotic fluid. It's still super gross.

The library has corridors upon corridors of books. The shelves are at least thirty feet tall, stretching almost five times our height, and so long I can barely see their ends. We speed down the long hallway between the rows of bookshelves. As we pass, I look down the rows and see many men and women standing idly in the corridors, looking at books, climbing ladders, casting minor spells, and napping.

We are making quite a ruckus, so many people stop and stare as we run by. They don't seem to care that I am being pushed down this hall by two monsters. They don't look scared, but they do that, "I smell something hot," thing I have grown accustomed to seeing people do. I'm probably extra smelly today—with my uterus trying to push its way out of me and all.

This building is enormous, and this hall runs deep into the library. We finally reach the end and find ourselves at two large doors. They remind me a bit of the door to Thadius' room. Just as I am thinking about him, I get a contraction. I get it uterus, you hate him. I hate him, too.

Al grabs a door and holds it open for us. We are in a hospital! "See, I told you they can take care of you here." Says Auggie.

Two women and a man look up, smell the air, and their eyes widen. They see me in labor, and their Hippocratic oath seems to kick in because they all rush around me to help me.

"Room thirty-two is open," one woman says. Gideon nods and pushes me to the left. The three are frantically grabbing supplies from shelves—clothes, buckets, and potions and placing them on a cart. They are quick because they are almost immediately directly behind Gideon, pushing their way in front of the trailing Al and Auggie.

I look back at the boys and smile at them. Al smirks and Auggie pulsates and changes to a lighter color.

They turn into a room that looks almost like a modern hospital birthing room. Sure, there are no electronics to hook me up to, but the linens are white and clean. One of the nurses that followed behind us, the man, rushes to open the curtains and prep the pillows for me. The others put all the various bottles and devices they brought in their proper place.

One of the women nurses approaches me with what looks surprisingly similar to the hospital frocks from my world—a thin cloth that ties in the back. "Okay, ma'am, let's get you changed." She walks me to an area behind a dressing wall.

She helps me remove my clothing and change. She folds my clothes and puts them on a table. She then returns me to the bed and sits me down on it. She covers me with the blankets. I like this lady. Something about being tucked into a bed is a key to my heart.

"How far apart are your contractions?" Gideon asks.

"Um, I don't know. I haven't been counting," I say.

Gideon looks at Augusten and yells, "Come on, man!? Doesn't your mom have, like, fifteen children? Don't you know how this all works? Why didn't you count for her?"

"Sorry, she didn't say she was in labor until we were right at the door," Auggie replies looking pretty ashamed of himself.

Gideon scowls at him and lets out a low growl. He takes my hands between his (I expected paws, but they're the hands of a man) and says, "Don't worry, we will take excellent care of you. This team has delivered over five hundred babies combined."

They all stop what they are doing to look back at me with a smile. Then get right back to work.

"I need to take a look to see how dilated you are. Are you okay with that?" I nod. Damn, his bedside manner is impressive. I know I am arousing him, but he is not letting on. I try very hard not to look down at his crotch.

"Okay, lean back a bit for me. I'm going to insert my fingers to measure your cervix. Don't worry. I trimmed my claws this morning." He grins. "There will be some pressure. I'm not going to lie to you. It will be uncomfortable." He places gloves over his hands while he describes what he is going to do, then moves to my side. He reaches under the blanket and gets his fingers inside me so fast that I am stunned.

He looks off to the side as he feels around in there, careful not to look me in the eye while he's doing whatever it is he's doing. I take this moment, while he is not looking at me, to examine him. His monster form is kind of adorable. He looks a bit like a kitten, a tiger, and a man combined. While his body is shaped like a man's, he has a tail sticking on the back of his pants. It's currently sticking straight up and swaying very slightly. I wonder if his tail expresses his emotions in the same way a house cat's tail does. His body is covered in orange fur with black stripes and I want to pet him so badly. I've always loved cats. His face is not quite as large and menacing as a tiger's, but looks to be shaped more like a common house cat. His eyes are beautiful. Their golden irises encompass the entire visible area of his eye except for the black slits of his pupils that expands and contracts as he looks around.

"Okay, she is about three centimeters dilated. So, we have a little more time. You'll start to push when you get to about ten centimeters," he says to us, punctuating almost every other word with a nod of his head.

"Boys, you might as well get comfortable." He gestures to Al and Auggie to some chairs at the other end of the room. "Al, I'm assuming you are the father based on the fact that you look like a human. Congratulations. We thought you were killed when you tried to save her, but I guess you just got too preoccupied to return." He's making kind of a naughty joke, but the inflection in his voice doesn't change. It's still that same monotone, reassuring silky voice he was using to calm me. So, he remembers me.

"He is not the father. The father is not here. He will not be coming." I say and look nervously at the nurses. He looks at me, perplexed. I can't tell them I'm carrying the future heir to the throne. They may report me. A look of understanding crosses his face, and I'm sure he knows Thad is the father.

"Okay, I'm sorry for presuming. Forgive me." He says, not pushing the subject. "Well, boys, we can catch up soon. Al, you have lots to tell me, but we have to get ready for this baby right now. First things first, ma'am, would you like some magic to numb the pain?"

"YES!" I say eagerly, then realize I should probably ask some questions. "Well, how does it work?"

"Thorin here is a master of paralysis magic," he says, gesturing at the male nurse. "He can numb you with extreme precision. Essentially, he can numb you from your belly to the top of your thighs. Pain has a way of finding its way out, though, and likes to travel to a place you CAN feel it, so Liza here can make the rest of you nice as cozy with her soothing magic. That way, you can still move your arms and legs but won't feel too much pain." Oh, so they're like magical anesthesiologists.

"That would be amazing. Thank you so much," I say looking right into those beautiful eyes of his. He smiles slightly revealing small fangs and his tail sways. I wonder if he knocks stuff over with that or if he's gotten used to it by now.

"Okay, it tends to wear off after a bit, and we don't want that to happen when the baby starts coming. So, they'll give you a little now, and then they'll increase it when you reach about eight centimeters. Does that sound good?"

"Great!" Bring it on! I am more than ready.

Liza and Thorin stand on opposite sides of me and wave their hands over various parts of my body. Liza waves over my whole body, but Thorin concentrates on my abdomen and crotch. Tiny tendrils of magic flow from their hands and land on my body before it spreads, leaving me with a warm and soothing sensation.

I am instantly calm and lean back, high as a fucking kite, and unable to feel my butt. "Ooo, that feels nice." I worry I'm going to piss myself. Not only can I not feel my butt, but I used to have this fear whenever I smoked pot in high school. Paranoia creeps in, and my heart races.

Liza notices the panic on my face and says, "Ah, you're one of those worriers, huh?" She waves her hand over my face. I feel much better. I look at her. She's the one who tucked me in earlier. "I love you, Liza," I coo. She giggles and blushes. She probably gets that a lot.

"There is a chamber pot room behind that door if you need to relieve yourself. Unfortunately, I cannot offer you any food or drink at this point," Gideon says as Liza blushes and rushes to the other side of the room to busy herself with something.

I think he's about to leave, probably to help someone further along in their delivery. "Wait! I'm really worried. This feels way too early. I thought I had at least another month." Maybe Liza needs to give me some more of that magic of hers, because I'm scared again.

"Oh, okay, we'll have Cinder take a look and see if anything is going on in there," Gideon says and motions to the second female nurse. I notice his tail sinks down and it reveals his emotions even when he's trying to suppress them. That sinking tail seems to express concern, I'm not sure why, though.

"Huh?" I ask. What does he mean by "take a look"?

"Cinder's magic lets her see through things," he responds in that same calming voice. The nurse I presume is Cinder approaches my bed. She has glasses on her head and moves them down to her nose. She moves up to me and stares intently at my belly. The glasses sparkle and shimmer.

She raises the glasses, rubs her eyes, and says in an even more monotone voice than Gideon, "The babies are both small, but they seem to be fully formed. They should have no trouble outside the womb. Both are in posterior position and ready for birth. The cords are well placed, with no wrapping. I don't foresee any issues."

"BABIES!? What do you mean babies?" I ask frantically.

"You're having twins. Early births are common with twins, but these two seem like perfectly healthy babies: one boy and one girl," she says calmly. Why are these doctors so calm?

Al lights up with excitement, and Auggie's smoke shifts and darkens.

Twins?! FUCK! Well, at least they don't have scorpion claws. She would have mentioned that, right?

20

I am exhausted. I feel like my entire life force was removed from me when those babies slid out. Slid is too nice a term. They clawed their way out screaming, it felt more like. They don't have any claws, though. Thank God. The first thing I did was check their little hands and feet for scorpion pincers.

I've tried to feed the babies, but I can't seem to accomplish anything. Gideon says my milk has not come yet, but to give it time, it will soon. He says some stuff called colostrum is coming out that should be sufficient. I'm scared my milk will never come in. I'm freaking out after my most recent attempt to feed them. I probably look like a deranged baby thief, just crying over these two newly stolen babies. They take the babies to another room to allow me some rest. I don't want to let them go. I wanted to sleep with their little heads against my skin, but I do need some sleep and have not been able to sleep in their presence—they make me so nervous.

I was worried I would hate them. I was afraid I would think of their father when I saw them and want to toss them out the window, but I don't. I see two tiny cuddly beings that need me and need protection at all costs. They're ugly gremlin-looking little things, but they're also the most beautiful creatures I've ever seen. They give me a bit of bravery. They give me calm—and worry. They are two little bundles of dichotomy.

Gideon was so kind. He saw the most horrid, disgusting, angry version of myself. I yelled. I screamed. I cried. I cursed … I peed. I spouted feathers around my entire body and cawed like a bird. But he kept calm with me. He treated me like I was the bravest, strongest woman to grace this earth and, most importantly, that every pain and frustration I was feeling was valid—I was allowed to feel it. I could feel it as loud and as mean as I wanted. I could take up the whole space, and he'd be there to push others out my way. I wonder if all women feel this way about the doctors that deliver their babies.

Yesterday Gideon and Cinder looked at my broken wrist and apparently it was super jacked up—my crappy splint and general inattentiveness were not healing it properly. They reset it for me (again) and put an actual cast on it. Gideon says it should be healed in a few weeks and I'm excited by the prospect of having my full dexterity back. I've never worn a cast before and it's really itchy. While I'm happy it will heal me, I'm not a fan of it.

I doze off and dream of Gideon licking my whole body with his scratchy cat tongue.

When I wake, it is morning. Wow, I slept for a long time. The babies are bundled up in little bassinets at my bedside.

Al and Auggie are asleep in the chairs they spent the last two days in. We are leaving the hospital area today. Apparently, the babies and I are perfectly healthy and no longer need to stay here under observation. When Cinder looked into my body and said they were small, I was worried we'd have to stay and wait for them to grow. Maybe they're not as cautious with here as they are in my world.

Al and Auggie scoop up the little bassinets and carry them as we walk. Gideon pushes me in a wheelchair, slightly behind the men. I watch them as they carry my babies in their arms. Their muscles ripple in their back. If my entire nether region wasn't shot to shit, I'm sure this sight would send me into a state of frenzy.

Gideon has an apartment in the library. We will be staying with him for a while. He told the hospital staff he will be taking a leave of absence. Once I am well enough to leave, we will return to Saloria and rescue Cordelia. Then, we'll figure out our next steps toward overthrowing Thadius.

We enter Gideon's apartment, and it is immaculate. Al gasps, "I've been living in a cave this whole time."

"And I've been living in a damn shack!" Auggie says.

"You could have come to live with me whenever you wanted. I told you where I was going, Auggie." Auggie looks genuinely surprised. He completely forgot Gideon had explicitly told him he was going to the library to take up residency. Al and I look at him, a bit annoyed. We can't be too mad; even though he forgot Gideon was definitely here, he still figured out that Gideon was probably here.

Gideon continues to explain how he came to work at the library, "I was the most well-respected doctor in the country before Thadius brought me on to help cure his curse. I trained with the lead physician here when I was in school. It didn't take much to convince him of who I was."

"You were Thadius' doctor?" I ask. I do remember Al telling me this, but I want to know more.

"Well, yes, until he assigned me to be Serena's doctor. She had multiple miscarriages in a very short period of time. He asked me to help them conceive."

"Oh, no!" I gasp. "She wasn't pregnant when he killed her, was she?"

"No, she had just lost another baby," he said. "Sometimes I wonder if … if I had been better at my job. If I had done a better job convincing her to stay in bed, would she still be with us? Would he have spared her if she was with child?"

I place my hand on his, still gripping the wheelchair. "Gideon, I don't think so," I say honestly. The babies held Thad back occasionally, but my complacency, my compliments—that's what saved my life.

He gives me a half smile and tries to change the subject.

"Anyway, when I first came here, all the doctors tried to cure me, but the curse wouldn't budge. One doctor said he was particularly fond of me and offered to try to remove my curse … sexually … but I think he just has a thing for cats. It didn't seem genuine. I'm also worried the feelings need to be mutual, and he was honestly insufferable," he laughs. I imagine a doctor with a furry kink entering Gideon from behind, lifting his tail, and pulling at his ears. I guess even a busted perineum can't stop this dirty perv from dirty pervin'. I see the sadness in Gideon's eyes and try to stop picturing him getting railed by a hot doctor that looks like he fell out of an evening television drama. Be respectful, Astrid.

Gideon gives us a tour of his apartment, which seems more modern than even the castle. It's how I'd picture a home in 1920s New York to look. He has so many books and many instruments. He shows us around excitedly and I notice his tone is different than it was in the hospital. He inflects his words more and doesn't speak as measuredly. I suppose he has a "doctor voice" and a "normal guy" voice.

He has enough rooms for us all to have our own room—even the babies. I worry about the babies being alone and try to insist they sleep with me. Everyone eventually convinces me it would be better for me to sleep if they had their own room. When they say they'd feel more comfortable going to the babies at night without worrying about waking me, I realize they were making some excellent points. I might get away with sleeping for the next few weeks while these dudes do all the work—every new mother's dream.

Cinder gave us a gift to watch over the babies at night: four portal mirrors that allow us to see from room to room. They're like magical baby monitors. I realize we can also use them to communicate with each other—like cell phones! I'm starting to think I should have told Cinder I loved her, too. A flash of me having a threesome with Cinder and Liza crosses my mind, and a tingle erupts in my crotch. Stop it, Astrid.

Each of us takes one of the mirrors, and we place the fourth in the babies' room. I enjoy watching them, the babies and the men, when I'm not with them. The babies sleep way more than I expected and don't seem to mind that I'm not producing any milk.

While I enjoy sharing a bed with Al, I appreciate that we have our own rooms. Right now, I need to heal, and I can't be tempted by him sleeping next to me and rubbing his hard cock against my leg in the middle of the night when I cannot use it to my advantage.

I am worried about Cordelia. I am afraid the townspeople are burning her down while I'm sitting here cooing over babies and waiting for my taint to grow back. I beg Gideon to go to her and leave the babies and me here, but he will not hear of it. He says he must be here to ensure the babies and I are okay. "They were born a little premature, after all," he says.

Al flies to the city daily to check on Cordelia to ease my worries, though, so I can at least relax a bit. I cannot have the responsibility of their friend's death on my head.

As the days progress, Gideon's protectiveness of the babies and me becomes more apparent. I think he's trying to compensate for his internalized failures with Serena through me. He hovers over us like a little helicopter kitty doctor, freaking out at every little movement. He reminds me of a cat of mine that had to take Zoloft who would jump at every sound. Despite his apparent anxiety, he doesn't make me anxious. He's good at calmly presenting himself—even if I know he's screaming on the inside.

I decided to name the babies Nathaniel and Katherine (Nate and Kate, yeah, I thought I was pretty clever with that). All the men are protective of them. The men say they have a smell similar to me and Serena, but not quite as strong. I can't smell it, too, so, I trust them on it.

One day we all sat around sniffing the babies, trying to figure out what their smell does. Giving them nose nuzzles on their tummies as we sniffed at them. Al said Kate smells like "coziness and hugs," and Auggie said Nate's smell is like "coziness and calm." They make you want to protect them. They make you feel comfortable and calm. I remember how sometimes I'd panic when I was pregnant, and their little kicks would calm me. Maybe I can still feel the effect even though I can't smell them.

Al is ecstatic to have a kitchen again and spends what seems like all his time making us food. He and Gideon brainstorm all sorts of concoctions that are supposed to stimulate breast milk production. It's been five days since the babies were born and I'm dry as a desert—a breast desert. I picture a desert filled with breasts instead of cactuses. Or maybe, penis-shaped cactuses (cock-tuses?), and it's the rocks that are shaped like breasts. Auggie spends his time hand-sewing little outfits for the babies and me. I spend my time trying to feed these babies, crying over the fact that I can't, and sleeping.

Taking care of twins is a full-time job, even when you have three other people around to help. I honestly don't know how the single mothers of my world do this. The men are all so kind. They always take the night shift. They draw baths for me, prepare meals for me, make clothes for me, and, best yet, change my babies' diapers. If I had the babies in the castle, I'm sure I would have had a group of people supporting me and doing all this work for me, but I wouldn't have felt as loved.

I wake up one morning to find that my breasts, which were double-D before pregnancy and probably pushing Es or Fs after (I have no idea, they don't have bra sizes here), are swollen to the size of fucking basketballs and hurt so much. I cannot touch my fingertips together when I cup both hands around a breast. They feel like they are going to explode.

Gideon and Al went to the library and hospital to get some books and formula for the babies since my milk still hadn't come in. Gideon has finally conceded it is taking quite a while, and we should consider feeding the babies something other than breast milk, so they don't lose any more weight. I'm just happy they have formula here. Auggie is in the living area with the babies, entertaining them with smoke twirls and a rattle. I howl in pain, and he comes running to me with one baby in each arm.

"What's wrong!? Are you hurt," he asks frantically.

"My breasts, they hurt so much!" I say.

"Oh, your milk came in! Here try to feed the babies," he gives me Kate, and I get her in position.

I hold Kate to my breast and rub my nipple over her nose the way the nurses showed me, but Kate does not seem interested. Maybe she's not hungry. I thought all babies would eat if you put a breast in their faces, like a dog with a bowl of food. She should be hungry! All she's had is whatever that thick stuff that oozed out of me up to this point was. And it hardly seemed sufficient. Gideon said it has been enough, but how much can a man who doesn't know about modern medicine really know? I do the same with Nate, and he too, is not interested.

"Please, babies! You're losing weight, and mommy is in so much pain." Maybe they're sick little sadistic fucks like their father. Can babies be evil? They both doze off in my arms, utterly disinterested. Fuck. Are they so hungry that they're too hungry to eat? Are they dying in my arms right now? I wail, utterly overwhelmed by the situation.

Auggie takes them from me and puts them in their cribs in their room. I sit on my bed, crying into my hands. I am a failure at everything. I can't even feed my fucking babies. The ONE thing I should be able to do as a mother. The whole reason I have these fucking tits.

I squeeze the sides of my breasts and look at Auggie desperately, "What can I even do!? They hurt so much." I flop down, sobbing uncontrollably. Auggie sits next to me on the edge of the bed and rubs my back like he did the day I went into labor. My clitoris pulses at his touch, but my taint screams. Fuck, I'm horny.

I turn to face Auggie, and he looks down at me. I can't tell what he's thinking—but his smoke color changes a bit. His shirt is perfectly fitted and shows the mold of his pecks. Why is a dressmaker so fucking ripped? I picture him lifting bolts of fabric, multiple at once, as his shirt bulges with muscle. His legs, they're big, too. I can see them stretch the material on his thighs, and I picture him pumping the pedal of an old-timey sewing machine with his foot, up and down, up and down, making me a beautiful dress, as I saddle up on his dick and kiss his neck.

"Auggie, will you help me?"

He clears his throat. "What do you mean?"

"Will … will you suck on them, please?" I plead. "The babies won't do it, but I need someone to."

He stands up—his erection in line with my face. He realizes this and turns to the side.

"Um, should I go get Al? Wouldn't you rather he do it?"

"No, I want you, Auggie. I need you, Auggie," I say.

He sits beside me on the bed and asks, "Are you sure?"

"Yes." I stand up and pull my sleeping gown off over my head. I feel so unsexy. My breasts look monstrous, and I'm wearing a diaper-like thing to stop the bleeding. The bed is the perfect height, so my breasts are right at his eye level. I use my knee to push one of his legs to the side and stand between his legs. I press my breasts onto his face so that it is squished between them. I rub my nipple against the spectral shape of a nose.

He wraps his arms around me and pulls me closer. He sucks on my left nipple—hard. I wail in agony and ecstasy. I am so fucking horny and so mad that I can't jump on his cock right now. I have wanted him for a long time, and to finally have him touch me but not be allowed to let him enter me is torture.

His smoke-like presence seems to fully engulf my body and flicks at my butt. I want to be with him. I want him inside of me. I can tell he wants that too. He's wanted that from the moment he set eyes on me—or smelled me, I should say. I lean over and unbutton his pants. His dick instantly jumps out without much coercion.

I grab his cock, hard. Auggie was there when these babies came screaming out of me, he knows how gross I am and still wants to fuck me. I want to pleasure him. I pump my hand up and down while rubbing my thumb over the tip. He stops sucking for a moment to let out a groan and then gets right back to work. I look down and appreciate the beauty of the scene in my hand. Yes, it's just a dick, but it's a dick engulfed in smoke that swirls around my hands as I pump up and down.

I might not be able to put it inside me, but I can still touch myself. I push hard against my vulva with my free hand, bucking at my hand. Being more gentle than usual because I'm afraid I'll hurt myself.

He gently smacks my ass and squeezes. I lean back in pure pleasure. I don't know if he's actually getting any milk, but I don't care.

I push him to the bed. He straightens out and puts his head on my pillow. I press my breasts into his face to let him keep sucking and grind against his abdomen, the tip of his dick poking at my butt. I come hard and painfully on his chest and claw at the headboard. Ouch. That kind of hurt. I pushed myself a little too far. Gideon never said I couldn't dry hump, but he probably didn't think he had to clarify.

I side my way down, so Auggie's dick is nestled between my breasts. He places his palms on their sides and presses them inward, so they squeeze tightly around his cock. I move my body up and down as he thrusts. He stops, gently pushes me upward with his right hand, and cups his left hand over his member. He lets out a sound of pure ecstasy as he ejaculates into his hand. I appreciate the gesture, because I do not feel like being came on. He squeezes my nipple while he does this. Milk shoots out. "It worked!" I say, exclaiming at the sight of milk spraying toward him.

"It worked," he says breathlessly as his body begins to solidify into that of a man. Well, I guess the definition of sex isn't so black and white according to this curse.

21

How are all the men in this world so attractive? I was lucky to pull a seven in my world. Here I'm constantly pulling twelves. They break the scale. Augusten's solid form has muscles that are so defined they look airbrushed. I could tell he had muscles in his smoke form when he wore clothes, but I did not expect to see this. He has shaggy blonde hair and soft blue eyes. I gaze into his eyes, excited to finally see them. His smoke form, unfortunately, had no facial features, and even his eyes were indiscernible. He is grinning at me with the jovial smile I would have expected from such a goofy guy.

I worry about what Al will say when he sees Augusten is a human. He'll know what we did. Will he be mad? Will he be jealous? What will Gideon think? He just met me, and now he's going to think I'm a dirty slut.

I hear Alistair and Gideon approach and jump up. "My clothes!" I say to Auggie. He grabs them for me, and we both hurriedly dress.

We greet them in the living room. There's no sense in trying to prolong the inevitable. They are so surprised to find Augusten in his human form they both drop the books they are carrying.

"Auggie!" Al exclaims and runs to hug his friend. Tears roll from his eyes. Augusten cries, as well.

"I know. I can't believe it. She lifted the curse." Auggie exclaims.

Al rushes toward me, and I am afraid he will hit me; instead, he grabs me and gives me a big bear hug lifting me from the ground.

"Careful with her! She just gave birth!" Gideon hisses while he picks up the books and stacks them on the table.

"Oh, sorry!" Al says, "Thank you! Thank you so much, M'Lady." I still get all tingly when he calls me M'Lady.

"Astrid, while I am grateful you cured my friend of his curse, you have put yourself in grave danger. The tearing. The infections. I think you should return to the hospital and get checked out."

"Oh, um, we didn't have sex-sex. I'm okay," I say bashfully.

They both look at me, and I can tell lots of dirty things are running through their minds. They look at Auggie, and he smirks in a "Yeah, I hit that" frat boy kind of way.

The babies start crying, and Auggie and Al both run to check on them.

Gideon asks, "Are you sure you're okay? He didn't take advantage of you, did he?"

"Thank you for the concern, doc. But I'm alright. If anything, I took advantage of him."

He looks at me doubtingly. You're next, cat boy. I giggle to myself. What is wrong with me? What is it about this world that has made me so fucking horny? Maybe my smell turns me on, too.

Auggie and Al come in with the babies. "I think they're hungry," Auggie says. I sit on the couch and untie the front of my nursing shirt. I rub my nipple on Katie's nose, and she instantly latches. I look at Auggie in pure amazement. The smile he returns is so warm and loving.

Al helps me position Nate so I can feed him, and he, too, instantly latches! I look at Auggie, and I start to cry. "Thank you so much, Auggie."

Al says, "What are you thanking him for!? Gideon and I made the milk-producing soup!?"

"Y'all did too good of a job. Look how fucking huge my breasts are! I have enough milk to feed two grown men, not just two little babies." I shouldn't have said that. That was a full-on boner trigger. Now they're all wondering which two of them get to do it.

I ignore them all, shifting uncomfortably to deal with their erections. I look lovingly down at the babies on my breasts. Gideon brings a stool over and lifts my feet. "I'm sorry my furnishings are not more comfortable, love," he says.

"No, it's perfect," I say without removing my gaze from my children. They both look up at me with my same gray eyes. "They have my eyes," I say. How have I not noticed this before?

"They do," Al says and leans over to stroke each of their heads, then kisses me on the top of mine. "They have your hair, too." Oh, yeah, I guess they do. They have a thin feathering of hair of head on top of their head, but it's not dark like Thad's; it's light like mine. I lean down and pull them toward my face. I breathe in deeply on their heads, inhaling their little hairs and giggling—I can't believe I could ever love anything as much as them. God, they're cute.

I look up at the three men who are lovingly watching me feed my babies and beaming at me. I loved the movie Three Men and a Baby when I was a kid. I think about how I've got a whole three men, two babies, and a woman situation going on.

The next day, Gideon takes me to a man named Silvester in the library. Silvester is a master of scent magic, and Gideon thinks he may be able to help me with my sexy scent situation. The man gets one whiff of me and says, "Oh, yes, I can see why this may be a problem. I can brew a potion that will neutralize the scent. You will have to drink it every 12 hours, though."

"What if I, um, want my scent to come back without waiting for the potion to wear off? Can you make an antidote?"

He clears his throat, struggling to be around me, "Yes, I can do that, as well, but the ingredients are not cheap or easy to find."

"I have money," I say and hold a jewel out in my hand.

"Oh, well, it will take me a few weeks to brew it."

"I have time."

"How much can you make?"

"For that cost, I can make enough to last you a year or so," he says while stroking his chin. I wonder if he's trying to hustle me somehow. He seems sincere, but I'm definitely not the best judge of character.

"How much can you make for this?" I reach my hand into my pocket, and when I bring it back out, I now have a second jewel, this one larger than the first.

He looks genuinely surprised, "For that much, I can make you enough to last a decade."

"Great, here's the deposit," I say. Placing the first stone on the table. "I'll give you the second after you give me the potions, and I test them."

"Deal," he says, and we shake on it.

We spend the next few weeks waiting for Sylvester's potion, tending to the babies, prepping supplies, and dry humping. Once the potion is ready, I can enter Sailoria without being harassed, and we can, hopefully, save Cordelia.

Gideon and I research how my and the babies' magic works, trying to learn more about it. We look for books that reference visitors from other worlds. We also discuss our theories on how the curse works, since my curing Auggie without penetration surprised us all.

Auggie spends his time playing with the babies, playing with me, and making clothes. He makes me a veil so I can hide my face when we return to Sailoria.

Al spends his time cooking, excited to have a kitchen again and have me as a new source of inspiration. I tell him about recipes I remember from my world, and we experiment to get them just right. I don't have the same cooking skills as Serena, and I don't know flavors as well as she did, but we have fun experimenting and taste testing.

One evening, while working on a heavily spiced recipe, I enter a sneezing fit. I sneeze, and golden feathers pop all over my body. I sneeze again, and turn into a gigantic golden bird, taking up more space than available and breaking bowls and plates. I sneeze again and float to the ceiling—my body dematerializes into a white cloud of smoke. I sneeze again, and feathers spray out of me. I assume I look like a cloud raining down feathers.

Auggie and Gideon come running in when they hear the crash of dinner plates. They all look at me bewildered, unsure what to do as I float there, sneezing out feathers.

After I stop sneezing, I weakly say, "Al, help me." He reaches out to touch me, and I fall downward—human. My clothes ripped to shreds at some point during this fiasco and lay on the floor. When I crash into the pile of clothes under me, all three men rush to my side.

Gideon pushes the others out of the way. "Don't touch her!" he screams. "If she's broken her back, we can't move her." He frantically inspects me, checking all my limbs for breaks. "Are you okay, love?" he says with that level of concern he tends to have in his voice that masks panic with a velvety blanket of reassurance.

"I'm fine," I say. "Just out of breath from all the sneezing." I know I hit the ground hard because I heard it, but I barely felt it.

He sits me up and pushes my hair out of my face. "You sure, love?"

"Yep, I'm sure."

"We have to figure out how this works," Gideon says.

"You're right."

Al and Auggie look at each other, utterly amazed I can use their powers. Gideon insists on trying various experiments with my powers to see how they work. He takes me to the field behind the library, and while my fear of open spaces has calmed a bit, it is not entirely gone. Should I tell him? He'll understand. But I can't turn into a bird again in the apartment; I'll tear it down. "From the research I did when I tried to cure His Majesty, it seems that when you cure the curse, you actually take some of it unto yourself. The strength of it is possibly correlated with the curse bearer's love for you."

"So, why am I turning into these forms when I sneeze?"

"And when you give birth." He reminds me.

"Oh, yeah."

"I suspect you're losing control of your human form, and these cursed forms are popping out. But there has to be a way for you to control it."

I think back on the various things Al and Auggie have told me since they transformed to humans. "Al said when he thinks about the feeling of being a bird, he can be a bird. Maybe I just need to try that?"

Gideon shrugs and says, "Won't hurt to try." I picture myself turning into a cloud of smoke and floating up into the sky. Oh, no. Will my worst fear actually come to fruition now? Don't think too hard about it, Astrid, or else it might happen.

"So, Gideon, I'm … I'm a bit scared of open spaces. I'm afraid I'll turn into smoke and float away. Is there somewhere else we can do this?"

"Oh … oh, forgive me, love. Yes, of course. Let's go find a large room in the library." As we walk back, I can't stop thinking about floating into the sky and flying away. Suddenly, I feel my skin ripple and cool. I feel my feet lifting off the ground. I look at my hand and see I am turning to smoke. I scream, "Gideon! Help me! Please don't let me float away!" He turns shocked, and lunges for my hand, but it passes through me. I am unable to give myself that slightly solid embodiment that Auggie could maintain.

I let out a blood-curdling scream as I look to the sky.

"It's okay, love! You can do this. Concentrate on the ground. Concentrate on my voice." Gideon says in that reassuring way he always does. "Think … think of Alistair. Think of becoming a bird and gliding to the ground." I squeeze my eyes shut … or at least I try to; I'm not sure if I have eyelids. I think of Al's smile. I think of his bird form. My bones creak and crack as they materialize and stretch into long wings. I feel the warmth and tickle of the feathers over my body. I stretch my arms wide and think of how much I love Al. I think of my babies and how I can't float away. I have to be with them. I look at Gideon, and he is smiling at me, reaching toward me. "You did it, love! You did it! You are marvelous!"

I land gracefully and run toward him. I wrap my wings around him. My feathers leave my body in a big poof. I'm naked, hugging him, sobbing into his chest. Snot is pouring from my nose. "Please take me inside, Gideon!"

He returns the hug, and I wrap my naked legs around his body. He lifts me and runs me into the library. He doesn't look particularly strong, but carrying me like this seems to cause him no issues. When we are safely under a roof, he places me on the ground. He removes his shirt and wraps it around me. I scramble and claw at him, not wanting to be let go. He scoops me back up and rushes me to the apartment. I rub my face against the soft fur on his chest, wetting it with my tears. A gentle purr vibrates from his neck and sooths me slightly.

I am still sobbing when Gideon places me in my bed—still with his jacket on—under the covers. Auggie and Al rush to the room, each holding a baby.

"What's going on?" Al asks.

"She … turned to smoke and started floating away," Gideon says.

"Oh, no. Are you okay, M'Lady?" Al sits beside me on the bed and places his hand gently on my arm.

"Oh, darlin', I'm so sorry. This is all my fault." Auggie says as he sits on the opposite side.

I have the covers wrapped around me tightly. I peek out from under the blankets and see the concern on their faces. Al and Auggie are bouncing the babies with one hand and stroking me with the other.

"Can you lay the babies next to me?" I ask. They lay them next to me, and I feel almost instant, but not complete, relief. I love laying here like this—flanked by family.

"I'm sorry, I did not know about your fear of open spaces. I feel so stupid that I didn't think to have you try this with a roof over your head." Gideon is pacing, unable to mask his anxiety this time. His ears are laid flat on his head and his tail is bushed out swinging frantically.

Auggie looks back at him and asks, "So, how did she get down?"

"She was able to transform into a bird and float down," Gideon says matter-of-factly.

"What!? Wow!" says Al.

"Please don't marvel at me right now. I need to work through these feelings first."

"Yes, yes, of course, M'Lady," Al says solemnly.

We all sit in silence. They watch me, waiting for me to speak.

"It … was pretty cool, though," I say.

- - - -`♥´- - - -

I'm back to isolating myself in a room again. The event has thoroughly traumatized me, and I spend most of my time curled up under my blankets. Auggie and Al both tiptoe into my room at various times to cuddle and dry hump. I am surprised there hasn't been any overlap yet. I'm not sure how they'd react if they stumbled upon each other. I find myself wishing the other would sneak in and join in on the fun whenever I'm with one of them. Gideon doesn't visit; I think he feels guilty. I want to tell him I don't blame him, but I can't leave my room just yet. I notice various books left on my bedside when I wake, obviously snuck in for me by Gideon.

After about a week, I'm finally able to leave my room. I find Gideon in the living room and make sure to tell him I am not mad at him. He breaks down into tears, and we embrace. I tell him we'll try again after I have some time to heal. "No, no, you don't have to. I don't want you to push yourself," he says.

"I want to," I say honestly. I really want to get this fear and these powers under control. I realize that for possibly the first time, I mean it when I say I want to conquer my fear. I spent years in therapy every week trying to beat it, but I didn't really want to. I didn't really try. I was comfortable with my fear. Comfortable in my home. I had no reason to get better. Now, I mean it. I do want to get better. I want to be able to look at the clouds with my children. I want to turn into a bird and fly. I want to flit around the world as smoke. I want to use these powers to murder Thadius.

Things get back to relatively normal. The men take care of the babies when I'm not feeding them. I sleep a lot. Al and I cook together again. Auggie and Al visit me often, and I have some of the best non-sex of my life. Gideon told me I had to wait at least four weeks before penetrative sex. Since I had tearing, he said "nothing below the waist," and gives me questioning looks every time I leave my room with either Al or Auggie.

Al and Auggie know precisely what is going on and express absolutely zero jealousy. I am baffled.

After three weeks of bouncing back and forth between them, my stress over the confusion of the situation builds up and I decide to have a chat with them. I find them both in the twins' room, lying on the floor, shaking rattles over the cooing babies. I am struck with an overwhelming sense of love. I could never choose between the two of them at this point, and I need to ensure they will never ask me to.

I sit cross-legged between them and make a silly face at Kate before saying, "I need to speak to the two of you."

They both sit up and continue to shake the rattles over Kate and Nate's faces but look at me with concerned expressions.

"Is something wrong?" Al asks.

"I just … I need to talk about us." I say, making a circular motion and pointing at the three of us with my hand, finger pointed to the sky.

They both wait expectantly for me to say something further.

"I … I love both of you deeply. Auggie, I'm not sure I've said that to you, but I hope you can feel that I do."

"You broke my curse. I felt it."

"Well, that being said. I cannot choose between you two, and I want to ensure that we will not find ourselves, months down the line, with one of you asking me to choose."

They look at each other knowingly. Al starts, "Forgive us, M'Lady, but we have discussed this without you."

"Oh," I say.

Al continues, "Yes, we have talked and are unwilling to give you up. We are also both willing to … sorry, this makes you sound like a possession, but I cannot think of a better word … share."

Auggie picks up where he left off, "We are happy to be with you in whatever capacity that means. We each understand that your love for the other does not diminish the love you have for us. Al is one of my best friends. I am happy to be with you and him, together, as a team—a family, forever."

I look at them and instantly think, "threesome." Is dick all I think about?

Al continues, "And, Astrid, I know what you're thinking right now. I can see it on your face."

"Oh, you do?" I say with a half-smile.

"Threesomes." Shit, he does. I blush.

"We are not opposed to that being something we do in the future," Auggie says.

Al continues, "But not yet. We might need a little more time to get comfortable with it. We've known each other a while and never really thought of each other like that. So, we ask that you let it happen naturally rather than ask about it or try to engineer some situation. We can talk about it again whenever you want, though. We just don't want to be pressured into it."

"Oh, of course, I would never push it," I say.

"Great, then, if you're happy with how things are? Then so am I." Auggie says.

"Me, too." Al says.

"I am," I say with a warm smile. I cannot believe my luck.

We all return to making faces and shaking rattles over the babies' faces.

Gideon approaches me one day and says, "So, you know what today is, right?"

"No, I don't have a calendar." I laugh. I probably sure learn how this world's calendar works. I'm sure Gideon will teach me whenever I care enough to ask.

"Well, today is the day you can probably safely have intercourse again. But take it easy! I don't want you to tear again. Please, please, come see me if you have any bleeding or pain." Is Gideon trying to get me to sleep with him? Is that why he's telling me I am cleared to get it on?

"Gideon, do you want–" he cuts me off.

"No, no. I would not ask you to do that for me. Plus, it wouldn't work. You don't love me." Do I love Gideon? He and I have the most in common. We honestly spend the most time together. Al is sweet and caring and makes food for me. Auggie is fun and funny, is excellent with the babies, and creates beautiful clothes for us. But Gideon, he's my friend. We discuss books and magic and perform experiments together. He delivered my babies and takes care of me. Maybe I do love him. Gideon notices the gears turning in my head and places his hand on mine.

"It's okay. I like my monster form. It's made me better and stronger. I had to wear glasses in my human form." He says with a chuckle.

Yes, but fucking me can make you even stronger. I don't push it. I can tell he's not ready. I bet he'd look so cute with glasses.

22

Silvester makes good on his promise. The potion he makes doesn't turn my power off completely, but it softens it enough to allow me to walk through the library without making every dick jump to attention. The antidote seems to work, as well. I take it while standing in the middle of the library and everyone begins staring at me and grabbing at their crotches uncomfortably within a minute. I take a sip of the potion, give Silvester the larger stone, and thank him profusely.

The ride back to Sailoria doesn't feel as long as the ride from Sailoria did—probably because I don't have to stop to pee every five minutes. We're already halfway back, and I'm surprised how quickly we've made time. We still have our wagon, and the babies and I ride comfortably. The rock of the wagon seems to keep Nate and Kate fast asleep. When they sleep, I tend to poke my head out the front to chat with the boys, careful not to get too good a look at the sky.

Al drives the wagon, and Gideon and Auggie ride beside on their own horses. Gideon plays his lute to entertain us, and the boys teach me different folk songs as we ride. I teach them some from my world. I never had an ear for music, but I've always had a quick ear for lyrics. When we're all trying to think of a song to sing, I sing some of the bars I remember from WAP. The men are astounded at the lyrics.

"Wow, is that really a song from your world?" Al asks.

"Yeah, it is," I say.

Auggie laughs, "This explains so much about you!"

"Hey!" I snap back.

"But what does stirring macaroni have to do with it?" Gideon asks, thoroughly confused.

Al laughs, "I think it's a reference to the sound it makes when you stir. It really is a great analogy." He and Auggie laugh uncontrollably, and Gideon remains baffled.

"Don't worry, buddy, you'll get it one day," Auggie rides up behind him and slaps him on the back.

"Wait! Do y'all have macaroni and cheese here? Al, can you make me some as soon as we get to town?"

"Of course, M'Lady," Al says.

"Yummy," I say very excitedly. The food here has been good, but it's been a bit too five-star for too long. I need some of my old staples.

"I'd like to try some, as well," Gideon says rather seriously.

Auggie and Al look at each other with a side eye and laugh uncontrollably.

"Sure, Giddy, I'll make you some, too," Al says.

"Let him stir it!" Auggie says, and they roar with laughter.

They really think they are hilarious. I hope I won't regret this little frat house I've inadvertently assembled. After they are out of breath with laughter and I can finally speak, I say, "I think it's time for us to set up camp. It's getting dark."

"Astrid, I think you should drink the potion if we're going to stop—especially if we'll be stopped by the side of the road. I don't want anyone to ride by and get any ideas." Gideon says.

I haven't taken the potion while we've been traveling. I know I have enough to last years, but I am scared to waste it. Plus, the boys said they have become used to the smell, and it doesn't bother them much now.

"I'm scared to waste it! You'll be up all night and see if anyone is coming from a mile away. If someone starts coming toward us, I'll take it," I say.

"You have enough to last you a decade. It's really better to be safe than sorry," Gideon says. I don't know why I don't want to take it. He's right; it is better to take it. I just don't like the way I feel when I do. If I'm being honest with myself, I like the power I exude when I don't. I like to think all the dicks jumping to attention are saluting their queen when I walk by. Plus, it tastes super gross, and I don't want to go to sleep with that taste in my mouth. We argue back and forth for some time. His reasons are always better than my excuses, but I hate losing an argument. He finally wins me over with a, "Please don't put Nate and Kate in danger over this." Damn him. He knows how to drive a stake through this stubborn heart.

"Okay," I say, finally conceding. In the time we've been arguing about it, it's already dark, and Al and Auggie have fully set up camp.

It's hot outside, so Al and Auggie have set up bedrolls for us to sleep outside the wagon under the stars. I'm scared a wolf will snatch the babies and insist on keeping them in the wagon. Tired of arguing with me at this point, Gideon doesn't fight me on it and nestles their carriers close to the back of the wagon so we can easily get to them.

"I'll keep watch tonight," Gideon says.

"But, aren't you tired? You haven't slept in two days?" I ask.

"I've got the best night vision. I'm not much of a sleeper, anyway." Gideon says.

I give him a concerned, suspicious look.

"I'll nap in the wagon tomorrow on the ride out," he says with a reassuring smile.

I get snuggly in my bedroll and cannot believe I am going to sleep under the stars. I am a person who can sleep under the stars now! I can't quite look up at them, but I can exist under them. Years of therapy, and I couldn't leave my house. Less than a year of this ultimate exposure therapy, and I'm sleeping under the mother fucking stars. I do a little cheer for myself. Go me. Gideon sits on the bedroll next to me and perks up his ears to get a good listen to things going on. His eyes reflect the fire in a beautiful yet eerie way, so I turn to watch Al and Auggie.

Al and Auggie are still fussing about getting ready to make a meal. Suddenly, Al wails out in pain. An arrow pierces the ground next to my head.

Al grabs at his arm and says, "Fuck". He never curses. What's going on? Where did that arrow come from? Did it hit Al?

Auggie seems to know what's happening before the rest of us because he instantly transforms into his smoke form and flies quickly toward some unseen villain. His clothes lay on the ground in the dirt where he stood. Al transforms into his large bird form; his clothes rip to shreds against the girth of his body and land next to Auggie's. Auggie will be complaining about the state of these clothes later; I know it. Al lets out a whimper when he pumps his arms to lift for flight. His arm must hurt, but it seems it doesn't hurt enough to stop him from flying. He quickly flies in the same direction as Auggie.

"Gideon, what is going on?" I ask frantically.

Gideon yells, "Behind you!" and lunges toward me. A knife presses to my throat, and a hand grips painfully around my arm. What? Who has me? How did the men not see him approach? Gideon was on high alert. Gideon freezes with his arms out in front of him. A nose presses in my ear and inhales deeply. "Damn, Your Majesty, I've been waiting to bury my face in that scent all day. You do not disappoint." A dick presses firmly at my back, and the hand that was on my arm is now grabbing at my breast—squeezing it aggressively and repeatedly. Fuck. I took the potion, but it doesn't entirely remove the smell. And it sounds like this guy has been following us all day. I didn't think about the fact that my smell could waft on the wind and attract others while we were moving—that, along with Gideon's lute playing and our singing, probably made us a giant bullseye.

Gideon is standing perfectly still, staring at the man holding me. "Let her go," he says. He hisses, while his claws and fangs extend to at least triple their normal length. He looks terrifying. I've never seen this side of him before.

Another man slinks beside the wagon, inching his way toward its back opening where the babies are. "Gideon, the babies! Don't worry about me." The knife pushes harder into my neck, and the hand at my breast moves to my arm. In a movement almost too fast to see, Gideon rushes toward the wagon. He leaps into the air and brings his hand down hard and fast on the arm of the man that's reaching toward the infants. The intruder's arm cuts clean off and lands on the ground with a loud thump. It takes the man a moment to notice what has happened to him. He grabs the place where his arm used to be attached and howls—almost like he's the animal. The babies start to wail, startled awake by the scream. Gideon growls so loudly I can feel the sound rumble in my own chest. The man Gideon attacked can no longer maintain his composure and falls to the ground. Gideon lunges toward him and plunges his extended claws deep into his chest.

Damn, I'm glad he cut those nails to birth my babies. His claws retract, and they are no longer visible as he eases his way toward the wailing twins. He licks the blood from his fingers and crawls into the wagon, shushing the babies. "Shh, now. Giddy's here. It's alright now," he says. He disappears into the wagon to check on them, and I can no longer see him. It is too dark. I cry, alone, about to be violated by a man with a knife.

The man with the knife at my throat says, "Queen Astrid. We are here at the behest of the king. Come quietly. The king wants you and the child alive."

Two eyes glow from the darkness of the wagon. Gideon wriggles to the ground, and I can now see him and the babies clearly in the firelight. He places them back in the wagon and turns to me, ready to pounce but obviously afraid if he does so the man will hurt me.

"There are two. Ha, maybe he'll double the reward," the man says.

"Let me go," I whisper, afraid if I speak too loudly, the knife will cut into my throat. I'm scared to move. Should I try elbowing him? Should I try to stomp on his foot?

"Call off your demons. He said you are the second priority. I can slit your throat right now and tell him the demons got you." He laughs and presses the knife harder. I feel a trickle of blood inch down my throat and to my breasts. His hand is on my arm, digging into it so hard that my circulation is cutting off in my hand.

"I'd still get my reward if I bring back your body along with the babies. Maybe the extra baby would make up for it. Or I could dash that one against a rock. The king doesn't know about it. I've always wondered what the inside of a baby's head looks like." He laughs maniacally.

A rage boils up inside me. Heat spreads to my face, and I sneer. I will not let this motherfucker touch my babies. The deep heat of rage turns to a cold chill as my body shimmers and turns to smoke. I slip through his fingers and away from the blade.

"WHAT THE FUCK!?" he says. I float to his eye level and turn to face him. How am I controlling my body? I don't understand this, but I'm doing it. I know exactly what to do. I want to rip this motherfucker's throat out. My bones creak and moan as I materialize. I feel the cold air on my naked body for just a moment before I am engulfed in a warm downy hug of golden feathers. My nose elongates to a hard, black beak. I spread my wings wide and caw loudly in his face. He is too stunned to say or do anything. He doesn't even scream—just whimpers. I instinctively lung forward and wrap my beak around his throat. I clamp down, and a quick gush of warm salty blood shoots to the back of my throat.

He falls back with a thud. I open my beak and let the mound of flesh in my mouth drop to the ground onto his chest. I slowly materialize back into my human body while staring at his lifeless form. I'm cold again, naked, standing on my pile of clothes. I spit blood from my mouth onto the body of the dead man. I stare, mesmerized by the blood pooling around his neck. The babies begin to cry again, but I don't turn to look at them. I keep watching the man's blood pool, confused by what I'm looking at. Did … did I just kill this man? His dick is still erect. Of course, I would notice that. I'm a damn dirty murderous perv.

I hear the woosh of Auggie around me and the loud thud of Al landing behind me. I still don't turn. I just watch the blood accumulate and soak into the dirt.

"Damn, darlin'. That was awesome!" Auggie says.

- - - -`♥´- - - -

Gideon and I wait in the wagon while Auggie and Al get a room for us in Sailoria. Gideon can't leave because he's perceived as a monster everywhere but the library. I could go, veiled and potioned, but I'm too paranoid after our encounter on the road to try. Even in the wagon, I won't remove my veil. I'm too afraid someone will peek in and spot the runaway queen and her tiny prince and princess. I learned my lesson about not taking the potion and have been taking it religiously every twelve hours.

Al and Auggie help sneak us into "the room" they acquired for us. It's not a room at all! It's the entire top level of the inn. It's a full suite with a kitchen, living room, and multiple sleeping areas. It's bigger than my three-bedroom house back in my world. "This is the best room in the whole city, apparently. Those jewels you have are worth a fortune." Auggie says.

"Hopefully, using them doesn't attract attention," Gideon says.

"How long can we stay?" I asked.

"So, when I showed them the jewel, they thought I was trying to buy the place. So … um … since I didn't have any smaller jewels, I just bought it."

Gideon yells, "Are you crazy? We can't own an inn."

"Why not? I thought it might be a nice place for us all to live once we find the others."

"It's a business! Are we just going to run a business now? Auggie, you are too impulsive. Al, why didn't you stop him?" Gideon asks.

"I got a little caught up in the moment," Al says bashfully while looking at his shoes. These two should not be allowed to go off on their own together. I can picture the two of them getting all excited, egging each other on while they flaunted their wealth.

Gideon looks at me, aggravated, hoping I'll chime in, but I'm too exhausted from dealing with the babies. I just shrug. Hm, if a jewel could buy a whole inn, maybe Silvester did rip me off. Whatever.

Gideon throws his hands up in frustration and starts furiously unpacking. Al and Auggie look at me helplessly.

"Look what you've done," I say and give them a scolding mother frown.

I hand the babies to Al and Auggie and walk over to Gideon. I place my hand on his shoulder. "Hey, what's this all about? Yeah, it was a boneheaded thing for them to do," I look over my shoulders at them, and they look like two super-hot deer caught in headlights, "but you seem extra worked up. Is something else bothering you?"

Gideon stops unpacking and sinks into a nearby chair. "I'm sorry, guys. I'm just really worried about Cordelia. I'm worried my song won't work. We don't even really know if the song is what took her out of this state last time. Maybe it was a coincidence. And now we have to figure out how to run an inn? It's just too much."

"I understand you're worried about her. We all are. We'll try the song, and if it doesn't work, we'll keep trying until something works. We can stay here as long as it takes—we own the place now, so there is no timeline." I giggle.

He looks at me and gives me that half-smile he does that shows one of his fangs, and I swoon a little. So adorable. I kneel in front of him and place my hand on his knee. "It'll be okay. Don't worry. We won't give up on her." He puts his hand on mine, and we look at each other for a few moments.

"Okay," I say, putting my hands on my knees and standing up quickly. "Let's do this!"

23

We decide to wait until very late at night to visit Cordelia. If the song works as we hope it will, we're worried her transformation into a human-shaped tree, rather than the big tree-shaped tree she currently is, in the middle of the day will arouse suspicion—more like scare people shitless. Al stays home with the babies.

Auggie, Gideon, and I are all standing at the base of the tree Al claims is Cordelia. I look up and am overwhelmed by her size. Oh, hey, look at me looking up. Don't peek at those stars, Astrid. My anxiety spikes, and I grab Auggie's hand just in case I accidentally turn to smoke and start floating away. He looks at me with a warm smile and pulls me close. He knows I'm freaking out. Concentrate on the tree, Astrid. She is gorgeous—in full bloom. The most enormous, most beautiful cherry blossom I have ever seen. Actually, I don't know if I've ever seen a cherry blossom in real life.

Auggie approaches the tree and places his free hand on her trunk. "Yep, that's Cordi, alright. Cordi, it's me, Auggie. Can you wake up for us, please?"

Not one to wait, Gideon pulls out the lute and immediately plays the song. Her branches and flowers shake, despite the lack of wind. Is it working? A look of hope crosses Gideon's face, and he plays more fervently, but nothing else happens. She won't return to her human form.

He plays so long that his fingers cramp. He stops and stretches his fingers. He looks at me, defeated. Benches surround the tree. Are we in some sort of park? She really picked a nice spot to root. He walks dejectedly over to one of the benches and sits down. I've never seen him look so exhausted and frustrated. He tosses the lute to the side of the bench, places his face in his hands, and sob.

I release Auggie's hand, no longer worried about myself, and sit next to Gideon. I embrace him and say, "It's okay. It's just the first thing we tried. We can keep trying. Do we know anything else she likes?"

"She liked Al's sweet cakes, she liked designing dresses with Auggie, she loved Serena," Gideon replies between sobs.

Serena. If only Serena were here. "Gideon, you said that even though my scent had a different effect from Serena's, it seemed like the same smell, right?"

"Yes," he responds.

"Maybe I should take the antidote while you play. Maybe that will stir something in her. Maybe she'll think I'm Serena. I don't know if a tree can smell, but it's worth trying, right?"

He looks up at me, hopefully. I can see the gears turning behind his eyes as the light flashes across them, making them glow. "Let's try that," he says seeming more hopeful.

I reach up my skirts to find the small vial of antidote strapped to my leg. If Gideon could blush, I'm sure he just did. He looks away so as not to see the flesh of my legs. I uncork it, make a little cheers motion toward Auggie and Gideon, and take a small sip of the antidote.

"Okay, the antidote is working," Gideon says, and I can see his pants bulge.

Auggie rubs at his crotch and says with a chuckle, "Yep, it's working."

The flowers rustle violently. Is it working on Cordelia, too?

Gideon notices the rustle as well and scrambles to grab his lute. He plays the song with such passion I almost feel like I can see the music. The branches shimmer and sway. The blossoms open wider and emit a pink glow. I hum along, knowing the tune by now. A tear rolls down Auggie's cheek as he watches the tree intently for any new movement.

After a few moments, the branches shake so violently that the flowers fall off showering us with petals. It gets so thick it feels like we're in a sea of petals. I can't even see Auggie or Gideon anymore. They dissipate, and I can see the tree again. The branches reach toward the heavens with a loud creaking noise. It pauses and begins to shrink as if it's being pulled down into the ground.

As it shrinks, the body of a full-breasted, nude woman begins to take shape in its trunk. Deep green eyes open within the bark. The white of the iris against the dark bark is breathtaking. It stops shrinking and has taken the shape of a gorgeous woman, made of bark and with cherry blossom branches for hair. She walks toward me and turns her nose upward. "You are not Serena. Who are you?" she says coldly.

Auggie leans in front of me and waves at her, "Hi, Serena, that's Astrid. I'm happy to see you again. I missed you."

She looks perplexed. "How long have I been asleep this time?"

"Months," Auggie says.

"No wonder my neck is stiff," she says as she moves her hand slowly to the back of her neck.

"Come on, Cordie. We'll take you home with us," Gideon says, through tears and reaching toward her hand. She seems a bit confused and disoriented but nods slowly.

We brought a large robe to help us hide the fact that we would be walking through the streets with a big tree woman. Gideon places the robe over her as best he can. Auggie, taller and a total fabric nerd, adjusts it further to cover her head fully and ensure there are no wrinkles.

Auggie places her arm over his shoulder and has her lean on him. She is very tall, almost as tall as Auggie. She's also very stiff and struggling to move. She doesn't fight the help and doesn't ask questions. She simply acquiesces. She seems too tired to do much else. Auggie and Cordelia walk toward the inn. As she walks, cherry blossoms fall out her robe behind her, covering the ground in her wake. Is she shedding? Gideon hangs back, waiting for me and watching them.

I start to follow them, but stop when I realize my scent is still uncovered. I need to take the potion before we trek through the city. I can't rouse suspicion. Or should I say "arouse"? I still have the vial in my hand. I take a sip and reach under my skirt to place it back in the belt on my thigh. Gideon gets visibly uncomfortable when I lift my skirts, covers his crotch, and turns away. What's with this dude? He birthed my babies, for Christ's sake. He has seen me walk around naked. Why is a little thigh getting him all hot and bothered today?

When we get back to the inn, Al rushes Cordelia and gives her a big hug. He begins rambling away at her, "Oh, Cordi! Thank God you're okay. Some townspeople were discussing burning you. You made people sad for some reason. I tried to convince people you were good luck every time I visited." I think he's overwhelming her because she stares at him blankly for a moment.

Her arms creak as she tries to lift them to hug him back, but she's unable to. "I need to sit down," she says. "I am exhausted."

"Are you hungry?" Al asks. He's so eager to help her. I might need to tell him to calm down a bit.

"No, I am okay, but I would like to hear the story of what's going on with you two." She points at Auggie and Al in their human forms. I guess she's getting her wits about her now. "And who is this?" she says as she points a thumb at me. "And who are those babies?" She motions toward Nate and Kate, lying on the floor at the other end of the room.

After we answer her questions, she looks at me and says, "So, you're from the same place as Serena? Did you know her?"

I find it a little funny she would think I know Serena, but I'd probably ask the same thing if I met two literal aliens from another universe. "Unfortunately, no. My world had a lot of people in it."

"That's too bad. I think she would have liked you." She says as she drifts to sleep in the chair.

"Should we put her in a bed?"

"No, let's leave her." I think of a stupid joke about "leafing" her, but don't say it.

Al and Auggie are playing with the babies in their room while Gideon and I fuss about the common spaces, straightening things up. We're both nervous cleaners, and I want the place to be spotless when Cordelia wakes. We cross paths in my bedroom while returning some of the things the twins had been playing with.

Gideon stops me from leaving by gently poking at my elbow. I turn to look at him. "Astrid, thank you. I couldn't have saved Cordelia on my own. Thank you for having faith in me and not giving up on me."

"You're welcome, Gideon," I smile.

He looks at my feet as he speaks, "I … I know you don't feel the same way, but … but, I love you, Astrid."

I look at the top of his head, stunned. His ears flick nervously, and his head remains bowed in submission, too afraid to look me in the eye. I wasn't expecting him to say that. Do I not feel the same way? Gideon and I have become incredibly close. I can confide in and converse with him in ways I cannot with Al and Auggie. He has protected me and cared for me. He's supported me. Of course, I love him. "I … I love you, too, Gideon."

He looks at me with tears welling up in his eyes. I feel like he's about to ask me, "But do you love-love me? Check yes or no". Instead, he slowly walks toward me. He places his hand on my cheek and kisses me so gently on the mouth that it almost doesn't feel like a kiss at first. He's the most timid of the men, but he somehow is the first one brave enough to initiate a kiss with me.

We slowly break apart, and I look at him, waiting to see what he will do next. We both look at each other, too scared to move. I want to grab him by the arm and throw him on the bed, but for some reason, I cannot. It's different with Gideon. It feels like anything we do next will ruin what we have. Do we want to proceed? Do we want to pretend like this never happened? I can't believe how scared I am. This damn dirty perv feels like a sweet innocent virgin right now.

Gideon walks to the door and closes it gently, trying not to make a noise. He turns the lock. He gently grabs my hand and walks me toward the bed. I tremble. I am afraid. But I want to do this. I do. I am surprised by how forward he is being. He notices me trembling, and lets go of my hand.

"We don't have to do this," he says. "Do you want to do this?" I am surprised that, despite his bashfulness, he is being so direct. He's initiating sex with me, not the other way around—Al and Auggie couldn't even muster up that courage the first time. He trembles slightly and seems unsure of his movements, but he's not stopping.

"Yes, I do. I'm just nervous." What is going on? Why am I scared? Maybe it's the cat thing. I've never had sex with a man-shaped cat before. No … that's not it. I'm nervous because I love Gideon. I care about Gideon. I love him so much that I am scared of what this will do to us.

He smiles, kisses me on the cheek, and pulls me close to his body. "I'm nervous, too," he says and his voice cracks. He's just a little taller than me, so when he pulls me close, I can feel his package against my clit. It wakes up in anticipation sending a shockwave of tingles across my body.

He reaches down to my waist and pulls my dress over my head. My nipples sparkle in the moonlight, wet with breastmilk. He leans down and licks my breasts. His tongue is rough like sandpaper, and a shiver runs from my breasts straight to my vagina. I am instantly wet. He walks me backward slowly toward the bed. When the back of my knees hit, I sit down.

He removes his shirt, and I run my fingers over his body, caressing his hair. It is so soft. He purrs. Oh, that's cute.

He grabs my breast and kisses and licks it. He rubs it against his face. I reach for his belt loop with my other hand and pull him toward me, pressing his body against my crotch. I wrap my free hand around and grab his lower back. I stroke his hair while I gently pull him into me.

I place my face against his chest and rub my cheek against the soft fur. This is nice. I wish I could stay like this forever, just cuddling on him.

I realize I am freezing. "I'm cold," I say, trying to bury my arms between our bodies. He's so warm and soft!

"Let me warm you." He goes to the head of the bed and pulls the blankets back to make space for me to get under the covers. I crawl under them and scoot to the side so he can lie next to me. He contemplates what to do for a moment and takes off his pants before getting in. I think he is embarrassed by his body because he does not give me a chance to admire his naked form. He's so different from Al and Auggie, who like to stand at the foot of the bed posing like superheroes while I drool over their muscles and fondle myself.

He pulls the blanket up to our chins and wraps his arms around my naked body. He doesn't do anything for a long while; he just hugs me and caresses my arms. I wait for him. I am eager to bring him into me, but I don't think being sexually aggressive will go over well with him right now. He's so nervous; I don't want to scare him off.

He strokes my breasts and kisses my neck. He nibbles at my ears and grinds gently against my leg. He is much less eager than Al and Auggie. Significantly less than Thad. He is gentle. He takes his time. He savors me. And the anticipation makes me so wet I swear there is a pool forming under me, soaking the sheets. This poor mattress will need to be replaced within a few weeks.

I gently pet his body, savoring the hair all around him. I turn to my side so that we are face to face and our genitals are pressed against each other. He moans in excitement, and his purring gets louder. To my surprise, the purring seems to make his penis vibrate. I could probably get off just pressed against him like this.

I run my hand down his back and reach his backside, where the base of his tail is. I run my hand from its base to the tip, turning it in my hands. He shudders and moans and presses himself hard against me. He turns me to my back and asks, "Can I be inside you?"

I lift my hips and grab his, jamming his cock into me. "YES!" I moan. I can't be timid anymore. I need this dick in me.

He reaches down and thumbs my clit while he pumps inside me. He licks, sucks, and bites at my nipples. The difference in texture between the top and bottom of his tongue is ecstasy.

He moves his head away from my nipple to look me in the eye. I lift my head and kiss him hard on the mouth, cutting my lip on his tooth, but I don't care.

I grab him by the shoulders and push him to the bed on his back. He grins so big I think his teeth get longer.

I throw my leg over his waist and easily slip him into me. I press my hands into his abdomen and move my pelvis in a circular motion. His hips are the perfect width; I can get the ideal friction angle against my clit. Skinny boys are the best for this position. His dick is just the right length. It reaches inside me and rolls against the sides of my vagina. I lose myself in pleasure, getting faster and more aggressive.

He stares at me in disbelief that I am doing what I am doing. He reaches around and sticks one of his tiny fingers in my anus. I scream in complete pleasure—the walls of my vagina squeeze against him. I fall toward him and bite his neck. I moan "fuuuuuuuck" as I come.

He grabs my hips and frantically moves my waist up and down, pumping my body quickly on his dick. I lie dead on his chest, still recovering from the orgasm, but not yet ready to have him remove himself from inside me. After a few short moments, he pushes so deep inside me that his butt lifts from the bed, and he cums. His dick throbs with each spurt. His body convulsed in pleasure. I'm falling asleep on his chest, his dick inside me. I notice the hair on his body receding. No! It's so cuddly. I look up and see an attractive man with golden hair, looking at the ceiling and smiling with that same wry smile Gideon always gave me, just without the fangs.

"Wow," he says. "I've never done that before. Like ever. Not even before the curse." I didn't know he was a virgin. I guess I was right when I called everyone at the library a bunch of "virgin bookworms." Damn, all that stuff he did with his hands didn't seem like virgin moves. I wonder if his doctor training taught him how to make a woman come. I kiss him on the shoulder and fall asleep.

I wake up to the sun shining through the windows. No one woke us or disturbed us through the night. They probably knew what we were doing. I take the time actually to look at him. He has a puffy coif of golden hair on top of his head. His skin is baby smooth and supple. I don't think this man has ever had a pimple; his skin is flawless. His face is narrow, starkly contrasting to the round shape it held in his cat form. I gently lift the blanket to get a peek at him. He's lean like he was as a cat. He has a thin swimmer's body—tight, sinewy, and boney. Hot as fuck. He makes a slight noise and turns to the side, giving me a good look at his firm little ass. Thanks for the show, Gideon. I stop ogling him and decide to let him sleep. I put my clothes on and sneak out, trying not to wake him.

Auggie and Al are feeding the twins breakfast. They're drinking more formula now, and while I'm a bit disappointed they don't rely entirely on me to eat, I am excited to have my tits back. I couldn't keep up with those voracious little boob-biters. Al and Auggie look at each other knowingly. I'm sure my hair screams, "Guess who just got fuuuuucked?"

"Where's Gideon?" Al asks with a slight smirk. Yeah, they must have heard us.

"He's sleeping," I say, motioning my head toward my bedroom door.

"Is he … human?" Auggie grins in that cocky frat-boy way of his.

Almost on cue, Gideon walks into the room behind me, fully naked, and wraps his arms around my waist. He kisses my shoulder and looks up, "Yep." I'm a bit surprised by this audacity. Have I created a monster by making him human? He usually has a bit more modesty than this. I can't believe he's just walking around swinging his dick like it's nothing. He never walked around naked in his cat form.

Auggie and Al stand up and walk toward him. They clap Gideon on the back and say things like, "Welcome to the family, brother! I missed that gorgeous golden hair of yours. Damn, you're still so skinny." They seem like they don't even notice he's fully nude. Boys are weird.

"Y'all are weird," I say and go to the breakfast table, stealing a small snack from Auggie's plate.

"Hey, now, no need to steal food; I can make you breakfast," Al says.

He comes over and kisses me on the head, "What would M'Lady like for breakfast?"

"Eggs. Scrambled. And toast, please!" I say, very excited about breakfast.

"And you, Gideon?"

"Same," he says, stretching arms in front of him, arching his back slightly, and yawning. He may not be a cat anymore, but it is a very cat-like gesture.

"Okay, but first you gotta' go put on some clothes. No dicks at the breakfast table. That's a new rule I'm instituting," Al says.

"But what if it's your dick?" I ask.

"No dicks but mine at the breakfast table!" He giggles. Is this really the nervous, apologetic man I met a few months ago? The man who seemed so scared of breaking things? Am I really the same girl who was scared of the sky and people? No. This quest has changed us all.

Gideon returns with some clothes on and a big smile on his face just as Al is placing some eggs on his plate. If I didn't believe he was a virgin before, that smile tells me otherwise. He is definitely smiling like a man who just got laid for the first time.

"Damn," Gideon says dejectedly.

"Something wrong with the eggs?" Al asks.

"No, it's just I'm going to need to wear glasses now that I'm human again."

"Well, you could just stay in your cat form all the time if you wanted," I say, thinking about rubbing his soft fir against my body.

"I'll think about it. For now, I think I'll spend some time wearing this form." He grins.

"We'll go get you some glasses today," I say with a smile. I give him a peck on the cheek, then take a bite from my toast.

He blushes and eats his eggs.

"Al can turn just parts of himself into a bird now. And I can turn just parts of my body to smoke. Maybe you can just turn your eyes." Auggie said.

We all look at him, waiting for him to try. He crosses his eyes, and nothing happens. He is so adorable.

"You'll figure it out," Al says. "It took me a few hours to get the hang of it. I just had to remember what it felt like for my body to be a bird. Then it just kind of became a bird again."

"YEAH! I was thinking about how it felt when my hand was smoke—how it would weave through a thing. Then my hand was smoke!" Auggie says.

At that moment, Gideon entirely turns into a cat. Then right back to a human. He looks very startled.

We all laugh uncontrollable at the expression on his face.

"What's so funny?" a voice came from the door.

Cordelia stands at the door. At least, I think it is Cordelia. She doesn't look monstrous at all. She is a tall, gorgeous woman with the same large, round breasts as the tree I met last night. She has the same voice, but she has human skin and flowing red hair. Auggie and Al explained to me once that Cordelia could use glamour magic to make herself appear human even though she is cursed. She must be using magic right now.

"Ah, got some of your magic back, have you?" said Auggie.

"Yep, I won't be able to hold this for too long, though," she responds.

She looks at Gideon. "Weren't you a cat yesterday?"

"Yes, I was," he blushes.

"Just fucking your way through all my friends, aren't ya, beautiful?" she says and grabs a seat next to me.

"Cordi … don't be like—," Gideon says. Looking a bit bashful at her rudeness.

"Sorry," she says, "I was just joking. I'm so happy for you, Gideon. You, too, Astrid." She hits my arm slightly with her elbow and winks at me.

Her apology helps, but I'm still bristling at her initial rudeness. Well, missy, guess who's not gonna get her curse lifted by this pussy any time soon. I can't stay annoyed long because I instantly picture burying my face between her tits.

24

It's been four months since we woke Cordelia, and we've made no progress finding Florian, Osric, or Lysander. The previous owners of the inn and all the patrons have fully cleared out and we have the entire inn to ourselves, but we still mostly just use the large upper-floor suite as our home. Our time has been engrossed in caring for Katherine and Nathaniel, but Al and Auggie have flown to other towns and areas of interest to ask about monster sightings. They've come home each time dejected and needing cuddles.

Cordelia and I became fast friends. We have a lot in common, and it's nice to have a bit of feminine energy around in this sea of erections and testosterone. We started a sort of romance novel book club, and we can spend all day chatting about the books we read. Gideon used to join in on the fun occasionally, but he would get a bit too analytical about it, read way faster than us, and find all the plot holes. We told him it's not always about the plot, sometimes it's about the feeling, but he didn't quite get it. We unofficially kicked him out of the unofficial book club.

Cordelia was a master of glamour magic before becoming a monster. Despite the curse, she is still able to use that magic. She can't hold her glamour for long, so she spends her time around the inn as her tree form. However, she can use it on herself and is also able to adjust my appearance so we can go on short shopping excursions in the city without worrying about being spotted or feared.

We like to leave the men with the babies and go and get ingredients on Al's shopping list or look at fabrics for Auggie to experiment with. Auggie is excited to have two women at his disposal for which he can create all of the latest fashions. He enjoys seeing us go out and model the clothes. He loves when we come back with compliments from passersby. He also makes clothes for the guys, but "they just don't appreciate a good ruffle," he says.

Today Cordelia and I are having a great time, walking through town linked arm in arm, chatting like we're old friends, and casually browsing the local shops. We're modeling Augustine's most recent designs, of course. People stop to stare at us constantly. I joke that we're hiding in plain sight. I enjoy seeing people stop and stare at me because of my clothes and knowing that if they're getting hard, it's not because I smell weird, but because I look hot in my dress. Even though Cordelia glamoured my hair and face, so I don't look exactly like my wanted poster, I still mostly look like me. She didn't touch my body, and Auggie, obsessed with my body and knowing its every curve, has made me an outfit that accentuates it perfectly.

As we walk into the opening of the square, multiple people stop to stare at us. We are stunning with our glistening fabrics and devil-may-care attitudes. None of these fools know that the two hotties strutting down the street are actually wanted criminals of the crown. I think about how we're the "it girls" around town and purr to myself. Since curing Gideon's curse, I have developed the ability and impulsion to purr when pleased.

Cordelia pokes me in the side and giggles while making that little cat paw gesture girls make when working at maid cafes, and I get all wet thinking about her in a maid outfit—putting ketchup on my omelets. Maybe, putting ketchup on herself? I snap out of it and realize she's telling me I'm purring too loudly and might start rousing suspicion. While my face may not look like the one on a wanted poster, purring like a cat would probably garner the wrong kind of attention—the, dissect me on a table, or, burn me at the stake, kind. This town is accepting of magic, but not monsters, unfortunately.

While I know I look fantastic, I do find it hard to believe anyone is looking at me while I'm standing next to Cordelia. I asked Auggie once if Cordelia uses her glamour magic to make herself look like her old self or if she improves upon her looks a bit. He surprised me by telling me she was actually a little more attractive in real life, and that her magic isn't quite able to get her pre-curse face exactly right. I looked at him like he must be lying. I cannot imagine a more beautiful creature than Cordelia's glamoured form.

Once, while walking through town, Cordelia told me Auggie was probably her best friend, but she was also quite close with Osric. They had been lovers at one point. They weren't compatible romantically or even platonically, "But, GAAAAAAAWD, could he fuck," she said with a loud chortle. As she stopped in her tracks, laughing loudly, everyone stopped and watched her. To command a room like that. To not be told to "pipe down" when you take up so much space. That must be nice. Next to her, I must look like a fat, frumpy potato. A fat, frumpy potato in a gorgeous dress.

Al and Gideon requested we pick up some herbs while we are out, so we stop at the herbs shop. When we entered the shop, the merchant who supply the shop is there chatting with the store owner very loudly, putting on a show for the whole shop. He thunders, "Yeah! And it had all these tentacles, tons of 'em! But the top of him was a huge naked man!"

Cordelia grabs my arm and whispers into my ear, "He's talking about Osric." Cordelia approaches the traveling merchant and asks him where exactly he had seen this sea monster. He told us he has been living near the south docks. "It hasn't hurt anyone, but you ladies shouldn't go out looking for it. He's a terrifying sight."

Cordelia looks at me with a level of happiness I have not seen in quite some time. Cordelia is that kind of beauty that strikes you through the heart. I've known her for months, and I am still in awe of her beauty. To see her smile not only stops my heart but also makes me wet. She would definitely be a Victoria's Secret model in my world. She stands a good six inches above me. She's quite tall for a woman, and even though I'm average height, she makes me feel like a pipsqueak. So, when she hugs me in delight, I can easily nestle my head on top of her breasts without revealing that I am a damn dirty perv doing a little motorboat on the top of my bestie's breasts. The two merchants watch, very confused about why we are so excited to hear of a monster sighting. They might also be enjoying the same tit bouncing show I am.

As her breasts smack me in the face when she jumps up and down, I notice that they are getting a bit hard—a bit wooden. "Um, Cordie," I say and point at her breasts. The magic is wearing down.

"Oh," she whispers. She pulls her shawl closed to cover her chest and says, "Thank you, gentleman," as we walk out. They probably think we're crazy.

We jog back to the inn, uncaring that two women running through town is both improper and a spectacle. One runaway queen and one tree woman would make even more of a spectacle. We stop in the entryway of our suite, out of breath. The men all stop what they are doing and look at us. "Having fun, ladies?" Auggie asks.

"We … know … where … Osric … is," Cordelia says through gasping breaths, arm jammed in her side, massaging out a cramp. Her breasts are heaving so much that we are all a bit mesmerized by them. Running reduced the swell in my vaginal lips that aroused when she jammed her tits in my face, but this new pose of hers has brought it back with a vengeance. Damn, I need to get off. I scan my men wondering which I should rush to the room and then remember the task at hand. Astrid, stop drooling over your friend's tits and thinking about riding three cocks, each with its own unique curvature and pleasure. Think about the quest!

Even the babies look hungry at the sight of Cordelia's heaving bosom. They aren't crawling yet, but they can sit up. They are sitting on the ground playing with some toys and bouncing on their little butts in excitement, reaching toward Cordelia and me. I pick up Kate, and Cordelia picks up Nate. They both claw at our breasts, obviously hungry. I wonder how much longer I have to breastfeed them. I'll ask Gideon later. I walk to the couch and remove my shirt to feed Kate. Cordie places Nate at my opposite breast.

"So," I say, having caught my breath before Cordelia—my stamina has been increased tenfold from receiving Gideon's powers, and Auggie's seems to have given me pretty decent lung capacity. "He's down by the south docks. A traveling merchant was talking about some tentacle, sea monster, half man, thing."

"Sounds like Osric," Al says. "Auggie and I can fly over there tonight and check it out. See if we find him."

We all agree that this sounds like a marvelous plan.

"I'll make dinner first," Al says.

When night falls, Al and Auggie prepare to leave. Auggie spent too many days furious with Al for transforming before removing his clothes, so now they have a special spot on the roof to disrobe before transforming and flying off. It's easy for me to reach from the balcony because Al built me a little ladder. I love to go up there and watch them take off their clothes, then give them kisses goodbye while rubbing myself on their naked bodies and fondling them just a little before they fly off. They only do this at night so others can't see them, so I tend to hang back and masturbate after the show. I can't believe I can masturbate on a roof under the stars! The fear of the sky almost makes me come faster, and I don't particularly feel like dissecting that new fetish. Also, the idea that maybe there's somebody off on a second-story window watching me and I'm not as hidden as I think, makes it even hotter.

Tonight, I kiss them for a long time and give them both a quick goodbye dick squeeze. I tell them the squeeze is for good luck. They laugh at me and fly off.

After I masturbate myself to completion on the roof, I return to the living area to find Gideon and Cordelia sitting on the couch together. It seems like Gideon was waiting for me, because he immediately stands up when I enter the room, comes over, and kisses me goodnight. He hadn't slept last night because he had been up all-night studying something. He gets hyperfocused, disappearing for days. I used to do the same thing. The babies are down, leaving Cordelia and me alone in the living room.

She's in her tree form, and I am honestly more comfortable with her this way. We spend so much time like this and, while she is attractive in this form, her beauty isn't so stunning it leaves me literally stunned and dumb. She can stretch and grow her body however she wishes, and when she moves, she looks like she has to "grow to where she goes" rather than move there. She moves a bit slowly, but the sound of her creaking is soothing. She likes to impress me by reaching across the room to get books or wine or whatever.

She pulls out the latest book we've been reading together and says, "book club?"

I squeal, "Oh, yes! I can't wait to talk about the latest chapter!" and hurry to the kitchen to get some cheese to go with the wine she already has set out for us.

I just finished masturbating. You'd think I'd be cooled down, but I'm not. As we discuss the latest scene of our current romance novel, I start feeling hot and bothered—shifting in my chair, considering reasons I can excuse myself to rub one out again. Maybe I should wake Gideon by sitting on his face? I wish my men were a bit more romantic. They're sweet. They're helpful, but maybe I gave away the milk for free a bit too early with them (literally with Auggie) because they don't particularly try to romance me. This scene from the book is hot, and there's no penetration or anything—just desire and expectation.

Today Cordelia has grown flowers around her head that almost form a crown. I try to distract myself from the pulsing between my legs and reach out to gently caress one, "these are quite beautiful," I say.

She shudders and says, "You know the flower is the sex organ of a tree, right?"

"Oh, God. I'm so sorry." My labia pulse with my heartbeat. If I were in a manga, the sound "badump" would emit in big letters right at my crotch.

"It's okay," she says. If she had a vascular system, I'm sure she'd be blushing. She looks down, her eyelashes batting. Her eyelashes are so long. Her eyes are so green. They are the same gorgeous eyes she has when in her glamoured form.

We both sit there, unsure of what to say now. She looks back at me and says, "You know … you could do it again if you'd like." And reaches her hand out to rest on my leg. At this moment, I realize an intense passion has been building up inside me. Our friendship has been blossoming around an erotic will they won't they dance. I have been lusting after her, and she has been lusting after me. We were both just afraid to say anything. I didn't know how Cordelia felt, but I had hoped. I hoped all those times she pressed her breasts into my face when she hugged me were deliberate actions to seduce me. Since we've been in the city, I have kept myself under the effects of the suppressing potion. So, the feelings she may have for me are truly for me. The real me, not the "smells like she's from another world and super fuckable" me. Maybe she's not interested in me. She's never expressed any interest in women. Perhaps she's just horny from the whole caressing her flower thing and this spicy book.

I've always been attracted to women, but I've never really been with a woman. I've made out with a few. Gotten to second base, but that's it. There was one time in college when I got awkwardly fingered by a fellow flautist in my car before practice, but she wouldn't let me touch her back and I didn't come. I think, "fingered by a fellow flautist" and giggle. There was also that time when Gen shaved me, but I don't know if that counts. Focus, Astrid.

The buildup of passion explodes all at once, and we lunge toward each other, pressing our mouths together hard. I push her back on the couch and straddle her, slipping my tongue into her mouth. Her lips are soft, even though they look like wood. Her tongue is wet. I place my hands on the sides of her face and gently stroke her flowers with my fingertips. She moans in pleasure through the kiss slowly grind on each other on the couch. We kiss for a long time. I'm not sure what to do. I'm not really sure where to concentrate my actions, so I focus on her flowers for now.

Her arm reaches behind me and lifts my dress overhead. She tosses it and pushes me back to admire my body. She licks her lips like a predator about to eat its prey. When I first came to this world, I did not like that they didn't have panties. I even had Auggie sew me some; I missed the security of it. But I am starting to appreciate the lack of an extra piece of cloth on my body to remove.

I quickly return my face to hers. Unable to withstand the desire to shove my tongue down her throat.

I stand, and she stands with me, unwilling to remove my mouth from hers. She has to bend awkwardly to do so, I'm so short, and she's so tall. She breaks away when I grab at her dress, trying to pull it over her head. She has to help me because … short!

Her body morphs and changes to that of her glamour. I look at her, dumbstruck and salivate a bit. Her hair is red and her nipples are small and pink. Her pubic hair is red, making a perfect composition of color. I look her in the eye and say, "Cordelia, you are gorgeous, but I know you drained all your magic earlier today. I know it's painful for you to do right now. You do not have to take that form to be with me." She smiles, and a tear runs down her cheek. I touch her face and brush the tear from her cheek with my thumb. I stand on my toes and kiss where the tear was.

She grabs my ass and lifts me so my legs are wrapped around her. She is as strong as a tree, after all. Her stomach glistens with my juices as I gently grind up and down on her stomach. She is the best kisser. I'm starting to wonder why I even like kissing boys in the first place when women's lips are much softer, their tongues less eager and more inviting. She slowly morphs back into a tree.

She whispers in my ear, "You know, I can, um, grow things wherever I want and in almost any shape." At that moment, I feel a protuberance grow on her stomach right where I am grinding her. I freeze. "Would you like that?" she asks.

"Yes, yes," I moan. She then slowly grows inside of me, rolling and flinching. I look down in awe as a leaf sprouts from the base. "That's not all I can do," she giggles and the leaf flicks at my clit.

Holy shit, this is like the vibrator I used to have at home. It does not take long before I lean back, bucking her so wildly that she has to hold tight to my lower back to keep me from falling. She giggles at me and watches me with an eager look. She stares at my tits as they bounce up and down while

I grunt and moan. After I come, she falls back onto the couch, still inside me.

"How is this a curse?" I ask. And we chuckle.

I look at her and examine her body. I realize she has a flower between her legs, approximately where her pubic hair should be. I have never seen this part of her. She usually keeps it hidden.

I crawl downward, my face inches from the flower. I press my nose into it and inhale deeply. An intoxicating aroma of cherry blossoms enters my nostrils. It is so sensual and lovely it warms my body. She shudders and runs her fingers through my hair.

She spreads her legs for me to position myself, and her lips glistening from beneath the lowest petals. She is eager for me and writhes on the couch.

I place my hands where her legs meet her body and feel under the petals with my thumb, rubbing the area around her opening. With my other hand, I lift the petals and see it in full view. A perfect set of lips. A cute little button clit. An enticing vaginal opening. While I look at it, she lifts her butt upward slightly almost hitting me in the nose. It is begging me to dive into it.

I slip my two fingers into her, and she moans, still holding my hair. I look her deep in the eyes and grin like an idiot. I dive in and press my mouth gently against her clit, wrapping my lips around it, sucking it, and wetting it with my tongue. I'm not sure if I'm doing this right. It seems to me like something I'd like. I'm sure she'll show me soon enough if I'm doing a good job.

She bucks at my face. BINGO. I'm doing a good job! I rub my face against her wet pussy and lick and kiss faster, firmer. Well, actually, I don't need to do much because she's doing most of the work. I just need to keep my fingers inside her and not let her buck my face so hard I lose my position. I reach my other hand up to her belly to press down. For a moment, I can't breathe because my mouth and nose are fully buried within her folds, covered by her flower.

She jerks and twitches and screams in pleasure as she slowly morphs into her human form. This time, not from the glamour, but because the curse is being lifted. She looks like someone who just had a large Thanksgiving dinner fully naked—spread eagle, slumped down, with her hand on her stomach. I wonder if she may never get up again as she lays there panting. Her red pubic hair glistens right in front of my nose, and it still smells like sakura flowers.

I get off my knees and kiss her nipples, kiss her neck, and kiss her mouth before flopping down beside her. She looks at me lazily, and I realize Auggie wasn't lying. She is more beautiful than her glamoured form.

25

Cordelia and I get dressed, and she rushes to a mirror to admire herself. She jumps up and down ecstatically and squeals like a little girl. "Thank you, thank you, thank you! I love you, Astrid," she says, kissing all over my face.

I place my hands on her hips and look up at her. God, she is gorgeous. "I love you, too, Cordelia." I hug her breasts against my face—now feeling confident enough to rub my cheek against them. We stand like that for a few moments, Cordelia weeping quietly and petting my head until the door flings open, startling us out of our embrace.

"Look who we found," Auggie bellows, arms motioning toward a cloaked figure in the doorway. The figure glides into the room, their cloak moving in waves. He lifts the hood revealing dark, piercing eyes under a shaggy dark mop of hair and big bushy eyebrows. He is devastatingly handsome because, of course, he is. Every cursed man in this world seems to be. He rubs his sharp jaw, stroking his stubble with a thumb, and smirks at us with the most devilish smile I've ever seen. This guy exudes hotness and cockiness. Why is everyone here so hot?

Cordelia backs away from me and runs toward the newcomer. She jumps on him, wrapping her legs around him, and planting kisses all over his face just as she did to me. The fact that he is holding her as she had held me is not lost on me, and I am jealous I cannot lift her like that. Tentacles slither their way out from under his cloak and cradle her ass to hold her up. I can't see his body, but I remember the entire bottom half was tentacled.

Oh, no, I'm in a hentai isekai anime. I half-expect, half-hope he will start probing her with his various tentacles right now. I picture him grabbing Al and Auggie, bending them over, and…

I'm awoken from my hentai fantasy by Osric bellowing, "Cordie! You're human!?"

"She wasn't when we left," Auggie chuckles and smiles at me. They really don't mind me fucking everything that breaths. I wonder if the jealousy emotion even exists in this world. A girl can get used to this.

Osric places Cordelia on the floor and slithers toward me; he strokes my face with a tentacle and says, "So, sweet thing, am I next?" And licks his lips.

Everyone freezes, waiting for me to respond. His tentacle has slightly stuck onto my face. When I pull it away, it makes a little pop—probably leaving a mark. I must admit, this is turning me on, and I don't quite know why. He pushes himself toward me, pulls me close, lifts me a few inches off the ground, surrounds me with tentacles, and presses his dick hard against my thigh. He grins so large and hungrily at me that I think I might actually let him probe me right here while everyone watches—touching themselves.

"Osric! Stop that!" Al says, walking toward him.

He puts me down gently on the ground, and I say, "Sorry, but I make it a rule not to fuck things that smell like seaweed." I'm lying because I do want to have sex with this sexy squid. But he's being an ass, and I'm not really into that.

"Ha!" he roars. "I like this one. I can see why you're all fucking falling over yourself for her. With tits and wits like that, what's not to like? Apologies, missy. I am just a forward guy. Some people like that about me, right Cordie?"

"Liked," Cordie quips back.

He chuckles and pulls up a chair that makes him look like some badass cowboy. He turns it backwards, spreads his tentacles across it, and rests his arms on the high back. Why does everything this guy does seem so cool and hot? Like, how does he make sitting on a chair look dangerous? I wish the chair didn't have a covered back, because I assume his dick would be in full view otherwise. I desperately want to see it again.

"Where's Giddy-boy? I thought you said he was here?" Osric asks looking back to Al.

He's sleeping," I breathe out.

"Knock him out, did you?" he says with a wink.

"No, he stayed up all night reading," I say, unsure why I'm insulted and turned on by everything this guy says. It's the smirk. It's the tone. I don't like this guy, but I also desperately want this guy to probe me.

"Of course," he says while shaking his head.

There's a moment of silence, and he slaps his leg.

"So, what's the plan? Florian and Lysander are in Laila, working as part of the Laila's special forces army. How are we going to get them?"

"You know where they are?" Cordelia exclaims.

"Course. I was with them until about a month ago. Until I was asked to leave by the captain."

"Why were you asked to leave?" Al asks.

"Fucked his wife and his sister," Osric bellows and laughs with such a roar I am afraid the babies will wake.

"WHAT!? Um, how are you not cured of the curse?" Al asks.

"Turns out they just had a thing for tentacles and threesomes, not so much me."

"What? You're kidding me. Some women didn't like you? I'm shocked," Gideon says sleepily from the doorway to his room.

"Giddy-boy! Come join us!" he says, beckoning him to us. "I've been trying my darnedest to get this curse removed. I've been fucking my way up and down this shoreline and throughout Laila. Turns out people really dig tentacles. Especially tentacles in a uniform." He winks at me. One of the babies starts crying. I think it's Nate.

"Shit, y'all got babies in here? You've been a busy little lady," he chuckles. I look back at him, annoyed, as I walk to the room to grab Nate. I coo at him and sing a short lullaby to him.

I hear Osric say loudly from the other room, "KING THAD'S FUCKING SPAWN!? Are you serious?"

"Keep it down," Auggie whisper loudly.

Osric continues, "Well, there's your ticket to Thad right there. Use the little brats and maybe the wench as bait. The prick will come running for his fucking offspring. All that fucker ever talked about was a damn heir. There a boy in there?" He chuckles loudly.

My blood begins to boil. I gently place Nate back in his crib, and I jolt into the living area smoke-like, my hand instantly at his throat, "Touch my babies, and you fucking die, squid." He wiggles underneath me, unable to move as tree branches curl around him, thorns cutting his flesh. Weird, Cordelia didn't have thorns. This new power kicked in fast.

Everyone looks at me with pure amazement as Osric chokes under my grip, failing to breathe and unable to save himself. Claws emerge from my nails and press against his skin. Thin trickles of blood drizzle down his neck as I puncture his flesh. I let out a low growl looking at him with my head tilted down.

The others rush toward me and try to pull me off, but I won't budge. I want to see the light drain from this motherfucker's eyes. I hiss and can feel fangs press against my bottom lip as they extend. If I don't choke him to death, maybe I'll bite out his throat. I'm good at that. This wouldn't be the first man I killed, and it probably won't be the last. A bloodlust overwhelms me as I envision the warmth of his blood gushing into the back of my throat and oozing its way into my belly.

Al tries to calm me, "Astrid, it's okay. He's an asshole, but I swear he was joking. Please, he'd never hurt your babies." He strokes my hair, and I regain my composure. What the fuck am I doing? Was I seriously about to murder this man and drink his blood? My branches rescind, and I release my grip, shaking my head as I return to myself. My torn clothes fall, revealing my left breast.

"FUUUUCK, THAT WAS HOT. I've never been so hard in my life," Osric says. "Has she always been able to do that?" he asks the others with a laugh.

"GET THE FUCK OUT OF MY HOUSE! NOW!" I scream as I point at the door. My voice is in a loud, booming, commanding tone. It doesn't sound like me. It sounds like a clap of thunder—my chest heaves, my body hot with anger. Cordelia even covered her ears slightly at the sound.

"Okay, okay. I'll be at the docks. You know where to find me," Osric replies as he slinks to the door. He leaves without an apology. Without even a hint of regret for being such a prick.

- - - -`♥´- - - -

"Lysander and Florian are part of the army of Laila? And the plan is to go to Laila and convince them to join us in fighting Thadius?" I ask Auggie.

"Osric says he's not sure if they'll come with us, they have made a good life for themselves there," Auggie says. I bristle a bit at the name Osric.

"We should at least go and feel it out. It's better than sitting here doing nothing," I say. Who the fuck am I? What happened to the girl scared to leave her room?"

"Well, the quickest way to get there is by sea," Gideon replies.

I croak out, "Um, I can't ride boats. I'm too scared of them." There she is. There's that girl scared to leave her room. They all look at me, wondering if the girl standing in front of them is the same woman who just tried to pull out the throat of their friend.

Al chimes in, "We *can* travel by land, but, M'Lady, it would not be safe. There are mountains that would be near impossible to cross with the babies. I can't even fly through that altitude. And it would be a significantly longer voyage. We'd have to pass through multiple countries to get there."

Fuck. I guess we have no choice. "I guess we need a boat, then," I sigh.

I realize getting a boat means we must go to the docks—where Osric is. "Osric *is not* coming with us," I say sharply.

No one protests, even though I can tell they want to. Why do they like that asshole?

We spend about three weeks preparing for the voyage. I still have quite a few jewels left from my necklaces. A few jewels easily buy us not just a boat but a ship. A ship with a full crew, which is great, because none of us can sail.

I am pleased because it is a very comfortable ship, with many rooms and fluffy beds. Al is pleased because it has a galley. Apparently, it had previously been a pleasure ship for some local nobility who had fallen on hard times and were more than happy to trade it for the jewels.

We board on a sunny day. The crew looks at us like we are a sight to see. I bring enough potion with me to last this voyage five times over. I don't need any cabin boys sneaking into my room at night. The ship's captain, Captain Cornelius, has a jolly nature about him and reminds me of Santa Clause. He doesn't seem like the rough and tumble sea faring type I had typecast all captains to be in my head.

As we board, I scan the perimeter looking for Osric. He must be around here somewhere. Al spoke to him last night and told him our plans—plans that did not include him. He wasn't too happy about it, as Florian and Lysander are his best friends, and he wants to quote, "Gut that pretty boy king like a fish."

"Well, maybe he'll learn not to joke about hurting my babies," I say in a sweet singsong voice as I bury my face in Nate's tummy and make a blowing fart sound. "Won't he?" I say as I wiggle his little feet. He giggles, and Al doesn't say anything else about Osric.

I panic a bit as I look out to the ocean. It is expansive and deep. I hate water. But my family will protect me. Also, Gideon got me some magic calming pills from the library courtesy of the nurse who helped with my delivery. I love that woman.

26

It's the third day of our voyage and I sit with the babies on the dock under an umbrella, bouncing a little ball as they laugh ecstatically. Gideon and Cordelia are lying next to us, soaking up the sun and avoiding the shade entirely. Even though they are no longer a cat and a tree, they still have cat and tree quirks. Their love of soaking up rays is one of them. Gideon is purring while dozing off, and Cordelia has sprouted a small flower in her hair. I point at them and ask Nate and Kate, "Aren't they cute?"

Being under the umbrella is helping my anxiety over the sky a little, but looking out at sea still freaks me out. I took one of my pills recently and the effect is peaking, so I am feeling pretty good right now, though.

The wind picks up, and the shawl I'm wearing whips me in the face. As I'm fighting with it, Captain Cornelius approaches me. "Ma'am, you and the little ones should get inside." He points at a dark cloud in the distance. "That storm is coming fast." My stomach sinks to the floor when I look at the cloud, and a cold sweat covers my body. My heart stops, and I slowly breathe in and out to calm myself. Fuck, I wish he hadn't pointed to the sea. I might need to take another pill. Can I take two?

Gideon and Cordelia help me gather my things and the babies, and we hurry into my room. My room is right off the deck at the back of the boat, and the bed is against the windows that take up the entire back wall. I would have assumed this was the "captain's chambers," but the captain sleeps below deck with the crew. I'm not sure if I purchased this pleasure with my jewel or if the captain is just a super nice guy. I'm not complaining either way.

Gideon, Cordelia, and I sit on the bed with the babies, and I get very nervous. This is the first storm we'll experience at sea, and I don't know what to expect. Surprisingly I haven't had a lot of seasickness, but I am bracing for it. I fetch a bucket to keep near the bed, just in case. The hanging lanterns cast a mesmerizing pattern on the floor as the boat sways. I might get sick. I try to count the books on the wall and stroke the various silks and velvets on my bed to focus my mind away from the storm, but it's not helping. I'm entering full panic mode.

The boat rocks harder, and I worry about Al and Auggie. Where are they? After the captain told us to go inside, he asked them for help tying things down to prepare for the storm. He hadn't asked them to help out before, but it makes sense to put the two big guys to work during a time of crisis.

I rock back and forth, and Cordelia and Gideon notice my disposition. They give each other a look as if they have some unspoken language between them and immediately work to console me. Gideon glides over to my dressing table and rummages through my drawers looking for my pills. Cordelia grabs the babies in both arms and snuggles up next to me. The babies really do have a calming effect on me, but they can't stop me from entering a complete and utter panic. Cordelia places Nate between us so she can wrap her arm around us and strokes my back while humming. The babies don't seem bothered at all, but I'm sure my energy will bring them down eventually. Gideon exclaims, "Ah ha!" and comes over to give me another pill. "Here, take this. It will help," he says while kneeling in front of me and stroking my knee.

Al and Auggie storm into the room, crashing the door against the bookshelf behind them. I'm not sure if they flung the door open or if the sway of the ship flung it open. Either way, the loud bang startles the babies, and they begin to cry. Al and Auggie struggle to keep their footing as they say, "Sorry, babies," and work to close the door behind them. It looks like a real struggle, and I am happy that I am sitting down. They run and slide around the room to secure various things, but they're too late as many things fall off shelves and crash to the floor.

I bring my knees to my chest and hug them close to me. I rock back and forth while visions of the boat being capsized rush through my mind. The water crashes hard against the cabin's window, startling me out of my stupor. I instinctively snatch my babies from Cordelia and pull them close to my chest. I continue to rock back and forth and chant, "We'll be okay, we'll be okay," over and over to myself and the babies. The water crashes against the large windows behind me again, and I scream in fear. Gideon motions for me to move away from the windows, saying, "I don't think it's safe by the—"

Before he can finish his sentence, a loud bang sounds behind me, but this time it's different. The crack is followed by a crashing sound as glass explodes all around me, cutting against my skin. I block the babies from the onslaught of glass and debris, taking a back full of it. It knocks the wind out of me, but I don't let go of the little ones. Before I know what is happening, the room fills with water. I close my eyes, and think I hear Gideon yell, "Astrid," but it's muffled. I'm fully submerged in water. I squeeze my babies close to me, perhaps too tight, and a current pulls us backward violently.

I open my eyes. They burn with seawater. It's dark and murky, but I can see the ship above me—a dark looming mass. How did I get outside of the boat? I try to swim upward as best I can, but I can't with the babies. I kick and kick, but I don't think I'm even moving. It's hard to tell how far up the surface is, and the boat is already much further away from me than it was when I first opened my eyes. Are we sinking? I feel the babies choking and sputtering in my arms. I begin to suffocate and let out a yelp. Water rushes into my lungs. They're on fire. My arms slowly release Nate and Kate as I drown. Are they already dead? This is how I die? In water? My dad would say, "Why'd I teach you how to swim if you're just going to fucking drown?" If I hadn't squeezed the babies so tightly, maybe they'd still be alive. I killed my babies. No one will ever find our bodies out here at the bottom of the ocean. We'll be fish food.

Suddenly, a warm hug wraps around me, and water rushes around my body. Am I going upward? Is something pulling me upward? Before I can tell what is happening, I am on the ship's deck, wrapped in a giant tentacle. I gasp for air and cough. I push against the tentacle. It feels like it is stopping me from getting all the air I need.

I hear a man's voice scream, "Come on, little ones, you're okay! Missy! You awake?" Osric's face is inches from mine. My hair is slathered across my face making it hard to see. Osric wipes my hair out of my face. "Thank God," he says when I blink back at him, trying to see through the heavy rain.

He turns his attention away from me and looks to the deck at something he has wrapped in his tentacles. "Come on, little princeling. You can do this," he says. I hear a baby wailing. Kate. Where is she? She sounds far away. The rain is so loud. I can't see either of my babies.

But … I only hear one baby. I don't hear Nate. Osric is pumping at the thing he's holding in his tentacle with his fingers. He bends down, places his mouth on it, and blows. It's my Nate! MY BABY. I try to scramble to my feet, but I can't. My feet slip from under me. I claw at the boards. Splinters pierce my fingers. A tentacle holds me down.

I scream and wail and try to crawl toward the thing Osric is focused on. As I get closer, I see Nate's lifeless body wrapped in one of Osric's tentacles. No! My baby is dead! Osric continues to give him CPR, and I scratch at him, trying to get to my baby. Osric pushes me away with the tentacles he isn't using for CPR and continues to work. Nate looks like a tiny limp thing while wrapped in the tentacles. He doesn't even look real.

Nate coughs. Osric pulls him to his chest and says, "Oh, thank God." He looks to the sky and lets water pelt him in the face. He weeps loudly and unabashedly. He notices me struggling to get to Nate and moves me close to his chest with the tentacle wrapped around me. Kate appears from the other side of Osric, wrapped in a smaller tentacle. He pulls us all to his chest and covers us all together. Tentacles group above and around us, creating a barrier against the rain. I wail as loud as the babies. Osric brings his arms around the three of us, and we all sob.

"You saved us. You saved him! Thank you. Thank you," I bawl.

Osric moves us all toward the back of the boat—toward the door flap that leads below deck. His movement is smooth; it feels like we are floating and gliding as he moves. When we are close to the door, Al and Auggie slam it open. Al reaches his arm toward us and yells, "Oh my God, Astrid. Come,

come inside." He pulls me from Osric's embrace and ushers me below deck. I turn to see Osric still at the opening of the hatch. He's slowly lowering the babies into Auggie's arms while bracing himself against the frame.

We gradually make our way to an empty storage room below deck, slamming against the walls as the boat rocks. Gideon and Cordelia are already in the room in a crouched position on the floor and hugging each other when we open the door. Their faces turn from fear and sadness to elation, and they stumble and crawl toward us. We shuffle into the room trying to reach each other. Osric is in the back, and when he enters the room, I notice he isn't having any trouble standing. He's using his many tentacles and their suckers to hold himself to the ground and walls.

The rest of us stumble and fall, and Auggie almost spills over with the babies in hand. Osric quickly reaches out his tentacles and steadies Auggie. Tentacles slither into the room, wrapping around us and making little pop sounds as they lift from the walls and floor. He holds us all together in a tight embrace. We all stand now with no issue, thanks to Osric's stability, and we hug and kiss each other in relief.

All seven of us sob uncontrollably. The babies and I receive so many kisses from so many mouths all over our faces it's hard to tell where they are coming from. Everyone, even the babies, calm before I do. My pills have been lost to the water. Not that it matters, I've probably already taken the maximum recommended dose. But I wish I had more right now. I continue to sob for the next hour until we all pass out in a giant people (and monster) pile of exhaustion.

I wake to find myself back in my bed in my room. The windows have been boarded up. My babies!? I frantically search around me in the bed for them, "BABIES!? BABIES!?" I scream. Al runs in with them both in-arm.

"It's okay. It's okay. They're here. They were just having breakfast," he says, a bit out of breath. They outstretch their little arms and reach for me. I rush to them and embrace all three of them. They both have what looks like smashed peas all over their face. They rub it in my hair, and I don't care.

"I think maybe you took too many of those pills. You've been out for two days." Al says. I fawn over my babies and nuzzle their little noses. I kiss their tiny heads and thank God they are alive. I hold my head between theirs. I breathe them in and start to cry. If it hadn't been for Osric, they'd be lost to me. I'd be dead. They'd be dead. We'd be at the bottom of the fucking ocean right now—one of my biggest fears realized.

"Where is Osric?" I ask calmly.

"He's on deck, helping with repairs," Al responds.

"Please bring him to me. I need to speak to him," I say solemnly as I return the babies to him.

Al looks at me curiously, unsure if he should do as I ask. "Okay," he says cautiously and exits the room.

I pace the room back and forth as I wait for Osric to enter the room. I bite my nails. What am I going to say? What can I say? I need to thank him. I need to apologize.

He opens the door and warily peeks in. He clears his throat and says, "You asked for me?"

"Yes, come in," I say.

He hesitantly enters and gingerly shuts the door. I seem to make him nervous. I guess I did almost murder him. He postures and pretends not to be scared, and stands up straight. "What's up?" he says, lacing his hands in front of his stomach, where his tentacles attach to his body.

I rush toward him silently. He flinches making his back slam against the door. The look on his face betrays fear. I'm sure he thinks I am going to rip out his throat.

I jump on him and kiss him so hard I almost stun myself on impact. I wrap my legs around his chest and my arms hard around his head. I claw my way up him, trying to keep myself up and engulf him with my entire body. I press my tongue in his mouth and bite at his lip.

"Oh," he says, now cradling me with his tentacles. "Well, you're welcome, missy."

"FUCK ME!" I demand.

"As you wish," he says and rips my clothes from my body with his various tentacles with a single movement. They lie in pieces on the floor. Auggie's going to be pissed. He liked this dress. I probably should stop wearing nice things. I get ravished too frequently.

He buries his face between my breasts, and I feel something slimy flick at the opening of my vagina. I look down, and he is smiling back at me menacingly. "If it gets to be too much, just say, 'calamari'," he winks. Har har. Very funny. The tentacle enters me with a sharp, piercing pleasure.

The tentacle wiggles and worms inside me. I convulse as it hits locations within me that have never been touched before—in places I didn't think were possible. He removes it from my vagina, slick with my white cream. Damn, he must have scooped it all out.

He replaces the tentacle with another, larger tentacle. I gasp, and it digs its way into me. It pulsates within my vaginal canal. Expanding and collapsing and flicking its tip inside me.

He tickles my anus with the wet tentacle he pulled from within me. I bite his lip, and he gently plunges the sopping tentacle inside my ass. HOLY SHIT, this feels good. The tentacle is wet enough that it slides in with minimal pushback.

He pulls me away from his body and holds me in the air. He doesn't touch me with his hands. He wraps me in more tentacles than I can count and watches himself penetrate me and stroke me. I grab at the one in my crotch, needing something to hold on to. Every part of my body is being touched with pulsating, slimy flesh.

He lowers me slowly, turning me so that I am almost horizontal, lying down, but in the air. My head points directly at his belly, and I look up at him. His tentacles open up like a curtain revealing his penis. He presents it to me like a prize. He folds his arms behind his head and leans against the door. He grins at me with all his teeth. I know that look.

I lean forward and grab this cock eagerly. I shove it in my mouth, taking it all in. There are so many tentacles on my body I can't tell where they are coming from. I don't care. This is pure pleasure.

Suddenly, I feel something sucking at my clit. I reach down to feel a tentacle press again me, fully covering my front. Is he using a sucker? I frantically grab for something to hold on to so I can press it hard against me. I begin to choke a bit—I'm getting distracted by my own pleasure. "Calamari?" He asks.

"Don't you dare fucking stop!" I bark. He laughs at me and brings me back up to his head. He sucks on one nipple with his mouth and sucks on the other with a tentacle. I scream. I literally scream in pleasure as I come and convulse wildly, unable to tell where to reach, my arms flailing uncontrollably.

He removes the tentacle from my vagina and easily slips me onto his dick. He kisses me on the mouth and moves me up and down vigorously, still sucking on my clit with a tentacle.

I am so exhausted. I can barely move, but…I feel a climax coming again. "Oh fuck" I say. He pushes deep inside me, filling me up, and I bite his lip as I come, again. I can taste the metallic twinge of his blood. He doesn't stop sucking with his tentacles immediately, but I am fully spent. "Calamari," I whisper as I begin to fall asleep.

He slowly and gently removes his suckers and tentacles from within me. He now cradles me within them and places me on the bed. He curls up beside me, and I notice his tentacles start to recede. He lays on his back, dick limp and wet, arms and legs spread wide, breathing heavily. He chuckles, "Looks like I was next, sweet thing."

"Shut up, you stupid squid," I say breathlessly as we fall asleep in each other's arms.

27

The rest of the voyage is uneventful. Well, if you call spending three weeks having some of the best sex of my life uneventful. Everyone was happy, but not surprised, to see Osric stroll onto the deck with two human legs. "Welcome to the family, brother!" Al said, clapping him on the back.

I may have bitten off more than I could chew with this one. Osric is knocking on my door so frequently that you'd think I had forgotten to take my potion. With him coming over every day and the others also stopping by, I'm darn near exhausted. We'll have to get a fuck calendar or something because this is getting to be a bit much for me.

The shore of Laila is in view, and I dare to lean against the railing and admire the scenery. I can use Osric's power at will now and make some little suckers at the bottoms of my feet to hold myself in place. Having all these monster powers coursing through my veins is giving me the confidence I need to face my greatest fears. The view is beautiful. I practice blooming flowers in my hand and letting them catch in the wind.

Osric saunters up next to me and places a hand on my backside. He looks at me with a raised eyebrow, and I say, "Not now. I'm exhausted."

"Fair enough," he says as he slides in behind me. He hugs me to himself and places his chin on my head. We both chuckle, and I turn to face him with my back against the railing. I wrap my arms around him, hands folded, resting on his ass.

"Laila isn't exactly a kind place to women. If anyone gives you trouble, we all have your back … even though," he rubs his hands at his throat, "you probably don't need it." He smirks.

I look at his throat. I don't see any marks where I punctured his skin the night we met. It's been three weeks, but I assumed it would have left a mark. He must heal quickly. He lifts his chin so I can see his neck clearly. I caress the area where I punctured him with my finger, and his penis throbs against me. I don't even feel a mark. I guess I didn't hurt him as badly as I thought I had. "Sorry about that," I say.

"I deserved it."

"Yeah, you did."

We both laugh then kiss—arms wrapped around the smalls of each other's backs.

"Oy, squid! Astrid!" Cordelia calls down, "Captain says we should start preparing to disembark."

- - - -`♥´- - - -

I feel silly for having previously banned Osric from our group because I don't know how we would navigate this place without him. He knew exactly where to land and exactly where to go. We dock at a port town a few miles from the military encampment that Florian and Lysander are supposedly at. The plan is for me, Osric, and Al to find them while Gideon, Cordelia, and Auggie stay behind with the babies. We're all terribly excited to be on land again, except for Osric, he enjoyed being on the water.

As we're walking down the pier, Cordelia rushes in front of the rest of us to a patch of dirt ashore. She leaps to the ground and sinks her hands into the earth while laughing maniacally. I walk up to her and look down at her hands. She exclaims, "Oh, God, I missed the ground and soil! Funny. Before the curse, I wouldn't be caught dead sticking my hands in the dirt. Now I crave it like food or sex." She grabs at her breast absentmindedly and grinds her crotch against her heels. What the hell is she doing? Is she masturbating in the dirt?

All of a sudden, I understand what she means. When I smell the dirt, I get a feeling of emptiness inside me. The feeling isn't concentrated in one place like my stomach or loins. It's everywhere. It's in my veins. I sit down next to her and softly place my hand on the ground submerging it ever so slightly into the dirt. The cold earth against my hands sends a wave of pleasure through my whole body. I guess now I'm a dirt lover, too. I stroke the dirt probing my hands into the ground. The feeling of it filling the spaces between my fingers brings me a pleasure I have never felt before. I want to fill all my spaces with it. My other hand instinctively shoots up to my nipple and pinches it through my top as I grind against my arm, which is shoved into the dirt.

Roots grow from my fingers and penetrate deep into the dirt. I feel the soil shift and move around my roots as it accepts me into it. I think I kind of have an idea of what it must be like for a man to bury his dick deep into something now.

I look at Cordelia and am overcome with lust. My whole body has never been so aroused. Small flowers sprout around our torsos as we look at each other like wolves, ready to pounce on prey. We grind against the dirt and salivate. I want to push her over and sit on her face. I want to fuck her face so hard that I push her and myself deeper and deeper into the dirt until we are buried in it—until it fills our lungs, and we suffocate in pleasure.

I lean toward her to do just that, when I feel a soft hand on my shoulder hold me back. I look behind me to see Gideon looking at me, his face wrought with concern. "Astrid! Cordelia!" he says in a hushed yell.

I am snapped out of my intoxicating trance. I realize that there are quite a few people here, and we are kind of making a scene: two ladies drooling over each other while sprouting tiny flowers about to fuck each other's brains out in the dirt.

We both stand abruptly and brush ourselves and each other off. We try to compose ourselves, but definitely linger longer than we probably should in public on genitals and breasts when we brush.

"Damn, Giddy! Why'd you stop them? That was about to get super fucking hot!" Osric laughs. He has this way of saying something that sounds like he's mad, but he's obviously not. This time I'm not entirely sure if he is or isn't angry.

"Because we don't need to get arrested in this town for public indecency," Gideon hisses in reply. "You told me how they treat women here. They definitely don't need to be catching so much attention."

"What the fuck was that, anyway?" Osric asks me.

"I'm … not sure," I say bashfully. I'm surprisingly ashamed. I am all for sexual freedom and empowerment, but I really lost complete control of myself for a minute there. I guess I'm not just a damn dirty perv anymore. Now I'm a damn dirty dirt perv.

"It's what I like to call 'dirt lust,'" Cordelia pants while brushing dirt off my ass. My ass is clean, Cordelia, but keep doing it. "Now that we've had some dirt, we'll be back to normal soon. I've never experienced it this bad before. It's been so long since we've been on land." I really want to grab Cordelia's hand, a pile of dirt, return to my room, and finish what we started, but I know we have things to do. I picture the two of us mud wrestling, and a burst of arousal drips down my legs. Yeah, I don't know how I will swing it, but we will definitely be mud wrestling one day.

"Well, now that you're done fucking the dirt, maybe we should head out?" Osric chuckles. "While I definitely wouldn't mind watching some more of that, Gideon's right. Maybe now's not the time."

I look at the others, and the blush on their faces tells me they wouldn't mind watching more of it, either. Gideon, Al, and Auggie stand there like three young boys trying to hide their erections. Osric doesn't bother hiding his. I wonder if the public indecency laws here have a problem with cocky dudes proudly displaying their erections.

Al and Auggie are holding the twins and the babies reach toward the ground, obviously wanting to play in the dirt, too. Now I feel horrible. I can't be a damn dirty dirt perv in front of them. I approach them, pet their heads, and kiss them. "Sorry, sweets. You can't play in the dirt right now. Maybe later. But … probably not with Cordie and me." I glance back at Cordelia, and her back stiffens in embarrassment as a deep pink blush covers her face. Her face almost matches her hair as she stands there, holding her breath, unsure what to say. I wink and give her a half smile. At this, she exhales deeply and doubles over with laughter.

"Yeah, probably not with us, little ones," she belts out between chortles.

At this, we decide it is time to part ways. Gideon, Cordelia, and Auggie take the babies into town with them to do some shopping and stretch their legs. Gideon is excited to see what kind of books they have. Auggie is excited to scope out the fashion. Cordelia is excited about both. I kiss everyone goodbye, giving the babies each an extra kiss. When I look back to see them watching me leave and waving, my eyes tear up with love. I am so lucky to have such a fantastic family.

Al, Osric, and I find a place to buy some horses and head out on the north road. The trip doesn't seem to take too long. Being on a horse rather than being dragged by them in a wagon makes the journey faster. If not actually faster, at least more interesting. Plus, Osric tells us a bunch of raunchy stories to entertain us. They sometimes make Al a bit uncomfortable and make me grind hard against my saddle. I'm still a little riled up from not finishing in the dirt.

"Osric, how exactly did you, Florian, and Lysander end up here?" I ask.

"As you know, Laila and Laerean are on the brink of war. We figured, even though we don't agree with the king of Laila's views, joining his army would be our best bet at being able to kill Thadius," Osric replies. I remember Thad telling me that Laerean and Laila relations were strained, but I thought they were in peace meetings.

"Oh, Thad said the king of Laila came to our wedding," I say aloud.

"Yeah, Thadius has been planning to take over Laila. It's a much smaller country, but very rich in spices and jewels. King Dorius, the king of Laila was trying to convince Thadius to marry his daughter to stop war … but that didn't happen," Osric trails off probably aware I will start spiraling and blaming myself for the war.

"Oh," I say and look at the ground. Would this world have been better off if I had not suddenly appeared in it?

"Hey, sweets! Don't go doing that thing where you blame yourself for the actions of that shithead. I've known him my whole life. That fucker was going to marry the princess and then still go to war. I'd bet your cute little ass on that." Osric moves his horse near mine and reaches a tentacle out to pet my head. I look back to him and smile trying to reassure him I am okay, but I guess I'm not convincing.

"Hey, stop moping. Do you need me to cheer you up?" the tentacle grows and wiggles its way to the tops of my legs.

I smile bigger this time and say as sweetly and pathetically as possible that I do, in fact, need him to cheer me up after all. "Maybe," I say and pout my lip out as far as it will go.

Al laughs and rides ahead of us while Osric sucks at my clit with a little tentacle.

"Wait!" I say before I can come, "Let's stop so I can get in the dirt!" Oh, shit this is going to be awesome.

We reach the encampment, and a guard stops us. We ask to see Florian and Lysander, but he refuses to let us proceed.

"Come on, Strandor! You know me! I'm just here to see my friends," Osric pleads.

"I do not know you, sir," Strandor retorts. He looks at Osric with a face that says, "How dare you to say that I know you." Pure disgust.

"Oh, yeah," Osric says. He transforms a part of his body into a tentacle. "Recognize me now?"

"Osric!? Where have you been?" They shake hands in that masculine way two men who want to hug but don't want to look weak tend to do. "Now that I know who you are, I still can't let you in. The captain is pissed." He laughs.

"Oh, he hasn't forgotten about that, has he?"

"Of course not! You fucked his wife, his sister, and his dog!"

"I DID NOT FUCK HIS DOG!"

"Well, that's what he's telling everyone."

"Shit," Osric says, looking back at us and kicking the dirt under his feet. The smell of the dirt excites me a bit. I hope this will not be something I have to deal with for the rest of my life. "Well, what about these two? Can you let them in?" Osric says as he points a thumb at us.

"Who are they?"

"If I say they're Florian's wife and brother, will you let them in?" Osric asks with a smirk.

The guard contemplates this request for a few moments while rocking on his heels. He obviously wants to help out Osric but it's clear he is not supposed to. A flash of an idea crosses his face and he says, "How about I just send for Florian and Lysander?"

"My man. I knew you were a good guy, Strandor. I promise I won't fuck your wife or your sister!" Osric grabs his hand and repeatedly pumps it up and down while holding onto his elbow. Strandor looks like he may shake right out of his boots from this exchange and can barely keep his balance.

"What about my dog?" Strandor asks while chucking.

"Now, that I can't promise," Osric says with that loud booming laugh voice he seems to always talk in. They howl in laughter, bending at the waist. I make a retching noise and roll my eyes at them. Boys are weird.

- - - -`♥´- - - -

Florian and Lysander are easy to spot as they walk toward us. They are both very large and very not human. They're a sight to behold. Florian is a furry's wet dream. He's a bipedal wolf with the build of an Olympian God. He wears no shirt, just some trousers that look to be military-issued. His fur is snow white and glistens in the sun almost blindingly. As he walks, the muscles in his lower abdomen expand and contract—their definition not compromised by a body fully covered in fur.

Lysander, in contrast, has not a single strand of hair on his body. He is covered in green scales with a golden sheen. He is dressed similarly, but his pants are slightly tighter. As he walks, I can see a large mass at the front of his pants, pushing the fabric to its limits as it stretches and sways with his movement. That's right! He had two dicks. I remember the shapes of his and Florian's cocks when they approached me in the woods. My eyes widen in lust at the memory paired with the current eye feast.

As I watch their large bodies saunter toward me, I catch myself fantasizing about different sexual positions they can put me in. I envision rubbing my hands over their bodies and relishing in the sensations brought forth by the different textures of their skin. I imagine the soft caress of Florian's fur between my legs and the slick coldness of Lysander's scales against my lips. It takes all my willpower not to jam my hands down up my skirts as I picture them both having their way with me simultaneously. Have I really just gotten so used to the idea of fucking monsters that I have literally no hesitation in my fantasies?

When they spot us, they quicken their step and rush toward us. I've never seen a wolf and a lizard smile before, but now I have. Light flashes on their fangs as their grins expose them for us to see. Their smiles are terrifying and menacing and weirdly erotic. I want them to rake their teeth over my body as I tremble at the thought of them ripping my flesh from my bones. Chill the fuck out, Astrid. How are you still so horny after what Osric did to you less than an hour ago?

The four men meet in a loud thump as they come together in a large group hug embrace. I'm not sure, but Florian may be crying. Al definitely is. I knew they were all friends, but I didn't realize just how close all these men were to each other. After they spend time catching up, Lysander looks at us and says in a cool, calm voice, "I know you lot didn't come here just to catch up. To what purpose did you come?"

"We hoped you could help us kill Thadius," I say firmly. I decided there was no reason to beat around the bush and figured I should just get to the point.

Their smiles fade and they stiffen in unison. They look at each other and back at me. "Listen, we want him dead more than anyone, but we're not strong enough. He's overpowered us multiple times. We can't keep trying," Lysander says.

"But we're stronger now," Al says. "When the curse lifts, your powers increase. Also, Astrid has absorbed all our powers. She's super powerful." He places his hand on my back and grins at me like the proud boyfriend he is.

"I'm not convinced it will be enough," Lysander says. I notice Florian doesn't participate in the conversation. He just sits silently, listening while a low hum that may be a growl builds up in his belly.

"Listen, lads," Osric says. "She … almost made me piss my pants when she showed me a fraction of her power, and that was before I gave her some of mine." He smirks at me. I blush a bit. "My power—I can control it at will and use it when I like. It's increased tenfold. I can lift the anchor of our ship, for fuck's sake! I couldn't do that before!" Osric says.

"Sounds like you don't need us, then," says Lysander dismissively. Florian lets out a little snort. I don't know what that's supposed to mean, but I think maybe he's agreeing with Lysander. Lysander leans back and folds his arms.

"Maybe we don't," I say. What's with this guy? Isn't he supposed to be some strong, fearless warrior? Why's he pussing out? I'm not in the mood to play games with him and really don't feel like trying to convince them. I begin to rise and leave. I'm not sure why I'm so annoyed, but I am.

Osric stops me by grabbing my hand and gently pulling me back down, "Listen, brothers. We need you. We can't fight without you. Don't you want to be there when we take the life from his body? Don't you want to …" he pauses and chokes up, "avenge Serena?" Florian lets out a whimper like a dog whining for his master. It's quiet and he stifles it, but I hear it. He glances up to see if I heard and back down to the ground quickly, when he realizes I did. Lysander shifts in his seat. All of these monsters can't hear her name without a visual reaction. I even see Al and Osric shift uncomfortably.

Osric takes a moment to compose himself then continues, "I don't know if we can defeat him this time. It might end like the others. It might end with us all lying dead on the ground, cut in half by those fucking pincers. But I'd rather die trying than live with this feeling any longer. Please, come with us." I've never heard Osric be so sincere before. He's always joking and crass. I suppose he was pretty sincere when he saved Nate.

Florian stands silently and looks Osric in the eyes, "I'll come with you," he says stoically with a voice dripping with masculinity.

Lysander stares at his friend in disbelief. "Fine," he concedes and hangs his head. He looks to Florian and says, "You realize this will make us war deserters, right?" Florian nods silently and Lysander just shakes his head baffled at what his friends seem to be getting him into.

Lysander turns to me and says, "I hope you're as strong as they say."

Osric lights up and shifts back to his usual happy, boisterous self. They all hug and cry.

It looks like I've got my full party.

28

We return to the port city with Florian and Lysander in tow. The trip back to town is even more raucous than the trip out. On top of Osric's raunchy stories, Lysander peppers in war stories. They are both getting me extremely hot as I picture them fucking and fighting in various states of undress.

The arrival of Florian and Lysander results in the necessity to celebrate—we have our complete monster-slaying party, after all. Osric buys barrels of spirits, and Al buys enough meat and bread to have a feast. We make it back to the ship before the others and settle Lysander and Florian into their quarters.

When Gideon, Auggie, and Cordie return, we, and the crew, are already well on our way to being seriously drunk. An eruption of laughter emits from our ship as all these old friends hug, catch up, and drink. The babies are wide awake and want to party, too. Captain Cornelius is not much for partying and retires to his cabin. He offers to watch the babies. I thank him profusely.

We dance and sing and rejoice. When the subject of what is to come next is breached, we silence the question and say, "That is a problem for tomorrow!" The trip from Laila to Laerean will be long, and we will have more than enough time to plan and scheme.

Florian and Lysander dance together, and I am surprised by their moves. They're quite good. The movement and gyrations of their pelvises are enticing, and I consider taking a sip of my antidote to see their cocks swell in their pants. I want to see Lysander's two cocks rip his pants in two. I think better of it and dance. Al and Auggie dance with me while Cordelia and Gideon play cards. Osric plays the wallflower, leaning against the edge of the boat, watching the party and sipping his mead.

I dance and dance and look back and forth between Al and Auggie. They are so handsome. I lean in and kiss Auggie deeply. Then Al. Osric looks toward us and raises an eyebrow. He holds his cup in the air to cheer us.

Watching Florian and Lysander's muscular, lean bodies has gotten me quite hot and bothered, so when Al and Auggie kiss me, I cannot stop myself from grabbing their hands and running them to my chambers.

I almost push them into the room. I slam the door and lean against it. I look at them ravenously. They look at each other as if to ask, "We doing this?" They both nod, smile, and walk toward me while removing their shirts. I've been waiting for this!

They kiss my neck and grab at opposite breasts. I moan in delight. Al gets to his knees and slips his tongue between my lips, flicking it teasingly at my clit. Auggie kisses me on the mouth, tongue flicking almost in unison to the beat of Al. I don't know what to do with my hands. They're pressed hard against the door as I push my pelvis forward onto Al's face.

I reach down with my left hand and grab Al's hair, not hard, just enough to get ahold of him. His hair is so soft. I reach down with my right hand and pump away at Auggie's cock. I like doing it from this angle because it allows me to pull at it. It's much easier on my wrist, which still flairs up from breaking during my escape.

I'm about to come but don't want to. I want these men inside me when I come. I pull Al's face from my crotch by the hair. I push Auggie back with a gentle hand to the abdomen.

"Lay on the floor," I tell Al, and he eagerly sits back and lays down. I walk over toward him and slide down on his cock. I place my hands on his belly and moan, head pushed back. I move in small circles and spread my labia so my clit can rub on his pelvis. Al grows feathers on the tips of his fingers. He gentle caresses my hips and breasts teasing me. When I'm not aroused and he does this, it tickles terribly, but when I'm on his dick it makes every sensation more intense.

Auggie stands there, unsure of what to do. I reach back and grab for him. He walks over to me, and I grab his dick, leading him to stand in front of me. He straddles over Al, and I place his dick in my mouth. I lick at it and kiss it. I cup his balls as I move my mouth up and down. This whole action is too distracting for me, and I am unable to really concentrate on what I'm doing on Al's cock below me.

I look up at Auggie and point to my dressing table. I say, "the blue bottle." The oils in there should work as a great lube.

He walks over to the table, and I lean down to kiss Al. He grunts and humps. He is always so restrained. He never wants to finish before me, and I can tell he's having a bit of a struggle. "You can cum in just a minute, sweetheart," I say and then kiss him hard on the mouth while I play with his nipple.

It takes Auggie a minute to understand what I'm getting at with the lube. He looks at me, confused. My mouth is still on Al's, and I lock eyes with Auggie. My eyes flick back to my ass. His eyes light up, and he understands the assignment. He pumps some of the oil into his hand and chuckles when he has too much. He rolls his dick in his hand, slathering it with the oil as he walks toward me. Fuck he looks hot. He gets behind me on his knees and scoots toward my ass. I stop gyrating on Al so that Auggie can get into position.

He rubs the tip of his dick around my anus, spreading the lube around the opening. He pushes gently at first but then harder. It takes a second before it pops right in and buries itself inside me. I scream in pleasure and a bit of pain and lean back to rest the back of my head on Auggies chest. He leans down and kisses me upside down. I put my hands up behind my head and grab his hair. He bites at my ear and neck.

I lean back down and put my hands beside Al's head. I need some leverage. Al grabs my breasts with both and kneads at them. I move in a deep, slow, methodical circular motion, rolling his cock inside me. Auggie doesn't thrust; he just lets my movement take over. I hear him moan, "Oh God," from behind me. Auggie bends forward, resting his chest lightly on my back. Auggie's hand turns to smoke and reaches into the crevice between me and Al, pressing against all the spots that Al and my anatomy aren't locking and completely enveloping the entire area.

Auggie pumps as my speed increases. He messes up my rhythm a bit as he finishes, stopping my movement so he can ejaculate deep inside me. He removes himself from me, and the feeling of removal is intense. I moan and then get back to work on Al. I circle and circle. Auggie remains behind me, keeping the pressure on my back and fluffy pleasure between my legs.

I moan, grunt, snort, and lose myself to the ecstasy of it all. I'm so close to climaxing, but I just can't. The only thing happening in the world right now is the bliss between my thighs. Al knows this look on my face, the look of me pushing hard to climax. He also knows this aggressive grunting thing I do when I am trying so hard just to fucking come.

"Come on, M'Lady. Come for me. I want to you to come." He reaches up and pinches my nipple and I'm not sure if that is what does it, but I finally reach orgasm. "That's it," Al says as he pumps harder into me. I collapse onto his chest, fucking exhausted. I don't know how he can perfectly time these things. He must have some magical control over his dick. Auggie stands removing his weight from my back and giving Al more room to lose himself. I close my eyes and let him finish inside me, inhaling his chest hair.

I'm falling asleep and barely able to stay awake. Auggie is on the other side of the room, wiping himself off when Al rolls me off of him. Al picks me up the way Thadius used to. Al places me on the bed, and I close my eyes. Al wipes me off with a cloth, cleaning me—what a sweet man.

They put the blankets over me and crawl into bed with me. Al is in front of me. Auggie is behind me. "I love you," Al whispers at my nose. "I love you," Auggie whispers in my ear. "I love you," I say to both of them as I fall into a deep sleep, rocked by the boat and soothed by their hearts beating in unison.

Now that we've partied our hearts out and fucked out brains out, we start to plan our attack on Thadius. I do not know my way around Thad's castle since I was in my tower the whole time, but the others do. Lysander and Florian can fill in my numerous blind spots of the castle and ground's layout that only members of the King and Queen's Guard would know. For example, they know of underground passages that lead to the king's chambers and his dungeon.

Lysander is a master strategist. Many nights, we all stay up, discussing how we will get to the king. One night Lysander sits silently as if lost in thought. A pained look stains his face and twists it with shame and fear. I place my hand on his and ask what has upset him. He swallows slowly and sighs wearily before answering. "I am ashamed to admit it, but I accompanied His Majesty on many of his … um … hunts." Lysander shudders as he remembers the horrors he witnessed. "He is most vulnerable during that time. He gets consumed with the task and does not notice things happening around him."

"But doesn't he have all of his guards with him?" I ask.

"Yes, but he usually runs off, leaving them behind." He pauses, contemplating his following words and bringing more definition to the plan stirring in his head. "They are not as strong as he is. We can … incapacitate them more easily than we can him when His Majesty has his full wits about him." He didn't seem like he wanted to say that last part. I am sure he doesn't want to kill the men who he once worked alongside.

"Will you be okay with murdering your friends that are just doing their job?" I ask, honestly not sure what his answer will be. We've spent the last few weeks together, but he hasn't revealed enough about himself for me to have a full grasp on his temperament or ambitions.

"My wish is that we will only incapacitate them, not kill them. But they are all fully prepared to die for His Majesty, as I was. They will feel honored by death." He folds his hands on the table and stares at them. His eyes glisten, and I wonder what he's thinking. I've already probed him about his feelings once tonight. I don't know if I can test him again. My mind whirls as I try to fathom his inner monologue. The way he talks about dying for the king makes me wonder how he was able to leave behind such deeply seeded, perhaps brainwashed, feelings.

After spending a few moments in silence, he seems to be more committed to the plan of finding Thadius while he is out hunting. He explains how we won't know precisely when Thad will go out hunting since his hunts happen sporadically. But Lysander suspects my absence has increased the frequency, so we shouldn't have to wait too long for one to occur.

"Should I have stayed? Because of me, all these women are dying," I say, tears rolling into my eyes. Everyone surrounds me and tries to comfort me. Lysander puts his hand on my knee, "It is easy for us to feel responsible when we are pawns in a villain's game. But you are not responsible for his actions. He is. You had to save yourself. Your babies. You saved all of my friends. You did the right thing." I don't know if I believe him. I have been gone for quite a long time. I picture the body count that has piled up because I left.

"I should have stayed. He's off murdering women because he's mad at me."

Florian doesn't speak much, but when he does, it is always to comfort and calm someone. "Don't blame yourself, lass," he says in that voice so deep it penetrates your diaphragm when you hear it. It has taken me a few weeks to convince him to stop calling me "Your Majesty" and I am happy in this moment he does not.

"He was going to find a reason to murder those women whether you left or not. He had a list … a list of women in the town. He would use it like a menu," Lysander says. I shudder. I knew Thadius was a monster, but every detail I learn of his life outside my little room in the tower still surprises me.

Everyone looks at Lysander with a "come on, man" look. Lysander seems to realize he perhaps has said too much. I am not a warrior, after all. I am just a scaredy cat queen.

"Please forgive me for putting that thought in your head. I did not mean to cause you distress or blame you for his heinous actions. I'm not—the best with words. I struggle to know how my words will affect others before I say them."

I look back at him and smile, wiping a tear from my eye. "It's alright. Thank you for being honest with me. I don't want to know these things, but I need to know them."

29

When we return to Sailoria, we find our inn-turned-home precisely as we left it. Al and Gideon immediately begin tidying up, and I put the babies down for a nap. Cordelia follows me to the room and puts her hand on my back. She seems sad, but I'm not sure why. I thought she'd be happy to be back in her room on solid ground. We were even able to find a nice place near the docks to have sex in the dirt while the men stood guard.

Cordelia leaves her hand on my back as she speaks to me in a somewhat hushed tone. "Gideon and I were talking, and we think he and I should … should stay here with the babies when you fight Thadius."

I look at her surprised. "What? I thought you both wanted to fight him."

"We do. We really do. But someone has to stay with the babies, and we're the weakest. We wouldn't be much help."

"That is not true. I've seen Gideon slice off a man's arm and then punch a hole through his chest. Your glamour magic could help disguise us. Your tree magic could hide us. I bet if you tried, you could rip a man in half with those branches."

"I'm not built for fighting. And I'm scared. I'm terrified of Thadius. When I saw what he did to Serena. I saw what he did to those women in the woods. I … I can't see it again. I won't recover this time."

I bring her in close for a hug, my cheek pressed against her breasts. "I understand. I won't make you go through that again." I feel like such a jerk for not noticing she felt this way sooner. I should have seen it when she sat quietly during our planning sessions. I haven't been the most attentive partner emotionally.

"Plus, who else is going to watch the babies? You weren't just planning on taking them with you. Were you?" I guess I kind of was. I make a face that seems to reveal my ineptitude because she laughs at me and says, "That's ridiculous. They'd give any stealth advantage away the moment they started crying. Or the moment they shit their pants." She looks at Kate, who is making her I am pooping my pants face while the room fills with a stench to end all stenches.

At that moment, Al walks in and looks at the two of us before asking, "Everything okay?" He can tell we are upset. Then the smell hits his face, and he grimaces. "God, no wonder you two look so sad. You're just going to leave her like that?" He scoops up Kate and takes her to the changing table. "Oh, my God, what have you done, little princess? This is atrocious," he says to Kate as he removes the diaper and wipes her down. Kate giggles at the faces of disgust Al makes. "You almost slayed me, Katie girl. You're a warrior princess of stinky poops!"

I go over to them and look at Kate. She is still giggling at all the faces Al makes as he pretends to be slayed by her. "Is daddy being silly, Katie? Did you kill daddy with your poopies?" I ask while making a scrunchie nose face.

"Daddy?" Al looks at me, confused. I have never called him that, and it's not really a term they say in this world. They say "father" or "papa" but not "dad" or "daddy."

"Well, yeah, you and Auggie and Gideon are their daddies. It's a term of endearment from my world that essentially means father. They don't need their biological father because they have their daddies," I say.

He smiles warmly. "I like that. Who's your daddy?" he says to Kate.

"Yeah, don't say that," I make a face and chuckle. "It … um … means something different when you say it like that."

Cordelia comes over, and we all hug.

We've prepared for our trip. We have supplies, weapons, and horses. Today's the day for us to leave, and I must say goodbye to the babies, Cordelia, and Gideon. The babies seem completely unphased by my impending departure, having no idea what's going on. Gideon wishes me luck and gives me a soft kiss while wrapping his arms around me. Cordelia, on the other hand, is a bit inconsolable.

We go to my room to chat and have some alone time. We leave the others in the living area—boots on, packed, and ready to go. They seem a bit impatient, but they abide. They, too, love Cordelia and don't like seeing her upset.

She's crying softly, sitting next to me on the bed. I dumbly assume this is about me being gone and say, "I won't be gone that long. I'll miss you, too, but we'll be back in a month—month and a half max."

She looks at me, annoyed. "I'll miss you, but that's not what this is about. I'm worried you won't come back. I'm worried he will kill you. Slice you in half the way he did Serena. You don't have the babies in your belly to protect you from his wrath anymore."

"Oh," I'm unsure what to say. "I can't promise that won't happen. I want to, but I can't. I wouldn't go if I didn't think we had a chance. Plus, I'm super strong," I say as I flex my non-existent muscle. She giggles at me, pushing my arm down.

"Hey, it's not that funny," I laugh. It is funny. I am monster-strong, but the rest of me is weak and soft.

"Please, just promise me you will come back," she pleads with her hands writhing in front of her.

"I will come back," I say and kiss her on the cheek, and finally consider that I may not come back. "Promise me you will care for Nate and Kate if I don't."

"You can't do that. You can't promise you will come back and then talk about *not* coming back."

"You're right. I promise. I will come back. I will kill Thadius for what he did to Serena and all those women." Images of the men who made him jealous an angry in the torture chamber flash through my head, "And for what he did to all those men. He will pay. I will take what he cares about most—himself. His power. His kingdom."

"If you get a chance, can you rip off his dick? I mean, don't make it a priority, but definitely keep it in mind," she says with a smirk.

I laugh and imagine the process of doing it. I picture pushing him to the ground and reaching into his pants while a look of pleasure washes over his face. I relish in the vision of pain and panic contorting his face as I pull too hard.

"And yes. Gideon and I will raise Nate and Kate. Of course, we will. We love them." She looks down at the floor, picturing her future without me.

I brush the hair out of her face. It sticks to the side, wet with tears. I kiss her tears and she giggles sadly. She places her hand on my thigh and says, "You look good in riding pants. You have such marvelous thighs." I don't really have marvelous thighs. I have large thighs, but if that's what she's into, I don't mind wrapping them around her head—for her pleasure, of course.

"Thanks," I blush and kiss her on the mouth.

I realize she got all pretty to say goodbye to me. She's wearing the red lipstick I always say goes so well with her hair. It has a sweet, waxy taste and rubs off on my lips. I pull back, and she giggles again; this time the giggle is flirtatious and not as sad. She says, "Sorry, hun, but that's not your color," and rubs at my lips with her thumb.

I playfully bite her thumb when it stops at the corner of my mouth. I stand to face her. She's much taller than me, so it's a weird dynamic we aren't used to—me being slightly above her and her having to be the one to look up to kiss.

She spreads her legs inviting me to come closer. I stand between them, pressing myself against her. I grab at her skirts and pull them up her thighs. We rub against each other, and I feel my pants getting wet from arousal. Fuck, I wish I wasn't wearing these pants. I place my hands on her thighs and rub at the swelling flesh of her labia with my thumbs. During breaths for air between kisses, she says, "What do you say? One time for the road?" Girl, you should know by now my answer is always yes.

"Yes," I exhale in delight and lust. We fall onto the bed, kissing and removing clothing until we are naked and humping at each other's legs pressed between our thighs.

She rolls over, bringing me with her, so I am on top of her. I slick her leg with my arousal, and she slicks mine. I kiss her nipples, making her moan in pleasure. She usually has a medium to high-pitched voice, but when she moans in pleasure, really moans, not just acting, she sounds like a woman who has smoked all her life. It is so hot, and I love that she has this easily identifiable trait that tells me I am doing a good job.

I move my body upward and straddle her chest. I place my butt on her boobs, and she smacks at my ass. I thrust my pelvis forward, and she eagerly buries her face in my crotch. She places a finger inside my vagina and pinkie in my anus, and I buck on her face. I put my hand on the headboard and am grinding away, about to come, when the door opens.

Osric walks in, saying, "Come on, girlie, I know you want to say goodbye, but we're all waiting." He's never been the knocking type. I think he does it in hopes he'll walk in on a scene just like this one. He takes in what he's witnessing and clears his throat. We both look like deer caught in headlights and scream, "Shut the door." He does, but he shuts it behind him, still in the room. He realizes his mistake and says, "Oh, sorry." And begins to leave.

"No, squid." Cordelia says, "Stay. I haven't gotten a chance to try out those new tentacles of yours that you're always bragging about."

I look down at her, momentarily confused. I thought she hated him. Her hands are wrapped around my thighs, and she gives me a wry smile. Her face is sopping wet from where I was just pressed.

"Don't get me wrong, I still don't like you," she says.

"Come on, Cordie, you used to tell me you loved me all the time. In that raspy voice of yours." I know precisely what voice he's referencing. He's talking about her horny rasp.

"You okay with that, hun? I'm fine keeping you all to myself right now, of course," she says. I nod and get off of her, moving to her side. Of course, I am down for this. If there were a way I could get all seven of them naked in this room right now, I'd do it. My mind wanders as I scheme ways to get the other five in here. I lay on my back and spread my legs. I instinctively press at my clit at the thought of all my lovers in here with me.

The sight of two women, spread eagle, beckoning him is all the encouragement Osric needed. He quickly removes his clothes and approaches the bed. "So, you want the tentacles, huh?" My attention snaps to him. I look down at Osric, and I want him to fuck me as soon as possible. I was so close when I was riding Cordie's face, and I'm a little annoyed he stopped me.

We both bite our lips and nod our heads at the exact moment his tentacles slink their way toward our lower bodies. He asks with that cocky voice of his, "One or two?"

"Two!" we say in unison as his slippery tentacles slide right into all of our holes. I love when he gets to me from both angles like this, and I am happy for Cordie to be able to experience it, too. It really does transcend a dick. It almost mimics some of the most expensive dildos and vibrators I have back home in my world. I've gossiped with her about it before. She's said on multiple occasions she wished she could try it, saying Osric was so good with his dick he must be good with those tentacles. She just had trouble finding a way to initiate any sexual contact with him—since all they ever do is bicker. Now she gets her chance. Osric stands at the foot of the bed, watching us writhe on his tentacles while he strokes his dick, licking his lips at us.

We close our eyes, and he says, "Look at me, please." We look right back at him.

He uses a free tentacle to grab my leg and pull me toward his cock. He removes the tentacle from my vagina and slides me onto his cock, leaning forward to bite at my nipples. I look back at Cordelia and reach for her. I want to be with her.

She removes the tentacles from inside her and crawls toward me. I pull her to me, so she sits right on my face. I close my eyes, and my nose buries into her pussy as she positions her clit on my lips. I don't even have to do anything. I just try to breathe as she gyrates in a circular motion on my face. I feel one of Osric's tentacles reach over my forehead and enter her anus. The only thing I regret about this position is I wish I could see what is happening.

Cordelia and Osric are face-to-face right now. And I hear her say, "Kiss me, you fucking squid."

I start to have trouble breathing, so I grab her ass and push it upward off my face. She seems disappointed. I think she was about to come, and I messed it up. But she turns to straddle me, puts her tits in my face and her ass in the air. "Eat me, squid."

"Yes, ma'am," he says. He slaps her ass firmly. It lets out a loud noise, but she doesn't cry out. She just leaps forward a bit in surprise and her tits hit me in the face. I hope he does it again.

She's bouncing her tits in my face while he eats her from behind, still railing me. We probably look like a dirty triangle to the outside world. Her tits bouncing in my face is the last piece of my coming puzzle. I wail loudly as his dick rolls inside me, with a sucker at my clit and a tentacle in my anus. When I finish, I pull away from him, unable to handle it much more.

He pulls out of me with a wet sloppy pop and then slides his dick into Cordelia. She wails. I reach up and rub her clit. Trying to lick her nipples as they quickly bounce back and forth, grazing my face. She comes, hard, screaming so loud I know all the other boys know what's up. A baby cries. I giggle. Oops. At this point, it seems like Osric is coming too, because he's jerking slightly, and all his tentacles stopped moving.

"Thanks, girls. I needed that," Osric says as he collapses to the floor. We all lie silent for quite a while, trying to catch our breath before rising.

We leave about an hour after our originally planned time. It takes us some time to clean ourselves up and redress. I feel guilty for leaving the boys waiting, but they don't seem to mind. I pictured them entertaining themselves by sucking each other off, a circle of boy on boy on boy on boy on boy. When we return to the room, Osric looks rather pleased with himself. Auggie rolls his eyes at him.

I hug the babies one last time before I hand them over to Gideon and Cordelia. I then embrace them in one big bear hug and tears well up in my eyes. I wish I could have also made love to Gideon before I left. "Come back to us. Come back to these babies," Gideon says as we embrace. Don't worry, kitty boy. I'll be back soon so I can have a turn at you. Why am I like this? I can't even have a nice goodbye without being a dam dirty perv.

30

The location Thadius hunts isn't far from the area where when they first found me, so we set that as our destination. It takes a few days, but not as long as it took Al and me to travel to Sailoria from there. Al and Auggie fly ahead and scout the way.

The longer we spend in the woods, the closer we get to our goal, the more anxious I get. Osric and Auggie both tried to initiate some sexy time with me, but I shut it down. I'm too scared. Al never does. He can sense my mood.

We've been at camp for three days, and the last two nights, Al and Auggie have come back with no news of seeing Thadius. They haven't gone out scouting yet tonight and we're all chatting around the fire, getting anxious and nervous. We hear the scream of a woman. We know what that means. We need to find her before Thadius does. He apparently lets them loose naked in the woods and then hunts them. Sometimes two at a time, but we only hear the screams of one.

Al and Auggie spring to action, but before they leave, I say, "WAIT. If you roll up on her looking like that, you'll be just as scary as Thadius. Bring me with you."

I climb onto Al's back, and he says, "You sure?"

"We have no time to debate this," I holler. I could probably fly myself, but I've been too scared to try, so I have no idea how to actually do it. Tonight's the night I face my fear.

He launches into the air, and it feels like my stomach stays on the ground while my body launches with him. His back pulses as his arms powerfully pump up and down. I'm terrified and excited. I'm stiff and wet in anticipation. My body can't seem to tell the difference between fear and arousal right now, especially with his back between my legs. Before I climax, we find the location of the screams and land nearby. She stumbles backward, naked.

I dismount Al and walk toward her slowly, hands out, in a calm-down motion. "It's okay. We are not here to hurt you. We are here to kill the monster chasing you." She looks at me wide-eyed and doesn't seem to trust me. I squat down, "We're not going to hurt you, I promise," I say and reach my hand out to her. She stretches toward me when suddenly she is lifted to the sky by a giant scorpion pincer around her waist. The claws close together, cutting her clean in half.

Her blood splashes on my face. I remain crouched, frozen in fear as Thadius' towers above me in his half-scorpion form. The metallic smell of blood enters my nose, followed by bile. I gag. My brain still hasn't processed what I saw but is processing the scent.

"BABE!" he says with a huge grin. His arms spread wide in a welcoming gesture. "Where have you been?" So casually. What is wrong with this fucker?

He notices my deflated belly and his personality changes. "Where is my child?" he growls. I am frozen in fear. "ANSWER ME!" His tone has shifted from the casual happy tone to absolutely terrifying.

Al lunges at him and is easily knocked aside by a large pincer. Al's head hits a tree, and he is knocked out. Fuck. Please don't die, Al.

I look back at Thadius. I am still frozen. I cannot move. My brain cannot think. It is still trying to handle the fact that a woman was cut in half in front of me. My cognition glitches at the sight of Al lying lifeless with blood splatted from his head.

"What did you do to your scent," Thad says while he leans toward me. His tone is calm again. "You don't smell as fuckable as you usually do." He sniffs again. "But I smell lots of men on you. What have you been up to, babe?" He winks at me with a smirk.

He motions over to Al. "Did he take you? Have you been with him this whole time?" his voice has shifted to annoyed, but not angry. I'm still too scared to speak when Auggie rushes in. He, too, is knocked away effortlessly.

He's hurled onto a tree spine first. His body wraps around the tree before he lands hard on the ground. His leg is bent backward, snapped in two. Please, Auggie, please be okay.

Fight, Astrid. Fight. Say something. Do something.

"You've been busy, babe." He says jovially. Why is he happy? He's swatted them away like flies, and they haven't even phased him.

He runs his claw down the side of my cheek and says sweetly, "I've missed you. I didn't realize how much I needed you. I've been crazy since you left. This woman, she's lying there, split in two because you left me."

He grabs me and lifts me off the ground. He pulls me close. He licks my neck, and I tremble.

"Oh, you like that? I know you're a horny little cunt," he says in almost a hiss. He pulls at my clothes and removes them with one motion of his claw. He dangles me completely naked in front of him and admires my body. His eyes widen, and he scoots his backside inward, revealing a HUGE hard dick. It's encased in a hard shell.

"Look how big it is, babe. I bet I can rip you in two with this." His grin widens to something maniacal. I begin to cry. He pulls me close against his chest, ready to bring me down on his dick. My body betrays me, and a tingle of excitement stirs within my loins as the blood rushes to my genitals. I am terrified and aroused. I hate myself for feeling even a fraction of desire for this prick.

"Please don't," I say as I weakly push on his chest. I won't let him have me.

"What, babe!? I thought you liked my big hard cock. You don't want it?" He whispers sensually in my ear, "Tell me you want it. Tell me you want me to fuck you until your eyes bleed." He hisses, and goosebumps spread across my body in fear and desire.

Tears stream down my face, and I turn away from him, unable to look at the horror between his legs. I am scared of what he will do—scared of what I might do if I lose myself to lust. He continues, "Let's make a deal.

Tell me where my son is, and I will let you go." I don't believe him. He won't let me go.

"I will never tell you where they are," I say so quietly it's almost a whisper.

"They?" He says, startled. Fuck. I'm such an idiot. He didn't know there were two. I didn't want him to know that, now if I escape him, he'll have his guards out looking for twins. But maybe I can keep him talking long enough for the others to get here—they're not nearly as fast as Al and Auggie. It will be some time until they arrive.

"Yes, I … I had twins. Nathaniel and Katherine.

"Katherine!? A girl," he grins.

"Yes," I whimper. His tight grip on me loosens, and his face softens. What is he thinking? He looks at the sky in a contemplative way. I study his face trying to guess his next move. He always insisted on a son, but something about the prospect of a daughter has shifted in him.

"Where are they? I want to see them. They deserve to live with me in the castle, not with you in the woods with these monsters. Are they close?" He looks around as if he may spot them.

"No, they are somewhere far from here, and you will *never* meet them." He slaps my face hard, but not as hard as he could. I know he could have knocked my head right off if he wanted to.

"Astrid. You WILL tell me where they are. You WILL come home with me and be my pet again." He brings his head close to my neck and inhales deeply. Why does this man still arouse me? I hate him with every fiber of my being, but his face at my neck hardens my nipples and causes the lips between my legs to pulsate. I moan in delight, unable to help myself.

"You've covered that scent of yours somehow, but it's still there," he says with a moan as he licks at my neck. I shudder in horror and delight.

He brings me close to him gently and presses my body against his, "I can tell you still want me. I can tell you want to come home with me back to your room. I've had it repaired and cleaned. It's back to the way it was before you left. Wouldn't you love to be back in that bed? In that bed with me? I promise I'll please you. Your leaving—it made me reflect on some things. I promise I'll make sure you come every time. I will be a better husband. I will be a great father. You could even leave the room, and I won't stop you."

"But you'll still be a murderer. You'll still murder women?" I say both as a statement and then a question. Would he really change for me? Could we really have a happily ever after?

"Well, I'll have to keep doing that, babe. I can't stop doing that! I will take it out on you and the children if I stop doing that. I can't do that! Astrid … I've realized … I love you. Please, come home. Please live with the children and me. We'll be happy. I promise." He's never told me he loves me. He's never spoken like this to me. Maybe he has changed. Maybe he can be better. Maybe I could be happy. But I'd have to be willfully ignorant of his extracurricular activities. I'd have to be complicit in his murder of all the women of the adjacent city. I can't do that. I will not do that.

At that moment, the others enter the clearing, "Astrid!" they yell.

"Look at you, My Queen. You've got your own little harem, haven't you?" He chuckles and looks almost proud of me. His tone changes to menacing as he says, "I will kill them all and bring you home."

"NO!" I scream and jam my thumb into his eye socket.

"YOU FUCKING CUNT!" he screams as he drops me to the ground and puts his hands to his face.

I scramble to my feet and stand tall, looking at him.

"We will kill you, Thadius! You do not deserve to be king," I say in the most intimidating tone I can muster. You can do this, Astrid, you don't have to be scared of him. You are strong.

"Deserve. Ha! It is my birthright. I deserve whatever I want. I own everyone and everything that steps on this land. I can do with it as I wish."

I growl, Gideon's claws extending from my hand. He's taken aback by this newfound skill of mine.

He quickly composes himself and rage fills his voice, "Ha, you're going to fight me? Fine. I don't need you and your brats. I can make more children. I'm going to enjoy watching those beautiful tits bounce in your blood."

His tail rushes toward me. He's going to impale me with it. At that moment, Florian jumps in the way, taking the strike. He yelps like a dog that had just been … well, stabbed in the chest.

"FLORIAN! No! Why would you do that?" I scream and drop down to him. My hands cover in his blood as I press at the gaping hole in him.

Thadius looks quite pleased with himself and laughs, "Ha, he tried the same thing with Serena and failed then, too."

I glare at him. He's smiling. He's ready to murder us all. He'll find my children and murder them just to spite my corpse. I look to Al and Auggie's lifeless bodies, transformed into their human forms, naked and bloody. Are they dead? I look at Florian on the ground before me, blood pooling on his chest. He coughs and blood spurts out of his mouth in a bubble.

Osric is rushing toward Al's body. Lysander is standing frozen at the edge of the clearing with a look of pure terror and uncertainty on his face. Why has he stopped? Is he scared? That can't be right. He's seen more war than any of us.

My heart screams in despair. I scream. The scream turns to a growl. I turn to smoke and flash toward Thadius' back. I mount him and wrap my legs around him. He doesn't know what happened. He doesn't understand how I got on top of him.

He tries to stab me with his tail, but wherever he stabs, I turn to smoke. My lower body turns to tentacles and I grab ahold of him hard, so he cannot buck me off. Branches with thorns tangle around his claws locking them in place. My face turns to a bird and I screech so loudly everyone covers their ears. I lunge at him, trying to peck out his eyes. I get one—the one I jammed my thumb into earlier. I wish I could have gotten the other one—effectively blinding him. I spit it to the ground. My face turns back and I smile at him, blood dripping from my mouth between my teeth. My hand grows claws long like blades and I shove it deep into the side of his neck.

He breaks his pincers from my branches, surprising me, and knocks me off of him. I land hard on the dirt. I slide across the ground. I wince in pain. He turns and runs, pressing one of his pincers against the socket that used to hold his eye. I try to get up, but I cannot. I'm in too much pain. I look at the sky above me. The same sky I saw the first night I was here and I pass out.

- - - -`♥´- - - -

I wake up groggy. My head is throbbing and my side stings.

I'm in the wagon—bleeding on a bed of silks. Next to me is Auggie. Next to him is Al. Both are breathing gently with their eyes closed. Oh, thank God. They're alive. Florian is on my other side, eyes wide open. "Florian, you're alive," I say and cup my hand around his snout. He winces in pain.

"Sorry I wasn't more help, lass" he says sadly.

"No, you were amazing. You saved me. You woke me to action."

"Happy to be of service," he chuckles lightly, winces, and then closes his eyes. I gently pet his head for a while and it seems to bring him some pleasure.

Osric is driving the wagon. Lysander trots next to him on a horse. Osric says, "You're awake. We're headed home. Fuck, I wish Gideon was here with us."

"We will not leave him next time," I say while stroking Florian's head.

"Next time? We just got our asses handed to us. I don't think there will be a next time," Osric says.

"No! I almost had him. He was scared. He ran away! I just need to get stronger. I need to train," I say.

I look down at Florian. My heart leaps for him.

"Whatever you say, girly," Osric sighs.

31

We return to the inn. There is no time for Cordelia and Gideon to express joy at our return because Al, Auggie, and Florian are all badly hurt. We are lucky we made it back without them dying. Osric and Lysander rode day and night without rest to get us home as quickly as possible. The poor horses were pushed to their limits and I'm shocked they haven't collapsed in exhaustion. I'm surprisingly just bruised and scraped. My most serious injury is a large scrape on my side from when I slid on the ground.

Al and Auggie have multiple broken bones, and Al has a concussion. Gideon says Al's lucky he didn't die from a brain bleed. Florian has a deep puncture wound to the stomach. They're all in their rooms, healing. I visit each daily and sit by their beds unable to sleep and worrying.

Al and Auggie can get out of bed after a few days, but Florian is still in a lot of pain. After a few days of his health deteriorating, I'm in the kitchen, preparing a snack, about to return to his side, when Gideon comes to me and says, "I don't know if Florian will be able to recover. The hole in him is quite large. I haven't been able to stop the bleeding." He clears his throat obviously afraid to say the next thing, "I don't know how he's held on this long."

"There must be something you can do!?" I yell.

He clears his throat again, "I don't think there is. I sent for my friends from the library with strong healing magic, but it will be days before they can arrive. He may be gone by then."

"No, no!" I plead.

Gideon looks down in shame and sadness. He's blaming himself for Florian's condition, I can tell. He perks up and makes the sound of a cat trilling. He does this whenever he has an idea. "Forgive me for suggesting this, but there—there may be something you can do."

I look confused. "Al told me how, before you cured his curse, he could not fly, his wing fully damaged, muscles severed. That got me thinking. When you cure our curse, do you cure us of other things, too? Then I recalled how I'd had cuts or bruises on my body, and they disappeared after we … made love. I think Al's arm had nothing to do with you curing the curse. I think it was about you. I think you can heal people—when you have sex with them."

Shit. Maybe I do. Cordelia had complained of neck pain, only for it to disappear after making love. We've joked that I can knock her bones back in place with my thighs, but maybe … I've bitten Osric's lip hard, made him bleed, and there's never a mark afterward. Al was getting a cold once, and I blew him. The cold never came to be.

"Now, I would never ask you to do something like that. Plus, we know you have to want to. You have to care for him for it to do anything for his curse. But who knows how your—um—sexual healing works." If this conversation weren't so grave, I'd laugh. I'll tell Gideon about the song later.

"I'm going to go talk to him," I say and return to Florian's room.

"Good morning, Your Majesty," Florian says. He's always so proper with me and really struggles to not call me Your Majesty—I have given up on trying to get him to stop. He was asleep when I left, so I'm happy to see he is awake.

"It's evening, Florian."

"Oh," he says wistfully, staring off into space.

"I have something I'd like to discuss with you."

He grunts as if to say, "What is it?"

"I spoke to Gideon, and he seems to think I have the power to heal—through my love." I'm not sure why I'm being coy about it.

"You mean the curse?"

"No—another thing. Yes, I can break the curse, but he thinks I can also cure wounds and ailments. I was wondering if—I could try. Try to heal you. Perform an experiment of sorts."

He laughs and coughs some blood.

"He told you I'm going to die, didn't he?"

"Yes," I say, grabbing his hand.

"I—I can't move. I'm in no condition to." He bashfully looks away from me. His puppy dog eyes look ashamed for some reason.

Still holding his hand, I place my other on his leg. There is a slight bounce as his penis reacts to my touch.

"You seem able," I say, eying the mound under the sheets that indicate his dick.

"I … I can't, My Queen. I cannot defile you in such a way. Not with this disgusting body. It is my job to give my life for my queen, and I am performing that duty. You do not have to take pity on me."

I look him in the eye. "I don't think you are disgusting. And I don't want you to die."

He says, "I will not lie. I have wanted to be with you since the moment I laid eyes on you. I lie awake at night, thinking of you. I dream of you. But, I … I don't want it to be like this. I don't want you to feel obligated. I want you to *want* me." What is with all these song lyrics today?

"Florian, I do want you," I say softly.

He chuckles and turns his head from me, obviously not believing me. He looks like a sad little puppy.

"I won't touch you if you don't want me to. But I want to touch you. I want you to touch me." I feel myself dripping down my leg.

He looks at me with tears, "Please, My Queen, do not lie to me. Do not play with my emotions like this."

I place my hand on his cheek and look longingly into his eyes. "How can I convince you?" I say and kiss the side of his snout. "I want this." I kiss the other side. "I want you." I kiss under his nose at the front of his snout. He doesn't kiss me back. When I pull back, he looks at me in pure terror. He cannot believe I had just kissed him. Fuck, I went too far. I was too eager.

"I'm—I'm sorry. I should not have without your permission," I say.

"You're—you're not disgusted by me?"

"No."

He places his hand on my face and gently lifts his body to try to meet me for a kiss. He stops short and winces in pain, making that sad dog whimper. Instead, I lay him down gently and kiss him. "Don't exert yourself. I can do everything."

He starts to cry, and I kiss the sides of his mouth, kiss his neck, kiss his fluffy ears—they tickle my nose. I'm still holding his hand, and I place it under my skirt for him to feel the wetness between my thighs. He seems extremely surprised and I say, "See, I want this." He slips his fingers inside me. That's a good boy.

I reach my hands under the blanket. He is naked but for bandages across his abdomen. I find his penis and stroke it. He bites his lip and moans and winces, making a sound a bit like a kicked puppy. "Am, am I hurting you?"

"No, no—this is good."

I move my hand up and down more quickly, and he moans, flicking at my clit with his thumb and pumping my pussy with his fingers. How does every man in this world know about a clitoris, but they're utterly ignorant of it in mine? They must have excellent sex ed here.

I push the blankets off him to see the bandage wrapped across his belly. I kiss gently at the area, careful not to put any pressure on it. I kiss the tip of his penis. I lick it like an ice cream cone and press my lips to it. I push down and cause it to part my lips. I place my lips on the side of it and move my mouth up and down. I cup his testicles and gently squeeze them with my hand while pressing the area where his taint is with my thumb. He's lying on his tail, but it's still wagging uncontrollably.

The bandage is high enough up his chest that I think I can get on top of him without hurting him.

"Can I get on top of you?" I ask worried it will hurt.

"Yes," he moans, "but—don't look at me." I think about how Osric always asks me to look at him, tentacles and all, and get a bit sad that Florian is so ashamed of his monster form. How sad this all must have been for him, living with this shame.

I carefully position myself so that my ass is facing him and bring myself down onto his dick. He yelps in delight and maybe a bit of pain. With one hand, I fondle his balls. With the other, I touch myself, pressing my hand hard against my clit.

He places his hands on my hips, and I roll around on top of him. His hands move up higher and higher. He sits up and grabs my breasts. Is he sitting up? Does that mean his stomach is healing? He kisses my neck. He plunges his tongue into my ear, and I can feel his hot breath. He moans in my ear and thrusts himself into me.

Suddenly, he grabs me by the waist and flips me around to all fours, positioning himself on top of me. He pumps quickly into me. He places his hand below my chest so that my nipples graze his hand as I move back and forth. His other hand is rubbing so astutely at my clit you'd think I was doing it myself. I turn to look at him, and I can see his tail wagging intently.

I hump back and forth against him and wonder if I'm hurting his stomach. He rests his chin on the back of my neck and breaths me in. He nibbles at my ear. His snout tickles.

I push my face into the pillow as I come. When I'm done, he removes himself from inside me and strokes his penis.

"You're done?" I ask. He doesn't want to come with me?

"I can't defile you with my semen, my queen."

"Fuck that. Yes, you can." I push my ass back, so I slip back onto his cock hard, and rock back and forth furiously. He cums inside me and lets out a quiet little howl. "Awooooo," he says softly into my ear.

He falls onto my back, and I can feel his body start to morph. His snout recedes against my ear. We fall to the bed and spoon. I'm little spoon. He's big spoon.

"Thank you, My Queen, you saved me," the man beside me says.

After we've had a moment to recover, Florian removes his bandage, and there is no longer a wound. We both stare at his waist in awe. My gaze easily moves from his waist to his face. I am dumbstruck. I thought I'd never see a more beautiful man than Thadius. I was wrong.

I stroke his belly where the wound was. I stroke his chest. I touch his face. "You—you are beautiful!" He has that same silver hair. His eyes are blue as steel. His jaw is chiseled. He blushes and looks away. He does not believe me. I understood his low self-image when he was a wolf, but now he's just being silly. No one in their right mind could ever consider this gorgeous slab of a man anything but.

We clean up a bit, and Florian is so revitalized he's ready to get up and conquer the world. I tell him he should probably wait in bed until Gideon checks on him, and he reluctantly returns. He still has that golden retriever energy, obeying my every command. I'm going to have fun with this one.

I get Gideon to come to the room, and he is flabbergasted. "I can find no problems with him."

Everyone is pleased to see Florian alive … and human! I explain the new power I've discovered, and everyone recounts times when they had been healed after having sex with me but hadn't thought anything of it.

Al perks up, "Oh, is this why the scar on my arm is almost completely gone?" He removes his shirt and shows everyone the nearly invisible scar where Thadius had almost severed his wing.

Florian lifts his shirt and says, "I have no scar at all" and points at the location where he had been impaled. Are they all going to take off their shirts now? Will I finally get my orgy?

Gideon, rubs his cheek and says, "Why would you have no scar but Al does? Maybe her power doesn't work as well on wounds already healed?" I can tell by the look in his eyes he is ready to run get his notebook and devise some experiments.

Al and Auggie saunter up to me, and both place their hands on the small of my back. Auggie says, "You know, this broken leg is quite a hassle." I look at them, and they are both smiling at me menacingly, jokingly. "Fine, come on. But can you bring out the smoke and feathers?" I say as I pull them both to my bedroom.

32

After everyone gets their turn being healed by me. I sit at the table with Lysander. I put my elbows on the table and lean my chin on my hands to look sideways at him. I have been so preoccupied with Florian's condition up to this point, I haven't spoken to Lysander at all since we returned.

"So, I guess we need another plan, huh?" I say.

"I guess so." He seems really down. I wonder if he's feeling left out of this massive fuck fest that is constantly going on around him.

"You, okay, Lyse?"

"I really thought you had him there. We were so close," he says.

"I think I need to train. Get stronger. Learn to control my powers. Then I think we should try again. Will you train me?"

He looks excited, "Yes, let's do it. We'll need a better place than here, though. The king will be looking for us in cities and there is no room in this inn to fight."

"The library?"

"I believe he'd look there, too. Didn't you say soldiers found you on the road between here and there? He probably has guards posted up the entire road."

"Yeah. Should we go back to Laila?"

"I don't think we need to go that far," he says.

We sit in silence for a long while.

"There is some abandoned land south of here. It's an old stronghold we used during the War of Absorption," he says.

"War of Absorption?"

"Yes, the last war of Laerean—the one that expanded the borders significantly. It's the war in which I got all my accolades."

"Oh, how far is it?"

"A couple weeks."

"Great!" We both look pleased with ourselves to have determined a plan.

"My Queen. I have something I'd like to discuss with you." He waits for me to respond.

"What is it, Lyse?"

"When you fought His Majesty. I just stood there and watched. I should have helped, but—I don't know if I can bring myself to hurt him. I protected him for so long, even when he performed the most atrocious acts. I don't think I can unlearn that."

"You fought him when you tried to protect me when we first met. You fought him when he tried to hurt Serena."

"I … I did not fight to wound, only stall. I … failed those women. I failed you. I failed Serena." He places his face in his hand and sobs silently.

I stand and hug him from behind, resting my chin on his head. "Lyse, you did not fail us. You did your best."

"I don't deserve to live. I am the monster I see in the mirror. I can never make it up to you. To them. To Serena." He sobs harder as her name passes his lips. This blatant display of emotion is a bit uncharacteristic of him. He must have been holding in this guilt for quite some time.

I bend down and take his face in my hands. His pupils are thin slits buried within golden irises. They are sparkling with tears. Dazzling. "If you want to make it up to us, you can do so by training me and teaching me how to kill him. We will avenge them. Together." I pull his head into my chest, and he reaches around to embrace me. He sobs deeply into my breasts.

We travel for two weeks south until we get to the fort Lyse described. Luckily the babies and everyone are in perfect spirits. I ask Gideon, "Hey, you notice how the twins never get sick?"

"Yeah," he says.

"I wonder if my magic works on them, too. Like, maybe it's not sex with me that heals you. Maybe it's just me loving you or something."

"It could be your breast milk."

"Oh, yeah, it could be that," I respond. I am still breastfeeding them, but only occasionally.

"Once all this is over, we'll have to perform some experiments to figure it out. I'm excited to try different things," Gideon says wryly. I push my shoulder into him and giggle. I am excited to experiment with him too. I'm going to experiment all over his adorable little face.

When we get to the fort, Lysander insists we immediately start training. Gideon assists by taking notes on different things I can do, feelings I had when I invoked my different powers, etc.

We find that even though my powers in battle have been purely driven by negative emotions, I can call them by recalling those emotions. Different emotions and memories can make different powers appear. Thinking of my lovers in a fond way brings their abilities to me in a form that is more sustainable than the ones I bring forth in a rage.

After two months of training, I can pull up any form I wish, even combinations of them. I also learn how to fight with a sword and some basic self-defense moves.

Lysander thinks I'm still not ready. Even though I am doing well with my powers, I need to be better with a sword. "I'm not going to be fighting him with a sword," I say one day to him, exhausted from training and trying to talk my way out of continuing.

Lyse replies, "True, but the guards will be fighting you with a sword. You need to defend against it. You need to learn how to fight to kill and fight to wound."

We spar all day, every day. My hands are blistered. My wrists are sore. I am left-handed and happy I broke my right wrist when I fell from that tower; otherwise, I don't know if I'd be able to hold this sword. It hurts so much at the end of each session that I can barely use my right hand. My sexual healing doesn't seem to work on me. I wish masturbating would heal my hands, but all it does is get me off and make my wrist sorer.

Lysander tells me I need to develop calluses on my hands to be a warrior. I don't have the heart to tell him I don't want to be a warrior. I am so exhausted from training I don't do much else. I can tell the others are feeling a bit neglected and missing sexy time, but I am too sore to initiate anything with them. That doesn't stop them from sneaking into my room at night and pleasing me, though. Cordelia has begun calling me her "pillow princess," as I tend to just lay around on a pile of pillows while she pleases me. I remind her I am, in fact, "a pillow queen."

However, I am not too sore to get extremely wet during my sparring sessions with Lysander. While training today, an icy rain begins to fall. Hard. I hoped the rain would get me a reprieve, but this dude is serious. He makes me spar with him in the covered barn instead.

I have not once been able to overpower him in the months we have been fighting, and I am starting to feel a bit disheartened. Damn, this dude is strong. Even when I conjure up some of my lover's strength, I still can't knock him down. The only time I can do it is if I use something like a tentacle or wings.

He knocks me to the ground, and I can feel the bruise on my ass get a deeper purple. I stay on the ground, defeated. "Get up," he says firmly. "Once more."

"I can't. I'll never defeat you. You're too strong, and I'm too tired." He grabs my arm and pulls me to a standing position. I slump.

"I'll tell you what. If you can knock me down, we'll call it a day. You can curl up next to the fire with some books with Gideon and Cordelia. I'll ask Al to make you some of those little cakes you love so much."

"Cupcakes!?" I say with excitement.

"Yes, cupcakes."

"Deal! I just have to knock you over?"

"Yes," he says and motions for me to come and get it.

I try a few times and am unsuccessful. A rage starts to boil up in me. I am furious with him. I want some fucking cupcakes. He swings his sword at me, and I rush him, shoulder to the chest, and knock him down as my sword deflects his. We crash to the ground together.

We lie together panting. I can feel his two dicks pulsing under his skirts, even through the padding he's wearing. I look at him.

"Gotcha!" I gloat.

"Got me." He smiles so wryly that I feel like I got tricked somehow. We lay there motionless for a minute, and the pressure of his dicks against me combined with the smell of the dirt sends me into a frenzy of desire.

I kiss him hard on the mouth. I have never seen a man (well, a lizard man) more surprised to be kissed in my life.

We claw and pull at each other's padding, trying to remove it as fast as we can, helping each other unbuckle and unstrap until we are in just our underclothes. His two dicks, side by side, are hard and very visible through his thin clothes.

"I … I only had one as a human." He says as he notices me staring at them.

"I assumed." The positioning is unfortunate on the two dicks. They'd be much better, one on top of the other. Oh, well, we'll figure it out. Maybe I'll stuff them both inside me at once. Would they fit?

We lunge toward each other in an embrace, and his erections press hard against my belly.

We skip the foreplay entirely. We've already done it with the fighting.

I lay on my back in the dirt and pull him toward me. Small roots extend from my back into the ground sending a pleasure through my veins. He places his left dick inside me and strokes the right with his hand. I wonder if there's a way he can put them both in me. I realize now they won't both fit inside my vagina. Maybe if I turn a bit.

I turn my body sideways, swinging my right leg over his head so that my anus is on the left side. "Put them both in me." He looks confused for a second and then understands. He removes himself from inside me and slips the one from my vagina, soaking wet with my juices, easily into my anus. At that exact moment, the right one slides its way into my eager vagina. He grabs my right leg and pulls it upward, thrusting against my two holes. I see stars with each thrust and hold myself in place with my roots. It's getting to be a bit much when he licks his palm and the inside of his fingers. He presses his moistened hand on my clitoris. Rubbing up and down and around vigorously and at a different speed than his thrusts.

I wonder if both dicks ejaculate at the same time. Yep. There it is. He cums in me, and I'm not there yet. He notices the slightly disappointed look on my face and just keeps going. What? He can keep going?

He smiles knowingly at me and keeps pushing and rubbing until I come loudly. When I'm done, I realize that I am covered in dirt and a complete mess.

Lysander laughs at me and brushes my hair down. "Your hair is standing straight up," he says, his voice softening.

As he pushes my hair down, he transforms into a human. "See? One dick." We both laugh.

I spend the next few weeks getting the hang of Lysanders powers and continuing to train with the sword. We have been training with less padding because every time I get a good hit on him, he has to fuck me after. Lysander is obviously aroused by pain. He calls me "My Queen" and likes it when I order him around and hit him a bit. In his human form, he can conjure up his second cock. On multiple occasions, we successfully get both cocks inside my vagina at once.

His human form is handsome in that extremely rugged and extremely dangerous way. You can tell his face is weathered by the violence he has seen and you can sense that he is not a man to be fucked with. Fucked, but not fucked with. I'm not sure how, but this tall, dark, scruffy, and brooding man is more menacing than the terrifying lizard. His strength and body mass are amplified in his lizard form, so he chooses to remain in it for most of our sparring sessions.

Today I still haven't gotten a good hit on him yet. I'm eager to do so because I am so horny and need a deep double dicking. But my eagerness has made me a bit sloppy in my fighting, and I've worn myself out from trying a bit too hard. I tell Lysander I need a moment to compose myself before the next round and we sit on a hay bale together. I am tempted to sit in his lap and grind on him now, but I know it won't work. He needs me to hurt him to get hard. I'll just have to be patient. I suppose instead of fucking him. I could just talk to him like a normal human being who sees people as people and not things to fuck.

"So, teach, how am I doing? Do you think I'm ready yet?" I ask as I pick at my nails.

"Almost. You're still fighting too much with your brain. You think too much before doing anything. I need you to react without thinking. It makes you easy to attack. You also need a bit more practice with my power." We learned that on my body, Lysander's scales make me nearly impenetrable to blades. Not impenetrable to dicks, of course. That would be a travesty.

We discuss Thadius' powers and how I could defend against them. Lysander hopes that if Thadius tries to stab me with his tail, the souped-up version of his lizard skin may stop me from being gored. We've been a bit too scared to stab me full stop to test it out.

"The tail is really the thing you should be most afraid of. His pincers are strong but slow. The tail is lightning quick. If he stabs you with that, he can poison you and incapacitate you."

I picture that tail. That fucking tail. How did he become so evil? I imagine him using that tail to paralyze women before having his way with them. My arousal for Lysander is replaced by rage at the thought of Thad. I think of that stupid half-smile of his. It boils inside me. It's an uncontrollable helpless rage. I stand up, hoping it will relieve some of my agitation.

Lysander looks at me and asks, "Ready to get back to it?" as I pace back and forth. He cocks his head sideways, trying to read me. He asks, "You okay?"

A rumbling growl vibrates my throat and chest. Maybe fighting will make me feel better. "Yeah, I'm fine. Let's do this." He grins, ready for me to beat and then fuck the shit out of him.

My rage has not subsided, and my hits are stronger and more determined. I keep seeing Thadius' stupid, sexy smirk flash in my head every time a jolt of pain travels through my body. Fuck. I hate him. I take my rage out on Lysander, and I can see the lust wash over his face as I hit harder and harder.

The side of Lysander's sword hits me in the same spot on my leg Thadius kicked me the night I found his dungeon. The feeling reverberates throughout my body as I am transported back in time. I freeze. Lysander moves in for another hit but stops when he sees I am no longer moving. I can see that night so clearly. I am almost reliving it. I watch Thadius transform in front of me as he screams at me, and this time I don't cower. I stand. I scream loudly and I feel myself getting taller, ready to fight him. My scream turns to a blood-curdling screech, and my skin feels like it is stretching and pulling. Something is tugging at my backside and my clothes rip off. What the fuck is going on. My mind returns to me and Lysander looks at me in horror. Why is he so small? I must have yelled very loudly because the others have come out to investigate.

"What was that noise?" I hear Gideon yell followed by a "Holy shit!" by Osric. I am calm, the blood in my veins is no longer boiling and I take in what happened. I am huge. My hands are clawed like a scorpion. I look behind me and I have a long scorpion tail.

What the fuck? I'm a scorpion? How did this happen? I've never been able to use Thadius' power before. Why can I now?

Lysander's face contorts from horror to excitement when he says, "I think you're ready. You can rest on the way there."

33

We return to Sailoria. Cordelia uses all her strength to disguise us all. We split into groups, careful not to have the twins together. There are guards everywhere with wanted posters, but they don't seem to notice us.

When we enter an inn, we decide that Gideon and Cordelia will stay with the babies again.

I begin vomiting, and everyone thinks I'm getting nervous. I laugh, "or I'm pregnant again." Everyone looks at each other with a start, and we know that I must be. You can't fuck like rabbits and not expect to make a bunch of baby rabbits.

I don't want to believe it, so Gideon gets the magic potion that Thad used on me last year. He and Cordelia assist me and I find that, yep, I'm pregnant. Fuck, not again.

"Do they have condoms in this world?"

"Huh?" Gideon asks.

"Never mind," I say dejectedly. Add condoms to the list of things I need to invent in this world.

"Whose baby is it?" Cordelia asks.

"I have no idea. It can be anyone's," I say, trying to do all the mental math.

"Well, it's not mine," Cordelia laughs.

We tell the others and everyone seems so excited—all congratulating each other.

"I don't know whose baby it is," I say.

"What do you mean?" Al asks.

"Like, who the father is," I respond.

"We're all the daddy!" Auggie says.

These boys are cute.

"Maybe we should wait until the baby is born to fight Thad," Gideon says. All the men seem to agree. I slam my hand on the table, my eyes alight with the fury of Lysander.

"NO! He dies NOW! This baby will be born in a castle." They do not fight me on it.

Auggie elbows Osric, "She gets sooo horny when she's pregnant. You think she's horny now. Just wait." Everyone giggles and looks excited. How does he know that? Only Al slept with me when I was pregnant. I guess Auggie was around those last few weeks.

Lysander looks disappointed and says, "I guess we'll have to cool it on the rough training."

"Well, I can still be rough with you, Lyse. You just can't be rough with me." He perks up in relief.

- - - -`♥´- - - -

We arrive in the City of Prailyra at nightfall and thick snow falls to the ground. I can't believe it's been a year since I left this city—since I left my plush prison. We waste no time searching for the secret entrance that leads to the king's chambers. There are no guards. That's weird. It's like he wants us to come in.

We are able to easily sneak through the corridors and find the door that leads to Thad's room. I tell the others to wait in the passage. If I call for them or fall, they can come, but they are no match against him. They protest but agree. I need to do this myself.

I enter the room I only saw on our wedding night. The big bed, rug, fire—it's all still there.

Thad is sitting at his desk writing. He looks up as I step into the light from the shadows.

"Ah, My Queen. I have waited for you. I hoped you'd come," Thad says.

I tremble and respond, "I'm here to kill you, Thadius." Be brave Astrid.

"Now, now. Let's talk this through." He stands and approaches me. He is wearing an eye patch. "I made sure there would be no one to stop you. I don't want to fight."

He continues, "You surprised me the night you did this." He points to his eye, "but it was the wake-up call I needed. I have been a monster. I have treated you poorly. I thought you were a weak pet, but you are strong. Stronger than me maybe. You, me, and our children—we can rule this world together. I have missed you. I love you. I find myself unable to sleep from thinking of you. That smell haunts me."

"I don't want to rule the world with you, Thad."

"You called me, Thad." He smiles and walks closer shaking his finger at me. "You're still into me." Why are you letting him talk? This is the part where the bad guy talks endlessly and then pulls the lever for you to fall into a pit of sharks. How does he still paralyze me in lust, and fear, and longing?

"Can—can you bring that scent of yours back for me? If you're going to kill me—which I'm sure you are. I can tell you are even stronger than before; you can at least give me this one last request."

"Why would I do anything for you?"

"Because you still love me. I can tell. Otherwise, you'd have killed me already."

"You're a monster. A murderer. A rapist."

"I—can change for you." He says and he reaches his hands out to hug me. What is wrong with me? Why am I falling for this?

"Please, babe. I will let everyone from the dungeons go. No more hunting. You can even bring your harem. I don't care. I will share you." He sounds genuine and sincere. Maybe he can change.

I reach into my belt and pull out a small vial. I hold it up in the light and turn it slightly to the side to show him. I drink it.

He looks at me quizzically and moans in delight as he sniffs loudly in the air. His dick gets hard and huge, and he presses his palm against his pants.

"Oh, babe. I knew you still loved me. I love you." He walks toward me and pulls me into a deep hug. Suddenly, I feel a prick at my neck. His tail is there, stabbing me, paralyzing me. He walks toward me, grinning. His grin isn't menacing, but loving.

I know from the experiments that Gideon and I performed, I have a few moments before the poison paralyzes me. Thadius looks smug as he removes his clothing. He licks his lips as he imagines the ravishing he's about to do to my body.

"Oh, babe, I need you so badly. I can't wait to be inside you. I'm sorry for the poison, but I knew if I didn't do it, you'd probably kill me. I need you to be docile tonight. Don't worry, I won't do it again. I mean it when I said I'll change. I'll take care of you. I won't hurt you."

The light bouncing from the fireplace casts shadows on his chest in a way that emphasizes every single crevice. A large part of me wants to let him fuck my brains out and wonders if I'd still be able to feel him inside me when the paralysis takes effect. Gideon and I hadn't tested that.

He's completely nude at this point and reaches toward me. He grabs at my clothing, pulling it down slightly and my nipples jump to attention. Oh, God, I want him. My labia pulse in desire and remembers the feeling of him between my legs. I bite my lip; I cannot be with him. He has not changed. I must do what I came to do.

He pulls me close and kisses my neck. He moans in pure delight and presses his cock against me. I moisten at his touch. While he's distracted kissing me, my body begins to morph into its strongest form. That of a scorpion. "Oh, babe. You taste so good. I missed you so much. I love you." He whispers in my ear.

He doesn't notice me growing in front of him until it is far too late and I tower above him. "I love you, too, Thad, but I cannot be with you," I say as a tear rolls down my cheek.

My legs are frozen in place, the paralysis taking effect. I reach my hand which is now a large scorpion claw and wrap it around his neck. He looks at me in horror as he realizes what is happening. I close my claw, severing his head from his body, decapacitating him instantly. The look of confusion is still on his face as I hold his head in my hand.

I fall to the ground, the paralysis fully affecting me, but not before I am able to yell, "Al!"

Epilogue

It's been three years since I killed Thadius and took the throne. When I emerged from his bedroom covered in blood, we expected the guards to try and fight me. The sight of their missing queen and presumed dead comrades shocked them to the point of stupefaction. Once they realized what happened, they all immediately kneeled and pledged their allegiance to me. The guards and castle staff knew what type of man Thadius was and did not fight me when I claimed the throne. They were happy to have the new ruler.

I suspect one day someone will challenge my position on the throne and either try to take it for themselves or force it upon Nathaniel. No one has yet and I'd honestly like to see them try. Nate or Kate will rule when they are ready and if they wish to.

The night of Thad's death we immediately released his prisoners and made sure they all received medical care. I've given them all large restitutions as well as honorary titles. I cannot right the wrongs Thadius did to them, but I can try.

The news of King Thadius' death at the hand of his queen spread like wildfire. The surrounding countries immediately sent envoys to congratulate me on my victory and determine if I too would be a land concurring tyrant like my predecessor.

Laerean had been on the brink a war with Laila when Thad died. I signed a peace treaty between our two nations. Laila's king, Dorius, is a royal cock, just like Thad. What is it with kings? They have everything but they have to be total assholes. He tried to take back Lysander, Florian, and even Osric during our negotiations, but my calm jovial queen veneer transformed into a deep, rumbling, monster when he pushed the subject too hard.

Lysander and Osric are convinced the peace treaty is just a ruse and King Cornelius will attack eventually. "He hates women. He fucks them. But he doesn't love them," Osric told me. They know he is fuming about a female leader with a harem bigger than his own. For now, I am fine with even the façade of peace. We'll cross the bridge of war when we get to it. I'm not particularly scared of their puny army and feeble king.

My reputation as both a monster and a lover have become local legend. My nickname among the locals is "The Queen of Hearts and Claws". I like it.

Once the confusion of taking over the throne subsided, I immediately wrote up schematics and plans for scientific innovation. First things Gideon and I developed together were toothbrushes and condoms. I missed the feeling of bristles between my teeth and couldn't keep getting knocked up. Three kids are more than enough and there was no way I was abstaining. We're currently working on the formula for some kind of chemical/magical birth control.

The twins are precocious little trouble makers. They have their father's radiant smile and his fucking pincers. It doesn't bother me the way I thought it would. I'm just happy they didn't stab their way through my abdomen. I explained to them their father was a scorpion and showed them the hall of past royalty. I've taught them their heritage, but not their father's bloody past. For now, all they know is that I loved him and he loved us, but he was not strong enough to control his scorpion form. I'll tell them the truth one day.

Violet was born about six months after Thad's death. It was immediately apparent she was Gideon's daughter. She came out purring and screaming. Gideon and I are still trying to figure out exactly how this curse works, but I told him I wasn't prepared to make more children for the sake of his scientific inquiry. The others were disappointed by this, I think hoping they too could have some children with their powers, but no one treats Violet like anything other than their own child.

I determined that, while Gen did not know the true extent of Thadius' evil, she did have suspicions, but was understandably scared to act on them.

We have rekindled our friendship, but I haven't trusted her quite enough to take her on as a lover. It's purely platonic at this point.

We're still trying to work out exactly what the royal status of my lovers should be. I want them to be kings and queens beside me, but they, my advisors, and my subjects aren't too keen on the idea. "Too many cooks in the kitchen," Al says. The current plan is to officially marry one of them and take him as my king (or queen), but I can't pick.

Today is the celebration of the anniversary of Thadius' defeat. I sit on my throne, crown on my head, lovers at my side. As my subjects cheer me, I look to my side to see the beautiful partners I have collected beaming at me with love.

At this moment, I reflect on how I came to rule this kingdom. How I came to be loved by seven gorgeous monsters. How I was able to finally leave my tower and sleep under the stars. Maybe tonight, I'll have them all at once. It is a celebration after all and every celebration needs a feast. I giggle to myself and whisper, "A feast of ass". God, what have I become? Even without the context of my inner thoughts, Florian gives me a knowing, sideways smirk. Fuck he heard me. I forgot he still had that super hearing. He knows me so well. I give him a little three-finger wave and raise an eyebrow as if to say, "You down?" and he chuckles to himself. That's not a no.

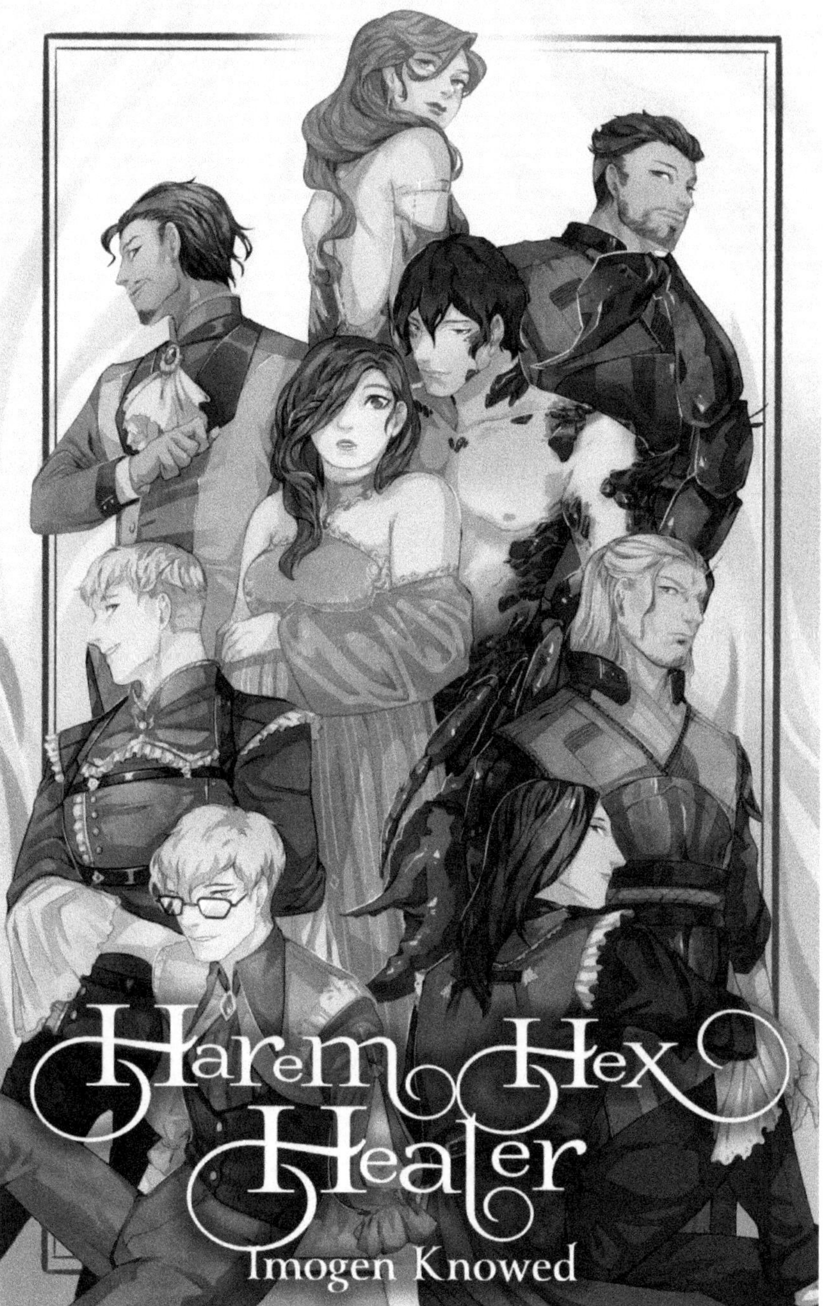
Harem Hex Healer
Imogen Knowed

A Note from the Author

Hello, readers! Thank you so much for taking the time to read Harem Hex Healer. I can't tell you how much it means to me that you made it all the way to the end!

It will mean so much to me if you review the book on Amazon and Goodreads.

About the Author

Imogen Knowed writes strong-willed and emotionally damaged heroines obsessed over by multiple suitors.
She enjoys reverse harem, slice-of-life, and shifter romances as well as cozy murder mysteries.

Sign up for her newsletter at:
https://www.imogenknowed.com/about

You can follow her on social media:
https://www.instagram.com/imogenknowed/
https://www.threads.net/@imogenknowed
https://bsky.app/profile/imogenknowed.com
https://www.tiktok.com/@imogenknowed

https://www.imogenknowed.com/

www.ingramcontent.com/pod-product-compliance
Lightning Source LLC
LaVergne TN
LVHW010605100826
845148LV00014B/2856